LAST WIT

Carys Jones

About *Last Witness*

The page-turning sequel to the best-selling psychological thriller *Wrong Number*.

Amanda Thorne is on a mission to avenge her husband. Restoring his honour and protecting his legacy will be dangerous, but she will not rest until all those who have hurt her loved-ones have been dealt with.

Her only option is to go undercover in the murky world of the gang kingpin McAllister. So, with her loyal companion Shane by her side, she heads back to Scotland to finish what they started.

McAllister's world is one of seedy nightclubs, drug deals and beautiful women, but he is a hard man to get close to. As

Amanda gets deeper and deeper into his dangerous world, what secrets from the past will come back to haunt her, and will she be able to protect the last witness to the truth?

A compelling, heart-stopping thriller that you won't be able to put down…

For my biggest fan, my dad. Try not to burn the chips when you read this one xxx

1

'I want to go home.'

Ewan's voice was plaintive, sorrowful, as he lifted his head off Amanda's arm and peered up at her through tired eyes.

Home.

The word pressed itself into Amanda's side like a thorn. Each time she breathed in she felt its barbed tip. What was home? A place? A person? For Amanda, home had been the beautiful new house she'd bought with her husband, Will.

Bending forward, she coughed to conceal the sob which trembled up her throat and burst from her lips. Will was gone. All that was left of him was the little boy at her side.

'Home.' Ewan smacked his hands against his seat and blinked back tears.

'We can't go home,' Shane briefly turned to look back at them from the driving seat. Amanda had watched his profile throughout their long journey, noticed the unrelenting tension in his jaw as he drove down seemingly never-ending motorways. Scotland was now in the rear-view mirror. The sun had started to dip in the sky and Amanda wasn't sure if she'd reach her mother's house before dark.

'Why not?' the little boy demanded of both the adults in the car, dividing his heated gaze between them. Shane was looking ahead once more.

'Because we can't,' Amanda wished she had a more concrete explanation to offer Ewan. She wrapped her arm around his slight shoulders and drew him back towards her. He was too tired to pull away.

'But why not?' his eyelids were drooping.

Because your mother and father are dead. Because the man who killed them may well be hunting you too.

'Because we can't,' Amanda repeated softly. A minute passed and Ewan's breathing deepened as he drifted off to sleep.

*

As Amanda had predicted, night had fallen when Shane's car pulled into the small driveway outside her mother's cottage. She could taste the salt in the air sweeping in off the Southern English coast as she stretched out her legs, trying to unknot them after the long drive down from Scotland. Thick, velvety shadows gathered where the vehicle's headlights couldn't reach.

'Are you sure she's going to be okay with this?' Shane's voice was dubious as Amanda yawned widely in the back seat and stretched out her arms.

'She has to be.'

'And if she isn't?'

'Well,' Amanda dusted a strand of blonde hair out of her eyes, 'you don't have a place of your own right now. I'm sure as hell not going back to my place. And that leaves hers.'

Even at night, the little cottage managed to look welcoming. A single outside light shone beside the front door. It banished away any shadows that lingered too close to the threshold. Amanda smiled a little to herself as she looked at its glow, remembering how that light used to be left on to help guide her back home during her teenage years, when she'd spent hours down on the beach with Shane and John. But who

2

was it on for now? Or did her mother just like to think that she was offering a guiding light to any souls that wandered along the cliffside?

It was cold out. When she opened her car door the slap of the night air against his cheeks roused Ewan from slumber. He made his hands into little balls and furiously rubbed them against his eyes. 'Where are we?' he mumbled the question as Shane scooped him up in his strong arms and rested Ewan against his chest. The boy promptly lowered his head and fell back asleep.

'I envy his ability to just sleep anywhere.' Shane smiled. It wasn't a hearty, natural one. More the sort of smile you use in polite company. But Amanda was grateful for it. It was nice to see someone else smile, especially since she doubted she'd ever be able to again.

Pushing back all her nerves and worries, she rang the doorbell.

'Are you even sure she'll be up?'

Amanda pulled her phone from her pocket and peered at the screen. It was a quarter to eleven. 'She'll be up.'

Sure enough it took less than a minute for the locks to turn on the other side of the door.

'Who is it?' Her mother's voice was tight, suspicious. Amanda could imagine her staring hard at the door, rouge lips pursed in annoyance.

'Mum, it's me.'

The door opened. Light flooded the porch, brilliant and bright. Amanda had to stagger back, briefly shielding her eyes.

Corrine was swathed in a floor-length navy silk nightgown which had long sleeves that billowed out at the wrists. She looked like she'd just stepped off the set of a BBC costume drama rather than out of her modest living room where she'd have been sat in front of the television, waiting to fall asleep. Amanda could hear the distant murmur of voices meaning that the TV was still on, playing to an empty room.

'Amanda!' Corrine said her daughter's name with a haughty air. 'What sort of time do you call this to come banging on your mother's door?'

'I didn't bang, I—'

'You should have called me! I'm a state.'

The latter part wasn't true. Even ready for bed Corrine was a picture of elegance and grace. Her hair was pinned into numerous curlers and held beneath a pale blue hairnet. Even without her make-up she looked strikingly beautiful. The lines that deepened with each facial expression only spoke of her rich life; they didn't remove the shine from the spectacle that was Amanda's mother.

'I wasn't sure what time we'd get here and—'

'Shane,' Corrine marched her bejewelled slippers out into the night, arms extended like she was welcoming home her prodigal son. 'Oh, how are you?' She stopped short when she spotted the little boy held against his chest, her own arms dropping against her sides in a ripple of delicate fabric. 'And who is this?'

'Mum,' Amanda placed a hand upon her mother's shoulder, 'this is Ewan. He's…' Closing her eyes, she stole a swift breath to steady herself, 'He's Will's son.'

'*What*?' The glamour was gone. When Corrine spun around to face her daughter there was fire in her eyes. 'Tell me this is one of your strange jokes, Amanda.'

'Mum.' She saw the judgement in her mother's eyes. The anger. It felt like facing a firing squad. 'Please, it's not what you think.' And then she crumpled into the confused woman's arms. Corrine held her, staring wordlessly at Shane who continued to hover near the front door while Amanda wept.

'Get the boy inside,' Corrine finally whispered. 'Put him up in Amanda's room. And sweetheart,' she took a firm hold of her daughter's shoulders and forced Amanda to stand straight so that she could deliver her order more directly, 'you need to get a hold of yourself. Whatever has happened, whatever has gone wrong, I'm sure you can fix it.'

He's gone. Will's dead. There's no bringing him back.

The words pounded in Amanda's mind like a drumbeat. Her husband was gone. Forever. 'It's...' she found her voice, but then closed her mouth. How safe was it to tell her mother everything that had happened up in Scotland? The men who had killed Will were gone but their puppet master was still at large. He could be pulling strings that very moment, sending eyes out into the world to find Amanda. To find Ewan. And truly finish what he started.

*

An hour later and the house was still. Ewan was sleeping up in Amanda's old room and Shane had stretched out on the sofa in the front room beneath a blanket Corrine had given him. Both he and Ewan seemed eager to rest, eager to conclude what must have been one of, if not the worst day of their lives.

'So are you going to talk?' Corrine was sat across from Amanda at the kitchen table. They were both nursing freshly made cups of coffee. The oaky aroma still lingered in the air, seeming out of place at such a late hour.

'Mum,' Amanda sighed and gazed into her cup.

'Okay then, I'll talk,' Corrine declared after a second of silence had drawn out. 'I want to know what on earth is going on here. You show up at my house at God knows what hour, with a boy who you claim to be your husband's *son*. And Shane can't seem to stand to be more than a few yards away from you, remaining in this house like some sort of lost puppy. You owe me an explanation, Amanda.'

'Will's dead.'

Corrine absorbed the information like a knife to the chest. She clamped a hand over where her heart resided and let her mouth fall open. 'Wh-what?'

'I can't,' Amanda's voice was uneven as it started to break. 'It's too dangerous to tell you more than that. But Ewan, his son, he's in danger. That's why I brought him here, to keep him safe.'

'Will's... gone?' Dead seemed too awful a word for her mother to repeat.

Amanda nodded woefully. Her heart felt so heavy and each time she formed a thought it hurt, like her brain had been replaced with sandpaper.

'Well, what... what on earth happened?' Corrine's words were pitched and slightly fearful. She tightened her hands around her cup of coffee.

'I've already said too much.' Amanda was aware that her shoulders were shaking, as was the rest of her body. 'Just... just help me keep Ewan safe.'

In a blur of navy and silk her mother swept around the table and pulled Amanda against her bosom. She held her daughter tightly until the sun started to lighten the sky and the shaking ceased.

'So I'm staying here?' Ewan cocked his head up at her as he stood barefoot on the beach.

'For a little bit, yeah.'

'What about school?'

'We'll figure that out come September.' Amanda guided him closer to the water's edge. The sun was shining, making the beach behind the cottage look especially beautiful. Light glinted off each of the waves that lazily rolled towards the shore.

'And I can't go home?' Ewan was still looking at her, ignoring the water which was now just a few feet from his little feet.

'I'm afraid not.'

'Ever?' There was hope in the question and Amanda hated to kill it. But she knew that Ewan needed to settle into his new life, needed to accept that there was no going back. She didn't want the changes that were about to be forced upon him to age him beyond his six years.

'No. Not ever. I'm really sorry, Ewan.'

She expected tears. Maybe even a tantrum. Ewan's face crumpled, his cheeks reddened with the pressure building behind them, but then, just as he was about to erupt like a mini geyser, a soft wave tickled the ends of his toes. Like flipping a coin, the boy's mood changed. He was still young enough to effortlessly bounce between elation and despair. He released a giddy bubble of laughter as he allowed himself to be swept up in the moment. He jumped up and down in the salty water, revelled in how his feet sank down in the damp sand.

And all the while, Amanda held his hand, kept him close, but she did not smile.

*

The day had been long. There had been a visit to a toy store at the nearest retail park where Amanda's credit card had taken a battering. But she didn't know how else to keep Ewan happy. Distracted. She bought him new bedding for her old room, new curtains, a black bike with red stripes, a bucket and spade set and a trolley full of toys.

'So your plan is just to spoil him?' Shane had wondered as he helped her bag up all her purchases in the store.

'Do you have a better one?'

'Not really, no,' he gave her a crooked smile. 'Kids aren't really my forte.'

'Nor mine.' Amanda hauled the last gift-laden bag into the awaiting trolley. 'Yet, here we are.'

'Can I ride my bike out when we get back?' Ewan was bouncing from foot to foot as they walked across the car park, unable to contain all his excitement.

'Of course.'

'Without the little wheels?'

Amanda frowned.

'The stabilisers,' Shane explained helpfully. 'Sorry, bud, but you need to keep those on for now.'

'Okay,' Ewan shrugged off any disappointment he might have had. 'But I want to be riding without the little wheels before my dad gets back.'

They'd reached Shane's car.

'Ewan,' Amanda locked eyes with Shane across the roof of the vehicle, 'you know that your dad isn't coming back, right?' She reminded herself that she was being cruel to be kind.

'Yeah, I know,' another dismissive shrug. 'But I figured that it's fun to pretend he is.'

Shane had climbed into the driver's seat and had turned around to help Ewan fasten his seat belt, but Amanda lingered outside, her eyes scanning every inch of the large car park as she breathed around the lump that had formed in her chest. Each time someone mentioned Will she felt like an iron vice was clamping around her lungs, trying to squeeze out her very last breath. There were vehicles everywhere, innocently parked up in surrounding bays. Amanda felt the sizzle of electricity in the air; it was all around her like an unstable mist that continued to spark. In any car there could be someone sat, watching them. Either one of McAllister's men or Turtle82. McAllister had been the man behind Will's death. A man Amanda had never met, but she felt his claustrophobic presence in every breath she took. And she had once trusted Turtle82, had let them guide her through online jobs when she was at university but they'd only ever been a name on a screen. Will's death had taught Amanda to take nothing at face value, even when it came to people she hoped she could trust.

There had been no new messages from her old darknet contact but still she kept logging in whenever she could steal a moment alone. But such moments were difficult to snatch in her mother's house with its poor internet connection and the continual presence of either Shane or her mother shadowing her every move, watching her like she was some china doll who could shatter against even the slightest gust of wind.

'You getting in?' Somehow Shane found the strength to sound positive, to keep a genial smile upon his face. Amanda wondered if his time working as a homicide detective had helped him become accustomed to death, to the ugly things people would do to one another. Maybe he had some secret way of coping with grief. If that was the case she wished that he'd share it with her. Amanda didn't feel like she was holding up well in the wake of Will's death. She felt like her favourite Linkin Park T-shirt which had once been jet-black but thanks to going through the washing machine one too many times had dulled to a sad shade of grey, the fabric becoming thin, almost transparent. She stopped feeling special when she wore the T-shirt. It started to make her sad, it just reminded her of how it had lost its former glory and of all the other things she'd lost. Like her dad.

Like Will.

This fresh pain had opened old wounds. Being in her mother's house made it harder to banish away memories of her kind father. Amanda knew that he'd have loved Ewan, would have unquestioningly taken him in and treated the orphaned boy like he was family.

'Amanda?' Shane's voice was thick with concern. 'You all right?'

She scrambled into the car. 'Yeah, I'm good.' It felt like the biggest lie she'd ever told.

*

Ewan tired himself out with his plethora of new toys. It wasn't even half seven when he yawned loudly and asked if he could go to bed. Amanda had to applaud his good manners. Evangeline, Will's first wife, had clearly done a good job of raising her son alone. And Corrine seemed equally impressed.

'He's so well-spoken,' she'd gushed to Amanda earlier. 'He always says please and thank you. He's a joy to have around, truly.'

That was something. It would have been more difficult if Ewan was a little tyrant making demands about the place. But he was genuinely the sweetest little boy Amanda had ever met. And he was Will's.

*

Amanda couldn't sleep. Corrine had kindly agreed to share her bed as Shane spent another night downstairs on the sofa. But after half an hour of tossing and turning, Amanda felt compelled to give into her restless feelings. She tiptoed out of the room and drifted down the staircase, out through the kitchen and into the small rose garden. She could hear the distant pounding of the ocean's waves against the shore. Dropping onto the small wooden bench that looked across the garden, out towards the sea, she sighed and breathed in deeply, filling her lungs with the rose-scented air.

'At some point you need to sleep.'

Amanda turned her head sharply back towards the house, where her mother was just stepping out through the back door, once again bundled up in her sumptuous navy silk robe. The fabric was so dark, so rich, that she almost blended in with the backdrop of the starry night sky.

'Sorry, did I wake you?'

'Yes.' Corrine sat down beside her daughter on the bench. Her Estée Lauder perfume began to overpower the natural scent of her beloved flowers. 'But it's fine. Wake me up all you want. I just want to make sure you're okay.'

'I'm okay.'

'You're not,' Corrine countered sharply.

Amanda looked out towards the moon which cast a rippled reflection upon the surface of the ocean. The little rose garden was always such a tranquil place, a place where Amanda could sit and relieve herself of whatever burden was resting upon her shoulders simply by absorbing the serene atmosphere that gathered amongst the rose vines. But not this night. She could feel her mother watching her, seeing through her words.

'Fine, I'm not okay,' Amanda conceded before her mother could say anything else. 'I've lost my husband and I feel like I've lost myself too.' She let her words drift away from them, out towards the open water. A pair of salty tears danced down her cheeks. 'I'm desperately trying to hold myself together for Ewan but…' Leaning forward, she dropped her head into her hands and then felt the calming pressure of her mother's hand against her back. 'How did you do it?' she coughed as she released one hand to glance back at Corrine. 'When Dad died, how did you carry on like you did? You always seemed so strong, especially back then.'

'I had you,' Corrine's eyes crinkled as she smiled, but they glistened in the moonlight with fresh tears. 'You were my reason to get up each morning. To tidy the house. To keep going.'

'And if you hadn't had me?'

Because Ewan wasn't truly hers, was he? The Scottish authorities could still track him down and demand Amanda hand him into their custody.

'Then I'd have done it for him. For his memory.' The tears that had fallen upon Corrine's cheeks sparkled like stars. 'He wouldn't have wanted me to wallow in my sorrow. And Will wouldn't want you to.'

'It's just not fair,' Amanda sniffed and sat up, furiously wiping at her eyes. 'I mean I've lost Will, and so has Ewan.'

'Life is never fair,' Corrine whispered pragmatically. 'But then you were forced to figure that out long ago.'

2

The waves roared beneath her like a hungry beast. Amanda's hands were glued to the arm that was holding her over the edge as she swung in the breeze like a pendulum.

'Daddy, help me.' It was difficult to speak the words through her chattering teeth. The arm pulled her higher and she peered over the top of the cliff and saw him braced on his knees, his face pinched in agony. Her father. Her hero. There was a powerful gust of wind and as it blasted them both her father's face changed. His hair became darker, thicker, his shoulders wider. He staggered forward, losing his grip on her.

'Will.' Amanda recognised the man holding her as her husband, felt her heart start to quicken with hopeful beats. Will Thorn was the strongest man she knew. If anyone could haul her up from the cliff edge it was him.

But Will was struggling. Amanda dropped further down the cliffside, heard the roaring beneath her grow louder. She clawed at Will's outstretched arm, dug her nails in, but she could feel herself slipping. 'Will!' She was screaming, looking up at him through the tears which had started to fall.

A shot cracked between them like a clap of thunder. Will let go. As Amanda started to fall she briefly glimpsed him tumbling to the ground, pressing his hands to his chest to try and stop the blood which was suddenly seeping out of him. The wind whipped past her as she kept falling. Any second she'd hit the rocks and—

Snapping open her eyes, Amanda sat up. She was breathing hard, sucking in air like she'd been deprived of it while she slept. Hugging her knees to her chest, she waited for the moment to pass, for the world to right itself.

'Amanda?' her mother stirred beside her. Corrine was hauling herself into an upright position, a hand cautiously checking the curlers beneath her hairnet as she did so. 'Sweetheart, are you all right?'

'I was having a nightmare.' Amanda's throat felt too dry. Too raw.

'Well, it's passed now. You should try and get back to sleep. You need your rest.'

Amanda looked towards the curtains on the far side of the room which swayed gently in a lazy waltz against a faint breeze which trickled in through the partially open window. The breeze carried in the rumble of the waves, the taste of salt, reminding Amanda that her nightmare would never truly pass, that it continued to exist all around her.

'I need to get up.' She swung her legs out of the bed and stood up before her mother could reach out and stop her.

'You really do need to sleep,' Corrine stated firmly.

'Whenever I close my eyes I see him.' Amanda was pulling a hoody on over her nightshirt.

'And when your eyes are open?'

Untucking her hair from her hoody, Amanda sighed. It was a deep sound which came up from the bottom of her soul. 'When my eyes are open, I feel him. It's like he's everywhere.'

'Because he is,' Corrine was rolling back onto her side, pulling the bed sheets up to her chin. 'When you love someone they never truly leave you.'

Amanda thought of Will. Of her father. Knowing that she'd never see either of them again made her ribs clench around her heart as though someone or something was applying pressure upon them, squeezing until they reached the point where the bone might snap.

*

Dawn was still far enough away that the stars were able to hold dominion over the sky. Amanda peered up at them from the little kitchen window as she waited for the kettle to boil. She needed coffee. Whilst her mind was willing to forsake further rest, her body was not. Her bones ached and her eyelids felt heavy.

'Couldn't sleep?'

Turning around, Amanda saw Shane slumped against the door frame, his hair ruffled from sleeping on the sofa.

'No.' The kettle whistled as it reached boiling point. 'You?'

'I've slept in more comfortable places.' Drifting into the kitchen, Shane pressed a hand against a knot in his back.

'Want one?' Amanda gestured towards her mug.

'Sure.'

'You know you don't have to stay here, right? You could find a place of your own, get on with your life. You need somewhere to stay after you were, you know, kicked out of your last place.'

'Don't you want me around anymore?' Shane stared at her, dejected. 'When you came to me wanting help back when Will first disappeared you opened up a door between us that had been closed for too long. Don't you want to keep that door open?'

'Yes. Of course. It's not that,' Amanda swiftly assured him as she passed him a fresh mug of coffee. 'It's just...' She sat down across from him at the kitchen table. The rough wooden surface was uneven in places and flecks of paint had come away, revealing the natural grain of the wood beneath. But the table fit the cottage. Shabby chic, that was the style people called it.

'Amanda,' Shane slid his hand across the table and found hers. He was so warm to the touch, like there was fire in his veins. 'I'm not going to leave you to deal with all this shit alone. You lost your husband and—'

'Do you think they're looking for us?' she interrupted, her eyes suddenly wide and wild.

'You mean—'

'McAllister's men,' Amanda finished for him. 'Do you think they know that we took Ewan? That we're here?'

'I don't...' Shane pulled his free hand through his untidy hair. 'No,' he concluded, his voice lacking conviction. 'Absolutely not. The trail would have gone cold up in Scotland, you saw to that with your darknet stuff.' He released her hand.

Amanda trusted the information she procured on the darknet. It was the ambiguous space on the Internet where there was no law – no reason. No ability to trace a user's movements. But as much as she trusted the darknet she couldn't ignore the uneasy feeling in her gut.

'But still. McAllister spent years hunting for Will,' she gazed sadly into her coffee, 'for Jake.' It was still so hard to reconcile her husband as being two men. She'd known Will Thorn, the sexy stranger who had been a gentleman to his core. That was the man she'd met and fallen in love with. The man she'd married. Then she learnt that Will Thorn was actually Jake Burton. And Jake Burton was a criminal, a dealer of drugs. A man on the run. Only Jake failed to outrun his past and it cost him dearly. And his first wife, Evangeline.

His real wife.

Amanda didn't like how she was starting to question everything about her relationship with Will. She found herself picking apart every moment, searching for clues she might have missed, for truths she might have ignored through blissful ignorance. Even when he uttered his vows to her he was repeating himself. Amanda felt like every truth she'd ever clung to was unravelling around her and scattering to the wind leaving her naked, alone. And scared.

'They're not coming for us,' Shane made a promise he couldn't keep.

'If he hadn't met me…' Amanda went to bat away a tear but none had fallen. For the time being she was all cried out. 'If it weren't for me, he might have kept running. Kept hiding. He might still be alive.'

'You can't think like that.'

'He's *dead*.' Her words bounced off the walls around them. 'And I had to watch him die, there in the woods, and then leave him so that I could…could keep Ewan safe.'

Shane got up, intending to come and comfort her, but Amanda was too fast. She hurried out of the kitchen, through the back door into the rose garden. Shane followed, his bare feet crunching against the little gravel footpath.

'I can't accept that he's gone,' Amanda admitted, keeping her back to Shane as her long hair billowed away from her in the wind like a scarf of sunlight-infused silk. She could see the sky finally starting to lighten in the distance, the stars beginning to lose their shine.

'But he is.' Shane's voice was soft as he placed both hands on her shoulders and together they looked out to sea. 'He's gone and there's nothing you can do about it. But you can do something about Ewan. You can keep him safe. You can give him a home. A life.'

'I'm not…' Turning, Amanda buried her face against Shane's chest, breathing in the familiar scent of sleep curdled with cologne. 'I'm not a mother.' She almost choked on the words. Shane's warm hands found her back and held her in a tight embrace.

'You're all that boy has left in the world.'

'I know.' Amanda's voice was muffled. 'And that's why I can't let him down. Why I have to keep him safe.'

'He is safe.'

'Yes, but for how long?'

*

It felt good to go jogging. It was familiar. Safe. As Amanda powered down the beach, kicking up sand with each step, she felt like she could almost pretend that she'd travelled back to a month ago, back when life was normal. Back when she thought she knew who her husband was.

Despite the early hour there were a few people scattered along the beach. Others out running, some with their dogs – throwing sticks into the waves for their four-legged companions to eagerly chase after. There was a weak sun in the sky. It seemed watery as it tried to shine out through the thin layer of cloud. It gave the new day a subdued feeling.

Amanda kept running. She felt an ache in her legs, in her muscles, and pushed herself to go faster. She'd always loved running. So had Will. Some mornings when he wasn't on an early shift he'd pull on his running shoes and join her as she paced through the woods. Amanda always knew that Will could easily outrun her. His legs were thick and powerful, perfect for acceleration. But he never raced off. He always jogged loyally by her side, throwing her occasional smiles as they moved beneath the leafy canopy created by the surrounding trees.

Her chest squeezed a bit too tightly and Amanda staggered to a halt. Placing her hands on her knees, she dropped her head and took deep, refreshing breaths. The air was damp; the blades of grass in her mother's garden would still be laced with dew. Slowly Amanda straightened and reassessed the beach around her.

There was a guy who looked to be in his mid-twenties walking in her direction with a black Labrador beside him who had a large stick held between his teeth. The dog's tail was wagging back and forth as it kept pace with its master. But Amanda was more interested in the beach dweller on two legs. Crouching down, she pretended to tie her shoelace so that she could subtly watch the man out of the corner of her eye. He wore baggy shorts and his head was shaved, but not close enough to hide that his hair was naturally black. He had a plain blue T-shirt loosely tucked into his shorts and his feet were bare, meaning that he must live close by.

'Come on, give,' he instructed his dog as he reached for the twig the animal was eagerly carrying. 'Wait now. Sit.'

The dog instantly sat, staring adoringly at the stick in his master's hand as his tongue lolled out of the side of his mouth as he panted.

Amanda continued to fidget with her laces, straining to hear even a hint of a Scottish accent in the man's voice.

'Okay now, fetch!' The man slung the stick into the waves and his dog bolted after it. He was now less than a few feet from Amanda.

'Morning.' He gave her a polite nod and a one-word greeting as he passed her by. Amanda stood up as the black Lab bounded out of the water, triumphantly brandishing the retrieved stick between its jaws. 'Good boy,' the man enthused, bending down to fuss his freshly wet dog.

Amanda turned away from them and continued jogging.

It could just be a front, she considered.

McAllister's men might be watching her in plain sight, scrutinising her every move as they decided when would be the best time to pounce. The man had held onto his grudge with Will for years. A drugs run gone sour and the price to pay had been Will's life. Jake Burton's life. And even Evangeline's, Jake's wife. Amanda didn't understand that kind of vengeance, she just knew to fear it. McAllister's men would surely be out there, searching. Perhaps they'd descend upon her mother's home in the dead of night, come crashing through the windows, and in the ensuing chaos steal Ewan straight out of his bed while he slept. Or maybe they'd just kill him there and then. A brutal single bullet. That was all it had taken to end Will.

Amanda stopped jogging. This time it wasn't because she'd grown tired. She sucked in air as she staggered away from the shoreline, feeling winded.

Will was gone.

The words were on a carousel in her mind so that she had to keep dealing with them over and over again.

Her man mountain. Her oak tree. The man whose name she had taken. He still existed in her memories. Will Thorn was still there but of course he wasn't. Not really. He was gone. Amanda kicked at the sand in frustration.

'Bring him back,' she demanded of the universe. But she knew it wouldn't happen. She'd made a similar plea for years as a girl after her father died and it was never answered.

*

'*Toy Story*? Again?' Corrine turned the DVD case over in her hands and frowned at the cheerful cover.

'Again, again,' Ewan was dancing in circles around the old woman, clutching his beloved Woody to his chest.

'He's watched it twice already today,' Corrine glanced over at Amanda who was slicing sandwiches for tea. Cheese and jam. The filling had been Ewan's choice.

'It's his favourite,' Amanda shrugged.

'But three times in one day?' Corrine sounded baffled. 'I mean, I love me some Robert De Niro, but even I couldn't look at that man's handsome face so repeatedly in one day.'

'He enjoys it.' Amanda plucked the DVD from her mother's grasp and headed into the living room with Ewan quickly at her heels.

'You'll sit and watch it with me this time, won't you?' he reached for her hand and gave it a squeeze.

Amanda knew she must seem distracted. She'd spent the morning sorting out her old room – turning it into a space more appropriate for a little boy. She'd put up the new curtains, emptied her books from the shelves and filled them with the toys they'd picked up for Ewan. It had been a bittersweet process. For so long her old bedroom had acted like a time capsule, a place she could escape to when her current life got too much. A place where she could pretend her father still existed. But as she'd taken down the final poster, she'd realised that she'd removed every trace of herself from the room. It was like she'd never been there at all.

'Well, I never thought I'd see the day,' Corrine had noted as she peered in from the landing.

'It had to be done,' Amanda rolled the last poster up. 'This is Ewan's room now.'

'So you have no intention of going back to that beautiful house of yours?'

'Not right now.'

'Because of all the memories of Will?'

'Yeah.' Amanda had nodded.

That and the fact that her home wasn't safe. It was there amongst her pristine walls and polished surfaces that she'd received the ominous call asking for Jake Burton. That call had been the first domino which had succeeded in toppling all the others. Even in her perfect home, she couldn't keep out the past. And if McAllister's men had known about the house back then, they still knew about it now. They might go there searching for Ewan and Amanda wasn't about to let them find the little boy. It would be easy enough for them to find the cottage with the rose garden beside the sea – even her mother's home wasn't completely safe. But they'd never been there, had never called. And Amanda was grasping at straws, taking what little consolation she could to try and silence the endless echoes of fearful doubt in her mind.

'You know, you'll have to go back eventually.' Corrine had been uncharacteristically quiet on the subject of Will. Perhaps because she knew from experience that only time would heal a broken heart. 'That's the problem with the world,' she'd added with a wave of her hand, 'it just keeps on turning.'

'This time, you watch,' Ewan was pulling Amanda over to the sofa which was currently doubling up as Shane's bed at night. 'Please.'

The boy's hands were already sticky with jam. Had he somehow snuck himself a sandwich? Or had one been leaked to him? Both Shane and Corrine were complete soft touches with him. Amanda was still having to adjust to being around the boy. The only instinct that had kicked in was to protect him. But she needed to try, to find the maternal parts of herself that had never surfaced before.

'Okay, I'll watch,' Amanda sat down on the sofa as Ewan settled himself on the floor, sitting cross-legged with Woody in his lap.

'Movie time again?' Shane came in, his hair still damp from the shower he'd just taken. 'What are we watching this time?'

'Guess,' Corrine deadpanned as she followed him through the door, bringing with her the plate of freshly made sandwiches.

'*Toy Story*?' Shane dropped down next to Amanda. He smelt fresh, like washing that had just come out of the dryer.

'*Toy Story*,' Amanda confirmed with a nod of her head.

'I love Woody!' Ewan yelled to them all by way of explanation for the marathon number of viewings.

'What about Buzz?' Shane countered. 'Are you going to leave him upstairs while you watch? It's his movie too.'

'Buzz!' Ewan jumped to his feet, his face crumpled with genuine despair. 'Ow, I forgot.' He raced out of the room, Woody momentarily discarded. During their toy-shopping spree, Amanda had slid all of the *Toy Story* cast that she could find into the trolley. Ewan had been most delighted by the addition of Buzz to his collection. She noticed that he'd written his name in felt-tip pen upon the base of the toy's feet.

She wondered what would become of his toys back in Scotland, of the little bedroom in the flat which now sat empty and abandoned.

'So how long are you planning on hiding out here with him?' Corrine passed a sandwich to Amanda.

'As long as I have to.'

'Well, you're always welcome here, you know that.'

'But I will go home. Eventually.' Amanda thoughtfully nibbled at her sandwich.

'You will?' Considering that Corrine had started the discussion about leaving, she seemed saddened by this response.

'Yeah, I mean,' Amanda quickly polished off her sandwich, 'when it's safe.'

'Safe?'

'Yeah.'

'And when will that be?'

When McAllister stops being a threat.

Amanda reached for another sandwich.

'So when will it be safe?' Corrine pressed.

When McAllister is dead.

The thought stunned Amanda. She held her sandwich inches away from her mouth, unable to take a bite. If McAllister was dead then the threat to Ewan would be gone, right? In Will's, rather Jake's world, there seemed to be old-school Western justice at play. An eye for an eye, and so forth. So if Amanda could find a way to permanently end McAllister, then Ewan would truly be safe, she could stop eyeing everyone up on the beach as if they were a potential threat. Then she could move forward, could stop living in the dangerous shadow of Will's death and start piecing her life back together.

'Soon.' Amanda shoved the entire sandwich into her mouth as Ewan came bursting back into the room, his little face wide with an excited smile.

'Now Buzz gets to watch too,' he declared jovially. But Amanda wasn't listening. In her mind she was already formulating a plan.

3

The house she had shared with Will was as she'd left it. It took barely twenty minutes to get there from her mother's cottage. There were still wooden boards covering the front-room window, blocking out the mustard-coloured glow of the late afternoon sun. The kitchen surfaces were bare, allowing the granite countertops to glisten in all their majesty. And it all felt so unbearably empty.

Amanda froze in the hallway, the kitchen just ahead and the living room to her left. Her perfect white interior doors were open; her pristine painted walls stared back at her with indifference. This was her *home*. But then why did it feel like she'd just stepped into a morgue?

'It's a bad idea going back there,' Shane had warned, keeping his voice low as they conducted their heated discussion back in her mother's kitchen. Corrine was distracted by Ewan, acting out a scene from *Toy Story* where she was the scared dinosaur and the little boy the brave Sherriff Woody. It afforded Amanda a few moments to tell Shane what she was intending.

'I have to go back.'

'It's not safe.'

'The Internet connection here is too slow. It's not secure enough.'

This caused Shane to take a step back. Amanda could see the thoughts racing behind his eyes as he tried to figure out what she was up to.

'Trust me,' she reached for his hand and squeezed it. 'Please, Shane. Just trust me. I know what I'm doing.'

'Do you?' He was wearing his cop mask – all fear and precautions.

'At least I think I do.'

'Amanda—'

'I have to keep him *safe.*' She hissed the declaration, throwing a quick glance back towards where her mother and Ewan were merrily playing. There was no keeping Ewan safe in a world in which McAllister existed, Will's death had taught Amanda that much. 'Just trust me, Shane,' she pleaded again.

Corrine had burst in then, puffing up red cheeks and dropping down into the nearest chair. Her sudden presence silenced any further protests Shane might have had.

'Who knew being a dinosaur could be so exhausting?' Amanda's mother exclaimed with a chuckle as she threw up both arms which were adorned with a glimmering array of silver bangles which caught the light as they musically trickled down to her elbows.

'We're not done discussing this,' Shane whispered his comment to Amanda as he scraped past her. But she knew that they were.

Amanda drifted up the stairs of her house, feeling like a ghost. She moved silently, reverently, afraid to disturb the eerie peace which had gathered amongst the magnolia and white walls. She dared to release a sigh of relief when she entered her study. A space that had always been predominantly hers. A space not permeated by Will's lingering presence. Yet as she sat down at her desk and booted up her laptop, she knew he was there too. She imagined him peering round the door as she worked, reminding her that it'd be dinner soon. After dinner they'd snuggle together on the sofa and watch Netflix. She'd rest her head against Will's strong chest until her eyes began to droop.

'I love watching you fall asleep,' he'd murmur as he tenderly stroked a strand of hair out of her eyes. 'You always look so peaceful.'

Amanda had never felt the same way about seeing her husband slumber. On the rare occasions when she looked across the bed in the shadows of night and noticed him on his back, eyes tightly shut, he never looked peaceful. He always looked far away. Unreachable. Did he used to dream of Evangeline and Ewan?

'Dammit,' Amanda swept her fingertips across her cheek, smoothing away the tears which had just fallen. This was her home. All the memories that lingered within belonged to her and *Will*. Not Jake. Jake had been the man Will had been before he met her. Jake Burton existed in another life, the one back up in Scotland.

With shaking hands, she logged into her darknet account. There was a message waiting for her darknet alias; Lambchop, a message Amanda had been expecting to find.

Turtle82 had made contact again.

As her heart crept into her throat, Amanda forgot about Jake Burton, forget about how hollow her home felt. Her eyes danced across her computer screen with keen interest. The message was simple. Abrupt.

> You can't catch a King Carp unless you're fishing in the right pond.
> Find the right spot. Then we'll talk again.
> T.

Fishing in the right pond.

So Turtle was still watching her. Still aware of where she was.

A car drove by outside, its engine murmuring distantly like a purring cat. Amanda chewed on her lip and tried to decipher the message.

Scotland.

The right pond had to be Scotland. Turtle82 was urging her to return up north, to Glasgow.

Amanda opened up a fresh window in her browser and started searching for hotels in the city centre. She'd been intending to return to Glasgow all along and now she'd been given the push she needed to commit to her plan.

*

'You can't do this.'

The sea lapped against Amanda's bare feet, its touch sharp and cool. She shuddered deliciously as the wave crept up towards her heels and then slid back.

'I'm serious, Amanda.' Shane was beside her, his own feet also resting on the shoreline. He was leaning back, his hands sinking into the damp sand. Above them a full moon shone like a perfect silver coin. Ewan had gone to bed almost an hour ago. The evening was theirs.

It was Shane who'd suggested a walk along the beach. Corrine had fully endorsed the idea of a moonlit stroll, shoving Amanda out of the cottage before she'd even had time to consider Shane's offer. But, she mused as she headed down the cliffside path, being alone with Shane, away from her mother's eavesdropping, would allow her to discuss her plan with him in full detail. To tell him that she was leaving.

'I'm going,' Amanda told him curtly. 'It's not up for discussion.'

Another wave kissed her toes but shied away from the rest of her feet.

'How can you even say that? Will *died* up there, Amanda. And now you want to put your life at risk too? You said yourself that you're all that Ewan has left! Why go back?'

'In order for Ewan to be safe, really safe, then McAllister needs to be out of the picture.'

'So what? You're going to kill him?' She could tell from his tone that Shane was mocking her.

'No,' Amanda's shoulders slumped shamefully. She couldn't believe she'd ever actually consider *killing* a man. She just didn't have it in her, no matter how much hate she had for McAllister. But there were other ways to remove someone from society. Prison for example. And Turtle82 had given her hope. Back in her student days she had done numerous jobs for Turtle which involved outing fraudulent investors, exposing people who were embezzling large sums of money. There was no way someone like McAllister was squeaky clean. He must have a digital trail of dirt over a mile long. All Amanda had to do was find it. And she knew that Turtle could help her do that.

'I have...' she dug her hands into the damp sand. 'A contact. A contact who can help me.'

Behind them a young couple strolled by hand in hand, oblivious to the conversation being conducted beside the waves. Amanda glanced at them as they walked away, wrapped tightly in one another's arms as if they didn't dare to let go of each other, even for a second. She envied their closeness, the

31

brilliance with which their love burned. She'd known that kind of passion before. In Will's arms and also in—

'Contact?' Shane grimaced as he said the word and climbed to his feet. 'Let me guess – it's darknet-related.'

He began stalking down the beach, having heard enough, all the old demons from their past relationship biting at his heels.

'Shane,' Amanda chased after him. She caught his hand and he allowed her to pull him back with little resistance. 'Yes, it's darknet-related. But it's too good an opportunity for me to just pass up. If I do this, I could ensure Ewan's safety for the rest of his life. A *long* life.'

Shane's hand remained in hers but he was looking down at his feet.

'I know it's dangerous. I know I'm taking a huge risk,' her voice was low, tentative. 'But that little boy, he's all I have left of Will. And he's worth it. He's worth saving.'

'So are you.' Shane raised his head and his green eyes held her in a steady gaze. In the moonlight his eyes shone as though he'd stolen some of the starlight for himself. With his hair ruffled by the sea breeze and the shadow of stubble framing his jawline, Shane looked so much like his younger self. Too much.

Amanda had spent countless moonlit nights such as this one pacing along the beach with him, hand in hand or pressed against a rock tangled together in a passionate embrace. Sometimes their friend John was there. Sometimes they built fires which burned late into the night and told ghost stories to each other from across the flames.

The beach remained the same. There was still the steep incline of jagged rocks which made up the cliff face. If you kept walking south, the tide would consume the beach completely after seven at night. The same moon was watching them overhead. The only thing that had changed was time. It had morphed them into different people. But Amanda could sense the echo of her younger self within her soul.

'Did they remind you of us?'

The sudden change in topic made Amanda feel disorientated. 'Who?' She looked further along the beach where the love-struck couple were just disappearing from view. 'That couple?' She hadn't realised that Shane had even been aware of them.

'Yeah,' he gave her a half-smile. 'I mean, that was us, once.'

'Yeah.'

A cold breeze darted between them, hinting at the frosty weather which was gathered out at sea. Amanda imagined tiny fishing boats being tossed upon furious waves as though they were nothing more than matchboxes. Nature could be brilliant but also brutal. Growing up by the sea, Amanda had learned from a young age to respect it.

'She can be unpredictable, the sea,' her father would say sagely as he walked his young daughter against the waves as the tide began to turn. 'Like any good woman,' he'd add teasingly. Only Corrine was never there to catch the joke, she kept her distance from the water for reasons which Amanda had never come to know.

'He always loved the ocean.' Amanda turned to watch the gentle lapping of waves which continued to break against the beach.

'Will?' Shane kept walking.

'No, my dad.'

Shane stopped. The shadows on his face changed. Amanda realised that he was regarding her with pity.

'I know what you're thinking,' she quickened her pace.

33

'What am I thinking?' Shane easily kept in step with her.

'You're thinking "Oh poor, Amanda. She's lost so many men in her life. She'll never be able to let a man in now. She's just fucked for the rest of her life." Because I mean that's right, isn't it? You thought I couldn't truly love a man because I placed my dead father on a pedestal.'

'Amanda—'

'And now Will, he's up there too. So where does that leave me, huh?'

'Actually,' Shane raised his voice, just slightly. Amanda stopped walking and turned her entire body towards him. 'I was thinking how strong you are. How, in spite of the incredibly shit hand that life has dealt you, you keep moving forwards. Losing Will could have so easily sent you into a downward spiral but you're still… you. And your main concern is Ewan. You're willing to put yourself in danger for him. Amanda, that's brave as hell. But then you always have been.'

'I have?'

'Yeah,' Shane shrugged, looking shy. 'I mean, you always pushed me, Amanda. You were never content to just stay in your comfort zone. You always wanted more from life and that… it inspired me.'

It was still warm out, the heat from the day lingering like a hangover. A short woman jogged past them with her Cavalier King Charles spaniel. The white and tan dog regarded Shane and Amanda with wide, excited eyes and slowed his pace, his tail wagging furiously, as if he were contemplating coming over to introduce himself.

'Come on,' the woman gave a command and a brisk whistle and her furry companion continued to run loyally by her side.

'I'm going back to Scotland and I don't want you to hate me for it.' There. Amanda had placed her cards upon the table.

'I could never hate you.'

'But?' Amanda raised her eyebrows expectantly.

'I refuse to let you go back there alone.'

'Shane, I don't have a choice.' She threw her arms up in frustration and took a step back from him as a fresh wave trickled over her feet, sending a fierce chill straight up her body as though she'd just sat on a poker made of ice. 'Urgh,' she moved out of the water which was growing colder with each passing minute.

'And neither do I,' the fire in Shane's voice pushed back some of the cold sensations that were sweeping along Amanda's skeleton. 'If you're going back to Scotland, then I'm coming with you.'

Amanda opened her mouth but no words came out. She snapped it shut again. She felt winded, stunned. And touched beyond measure. This was the Shane she'd grown up with, the loyal, kind, brave guy who seemed genetically destined to be a policeman. He was always putting her first, always keeping her safe. It'd made it so easy to fall in love with him back then.

'I'm serious.' Shane moved towards her and rested both hands on her shoulders.

'You... can't,' Amanda croaked over the lump which had formed in her throat. 'You've done so much already. I can't ask this of you.'

'You're not asking, I'm insisting. There's a big difference. Trust me.'

'What about work?'

'How long do you need?'

There was an intensity behind his eyes that Amanda rarely saw. He looked focused and alert. It was the attitude which had helped him rise so high within the ranks of the police force. Gone was the student, the dreamer, who Amanda used to play *World of Warcraft* with until their eyes burned and their wrists ached. Here was a man – strong and determined. And looking at him, into his confident, assured gaze, reminded her so much of when she'd first fallen for Will. Of how he'd made her feel so safe with just one look.

Amanda tilted her head away from his green eyes, needing to focus. Most jobs she did for Turtle82 didn't last longer than a few days. But she knew she had to be generous in her estimations. 'Um, a week. Two at most, I reckon.'

'Two weeks. Got it.' Shane nodded.

'Are you sure you want to do this?'

'I'm sure,' he pulled her towards him and softly kissed her forehead. 'When it comes to you, I'm always sure.'

*

'Vegas?' Corrine looked like she was somewhere between appalled and delighted as she repeated the destination Amanda was using as her cover for the next two weeks.

Two hours back at her house and on the darknet had placed her and Shane on the next Vegas-bound flight out of Heathrow. With some digital wizardry, she'd have them both checked through customs in just over eighteen hours and then checked into Caesar's Palace at the Las Vegas strip. For fourteen nights.

Amanda had chosen the location for their cover carefully. She needed somewhere busy. Somewhere they wouldn't stand out, where, if questioned, people would just assume they'd seen them since there was an abundance of tourists. And in a place like Vegas it was commonplace for people not to return to their rooms at night. They were too busy gambling or taking in a show or just being overwhelmed by the spectacle of it all.

'Vegas?' Corrine stared at her daughter, her mouth agape.

Amanda knew what her mother was picturing – an Elvis impersonator at some tacky little chapel.

'Shane and I just need to go somewhere and relax. Then when I'm back I'll sort out moving Ewan into my place and enrolling him into school.'

'Vegas?' Corrine's eyes were side as she imagined showgirls, strippers and shotgun weddings. 'Are you and Shane?' she pursed her purple lips together.

'Friends in need of a holiday? Definitely,' Amanda smiled falsely. The lie tasted sour upon her tongue as she told it. She wished she could be honest with her mother but the truth was too dangerous. It was better to have her mother believe she was lounging on a sunbed beside some turquoise swimming pool surrounded by faux-Roman columns.

'Is this...' Corrine clasped Amanda's hands between her own from where she was sat across from her at the small kitchen table. Yellow sunlight flooded the room, exposing every speck of dust which had skilfully avoided the depths of the hoover. 'Is this what you need to do to help you grieve?'

'Yes.' That was no lie. Amanda did need to get revenge on McAllister in order to grieve. In order to get closure. To heal.

'Then I support you.' Corrine leaned back in her chair, releasing her daughter from her grasp. 'I'll take care of Ewan, you don't need to worry about him. Two weeks you said, right?'

'Right.'

Amanda told herself that if McAllister's men hadn't come yet then hopefully they wouldn't come at all. She needed to believe Ewan was safe else she'd never leave, never put an end to the ever present threat of McAllister. And she couldn't take him with her. He had to stay.

'That's a lot of Happy Meals.'

'And think how many times you'll get to watch *Toy Story*,' Amanda teased.

'He's a sweet boy,' Corrine commented tenderly. 'And you're an even sweeter girl for taking him in so readily. Regardless of, you know, the *implications*.'

'Well, the legality of it all isn't really an issue at this point,' Amanda shrugged modestly, almost admiring her mother's ability to subdue a compliment with concern. Corrine only knew half the story and Amanda was determined to keep it that way. She was just doing what was right. What anybody else would have done.

'This morning Ewan said something strange.' Corrine wound her fingers together, looking thoughtful.

'He did?' Amanda sucked in her cheeks, suddenly feeling tense.

'We were walking down towards the beach and he said he spotted one of his mother's friends. But it was just Mrs Porter from down the end of the lane.'

'Oh,' relief shuddered through Amanda.

'It just struck me as odd,' Corrine continued. 'I mean,' she tilted her head and let her eyes bore into her daughter, 'is anyone looking for him, Amanda?'

'No!' Her chest tightened and the word came out much sharper than Amanda intended. She saw her mother flinch and lean back. 'I mean, of course not. He doesn't have anybody. Me and Shane, we're all he's got.'

Her heart was manic in her chest.

It was just Mrs Porter.

The old woman was almost as permanent a fixture in their neighbourhood as the imposing cliffs which snaked their way down the coastline.

But what if it wasn't? What if someone *was* looking for Ewan? And not just someone – McAllister. She felt more resolute than ever to take matters into her own hands.

'The way Shane has stood by you through all of this,' Corrine gave a wistful sigh and pressed both hands against her chest. 'He's always been a good egg that one, don't you think?'

'Uh-huh.' Amanda tried to sound flippant. She didn't have the energy to listen to her mother belt out one of her team Shane ballads.

'He still loves you, you know. I see it every time he looks at you, clear as day.'

Amanda's cheeks began to burn.

'The flame between you two never went out,' Corrine continued. 'It just needs the right spark to reignite it.'

4

It was raining when they arrived in Glasgow. A soft, light rain that silently soaked Shane's car as he navigated the busy streets. Amanda peered out of her windows at the bustling city centre. Brightly coloured storefronts broke up the gloom of a wet afternoon.

'We're almost there.' Shane nodded deferentially at the satnav perched on his dashboard.

'So we are.'

Amanda had selected a hotel in the heart of the city, amongst all the shops and restaurants. It would be teeming with tourists. It would provide the perfect cover for her and Shane – a place where they could be at the pulsing centre of all of Glasgow's activity but still hidden in plain sight.

Stay central.

That had been the single piece of advice Turtle82 had given Amanda when she queried where she should stay. She'd considered booking an isolated cabin out in the Highlands, but that felt too close to where Will had stayed. Where she'd found him. And the Internet connection in such remote places would be dire at best.

Shane swung the car round a sharp turn, down into the depths of their hotel's underground parking system. The grey light of day quickly slipped away, replaced by the murky yellow glow of the overhanging strip lights which stretched across row upon row of parked cars.

'Are you sure you're ready for this?' Shane asked after he'd slid the car into an empty bay and killed the engine. The silence around them pressed against the windows. Amanda leaned forward to turn off the satnav, noticing the shadows which gathered in the corners of the car park where the lights failed to reach, each one potentially pregnant with danger.

'I'm sure,' Amanda swallowed down her fear. 'This is where I have to be. From here I can use the Internet and search the city for McAllister.'

'And if he finds us first?'

Ignoring the question, Amanda opened her door and climbed out of the car. Cold air greeted her, wrapping itself around her like an icy cloak. She shivered, dressed in just jeans and a baggy white T-shirt.

'Jeeze,' Shane rubbed at his arms as he got out too. 'I wish we really were in Vegas,' he declared as he slammed his door shut.

'It'll warm up once the rain stops.'

'I hope so.'

As Shane unloaded their suitcases from the boot, Amanda looked around at all the gathered cars, at all the dark corners. Was McAllister lying in wait somewhere, looking for her as keenly as she was looking for him?

*

The hotel room contained just one bed. Amanda was through the door, attracted by the impressive view of the city the window offered, completely oblivious of the solitary sleeping space.

Shane remained in the doorway and cleared his throat.

'You okay?' Amanda turned back to face him.

'Um…' he gestured at the bed and raised his eyebrows. 'I think the hotel must have made a mistake with the booking. I'll go back down and ask for a room with twin beds and—'

'No.' Amanda raised her palm towards him, urging him not to leave.

'But there's just the one bed.'

'If we go down, if we make a fuss, we become memorable. We need to remain as incognito as possible, remember?'

'I'm not sure I want to sleep in a chair for the next two weeks.' Shane placed their cases on the bed and crossed his arms against his chest. 'Let me at least request a foldaway bed or something.'

'We can share.' Amanda turned her back on him to once again look out at the city. It stretched away from her, a sprawling maze of streets and skyscrapers. This was Will's city. His home. How many of these streets had he walked down? The buildings that rose up in the distance, almost obscured by the drizzle that misted the air, was one of those the block of flats where Will had lived? Where Evangeline had lived? What had become of their home? The police had surely moved on. Was the flat empty? Did it have new occupants? So easily a life could be erased, forgotten.

'Share?'

In the window, Amanda saw Shane's startled reflection.

'Yes, share.' She gave him a warm smile as she drifted over towards the bed and sat down upon its crisp white sheets. 'It's a big bed, Shane. There's more than enough room for us both.'

And I don't want to sleep alone.

She didn't share this last part of her rationale with him. Since losing Will, she'd yet to sleep alone. Her mother had been beside her each night, there when she woke up from a darkened dream to comfort her. Amanda wasn't sure she was ready to wake up to an empty bed. Not yet.

'I'll... um,' Shane was pulling back the sheets on the other side of the bed, assessing the space available. 'I can put a pillow in the middle to act as a divider.'

'Okay, sure.'

'And you're sure you're okay being here? Because just say the word and we could actually be in Vegas. You don't have to do this, you know.'

Amanda thought of the little boy back at her mother's, of his head full of dark hair which he'd inherited from his father, of his bright blue eyes that were all that remained of his mother. Ewan was probably sat with Corrine on the sofa, enjoying another viewing of *Toy Story* whilst they ate fish and chips out of newspaper baskets.

'No,' she hoped that Shane could see the strength in her gaze. The resolve. 'I do.'

*

'What's the plan?' Shane asked as they stepped out of the lift and into the lobby. Amanda remained at his side to ensure that to the outside world they looked like any other couple enjoying a city break. He might as well have asked her about the weather. The plan was a tenuous thing, subject to change at a moment's notice, at the whim of forces beyond their control.

'We need to just get a feel of the city.' Amanda wore a shoulder bag, into which her beloved laptop was stowed. 'Walk around a bit, get a sense of the place. Maybe sit somewhere and have coffee.'

'Use their Wi-Fi, anonymously hack social media accounts in the area to search for leads.' Shane's voice was soft and he almost sung the words.

'Okay, fine.' Amanda strode ahead of him, pushing her way through the revolving glass doors which led outside. 'But unless you have a better plan for how we can get some intel, I'm going with mine.'

The rain had stopped and the sun had managed to punctuate part of the cloud cover, allowing golden beams of light to thread their way down into the city. The air smelt of damp earth and asphalt.

'I'm kind of at the mercy of whatever you decide to do.' Shane walked alongside her, his hands deep in his pockets. His shoulders were high and his chin was bowed towards his chest. He looked awkward, like he didn't really want to be there. In contrast, Amanda was doing her best to walk with light, buoyant steps, her hair swaying upon her back as though she didn't have a care in the world.

'I thought you came here to help, not just spectate.'

She heard Shane sigh loudly as he contemplated this. 'It's just that my hands are tied. I can't risk doing anything that will cost me my job.'

'And you won't, since you're in Vegas, remember?'

'People are going to talk. You do realise that, don't you? Back home, no one knows what happened to Will. They'll just think that you and I have eloped on some romantic getaway.'

'Let people think what they want.'

'You don't care what they say?'

'When have I ever cared what people say about me?' Amanda asked as she stopped in front of a Starbucks. Inside, it was moderately busy but she noticed that several tables were empty, including one in a booth at the back of the café which would be a perfect spot for them to set up to conduct a bit of cyber-stalking.

'I always admired that about you,' Shane commented as he followed her inside. 'The only time you ever cared was when...' his voice trailed off and he nervously cleared his throat. Amanda knew what he was about to say.

The only time you ever cared was when people were speaking badly about your dad.

People being Jayne, Shane's ex-girlfriend and Amanda's former classmate, and others like her. Amanda could take every insult thrown at her on the chin, but she'd defend the people she loved until her last breath. Her father had been a hero in every sense of the word, she'd gladly risk the fires of hell to pull apart anyone who would dare to suggest otherwise.

The café was noisy and carried the intoxicating scent of coffee beans mixed with something softer, sweeter, like vanilla. The drinks machines hissed and gurgled as the baristas diligently prepared fresh orders. Amanda told Shane that she'd have a coffee. Black. Then she went to procure her coveted table while he waited in line. From behind her laptop she watched him waiting patiently in the queue, saw him massage his neck a couple of times when he wasn't thrusting his hands into his pockets. He was nervous. But no one else would see that. No one else knew Shane inside out like she did.

She connected to the local Wi-Fi and then started to work her magic. Scanning through nearby social media accounts was easy for a seasoned hacker like Amanda. The skills she'd learnt as a teenager were still sharp in her mind. She ran a number of searches for keywords. Some were more obvious than others—

Gregg
McAllister

Drugs
Jake Burton

Her laptop hummed against the dark wood table as it went to work.

'One coffee, black.' Shane placed down her drink and then slid into the booth beside her. He dropped a cursory glance at her computer screen. 'Are you sure it's safe to do that here?'

'Safe as houses,' Amanda absently reached for her drink and took a small sip. 'We'll be long gone before anyone could even get a bit suspicious. Look around, there's too many people using the Wi-Fi to be able to pinpoint one user and their activity.'

At every table there was someone either using their phone or laptop, heads bent, engrossed by whatever they were reading or typing. They were all connected by an invisible web which ran between tables, wrapped around their ankles, wrists, hearts and bound them all together.

'I was thinking,' Shane leaned back against his cushioned seat, drink in hand. 'We should check the latest police reports, things in the press. Look for stories about people being arrested on drunk and disorderly charges.'

'Not drug possession?'

'No, that's too obvious. A guy like McAllister would surely have the police and the press in his pocket to some extent. When business goes sour, he'll pin it on something else, probably drink.'

'Okay,' Amanda updated her searches.

Their drinks were lukewarm and only half consumed when her laptop pinged.

'Find anything?' Shane leaned forward with interest. Amanda caught a blast of the cologne he was wearing. It smelt stronger than it had in the car, the notes of cedar and lime more pronounced. Had he topped it up before they'd left the hotel?

Of course he had, he's making an effort to blend in.

Amanda pushed her hands through her hair, removing her questions about Shane's scent from her mind. She focused on her computer screen. There were a number of search results for her to look at. They were mainly news stories, a couple of Facebook posts. And they all related to the same thing – the Glasgow nightlife scene.

In the past week alone there had been five drink-related arrests. All upon one particular street that ran through the city centre like a scar. Amanda ran a search on all the clubs there.

Moxxi's was, by the looks of it, a high-end strip club. After Hours was a popular nightclub that played trance and house music. Hooked was also a popular nightspot which had live bands every Thursday and an R & B night on a Sunday. Rumours looked like a hybrid between strip club and dance venue. All of the clubs were within a half-mile radius of one another.

'So, I guess we need to start looking in these places,' Amanda tapped at the list of venues on her screen.

'Hmm.' Shane didn't sound impressed.

'What?'

'Somewhere like this,' he nodded at the surrounding tables, 'we can blend in no problem. The hotel, that's easy too. But a nightclub,' raising his eyebrows, he paused for effect. 'I mean, come on, when was the last time you went clubbing?'

'I…' the word *never* almost tumbled from her lips. Amanda had never really been the clubbing kind, unless you counted the Student Union back when she was at university. But even then she went to drink shots and play pool. She'd never danced beneath strobe lights, never sashayed across a sticky floor.

'That's what I thought,' Shane shook his head at her but his mouth was lifted in a half-smile. 'I can't imagine you in some little miniskirt and heels on a night out.'

'Is that what people wear on night's out these days?'

'I'm afraid so,' he looked down at her legs, 'jeans just won't cut it.'

'Since when did you become so knowledgeable? I don't remember you ever being Mr Club Med.'

'Um,' Shane loosened the top button on his grey polo shirt. He looked effortlessly smart in that and dark jeans.

'Oh.' Amanda closed her eyes and sighed. Deeply. 'I guess she was the type, huh?'

'Jayne loved to go clubbing with the girls,' Shane recalled flatly.

'Have you heard from her?' Amanda tried to sound impartial although the way her heart clenched in her chest told her that she wasn't.

'No. I don't expect I will.'

'She'll be pretty pissed when she hears that you're in Vegas.'

'That she will. And she cares an awful lot what people say about her.'

'Then maybe she shouldn't have said such horrid things about other people.' Amanda slammed her laptop closed, feeling that her recon session was well and truly over. 'I'm heading back to the hotel.' She didn't wait for Shane's response. Slinging her bag over her shoulder, she powered towards the doors and was grateful for the fresh air that filled her lungs as soon as she stepped outside.

'Hey, wait up,' Shane was swiftly at her side, his face pinched with concern. 'Look, I know you hate her and with good reason but—'

'She talked trash about my *dead* dad, Shane. There is no but.'

'But,' Shane reached for her arm and drew her to him, placing extra emphasis upon the word. 'She was jealous of you, Amanda. And she had every right to be.'

'I'm not going to listen to you defend her,' she shrugged him off and started marching in the direction of her hotel.

'She loved me,' Shane was hurrying to keep up with her, speaking quickly.

'Good for her,' Amanda retorted bitterly.

'And you were the reason I could never love her back.'

They'd reached the hotel. Amanda stiffened before the revolving doors. She could see people drifting around the lobby, pulling dark suitcases in their wake.

Will.

The wind that whipped past her almost seemed to whisper his name. This was where he'd been a boy, when he'd grown into a man. Where he'd become a father. With every step she took, Amanda felt like she was intruding, walking on his grave.

'Let's go inside and study the nightclubs some more.' Amanda couldn't acknowledge what he'd just said in Will's town, where it felt like his ghost lingered on street corners, it would be like stamping on his grave and she didn't wait to see the dejected look on Shane's face so she just hurried through the doors, allowing them to swallow her up like a whirlpool.

*

When darkness fell, the city sparkled. Amanda stood at her hotel room window, admiring all the glistening lights. The streets had been claimed by the night. The clubs which Amanda had researched online would now be opening their doors, welcoming in familiar faces along with new ones. Would McAllister be there? Or did he remain a king in his castle, hidden away in the Highlands? He lived in a vast mansion, that's what Amanda had learned about him, a vast mansion where there had once been a great fire.

Her gaze settled on a white van parked up in front of the hotel. The lights of the city gleamed against its clean roof.

'We need a plan,' Shane said from where he sat on the bed watching TV. 'Like, a serious, methodical one. We need to hit each club, figure out the clientele.'

'And what if he doesn't show?'

'If not him then someone who can lead us to him.'

'We could just go straight to his house. We know where he lives.'

'That's far too risky,' Shane raised his voice. 'I'm here to keep you safe, Amanda. And I intend to do my job.'

Amanda rubbed at the plush towelling robe that covered her arms. Her hair was still damp from the shower she'd just taken. She felt conflicted. She knew that she should be down there, out in the city, amongst all the lights, walking the streets that Will had walked. She should have been searching for McAllister, peering into every darkened corner until the rat presented himself. And then what?

Amanda softly trod her way over to the desk where she'd left her laptop. The carpeted floor was coarse against her bare feet. She popped the laptop open and logged into the darknet. Shane kept watching the TV, pretending not to notice.

They only had two weeks, a finite amount of time to find McAllister. Then it was back home, back to the real world, and Amanda refused to leave Glasgow until she'd removed the threat to Ewan for good. She needed to work swiftly, efficiently. She couldn't waste time traipsing from club to club, potentially following dead ends.

She typed out her message to Turtle82 and hit send without even waiting to consider her actions.

Let's be real. You want me to catch this King Carp
– tell me where it was last sighted.

5

At night the city stirred. As Amanda lay in bed she could hear the distant drone of car engines occasionally punctured by the shrill shriek of a siren as an emergency vehicle dashed down the streets in a blaze of blue lights. And closer than the sounds of the city, she could hear Shane sleeping. He was on his side, facing away from her, his deep breaths slow and steady. It would be so easy for Amanda to stretch out across the distance between them, to place a hand upon his shoulder, against his back, to wedge herself up close, to feel his body heat press against hers.

She missed Will so much that her body ached. She wanted to curl up in his arms, to rest her head upon his chest, to see his eyes crinkle at the corners when she made him smile. But her husband was gone.

The lies surrounding Will's death caused her inner wounds to sting. When she thought about who he'd really been – Jake Burton, about how he'd had a son and a wife, her chest constricted as though she was about to be choked by her own despair.

Pushing back the crisp white covers, Amanda got up. She grabbed a hoody that was draped over a nearby chair and pulled it on. After tiptoeing towards the window, she carefully drew the curtains back just an inch and looked out at the city. She felt as restless as the souls that wandered the streets so late at night. Above the towering buildings the sky was a thick black blanket devoid of stars. Amanda leaned her head against the window and released a tense breath which misted the glass.

Her gaze dipped and she stared dead-eyed at the white van, parked in the same position at the side of the road. The only vehicle on a busy street. Surely it was illegal to park there? Amanda considered focusing on its presence but couldn't. This wasn't her life, how could it be? She was meant to be in her perfect home sleeping beside her perfect husband.

Had anyone even found Will's body?

In these quiet moments, when most of the world slept, this was the question that haunted Amanda the most. She imagined him still slumped on the damp ground of the forest, the blood which had once flowed freely from his chest dried and congealed around him growing darker by the day.

'I should never have left him,' Amanda pressed her fingertips against the window. But she'd had no choice. There had been Ewan and she had to protect the boy. She had to—

'Amanda?' Shane's voice was clotted with sleep as she heard him sit up in the bed behind her.

'Did I wake you?' She turned away from the window and let the curtain fall back into place, sealing out the lights of the city that continued to twinkle like a thousand artificial stars.

'You okay?' Shane pushed his hand through his messy hair. Amanda noticed that his chest was bare. Her gaze dropped to the outline of lean muscles and when it kept dipping she forced herself to look up, to lock eyes with Shane.

'I just couldn't sleep.'

'You should try and rest as much as you can.' He got out of bed, revealing the low-slung pair of joggers that he'd been sleeping in, and trod a path towards the bathroom. 'Sleep deprivation can dull even the sharpest mind,' he threw over his shoulder before closing the door.

Amanda massaged her temple. She understood the importance of staying sharp. If she lowered her guard, even for a second, she risked McAllister finding her first. And given what she suspected he'd done to Evangeline she doubted he'd show her any kind of mercy. By all accounts the man was a monster, an animal, who deserved to be behind bars.

Or dead.

The vitriol which suddenly bubbled inside Amanda actually scared her. She clenched and unclenched her hands into fists as she went over to the desk. Opening up her laptop, she instantly saw that she had a new message from Turtle. Amanda pressed down hard on her mouse key, overly eager to read the reply.

Rumour has it that you need the right hook.
    T

Amanda's eyes danced over the message as Shane emerged from the bathroom.

'It's a little early for that, don't you think? You should really try and get some rest, Amanda.' He stood behind her and gestured towards the bed. The smell of his cologne had grown stronger, seemed fresher. 'I can head down to the hotel gym for an hour or so, if, you know, me being in the bed is making you uncomfortable.'

'Rumours and Hooked.' Amanda tapped a finger against her laptop screen.

'What?' Shane leaned forward to peer at the message.

'Those are the two clubs that McAllister frequents.'

'Amanda—'

'We just need to go there and suss him out. Assess how much security he has around him.'

'Okay, but—'

'Figure out which night's he's usually there. How long he stays for.'

'Can you even trust this,' Shane scrutinised the screen with increased intensity, 'Turtle82?' His lips curled down with disgust as he stated the username. 'For all you know they might be working for McAllister. This might all be some kind of trap.'

Amanda shook her head. 'No way. I've known Turtle82 for years. I worked with them when I was a student.'

'What if their account has been compromised?'

'Impossible.' Amanda didn't even take a second to entertain the idea. 'Turtle82 is the best there is when it comes to hacking. Their account is an impenetrable digital fortress. Trust me.'

'*You* I trust,' Shane pointed at the laptop, 'but this Turtle. We don't even know who the hell they are. They're just a name on a screen. And why are they even keen on taking down McAllister? What's in it for them?'

'Money, probably,' Amanda shrugged. 'McAllister must have pissed off the wrong person. Now they want him locked up but for their hands to remain clean. I used to work jobs like this all the time – sort of digital espionage, if you like.'

'It's *hacking*, Amanda, don't try and dress it up.' Shane's nose crinkled with disgust like it always used to whenever the topic of discussion was the darknet.

'And you devote your life to trying to find justice for dead men.' Her voice hardened. 'Talk about a lost cause.'

'Isn't that exactly what you're doing?' Shane took a step towards her, she could see his chest rising and falling with every beat of his heart.

'This is about more than Will,' Amanda retorted, raising her chin. 'This is about Ewan. About his future.'

'This is about revenge and you know it. McAllister might not even be looking for Ewan.'

'I'm not going to live my life beneath that shadow of doubt. If McAllister is behind bars then he can't hurt Ewan.'

'I've seen a man's reach extend far beyond the walls of his cell.'

'Then what am I supposed to do? *Kill* him?' Amanda noticed that the thought didn't chill her the way it should have. Disturbed, she moved away from Shane, back towards the bed where she dropped down upon its edge, head pressed against her chest.

'Jesus, Amanda, no!'

'Turtle82 has a plan. They know the way to take McAllister down. And yes, they're in it for different reasons than I am, but so what? We don't exactly have many people on our side, Shane. At this point I'm willing to take all the allies we can find.'

'But you're playing a dangerous game.' He came and sat beside her. 'You're trusting strangers, putting yourself in harm's way.'

'If I don't then who will?' She peered up at Shane as he looped an arm around her waist and pulled her close. She leaned her head against his shoulder and closed her eyes. 'Ewan deserves to have someone who will fight for him.'

'And I'll fight for you. No matter what.' Shane sounded far away, like he was speaking underwater. Amanda breathed in his cologne, felt the warmth of his body merge with her own as she fell asleep against his shoulder.

*

'So we go to the club, what then?' Shane asked the question through the bathroom door. Amanda was staring at her reflection in the large mirror that hung over the sink as she carefully applied a thick layer of mascara. She wore dark skinny jeans, black ankle boots and a silver vest top. Her hair was slightly curled as it tumbled down her back and lazy golden waves.

'We look around,' she shouted back before pouting and tackling her other eye.

'I still don't know about this.' Shane was in the centre of the room when she came out of the bathroom, his shoulders raised and his body a coil of tightly wound nervous energy. But he looked good. His black jeans had been matched with a white shirt and grey blazer. He looked handsome, casual. His hair was loosely styled with some gel and his face freshly shaven.

'You look...' Amanda froze just beyond the bathroom, feeling like she was fifteen again. She remembered all too well the butterflies which had erupted in her stomach when she saw Shane all dressed up for their school disco. Back then it had been jeans and a Ramones T-shirt, but with his hair styled and a cloud of cologne flanking his every step Amanda had seen her friend for the first time not as the boy she played computer games with and made bonfires but as the man who might one day steal her heart. And that was the man who was looking at her now.

'Stunning,' Shane's eyes widened as he took her in. 'Truly, Amanda, you're a vision.'

She gave him a nervous smile in gratitude. 'Well, let's get this over with, these things are already killing my feet,' she kicked out one of her boots and playfully scowled at him.

'Yes, but like I told you, they wouldn't let you in if you wore your Converse.'

'Maybe we need to test that theory,' Amanda teased as together they went out the door.

*

A chalkboard sign on the street, though rain-splattered, told them that it was live band night at Hooked. The Decadent Dominoes were playing. The path was littered with cigarette stubs and discarded pieces of chewing gum. A plastic bag sagged in a nearby drain like a used-up washrag.

'I think we should try Rumours,' Shane's hand was on the small of Amanda's back as he helped her pick a path along the street. Since leaving the hotel, she'd almost fallen in her heels three times. 'McAllister doesn't strike me as the kind of guy who enjoys listening to indie bands live.'

When they got there, there was a queue outside Rumours which snaked its way along the street. Women in miniskirts with legs for days giggled in groups as men openly flirted with them. The air was full of excitable, drunken chatter and Amanda felt completely out of her depth. People swore, turning the air blue and then cackled in delight. A litany of words Amanda didn't even understand tumbled from rouge lips. The laughter was always raucous. Always dirty. The glimmer of smouldering cigarettes lit up the line like cat's eyes. Amanda almost choked on the cloud of smoke which twisted in a halo around her head. This wasn't her scene. The second they reached the front of the line the bouncer would take one look at her and know why she was there. They'd read the heartbreak on her face, see the desire for revenge lurking behind her painted eyes.

'I can't do this,' she tried to drift away but Shane held her close to his side as they joined the back of the queue.

'Yes, you can,' he told her quietly. Confidently. 'We're just going to go in and have a few drinks together. Look around. That's it.'

'I don't know.' Amanda felt so socially awkward, like a teacup surrounded by champagne flutes. She stood out, seemed misplaced.

'If you want to go back, say the word,' Shane's hand was in hers and their fingers threaded together like it was the most natural thing in the world. Amanda looked down at their palms clasped together. She used to think that she and Shane fit together perfectly, like when she placed her hand in his it just seemed meant to be.

With Will it had been different. In his huge hands her own had almost disappeared and she loved that. He was a giant. *Her* giant.

She squeezed Shane's hand. He was right. She wasn't sure who she was really there for anymore – Will or Ewan. It was probably both of them. And so for the man she'd loved and for boy she'd vowed to protect, Amanda pushed back her shoulders and did her best to look like she belonged. 'I can do this,' she whispered to herself more than to Shane.

*

Twenty minutes later and they were in the club. In the dim lighting, Amanda could make out the red-cushioned booths which lined the outer walls. On the far wall there was a long bar where the optics were displayed beneath neon blue lights. Several bartenders darted about, all wearing white shirts and black waistcoats.

In the centre of the club was the dance floor. It seemed to absorb all excess light in the room. Whilst the booths were shrouded in shadows, the dance floor was ablaze with spotlights. Even the chequered floor was lit up.

'This place feels like the eighties threw up in here,' Shane said into her ear as he guided her towards an empty booth. Amanda sat down and looked around. There were mainly women on the dance floor, sexually moving their bodies in time with the music as if they knew every beat, could pre-empt every change in tempo. They all looked so at ease, moving with confident fluidity. And they all looked beautiful. Every woman dancing could have been a model. They had long legs and an ethereal, graceful elegance, even when clad in small skirts and wearing too much make-up.

Rumours felt nothing like the clubs Amanda had dared to visit back home. Those had also been full of shadows, but the people who danced within them seemed more… real. The people within Rumours looked like they'd fallen out of the pages of a Victoria's Secret catalogue. They were beautiful, exotic.

'This is definitely where McAllister will be.' Shane was still standing, glancing between the dance floor and the bar.

'You think so?' Amanda had to shout to be heard over the pulse of the music blasting out from the DJ booth, which was so loud it felt like it was replacing her own heartbeat echoing in her ears.

'This place seems exclusive.'

Amanda arched an eyebrow at him which made Shane grin. He flashed her a boyish smile and leaned in close. Close enough for his cheek to graze against her as he whispered in her ear, 'Don't worry darling, I've got eyes for no one but you tonight.' She knew he was teasing, but as he walked away towards the bar Amanda was still blushing.

The music kept pounding as the beauties danced. The air was thick with the lingering scent of stale beer laced with overpowering perfume. It was the kind of aroma which sunk into your clothes so that you ended up wearing it long after you'd left the club. Amanda drummed her fingertips against the table and waited on Shane. She kept darting her gaze around the club, peering into each shadowy corner. And then she saw him.

It took a second for her mind to catch up with her eyes. But there was no mistaking that the man sat on the other side of the club in what appeared to be a raised VIP area was Gregg McAllister.

He was in the centre of a booth like the one Amanda was sat in, only his had plump purple fabric instead of red. And his booth and two others were higher than any of the others in the club and two burly security men in black suits with earpieces lingered close by, flanking a red velvet rope which one of them occasionally moved away to allow one of the women from the dance floor to sashay over to McAllister.

He was surrounded by women, wearing a dark grey suit and clutching a glass of what looked like whisky in one hand. His black hair was slicked back and when he laughed, which he did often, it was easy to miss the telltale scars which gave him away. But when his face was resting, when he looked thoughtful, the long scars which pulled away from the corners of his mouth and crudely extended up towards his cheeks were obvious, even in the dim light of the club.

There was no doubt that he was handsome in a suave way. He exuded rugged charm, but in his suit he was the picture of old-school elegance, like Cary Grant in old Hollywood movies. He moved with ease, with confidence. The more people around him, the more animated and illuminated he became. He was like a black hole – stealing the light of all those nearby as he drew them close.

Amanda's heartbeat became too quick, too erratic. She could feel herself growing hot, her palms slick with sweat. This was the man who had hunted down her husband. This was the man who had taken her perfect life and shattered it.

Amanda thought of a snow globe she'd once broken. It had happened during a winter when the snow had come in thick, icy storms and settled waist-deep even in villages along the coast. A cool mist had settled atop the sea and didn't leave for weeks. The globe had sat on the mantelpiece in her mother's living room. In it there was a beautifully ornate little gingerbread house and when you turned the globe upside down and then righted it again the house was in the midst of its own snowstorm. You could even wind a gear on the base of the globe to have it play 'The Christmas Song'. Amanda had loved that globe. But that particularly cold year she'd gotten a Nintendo Wii and during a very boisterous game of tennis with Shane she'd knocked the globe flying off the mantle. It smashed against the dark wood of the floor, its precious liquid seeping out, the beautiful snow clotting in lumps.

'It's ruined,' Amanda had wailed as she scooped up shards of glass and stared down at them in dismay.

'The house is still okay,' Shane had knocked any remaining glass off and showed her that the little gingerbread house still stood. But it had lost its protective glass dome, its own personal snowstorm, its magic.

'Yes, but being just the house isn't the same,' Amanda had shook her head woefully. 'It's ruined.'

'One gin and tonic,' Shane placed her drink in front of her before sitting down. He sipped his Jack Daniels and Coke and then noticed her troubled expression. 'Amanda, you all right?'

'He's here,' Amanda nodded in the direction of McAllister and the bevvy of beauties who filled up the booth around him. They laughed along with him and seductively stroked their hands up his legs, along his shoulders, as though he were some sort of idol to them. 'That's him.' Amanda reached for her drink and consumed its contents in one single gulp, then she wiped the back of her hand across her mouth and continued to stare at the suited McAllister. 'That's the man who broke my snow globe.'

6

That night, Amanda saw Gregg McAllister when she closed her eyes. She lay in her hotel room, her body stiff, as she remembered the way he threw his head back with jovial abandon, how he laughed so heartily that his whole body shook. He had been the life of the party, the light source which everyone was drawn to. No one cowered when he raised a hand to make a point, no one paled when he locked eyes with them. To the people in the club, Gregg McAllister was not a monster, he was simply a man. And a popular one at that.

Is that how he'd once lured a young and impressionable Will, back when he'd been Jake, into his cause? Had Amanda's late husband watched McAllister in clubs with envious eyes, wishing he had his money, his success?

McAllister was a man in his late forties, early fifties. A man who was wealthy, powerful. Popular. A man who elevated himself to be something more than his peers.

Shane hadn't been impressed by the suited man with the Glasgow smile. 'He certainly fits the profile,' he'd muttered as he drew his glass up towards his lips. He'd looked unsettled. Did he too feel sickened to gaze upon the man behind Will's murder? McAllister hadn't been there, his finger hadn't been on the trigger of the gun which fired the killing shot, but Amanda knew it might as well have been.

At some point, Amanda's troubled thoughts drifted into dreams. She was back home, walking along the cliffside with her father next to her. Though she was grown, he was frozen in time, forever forty-five. They walked together in an easy silence as a salty breeze blew in from the ocean and whipped through their hair. Amanda joyfully filled her lungs with the crisp, clean air. In the distance she saw someone running, moving away from them. Looking at the dark hair and broad shoulders, her heart gave a squeeze as she instantly knew it was Will. Amanda started hurrying after him. She broke into a sprint as Will kept running, kept moving away from her.

'Will!' she yelled for him in between breaths as she kept sprinting. 'Will!'

A hand grabbed her arm, forcing her to a halt. Amanda spun around and looked into the kind eyes of her father.

'You can keep running,' he said, 'but you'll never catch him.'

'Amanda?'

She felt pressure on her arm. Real pressure. With a gasp, she opened her eyes. A soft grey light covered the hotel room. It was morning. Turning her head, she saw Shane sat up beside her, one hand still on her arm which he'd been shaking.

'You were having a nightmare,' he said apologetically. 'You kept calling out Will's name.'

'Oh.' The dream was still in the room, still fogging up her thoughts. Why had Will been running from her? And why couldn't she catch him?

'Why don't you shower while I go grab us some breakfast?' Shane suggested kindly, already slipping off the bed and pulling on a jumper and jeans.

'Sure, thanks.' Amanda rubbed at her eyes, she wanted to retreat back into the dream, wanted to ask her father what she should do. Because he always knew best, always knew which direction she should take with her life. But he was gone, just like Will.

*

During her reconnaissance mission to the club, Amanda had learned several things about Gregg McAllister. He was clearly social and well-liked by those around him. He liked to drink. Amanda hadn't lingered in the club for long after sighting her target but during that time he'd drained several glass tumblers of whisky and eagerly gestured to a waiter for more. But more than drink, McAllister liked beautiful women. Each time a fresh face twisted out some moves on the dance floor he'd call them over to his booth, draw them into the fold.

'So which way is our in?' Amanda asked, looking thoughtfully at Shane. They were back in the Starbucks just down from their hotel. It was late morning and the bodies inside had thinned out so that only a handful of tables were occupied. Amanda had been sipping on the same cappuccino for almost forty minutes.

'Our in?'

'Ideally I need to get close enough to him to get to his phone. If I could clone it I could access to all his files. His contacts.'

'And how are you going to get close enough to him to relieve him of his phone?' Shane sounded annoyed. 'If your plan is to get a job at the club and pinch it at the coat check, I'm not sure time is on our side.'

'He likes his drink. He likes his women.' Amanda listed the facts off on her long fingers.

'So at this point he's pretty much your average guy.'

'But one of those has to create an in for us.'

Shane leaned back in his chair and gave her a long, levelled look. He clearly already knew where she was going with the conversation. 'No,' he concluded flatly, his jaw clenching.

'Just let me—'

'No. Absolutely not.'

'But, Shane—'

'You are not tarting yourself up to get that man's attention. Why the hell would you even want to do that?'

'To get to his phone,' Amanda deadpanned. 'That's the goal.'

'Is it?'

'If I can clone his phone, I can give Turtle all the information they'd need to take him down. I'm sure of it.'

'Watching McAllister is one thing,' Shane lowered his voice, 'but *engaging* with him… Christ, Amanda, do you have any idea how dangerous that is? The man's a criminal. A killer. And for all you know he already knows exactly what you look like.'

'It's a risk I have to take.'

'Amanda,' he sighed her name and looked down at his hands in despair.

'I'm doing this.'

'You always do this. You always take things too far.' Shane had tears in his eyes.

'Do you have a better idea of how to get his phone? Should we mug him in the street? Do you want to shadow him when he goes to take a piss? My plan is the one least likely to get us both killed.'

Shane said nothing. Amanda took his silence as compliance.

*

Now that Amanda had a plan she wasn't sure how comfortable she felt about following through with it. She was in a department store across from Starbucks browsing the racks of their more fashionable designer section. Shane had sulked off back to the hotel, heading to the gym to work out his frustrations. Amanda was glad to be alone. As she eyed a short leather skirt, she knew that if Shane had accompanied her on her little shopping trip he'd just have vetoed every outfit. Amanda needed to do more than blend in at the club the next time she went – she needed to catch McAllister's eye and that wasn't going to be easy. The club had been packed full of gorgeous women, all of them slim and doe-eyed.

A red sequined top with a plunging neckline caught Amanda's eye. She grabbed her size and held it against the leather skirt. She feared that the combination would make her look more cabaret than sexy. With a sigh, she placed the garments back and kept searching, drifting amongst the clothes racks like a piece of tumbleweed.

Clothes shopping was certainly not her forte. She always opted for function over fashion. Her mother, on the other hand, would have been in her element. She'd have cooed over every item that sparkled, held up countless dresses against Amanda insisting that her daughter would look fabulous in each and every one. Corrine loved to shop, loved to accessorise with anything that twinkled. Amanda had inherited her father's pragmatism when it came to clothes. She wished that her mother was there to guide her, or at the very least pick out an outfit which would make her look more seductress than stripper.

Thinking about her mother made a thread of guilt knot its way across her chest and creep up her throat. She should call home. Pulling out her mobile, Amanda quickly figured out what time it was in Vegas and withheld her number before selecting the landline for the little cottage by the coast. Her mum answered after four rings.

'Hello?' Corrine sounded uncertain, caught off guard.

'Mum, hey, it's me.'

'Oh, Amanda,' instant jubilation on the other end of the line. 'It's so lovely to hear from you, sweetheart. We were just wondering how you were, weren't we?'

For a split second she assumed Corrine was referring to Amanda's father. That had been the 'we' which dominated her early life. But of course the old woman was talking about Ewan. Cracking a smile, Amanda wandered towards a clothes rack filled with cocktail dresses.

'I hope he's behaving for you, Mum. Not being too much trouble.'

'Not at all,' Corrine insisted brightly. Then, lowering her voice, 'I managed to convince him to move on to some of the old movies you loved when you were little. I even dusted off the video player and hooked it back up.'

'Way to go, Mum.'

'He's been loving the American tale with the mouse. And *Land Before Time.* Oh and *Labyrinth,*' Corrine's voice was rosy with nostalgia. 'He's loved them all, Amanda. Just like you used to. I told him that, tonight, if he keeps being a good boy, we'll watch *Dark Crystal.* Your father always loved that one.'

Amanda was surprised that her mother had kept the old stack of VHS movies that she'd watched repeatedly as a little girl every rainy afternoon after school.

'How's Vegas?'

The question drew Amanda back from the past.

'It's...' She looked around at the department store, at the high ceilings and well-lit displays. 'Very hot. And busy.'

'Is your hotel nice?'

'Lovely.'

'What time is it there?'

'Very early. I'm just about to head down to breakfast.'

'And Shane? How's he?'

'He's gone to the hotel gym for a bit.' It felt good to be including some truths in her response.

'That sounds about right. He's become such a dedicated young man, always taking himself and his fitness seriously.'

'Uh-huh.'

'And you two,' Amanda heard a door close on her mother's end of the line. 'How are things between you?'

'They're... complicated. It's all just difficult, Mum.'

'I see.' Corrine sounded disappointed, but she quickly recovered. 'I wanted to ask if there was anything I could be doing to help with the funeral. I assume it will happen when you're back.'

'Funeral?'

'For Will.'

Amanda circled the cocktail dresses twice, pulling in nervous breaths and willing herself not to cry. She hadn't even thought about a funeral. About letting his boss at the warehouse know that Will wouldn't be showing up for his next shift. Or any shift. To start going through the process of tying up loose ends, it felt too final.

'The funeral will be in Scotland. A very small affair since he has no family left.' Amanda coughed to clear her throat. Will deserved a funeral, a proper burial, but he wouldn't be getting one. There had been nothing in the news about a trio of bodies discovered in woodlands. McAllister must have gotten there first and Amanda didn't even want to consider how he'd have chosen to dispose of the bodies.

'I see.'

'I'm coming back from Vegas a day early to attend. And then I'm coming home.'

'I know this is a very difficult, very confusing time for you, sweetheart.'

'It sure is.'

'I'm just glad you've had Shane by your side through it all.'

'Yeah,' Amanda agreed softly. 'Me too.'

*

Amanda eventually decided on a black cocktail dress and peep-toe shoes which had red soles and promised to give her maximum comfort, at least according to the enthusiastic sales guy in the footwear department.

When Amanda returned to the hotel room, Shane was sat on the bed watching TV. His head shot up when she walked in and though she saw relief in his eyes his mouth remained held in a tight line.

'How was the gym?' she wondered politely as she dropped her bags down beside the desk.

'You been shopping?'

'I had to get a more… appropriate outfit.'

Shane grunted and said nothing more.

'I called my Mum and she's good. She said that Ewan is good too. He's found some of my old videos and—'

'I'm going to shower,' Shane leapt off the bed as though the covers had suddenly caught on fire.

'Shane—'

'Don't worry, I won't be long. Then you can take all the time you want to preen and make sure you look real nice. We need our bait to work after all.' He slammed the door behind him as he disappeared into the bathroom.

Dejected, Amanda went over to her laptop. She knew that Shane had every right to be mad at her but she wasn't about to back down. McAllister needed to be brought to justice and if she had to smear on some lipstick and show a little leg to do that then so be it. She was just playing the hand she'd been dealt as best as she could.

On her laptop, Amanda quickly ordered a few items from Vegas to be delivered to the hotel. Souvenirs for her Mum and Ewan. Items to help solidify her story that she'd spent these two weeks in the gambling capital of the world. Pictures were going to be an issue, which was why Amanda planned on sabotaging her phone on the way home, thus opportunely losing any pictures she might have taken whilst on holiday.

While she was shopping for gifts, she got an alert. There was a new message fromTurtle82. Amanda hastily read it.

> To bring down the man you bring down the mainframe. Find out where it is.
> T.

She read the message back, cradling her head in her hands as she rested her elbows upon the desk.

The mainframe meant his hard drive. The place where he housed all his most sensitive digital material. That would not be kept on his phone. It would be a computer or laptop somewhere, probably at his house. Amanda groaned and closed her eyes. Turtle wasn't just asking her to spy on McAllister anymore, he was asking her to get access to the man's home. And how the hell was she supposed to do that? Flirting with him was one thing, diverting his attention so that she could slip his phone from his pocket and run a cloning scan on it was do-able. Getting an invite back to his place – that was taking things to a whole other level.

Amanda leaned back in her chair, glancing towards the bathroom where she could hear the shower running, the hot water hissing angrily as it helped rinse away some of Shane's tension. How would he respond to this development? He'd surely be furious. He might even veto Amanda's plan altogether. Because it was getting dangerous.

The hair on Amanda's arms rose up as though the air around her had become electrified. She wasn't just going to meet the wolf, she was going to ask it to take her back to its den. How was she supposed to come out of such a situation alive?

Her fingers started to dance across her laptop's keyboard, her mind having already arrived at a solution. She remained on the darknet, which was a digital marketplace for anything and everything illegal. Drugs, guns, even murder, could be purchased on there for the right price. And the price was usually bitcoins. They were a digital currency which couldn't be traced and were extremely high in value. Amanda had bought some two years ago when they were new and going cheap. She was always drawn to any new technology or developments in the online world. The bitcoins that she had she'd intended to save for a rainy day.

Beyond her hotel window the sun was shining and the sky was a clear sea of blue. Amanda didn't need to get up and check to know that the white van was outside. Each time she caught a glimpse of it in her peripheral vision she felt ice slide down her spine. She couldn't ignore the crippling unease which told her not to trust its presence there. She tapped her hands against her laptop, drawing herself back in to the moment. Amanda knew she'd need to part with at least some of her coins. She didn't want to face McAllister unprotected.

Her screen was instantly filled with images of guns – all for sale. There were handguns, discreet enough to fit inside a handbag, assault rifles and even mini guns. All were available for the right price. Amanda felt sick just looking at them. Will had carried a gun when he'd gone on the run, had even aimed it at her when she'd managed to track him down. She swallowed as tears began to silently fall down her cheeks. He'd felt driven to arm himself and now she understood why. McAllister was a dangerous serpent in an expensive suit.

Amanda's stomach churned as she continued browsing the weapons. There were so many guns. The choice was staggering. Each buyer promised discretion. To buy a gun felt like crossing a line, like she was truly committing herself to this other life, the one she'd created on the darknet, the one that existed outside the usual boundaries of society.

The bathroom door opened and she exited the page and slammed her laptop closed. The weapon would have to wait. For now her focus was to make herself look as pretty as possible. It was time to dangle her bait in front of the King Carp in the hope that he'd bite.

7

'I just don't like this.'

It was the fifth time Shane had complained since they'd left the hotel.

'What's to like?' Amanda tottered beside him in her new shoes which were already starting to pinch against her toes.

'Maybe there's another way. We just need to think it all through, find an alternative solution.' He was talking fast, sounding like a man making a desperate final plea on death row. Amanda looked up and saw why his nerves were suddenly jangling like a set of jailor's keys. Rumours was just up ahead, its name spelt out in neon lights.

'It's going to be okay, I've got this,' she rested her hand on Shane's arm. He looked down at her hand and then slowly raised his gaze to meet hers.

'I'm just worried it's going to work *too* well. You look…' he sucked in a nervous breath of air. 'And he's – he's the worst kind of criminal. I'm scared for you.'

'I'll be fine.' Amanda gave his arm a gentle squeeze.

'I'll be right inside, by the bar, in case you need me.' Shane was starting to sound like a cop. His features settled into an intense expression. He was pushing back his fear to be brave, to be a pillar of strength she could lean against if she needed to.

'Got it, thanks.' Amanda's lips curled up into a tense smile. She couldn't believe that she was actually going to do this – to parade herself like a piece of meat within the lion's den. But what choice did she have? Time was not on her side and it was running out.

Inside, the club was just as busy as the previous night. Beautiful bodies moved in time with the music upon the illuminated dance floor as eyes peered out from the shadows of the surrounding booths. The music invaded her senses from all sides.

Amanda entered alone. It had been her idea, but as she stepped past the heavyset bouncer in black she started to regret it. Shane was back in the queue, still waiting to get inside. Amanda looked around, making sure she kept her shoulders back and her chin held high. She had to look like she belonged, like she was as self-assured as all the other women in there. During her walk across to the bar she knew it wasn't working. Her whole body had broken out in a cold, nervous sweat and she kept wringing her hands together like she didn't know what to do with them. She looked more awkward than alluring.

'What'll it be?'

The second she placed her hands against the smooth surface of the bar one of the waistcoat-wearing servers was in front of her. A short guy with cropped black hair and the beginnings of an impressive beard was staring at her, waiting on her order.

'Umm.'

She needed to be tipsy, not drunk. She needed to reach that place where you believe yourself to be infinite.

'A shot of tequila.' Then, on reflection, 'Actually, make it two.'

The guy nodded and briefly turned his back on her. Amanda pulled in a long, uneasy breath and then slowly released it. She kept telling herself that she was fine, that this was just any other club and that there was nothing to fear, but her body didn't believe a word of it. Her heart thumped louder than the music and kept trying to jump up into her throat. She was afraid. And what was worse was that she wore her fear. Her glamorous dress and expensive shoes couldn't conceal that she was a sheep in wolf's clothing. What if her fear was seeping into the air around her, drawing all the sharks close as though it were a drop of blood in the ocean?

'Two shots of tequila.' The bearded guy slid two small shot glasses towards her, each adorned with a wedge of lime and salted along the rim. He turned to address his next customer.

'How much?' Amanda leaned across the bar and raised her voice to get his attention. She gestured at her two drinks.

'Don't worry about it,' the guy waved a dismissive hand at her. 'It's on the house.'

When Amanda frowned at him in confusion, he explained further. He gestured behind her, at a distant purple booth and she felt her stomach drop to the floor.

'You caught the boss's eye so you get free drinks all night.' And then he was on to his next customer.

Amanda straightened and reached for her drinks, not daring to turn around. She hadn't expected things to be so easy. Or to happen so quickly. She was suddenly aware of the heat against her back, of someone staring. Had McAllister been watching her all along? Was he immediately attuned to the presence of someone new and glamorous within one of his clubs? Had he seen her anxiously make her way across the club, towards the bar? And as she placed her order had he made some signal to the bar staff that she'd missed? Was there now a huge scarlet letter emblazoned upon her forehead? Her palms felt clammy and Amanda had to remind herself how to breathe, that this was what she'd been hoping to achieve.

Out of the corner of her eye she saw Shane leaning up against the far side of the bar. She turned away from him, a drink in each hand. It was too dangerous to even make eye contact with him since McAllister was probably watching.

Amanda downed her first shot. It burned as it slid down her throat. With a grimace she put the glass back down on the bar and then downed her second drink. It went down marginally smoother than the first. With a gasp she returned the glass to its partner and then bit down on one of the wedges of lime. The sharp citrus flavour was a welcome respite from the burn of pure liquor. She waited for the drinks to work their magic, for the alcohol to curdle with her blood and give her some much-needed Dutch courage.

It must have worked because ten minutes later she looked up, turning towards the raised purple booth in which McAllister was sat, surrounded by women as usual. Only he wasn't looking out towards the dance floor or laughing heartily at some joke, he was staring straight back at her. Amanda tensed under the scrutiny. He kept staring, his mouth widening into a confident grin as he used one hand to beckon her over. She looked into the eyes of the man who had been behind Will's death and somehow kept her spine straight, her lips pressed together, willing herself to focus even though she just wanted to fall apart.

Amanda's mind and body disconnected. Whilst her head was screaming at her not to move, to just go over to Shane and leave, her legs drifted over towards the VIP area. With a nod from McAllister, the red velvet rope was moved aside and she was granted access to the most exclusive booth in the club.

'Well, good evening, gorgeous,' McAllister spread his arms across the back of the booth and looked up at her, ignoring the other women around him. He was focused only on Amanda and she found the intensity of his attention dizzying.

'Thank you for the drinks.'

'Anytime.' McAllister dropped his gaze for just a second and the brunette beside him knew what it meant. Pouting, she scooted further down the plush purple booth, making space for Amanda. 'When a beautiful woman walks into my club the least I can do is buy her a drink.'

'Your club?' Amanda did her best to sound surprised and, more importantly, impressed.

'This and a few others,' McAllister shrugged modestly. 'Why don't you sit down and tell me a bit about yourself, like your name?'

Amanda sat, doing her best to avoid the daggers which the other girls in the booth were throwing at her with their steely gazes. McAllister's suited leg was pressed against her own. A wave of nausea swept over her. She wished she had another drink to push it away, to stoke up her bravado. His arm was still across the back of the booth, just above her shoulders. He smelt good. Amanda hated that he did, and she hated herself for noticing. He smelt of expensive cologne, the kind that you take time selecting to ensure that it complements your body's PH, and then you expertly spritz it in the places it will be most effective. McAllister wasn't a man who just doused himself in aftershave bought at the supermarket. His scent had been carefully orchestrated. His suit was also a testament to his meticulous nature. It fitted him like a glove. The fabric was a deep blue that had a sheen to it, like it was crying out to be touched. He also wore a crisp white shirt which was tucked into his trousers and his hair was slicked back with mousse.

'So, your name?' He leaned into her, his breath a mixture of whisky and mint.

'Amanda.' She wanted to stab herself. There and then she wanted to stab herself firmly in the chest for her outright stupidity. The tequila had made her thoughtless and she'd responded to his question out of instinct. Gathering a hold of her thoughts, she did her best to salvage the situation. 'Amanda Preston.'

It felt strange to take Shane's name as her own, especially since she'd dedicated so much of her teenage years daydreaming about doing just that. She'd scrawl Mrs Preston over the back of her exercise books at school, circling the name with pretty hearts. Then, before anyone could see, she'd scribble through it all and paste a sticker over the embarrassing declaration.

'Amanda Preston.' McAllister said her name with a smile. 'Well, Amanda, it's lovely to meet you. I'm Gregg McAllister.'

I know.

'Hi,' Amanda nervously fluttered her eyelashes at him. She didn't know if she was flirting or just being polite. She'd never been great at seduction. Shane had been a friend who, over many years, moved over from the friend zone, and with Will... well, Will had been a force of nature, like being swept up in a hurricane. She'd been powerless to do anything other than go along with what was happening between them. It was the first time her heart had completely overridden her mind.

'You're not from round here, are ya?' Gregg's eyes were grey, the colour of early morning mist on a winter's day. They regarded Amanda with interest, like she was some exotic bird that had just flown into his garden.

'No,' Amanda politely clasped her hands in her lap. 'I'm from down south.'

'I can tell.'

Her eyes flew open and she held her breath. Was this the part where he said that he knew her? Was the bodyguard close by about to haul her out of the booth and evict her from the club?

'Your accent,' Gregg leaned in close to explain, pressing his body up against hers as if they were well acquainted. 'You're very well-spoken.'

'Oh,' Amanda blushed and her body crumpled with relief. 'Thank you.'

'See, thanking me for a compliment,' Gregg grinned at her, his eyes crinkling at the corners the way Will's used to. 'The girls round here should take note of how to be a well-mannered lady. Too many of them look like princesses but then talk like bloody lorry drivers.'

The thought of Will had crept up on Amanda once again. She could feel a downward spiral staircase opening up beneath her. If she went down it she'd descend into endless darkness. This was the man who had hunted her husband, who had ruined her whole life. How was she supposed to sit here and play nice with him?

'I know that look.' Gregg lowered his arms from the back of the booth and smacked both palms against the table in the centre of the booth, drawing the attention of a nearby server. 'This lady needs a drink,' he deferentially raised a hand in Amanda's direction.

'I… um.' More tequila felt like a bad idea. She'd already made an epic slip-up when she'd blurted half of her real name. It was time to rein it in. 'Can I have a Diet Coke please?'

'Diet Coke,' Gregg mulled this over, pulling his lips into a tight line. 'So you not only look like a lady but you drink like one too? Bet you never end the night tumbling out of a cab and falling on your arse in the middle of the street.'

'I save that kind of behaviour for special occasions.'

'Ha.' Gregg laughed. It was an annoyingly infectious sound, full of carefree mirth. 'So, tell me, Amanda.' He said her name carefully, as if he liked the sound of it. 'What brings you to my city?'

Revenge.

'Work.' It was basically the truth. She had previously worked for Turtle82 and it was partly at their behest that she'd returned to Scotland.

'So what do you do? Let me guess, you're a model.' Gregg's eyes twinkled at her.

'No,' Amanda shyly tucked a strand of hair behind her ear. 'I work in IT, developing websites for companies as a freelancer.'

'Huh. Beauty and brains. I'm impressed.'

Her Diet Coke arrived and Amanda quickly reached for it, grateful to have something to hold and occupy her hands, even if the glass was almost too cold to touch. She let her gaze flicker over to the bar, trying to locate Shane. She thought she'd almost found him when Gregg coughed to get her attention.

'How long are you here for?'

'Just a few weeks.' Amanda took a dainty sip of her drink. 'So you own nightclubs?' she enquired sweetly.

'Amongst other things,' Gregg replied with a dark chuckle. A chill entered the booth, coming from more than just her cold Coke. Amanda clutched her glass tighter, doing her best not to give in to her hatred. She yearned to thrust her drink into Gregg's face and call him the monster that he was. But she had to keep it together, stay composed, she was working towards a bigger goal.

'Other things?' she arched an eyebrow at him.

'Property.' A new drink arrived for Gregg, one that Amanda hadn't even noticed him order. He took a sip from his Scotch on the rocks and then expanded on his reply, 'I buy and develop old buildings. It was how I came to own this place.'

'I see.'

'It was an abandoned butcher's when I bought it twenty years ago. Whole place smelt rancid. Took months to air out all the brickwork.'

'And look at it now,' Amanda swept her gaze across the darkened nightclub.

'Are you really impressed?' Gregg came closer to her, his eyes searching her face. 'Because something tells me that a girl like you can be mighty difficult to impress.'

His scars were prominent even in the shadows of the booth. They pulled away from the corners of his mouth, eerie extensions to his smile.

'How does a property developer get such a scar?' The words were out of her mouth and in the booth before she could bite her tongue and stop them. The tequila had let her down again, had made her lips too loose.

Gregg gave an airless chuckle and stroked his face with one hand. 'Adds something to my charm don't you think?' he wondered cheekily.

Amanda kept her face serious, her eyes never leaving his face.

'I'm doing well now,' he lifted an arm across the back of the booth again, across her shoulders. 'But I didn't come from money. When this place was still a butcher's I was a young man making stupid mistakes. One day I pissed off the wrong person, they followed me home one night pulled me into a dark alley and took a rusty blade to my face.' The confidence seeped out of him. He was no longer a self-made man in a suit, he was a boy still haunted by the ghosts of his past.

'That sounds awful.'

But not nearly as awful as watching the man you love die in the middle of nowhere.

Amanda forced herself to place a hand on McAllister's knee. The fabric of his suit was soft to the touch, almost like silk. He looked at her and she heard his breath catch in his throat. A thousand thoughts swarmed in her mind like a hive of angry bees. What was she doing? Had she just made Gregg McAllister think that she wanted to sleep with him? Why had she touched him? Had she taken it too far? How far could she take it? Could she kiss him? *Sleep* with him?

Amanda withdrew her hand as her body gave her the answer. She felt sick and light-headed, but not in a good way. To kiss Gregg would be a step too far. She could never go to bed with him. Her soul would never recover from such abolishment of all that she stood for.

'You're very beautiful.' Gregg gave the compliment softly, respectfully. 'Sit with me a while won't you? I'd love to get to know you better.'

As much as Amanda loathed McAllister she couldn't deny the magnetism within him, how when he looked at her she felt compelled to gaze into his silver eyes. How when he asked her to stay it felt like a heartfelt request rather than an order.

8

The calendar date turned over as night became early morning. Gregg ordered more drinks, though Amanda stuck to her Diet Coke. All around them people danced, laughed, drank. It was a hedonistic atmosphere that Amanda could feel herself getting swept up in.

Excusing herself from the booth, she had to take a bathroom break. The heavy atmosphere in the booth was choking her. Despite the early hour, the club was still alive with energy. Amanda squeezed her way past drunken revellers and picked her way towards the bathroom.

The theme for the restrooms seemed to be indulgent gothic. There was black and red everywhere, like the whole place had been lifted straight out of Dracula's castle. Ornate black framed mirrors were hung above deep-set silver sinks. The door to each stall was thick wood, painted black. The walls were a shade of red which was almost dark enough to look like they'd been painted with blood.

Amanda steadied herself against a vacant sink and stared at her reflection. A stranger stared back at her. A stranger with long golden hair, painted lips and eyes framed with thick coats of mascara. The stranger who looked perfectly at home amidst the decadence of the restrooms.

Turning on the cold water, Amanda soaked her hands and then rested them against her neck. It was hot in the club. It felt like beyond the walls there was a fire raging and if she stayed too long at McAllister's side she'd end up getting burned alive.

'This club is the best.' A group of girls stumbled in, their make-up blurred around their eyes, their steps awkward and uncoordinated. They'd been laughing together as they came in. But the sound wasn't pleasant like the tinkling of silver bells, it was more like the cackle of a trio of witches around a cauldron. And when they saw Amanda they regarded her with dead stares and ceased laughing.

'Excuse me,' Amanda slid past them, making for the exit before they could engage her. She felt their eyes stalking her every movement until she'd pushed her way through the heavy black door and was back in the club. The music instantly blasted against her. For a moment she was disorientated. Leaning against a nearby wall, she pressed her chin to her chest, waiting for the moment to pass.

Her Diet Cokes had been just that, hadn't they? She felt oddly out of sorts. She was too hot and her skin felt too tight against her bones. Was she still drunk off those two tequilas? Or had there been vodka in her soft drinks? Was it an unspoken rule that all the drinks that arrived at McAllister's table had to be laced with alcohol?

'Okay, we're going.' A strong hand clenched around Amanda's arm, jerking her upright.

'Wait, what?' she instinctively pulled back, withdrawing from the grip.

'Amanda, it's almost three a.m. and you're drunk. We're done here, we're heading back.' Shane's shirt was crumpled and there were shadows beneath his eyes which dulled the lustre of their natural green.

'Um, wait.' Amanda squirmed away from him, angling her body in the direction of McAllister's booth. She felt like she was chewing on cotton wool. Why was it so hard to talk?

'Christ, you're pissed out of your mind.'

'I'm not,' she seethed. But there was some truth to Shane's words. Why else was she struggling to bring any clarity to her thoughts, her actions? 'I need...' she pulled in a deep breath of the club's stale air. 'I can't just leave.' There, things were becoming clearer. 'It will look weird. I need to at least say goodbye.'

'Five minutes,' Shane raged. 'And then I'm coming over to that damn booth and I'll drag you out of here if I have to.' He was so riled up. Amanda backed away from him, wondering how he'd gotten so mad.

'I was starting to fear you wouldn't come back,' Gregg commented as Amanda approached the edge of the booth. Had she imagined it or was there a challenge in his tone? 'I thought you'd perhaps done a Cinderella on me and dashed out into the night.'

'No,' Amanda gave him her sweetest smile. 'I wouldn't do that. Although,' she chewed her lip, looking conflicted, 'I do have to go. It's so late and I have work tomorrow. Well, today really.'

Gregg laughed, widening his mouth to reveal a set of perfect white teeth. Unlike Shane who was crinkled and weary, Gregg was still polished, his shirt smooth and crisp against his shirt as if he'd just arrived at the club.

'Dinner.' His silver eyes shone against the shadows of the booth.

'D-Dinner?' Amanda stumbled over her response, wondering if she'd misheard him.

'Yes, dinner. Have dinner with me. Tomorrow night. Or,' he pulled his smile to one side. The expression took decades off him, revealing the cocky boy who resided within the successful man. 'Technically it's tonight.'

Dinner. He was asking her out. On a date. The club grew hotter, the air stickier so that it almost became an impenetrable mist that was holding Amanda in place, preventing her escape.

'Tell me where you're staying and I'll pick you up at eight.'

He wanted to know the hotel she was staying at. A giant red flag unfurled itself in Amanda's mind. She blinked away her drunken haze and wiped the back of her hand across her mouth, stalling for time. Stating the name of her hotel was going too far. She'd already given away too much information about herself as it was.

'I'll meet you there,' she dropped her hand to her waist and adopted what she hoped was a confident, powerful stance. 'I loathe being chauffeured around. I prefer to make my own way to places.'

'An independent streak.' Still smiling, Gregg gave a slow nod of approval. 'Very well. Marco's, at half eight. It's a few streets away from here. I'd give you some more details but something tells me you enjoy figuring stuff out on your own.'

'Great,' Amanda replied breathily. She was suddenly eager to leave. She was sure there was something in Gregg's tone, a taunt. But when she looked into his eyes and saw his smile there was no malice there, just openness and flirtation.

'I'll see you later, Miss Preston,' he raised his glass to her.

Walking away, Amanda didn't look back. She kept her head high and mainlined for the doors which led out onto the street.

The cold night air met her like a slap in the face. Wrapping her arms around herself, Amanda started hurrying down the street. There were too many shadows, too many back alleys, and she didn't feel safe.

'Hey, wait up.'

She'd barely reached the sanctuary of the first lamp post when Shane came hurrying after her.

'So, are we all done with this now?' He was searching her face for answers.

'Let's just get back to the hotel.' Her teeth were beginning to chatter as the cold seeped into her bones.

'Amanda,' Shane eased into her stride and pressed a hand against the small of her back. 'Are you all right? What happened in there? Did you get what you need?'

'Dinner.' Amanda was fishing in her purse for her phone. It was too cold to walk all the way back to the hotel, she needed an Uber.

'You're hungry?' With his hand still held against her, Shane glanced up and down the street. All of the shops around them were closed up for the night, their frontages hidden behind heavy metal shutters.

'No.' Her stomach gave a loud grumble. 'Yes.'

'Then we'll find somewhere to go. I think there's a twenty-four hour McDonald's close by.'

'He invited me to dinner. Tonight.'

'Who did?' Shane dropped his hand. 'McAllister?'

'Uh-huh.'

'And you said no, right?'

Amanda looked at her feet which throbbed within her new shoes.

'Tell me you didn't agree to go to dinner with him,' Shane's voice was rising.

'I need to find where he stores all his files. His information. At the very least I need to clone his phone.'

'And you didn't manage to do that tonight despite how cosy you two got?'

'What? No. There was no sign of it. That better not be jealousy in your voice,' Amanda stepped back, creating a space between them. 'Because that man in there helped kill my fucking *husband*. Don't think I've forgotten that. Yes, he's charming. Yes, he's sort of fun to be around. But that doesn't stop him being an absolute monster, Shane. I'm here to do a job, that's it. And I expect you to support me.'

'What the hell do you think I'm doing here?' Shane snapped back. 'Do you think it's fun for me to watch you flirt with that… that *prick*?' Pushing his hands through his hair, he paced away from her. 'I'm here to support you.' He doubled back and cupped her chin with his hands, raising her face up towards his. 'I will stay by your side through all of this. I swear.'

'It's just dinner.' Her mascara became clumped with tears.

'No,' Shane smiled sadly at her. 'It's never just dinner. You know that.'

*

'I still don't like it.'

Amanda had slept away most of the day. It had felt good to peel out of her dress and envelop herself in the soft white sheets of her hotel bed. There had been no dreams, no nightmares. Just blissful, rejuvenating darkness.

'What if he expects something from you?' Shane continued. He'd just come back from the gym, his hair flat and damp with sweat.

'Like what?'

'Don't pretend to be naïve,' he said through gritted teeth. Even though he'd spent the better part of two hours down at the gym his whole body was still tight with tension. He sat down on the bed beside Amanda but didn't look at her.

'I'm not going to have sex with him if that's what you're getting at.'

'There's a lot of other ways to be intimate with someone.'

Amanda could feel the waves of heat radiating off Shane's body. His arms looked sculpted and muscular in the tight fitting T-shirt he wore. He was the first person she'd ever slept with. Together they'd explored every recipe in the sexual cookbook. He had been the subject of all her firsts. And together they fumbled through the basics until they became good at what they were doing. With Will there'd been no dress rehearsal. They just went straight for the main act and then stayed for the encore.

'I'm not going to do anything other than have dinner with him.'

'And if he pushes for more?' Shane titled his head slightly to watch her out of the corner of his eye.

'You think I can't handle myself?' Amanda challenged haughtily.

'I think you risk being blinded by your goal. You want to get access to his phone. What better way to do that than to separate the man from his trousers?'

'Shane!'

'Then what is your plan?'

'I don't...' Amanda picked at the ends of her fingernails. 'I don't really know. Yes, I need to clone his phone, but really I need to know where he keeps all his main data.'

'So you want an invite back to his place?' Shane stood up and turned around to face her, leaning against the unit which the flat-screen TV was sat upon.

'I didn't say that.'

'You're going to string him along, bat your eyelashes at him and suggest that you're as in to him as he is into you. You'll be a tease until you get taken back to his place. Then what?'

Amanda opened her mouth but Shane ploughed on before she could respond.

'Then what?' he repeated. 'You'll be at his *house*, Amanda. Surrounded by all his guards. You think he'll just let you leave without giving him what he wants?'

'I'll sound the alarm.'

'What?'

'I can set off his alarm system at just the right time, give me a chance to get away. And Turtle can help.'

'Christ, you're serious about this.'

'Do you have a better idea?' Amanda stood up and stared at him. They were just inches apart. She could feel the electricity crackling between them. 'He doesn't know who I am, so the only hand I have to play is my sexuality. I need to get access to him, Shane. I need him to lower his guard around me.'

'Letting you be close to him like that, it's killing me.'

'Shane—'

'When you showed up at the station looking for Will I thought,' he reached forward and took her hand in his, 'I thought that maybe…' He gave her hand a squeeze. Amanda felt the pressure through her entire body. Closing her eyes, she tried to imagine a more perfect moment, one where they weren't in Scotland trying to avenge her dead husband. If only they could go back to simpler times when there was sand beneath their feet and hope in their hearts.

'Love is being willing to do anything for someone.' Will had uttered the words to her on a balmy summer evening the year before. They were sat out in their back garden. The scent of fresh paint and wood drifted out from their shiny new home via the French doors which had been thrown open. Will was on his third beer and his eyes had misted. He stared dreamily out at the newly planted grass, at the bare wood of the fence which he still needed to varnish.

'Would you do anything for me?' Amanda had flirtatiously traced her fingers up his arm, loving how she saw him tense appreciatively.

'I'd do anything to keep you safe.'

'Anything?' Amanda queried teasingly.

'Anything,' Will clarified stoically.

'Would you wax your chest for me?'

'I'm not sure how that's keeping you safe.'

'Would you watch a musical with me?'

'Again, what's that got to do with your safety?'

Amanda slid off her chair and climbed on top of Will, facing him. His hands expertly gripped at her waist as she pressed herself against him.

'Would you take a bullet for me?' she wondered as she leaned down to kiss his neck. His grip against her waist tightened and his breathing quickened.

'Yes,' he told her as he lifted a hand to the back of her head and pulled her in for a deep, passionate kiss.

Amanda stepped back from Shane now, leaving the tension sparking in the space she'd just vacated.

'I need to get ready for dinner.' Her tone was oddly cold, detached.

'Have I...' Shane's hurt was splattered all over his face. 'Have I done something wrong?'

'No. God no. You've done everything right. It's just...' she folded her arms against her chest and sighed. 'Right now I need to focus on bringing McAllister down. I don't have space in my head, or my heart, for anything else.'

'And once that's all done and over with?'

'I think you already know the answer to that one,' Amanda made her way towards the bathroom.

'Maybe I need to hear it from you,' Shane called after her.

'Maybe you just need to trust how you feel.'

*

Marco's was a small, independently owned Italian restaurant located about five minutes away from *Rumours*. It had bright red awning over its front window and all the tables were covered in green gingham tablecloths. There was a real bistro vibe about the place. It was small, intimate. Unassuming.

Amanda had expected a guy like McAllister to take his dates to fancier places, to restaurants which had Michelin stars.

'Maybe he's trying to show you his more humble side,' Shane considered, his tone flat.

'Maybe.' Amanda felt more comfortable in her skinny jeans and T-shirt than she had in the cocktail dress. The outfit was more her. And so was the venue. *Marco's* looked like a genuinely nice little place to eat.

'I'll be at the Starbucks just up the road,' Shane promised. 'You need me, you call me, got it?'

'Got it.'

'Else I'll just meet you back at the hotel at eleven thirty. Any later and I'm calling the cops. I swear to God that I'm not messing around here, Amanda.'

'Eleven thirty, I heard you. I've even synchronised my watch and everything.'

'Don't make light of this.'

'I'm not.' But she couldn't resist flashing Shane a playful smile.

'And don't drink; you'll need a clear head if you want to make a play for his phone.'

'Yes, absolutely.'

To clone McAllister's phone Amanda needed at least five minutes with it. Her own phone was all set up with the technology and ready to go. She just needed to plant it down on top of her target, enter a code and her phone would start wirelessly cloning all of the data within McAllister's. She'd get access to his contacts, messages, emails. And she prayed that would be enough. She didn't want to go to McAllister's mansion, to be truly alone with him. He intrigued her but he also scared her. The charismatic gentleman in the suave suit was just one of the masks he wore. Which one had he had on when he ordered his men to hunt down Will? Amanda hoped she never had to see it.

The walk over to *Marco's* went by too swiftly for Amanda. She'd hoped to linger along the streets, to prolong the inevitable. The little restaurant was nestled in a corner and looked just as cosy and inviting as its online pictures had suggested. Tentatively, Amanda approached the main window and the red awning.

'Ah, Miss Preston.' The front door was swung open with the tinkling of a bell the second she approached. A smiling waiter greeted her from the other side. The warmth of the restaurant drew her in. The air was rich with garlic, bread and the sweetness of chocolate. 'Your date is waiting for you.' Ice slid down Amanda's spine at the word *date* but she managed to keep her head held high, her panic hidden as she glided past the waiter.

In a small booth at the back of the restaurant sat Gregg McAllister. There was a candle burning in the centre of the table and a dozen red roses lay upon what Amanda assumed was her seat.

She pasted on a bright smile and went over to him.

9

'Oh wow, the flowers are beautiful.' Amanda carefully lifted the bouquet of blood red roses and sat down.

'They are my favourite flower,' Gregg smiled at her.

'They are?' He didn't strike her as the kind of man who had a favourite flower. She assumed he'd be like Will – to him all flowers had been the same. McAllister wasn't supposed to a flower enthusiast, he wasn't supposed to possess any grace at all.

'I like how they are beautiful but also dangerous. You really have to watch that you don't get caught by a thorn.'

Thorn.

The word pricked against Amanda. *Preston.* She was Amanda *Preston.* At least that's what McAllister believed. There was no way he could know that her real name was Thorn. That it had been the name Will had chosen years ago when he tried to shake off his old identity. Or did he know? Had Amanda foolishly walked right into some kind of trap?

'I keep some at home.' Gregg's eyes sparkled at her from across the table.

'Some what?'

'Roses,' he dropped his glance towards the bouquet now resting against the table. 'I find something soothing about pruning them.'

Amanda tried to read his expression, tried to find something sinister behind his grey eyes. He was casually leant back in his chair, regarding her with warm attentiveness. He wore a dark grey suit which sharpened the silver of his eyes.

The black silk shirt beneath his jacket gave him a timeless sophistication.

'My, um…' Clearing her throat, Amanda reached for her menu. 'My mother has a little rose garden.'

'She does?'

Amanda clenched her fists behind her menu, worrying that she'd said too much. She needed to keep her tongue on a tighter leash.

'It's kind of her pride and joy.' She added nervously.

'Sounds like your mother and I have a lot in common.'

Amanda was extremely doubtful of this as she scanned the laminated menu.

'So what do you think of the place?' Gregg was gesturing towards the other tables.

'It's nice.'

'I love to come and eat here. I'd rather be here than anywhere else in the city.'

'You would?' Amanda found her attention being pulled away from the menu, towards Gregg. He laughed at her question and smoothed a hand down his shirt.

'Why so surprised?' he chuckled.

'I don't know,' Amanda felt sheepish as she looked back at the food choices. 'I mean,' with a frown she placed down her menu and pressed her palms against it, 'you wear designer suits. You own a nightclub. I saw you as being a guy who eats in fancy restaurants hidden away in exclusive hotels.'

'You saw me as a snob.'

'I didn't—'

'It's okay,' Gregg raised his hands at her in submission. 'Once people get to know me, they find that I'm rarely like they expected me to be. Maybe you can take the boy out of the slums but you can't take the slums out of the boy, I don't know. I just prefer to be somewhere that I'm comfortable, where the food is good and the service is with a smile. What's so wrong with that?'

'Nothing. Nothing at all.'

'I hope you'll come to realise, Amanda, that I'm nothing like the man I appear to be in the club.'

*

By the time Amanda's tiramisu had arrived she'd learned a lot about Gregg McAllister. He was raised by a single mother after his father died at sea whilst working as a fisherman. He dropped out of school when he was twelve so that he could start picking up odd jobs and support his mother. He was an avid Glasgow Rangers fan and had never been on an aeroplane. She knew all this yet she still hadn't managed to get access to his phone. Amanda feared her mission was destined to fail.

'It's not natural to fly.'

'So you've never been to somewhere like America?'

'Oh no, I've been.'

'How did you get there?'

'I took a cruise to New York.'

'Even though your father died on a boat?' Amanda deadpanned. 'Seems like flying might be the safer choice, don't you think?'

This had caused Gregg to laugh outrageously. He briefly abandoned his food to point his fork at her. 'You, girl, you got fire in your belly. I like that.'

The sweet taste of her coffee-laced dessert was still lingering in her mouth as a waiter appeared with a small pot of tea.

'I still know barely anything about you,' Gregg kept his eyes on her as the waiter poured them each a cup. 'I know that you're in the city for business. I know that your mother grows roses,' this made the corners of his mouth lift. Even with the garish present of his old scar he still had a warm, welcoming smile.

Don't be taken in by his welcome grin. The lyrics to *Never Smile at a Crocodile* fluttered through Amanda's mind. She knew she should be keeping Gregg at arm's length, not revealing too much about herself. But she wanted to get to his phone, and to do that she needed to gain his trust, at least partly. He needed to feel confident that he could leave it in her presence. Even for the briefest of moments.

'My dad also died when I was young.' Talking about the event which had marked her soul so deeply during her formative years always made Amanda uneasy. Her stomach started to swirl with grief and sorrow.

'He did? I'm so sorry.' Gregg's hand stretched across the table and found hers. His touch was warm and soft. But it wasn't reassuring. Amanda fought the urge to recoil and place her hands within her lap, away from his reach. 'What happened?'

'Car accident.'

It always amazed Amanda how two words could so succinctly sum up something so devastating.

'That's rough.' Gregg squeezed her hand and in his eyes she saw only concern. And he looked so handsome in the candlelight in his decadent suit with his thick hair smoothed back off his face, revealing how the shade of his eyes had softened in the gentle glow to the colour of a pale winter sky; grey yet heavy. The scar that bordered his smile sharpened all his edges, made him seem dangerous. It reminded Amanda of the danger and mystery that had surrounded Will and initially drawn her to him. But this was not Will. This was the man who had stolen him from her.

'He was my hero. Once, I almost fell off the cliffs near my home, but he saved me. From that day on he always seemed larger than life.' The admission tumbled all too easily from her lips. Gregg kept his hand on hers, drawing her into his silvery gaze.

'I sensed that we had a connection. We both know what it is to suffer an immeasurable loss in our lives.'

'Yes.'

'Sadly I've lost many loved ones over the years,' Gregg withdrew his hand and Amanda remained frozen in place, still feeling the heat from his touch.

'Me too,' she agreed softly.

Thinking about Will brought the moment into a clearer focus. Amanda saw through the magic created by mood lighting, the roses. Blinking, she saw just a man in a suit who was the reason that her husband was dead.

'If you'll excuse me I need to visit the little boy's room.' Gregg stood up and nodded at her before walking away from the table. Amanda watched him leave, watched how he addressed every waiter that he passed with a shoulder clasp and handshake. Then she looked back at the table and spotted his phone. It had been left so nonchalantly beside where Gregg had been sitting that for a moment she thought she must be mistaken. It must have been in his pocket prior to this point. But now it was out on the table. Vulnerable. Leaning forward, she took a better look and saw that it was most definitely Gregg's smartphone, briefly abandoned whilst he went to the toilet.

Amanda leant down and fumbled in her bag. Nerves made her movements sluggish. It took seconds for her own phone to be in her grasp. Straightening, she pressed in her passcode with shaking fingers.

How long until Gregg returned? A few minutes? Less? She could hear her heart pounding in her ears, marking every passing second. At its very fastest the transfer could take five minutes. Amanda needed to hope that time was on her side for a change.

And would he somehow know if she'd cloned his phone? Were all the waiters watching her, schooled to spot her slipping up in this very way?

But this might be her only chance and Amanda was determined to take it. She accessed the software on her device and then dropped her phone directly on top of Gregg's. A green information bar on her screen began to slowly fill up.

Eight per cent.

Ten.

She was sat in Marco's brazenly cloning McAllister's phone.

Twelve per cent.

Her eyes anxiously darted around the small café. There were no waiters nearby. A couple drifted around occupied tables which were at the front near the main door, looking out on the darkened city of Glasgow. No one else was seated at the back near Amanda and McAllister.

Fifteen per cent.

'Come on,' Amanda urged through gritted teeth.

Twenty.

Gregg could return any second and how could she explain away what she was doing?

I'm a reporter.

It seemed the most plausible lie, but then he'd shut the door in her face and all access to him would be cut off.

Thirty-two per cent.

Forty.

'Hurry,' Amanda stretched out her hand and let it linger beside the pair of phones which were stacked on top of one another like building blocks.

Forty nine.

Fifty.

What if losing his father had darkened Gregg's mind at a young age? What if the pressure of trying to support his mother had pushed him to do terrible things?

Fifty-five.

'Dammit.' Amanda squeezed her eyes shut, willing her mind to stop messing with her. She shouldn't be making excuses for McAllister. There were no reasonable excuses for what he'd done.

Will ran drugs to support his family. He ultimately abandoned them and faked his own death to keep them safe then he met Amanda and lied about his identity before marrying her.

Sixty-eight per cent.

Her husband had been no saint but he'd not been a killer.

Until the woods.

And when Amanda had first found Will out in that little sun-bleached cottage she'd known by the way he held the gun he aimed at her that it was not his first time brandishing such a weapon. She'd seen first-hand that he had the capacity to take another life.

When pushed.

What if all McAllister's sins had been committed when pushed? What if he was just like Will?

Eighty-nine per cent.

Amanda tapped her foot impatiently, feeling like she was going mad.

Transfer complete.

She snapped her phone up and shoved it back into the depths of her handbag with one fluid motion. As she sat with her chest heaving, Gregg sauntered back to the table. The scent of his cologne had strengthened. Amanda felt strangely flattered to imagine him in the small bathroom of Marco's applying a fresh spritz for her benefit. Their meal was drawing to a close. Was this the part where he'd assume that she was going back to his?

'I don't know about you but I've had a lovely evening,' Gregg caught a waiter's eye and gave a nod to request the bill. 'It's rare that I find a woman as beautiful as yourself who I can really talk to. Divorce can make a man bitter, but you've been like a breath of fresh air.'

'Yes it's been nice.' Amanda was surprised to find that she wasn't having to lie. Dinner had been nice. From the outside Gregg McAllister was a handsome, worldly man who was enigmatic and confident. But she knew the dangerous truths housed within the beating heart that he dressed up in designer suits.

'And it's just past eleven,' Gregg checked the Rolex on his wrist. 'The night seems to have run away with us.'

'Past eleven, wow, that's late.' Amanda forced a yawn.

'Might I be so bold,' as Gregg leaned forward, looking deep into her eyes, Amanda held her breath, 'as to ask you to join me for a drink tomorrow night? There's a bar that offers truly breathtaking views of the city and I'd like to take you there. That is, unless you're already bored of me.'

He looked as nervous as a fifteen-year-old boy asking a girl to the school disco. It was hopelessly endearing and Amanda couldn't help but smile at him.

'Drinks sounds lovely.' Standing up, she grabbed her handbag and thought of her phone within it, of how she might already have all the answers she sought. If so she could cancel their next date, head back to Ewan and put this whole mess behind her. Else...

'I took the liberty of writing the address of the bar on the card in your bouquet in the hope that you'd agree to see me again. Shall I meet you there at, say, nine?' Gregg was walking through the restaurant with her, his hands respectfully at his sides. 'I promise that it offers the best views in the whole city. You won't be disappointed.' He held the door open for her as she passed through it, her roses held against her chest.

'I look forward to it.'

If the cloning hadn't work, a second date with McAllister wouldn't be the worst thing in the world. Amanda chewed her lip as she walked away from him, the floral scent of roses coating her senses. No, another date with McAllister really wouldn't be so bad at all.

*

The cloning had worked. Up in her hotel room, Amanda pulled the data file she'd collected and sent it over to Turtle82, not wanting to risk deciphering its contents on her own laptop. Her roses were displayed on the desk in a vase the receptionist had kindly sent up for her when she'd seen her walk in with the impressive bouquet.

'Flowers are so clichéd,' Shane had noted with scorn when he saw them.

'Mmm, totally.' Amanda wasn't the kind of girl who loved receiving chocolates and flowers. She'd rather a guy buy her a DVD and some jelly babies. But she couldn't deny the flutter she'd felt in her stomach when she saw the roses there waiting for her at the restaurant. It felt like walking into the scene from a movie where she was the star.

'Was he insanely sleazy?' Shane's breath was laced with whisky. 'I imagine he spent all night trying to grope you.'

'Actually,' with her message sent, Amanda turned away from her laptop, 'he was a real gentleman.'

'He's no gentleman. He's just good at pretending to be one.'

'That's... that's what I meant.'

'Well, at least it's done,' Shane glanced over at the laptop.

'Hopefully,' Amanda stretched her arms up above her head and tilted her neck from side to side. 'As long as there's enough information held on his phone we can get out of here and head home.'

'You don't think there will be.' Shane was standing by his side of the bed, his voice flat. It was a statement, not a question.

'I... I'm hopeful there will. But,' Amanda pulled back the sheets on the bed, 'let's just wait and see. I don't want to risk being disappointed.'

'Are you seeing him again?'

'If I have to.'

'Amanda,' Shane released a deep sigh as he dropped into bed. 'I know guys like McAllister, how they operate. He's just a snake in a slick suit. His charm is all a mirage. Beneath the shine and polish he's a thug. And he's dangerous. Please don't go forgetting that.'

'He's really not all bad. He lost his dad too when he was young.' Amanda was surprised by her own words. Was she really making excuses for McAllister?

'Do not get pulled in by his bullshit. He's the reason your husband is dead. And why Ewan's poor mother was made to look like she'd OD'd. He is not some troubled, misunderstood soul. And just because there is never any blood on his hands doesn't make him any less accountable.'

With a grunt, Shane rolled onto his side and left Amanda staring at his back.

Was Gregg McAllister rotten to the core? Or, like Will had been, was he just a victim of unfortunate circumstances? Despite her mind being conflicted, Amanda managed to quickly slip over the precipice into slumber where she dreamt of running through endless rose gardens.

*

There's not enough data. There's contact numbers but no messages, no files. He's being careful. You need the mainframe access. Find the main computer he uses. Load all hidden files onto a USB and then get your ass out of Dodge.

T.

Amanda sat on her chair with her knees drawn up to her chest as she peered sleepily at her laptop screen.

'So, did they get back to you?' Shane stepped out of the bathroom, freshly showered with just a towel wrapped around his waist. Droplets of water still clung to his hair.

'Yep.'

'And?'

'And it's not enough data. I need to access his main computer.'

Shane said nothing. His jaw set in a firm line, he marched back into the bathroom and closed the door behind him. A second late Amanda jumped in her seat when he yelled 'fuck'. She imagined him amongst the steam that lingered in the room, hands clenched into fists of frustration at his sides. He just wanted her back home and safe.

Amanda closed her laptop and dreamily gazed at her vase full of roses. Their velvety petals had started to droop overnight. She knew through her mother's experiences that they were as delicate as they were beautiful. Her bouquet would not last very long.

'And you can bin those bloody flowers.' Shane burst back out of the bathroom, still draped in just a white towel. He pointed over at the vase, his features contorting with anger. 'If you want flowers, I'll buy you flowers.'

'Shane—'

'Bin them. I mean it. I don't want anything of *his* in here.'

'Okay, okay, relax.' Amanda reached for the vase.

'I can see you slipping under his fucking spell. You're such a sucker for strong men that seem wounded.'

'Shane—'

'Tell me I'm wrong,' he demanded, his voice like thunder. 'Tell me that you see who McAllister really is, that you're not being taken in by his charm.'

'I see who he really is,' Amanda calmly assured him. 'I'm completely on top of this. You don't have to worry.'

'Fine.' Shane stormed back into the bathroom and Amanda released her grip on the vase, leaving the roses be. It seemed pointless to throw away something so beautiful. It was only when she drew away that she noticed that she'd caught her finger on a thorn and had managed to draw blood.

10

The elevator doors eased open in front of her and Amanda paused, unsure if she should get out. McAllister was waiting for her in the bar just metres away. Another date. Another night of playing pretend.

'Remember why we're here,' Shane had stared into her eyes and placed his hands on her shoulders, applying pressure before letting her go and blinking back tears. As Amanda walked away from the hotel she didn't turn to look at him, couldn't bear to see the pain etched onto his face. She knew that each time he let her walk away to meet McAllister he wondered if she'd be coming back. If the man would morph into the monster and she'd meet the same fate as Will.

Will.

The scars on her heart had threaded together to spell out his name. What would he say if he could see her now – all dressed up for the man who helped kill him? He'd tell her to run.

'Just run, Amanda. Get away and don't stop running.' Because that's what he'd done – he'd run away. A decision which had ultimately proved fatal. Will had proved that running wasn't the answer.

Drawing in a breath and pushing out her chest, Amanda left the elevator. The top floor of the hotel she was in opened out into a luxurious bar which offered stunning views of the city through floor-to-ceiling windows. Amanda strode purposefully towards the slick ebony surface of the large bar and then stopped. Behind the bar stood two servers. Around her were dozens of tables and plush velvet sofas. Amanda turned, taking in every inch of the room. Every table, every sofa, was empty.

It was a trap.

Amanda spied the silhouette standing against the glittering city skyline, peering out on their domain. McAllister was already there, suited up as usual. He'd lured Amanda here, away from prying eyes. Did he know she'd cloned his phone? Did he intend to launch her from one of the vast windows and watch her plummet down into the shadows below?

'Good evening, Amanda.'

McAllister turned away from the window, sensing her presence. He held a Martini glass in one hand and, standing in the empty bar, he looked like some sort of Bond villain. Amanda began to calculate how quickly she could be back in the elevator, punching on the button to close the doors.

Her mind was too slow, panic making her thoughts foggy. McAllister strode over to her, smiling. His free hand in his trouser pocket.

'Where…' Amanda cleared her throat and smoothed her clammy palms against her dress. She wore a bright red bondage number which she felt was far too clingy, but Shane had begrudgingly assured her that such a dress would ensure an invitation to McAllister's home.

'You're going in all dressed up like some fancy present,' he'd muttered grumpily when Amanda stepped out of the bathroom in the dress, 'he'll just want to get you home and unwrap you.'

'Where is everyone?' Amanda's question came out like a whimper.

'Wow.' McAllister stopped a few paces short of her and his steely gaze swept over her dress which exposed her long legs and modest curves. 'You look,' a blush crept into his cheeks, 'stunning, Amanda. Truly.'

'Thanks. The, um…' she nervously wound her hair around her fingers, 'why's the bar so empty?'

She kept her eyes on his pocketed hand, waiting for him to produce a gun, steadily aim it at her and tell her that it was all over, that he was on to her ruse.

'I might have hired out the whole place,' he explained with a modest shrug, his hand remaining in his pocket. 'I admit it was something of an extreme length to go to, but I figured,' another shrug, 'it'd be nice to have a bit of privacy.'

He'd hired out the entire bar? Amanda's eyes widened. She was stunned. No one had ever done anything like that for her before.

'Come,' Gregg finally freed his other hand and gestured towards the windows where he'd been standing. 'We've got the best table in the place.'

*

Amanda had never been a connoisseur of wine. She knew three varieties – red, white and rosé. Her date for the evening was much more informed. He ordered them a bottle of something red and rare which he was certain Amanda would love. After the waiter had uncorked the bottle and poured them each a glass, Amanda took a sip and as it slid down her throat it felt like berry-infused silk. It was truly delicious. So delicious that she keenly drank two glasses before realising by her third that she needed to slow down a little.

'Do you come here a lot?' Amanda wondered. Gregg was sat across from her, leaning back in a sofa with one elbow resting on the chair's arm.

'As much as I can,' he admitted with the dreamy malaise that always followed several glasses of good wine. He turned his head to look out at the glittering city. 'There's something very serene about being up here. It calms me.'

'Do you need calming?'

'Sometimes.' His smile became mischievous. Then it dropped altogether. 'I mainly come here when I'm trying to outrun my demons.'

'Do you have many demons?'

'Too many.' With a sigh he leaned forward and reached for his glass of wine.

Amanda polished off what remained of the crimson liquid in her glass, savouring the rich taste. She knew she should be needling McAllister for information. But he seemed so vulnerable. Whilst hiring the whole bar made him look like a giant, as he sat in his plush sofa surrounding by empty chairs he looked woefully lost. And small against all the emptiness.

'Do you have any children?' She told herself it was an acceptable question to ask, relevant date talk even though Amanda was fully aware of what a loaded question it was. Gregg's silver eyes turned to stone as he placed down his glass without having drunk from it.

'I did. Once.'

'What happened?'

'I had two beautiful girls. They were everything to me. But there was a fire and,' he looked down at his hands, 'they didn't make it out.'

'My God, how awful. I'm so sorry. What were their names?'

'I can't,' Gregg shook his head as a single tear danced down his cheek and reached the tip of his scar. 'I can't say their names. It's too painful.'

Amanda joined him on his sofa. She knew she needed to stay close to him but she was also drawn to his pain. Few people had felt loss on such a scale as she had. She silently reached for his hands and held them tightly, pressing her body against his. He smelt like cedar, wine and secrets.

'I come here to forget,' he told her tearfully. 'I come here to try and get some distance from all my nightmares.' Squeezing her hands back, he turned so that his head was inches from hers. Then he leaned forward, letting their foreheads touch. 'And I run,' he whispered.

Arrows of despair pierced Amanda's heart and she had to fight the urge to flinch. Why was he talking about running? Was he alluding to Will?

'Every morning at sunrise I go jogging through the woodlands that border my home. I run until my lungs burn and my legs go numb and I find that it helps.'

'I go jogging too.' Amanda's voice was soft and seductive. 'I run every day if I can.'

'We have so much in common.' His gaze lowered to her lips and his breathing became shallow.

Amanda had been intimate with a man enough times to know what was coming next – this was all the prelude to a kiss. Biting her lip, she eased back from him, destroying the moment. This was all still a game and she wasn't about to show her hand just yet.

'Tomorrow,' she kept her hands on his, her voice sweet. 'Why don't we go somewhere where we can be *truly* alone?' Amanda pointedly glanced back towards the ebony bar and the pair of servers who were busying themselves polishing glasses.

'It's like you read my mind.' Gregg's voice was firm yet delicate, like the crunch of autumn leaves underfoot. 'Maybe you'd like to come over to my place?' he released one of his hands from her grasp and slid it over to her leg, resting it on the exposed skin just beneath her revealing dress's hemline.

'That sounds perfect.' Amanda hoped that her nervous breathing looked more like sensual excitement.

Gregg kept his hand on her leg. 'I feel like I can truly be myself around you, Amanda.' He inched his hand a fraction higher, pushing it beneath the red fabric. 'You don't play games like most other women do.'

She was too aware of his hand on her leg. His touch was starting to burn, to sear through her skin, corrupting her soul with every second they remained connected. Amanda reached for his face, cupped his cheek and drew his lips towards hers. It was a soft kiss, planted briefly against the corner of his mouth with enough pressure to leave a red mark. A signature.

Amanda stood up before Gregg could seize the opportunity to deepen the passion of the kiss. She smoothed down her dress and put on her most flirtatious smile. 'Until tomorrow,' she told him breathlessly. She hoped he'd just let her go, perhaps watch her walk away from his position on the sofa but he followed her like a lost puppy, out towards the elevator.

'You sure know how to leave a man wanting more,' his eyes were full of desire but he didn't touch her. He remained a few inches away, both hands pushed into his pockets.

'What more could you possibly want?' Amanda teased as the elevator doors glided open.

'Everything.' Gregg looked at her like she was all the wonders of the world rolled into one. 'With you I want everything.'

He was still staring at her as the elevator doors closed, leaving him alone up in his empty bar.

*

The night carried the scent of a thousand parties. Amanda carefully wandered down the street in her high-heeled shoes and breathed in cigarette smoke infused with wine, beer and vinegar-soaked fish and chips. Couples staggered close by, wrapped tightly together as though they were on a sinking ship. Amanda could see the lights of her hotel in the distance. It was a welcoming sight.

Once she'd drifted through the brightly lit lobby she went up to her room expecting to find Shane. But he wasn't there. Both the bed and the bathroom were empty. Amanda checked the clock on the bedside table. It was just after eleven. Was he not expecting her back so soon?

Her insides knotted themselves together in panic. She remembered all too well the feeling of waking up one morning and finding that her husband was gone. She looked at the crisp sheets of her hotel bed and bit back tears. Shane would never just up and leave her, would he?

But then she'd never have thought that Will would. Up until the day he'd left he'd been as solid and reliable as her late father had once been. He never missed a date, always came home on time.

Amanda burst out of her hotel room and into the corridor. She couldn't accept that Shane would just leave. That wasn't him. And she knew him. He'd been there her whole life, why would he bail now?

Back in the elevator Amanda could barely read the information about what was contained on which floor. She spied the word gym and pressed the relevant button on the keypad and prayed that Shane was there. Because if he wasn't…

Had McAllister taken him?

Maybe the empty bar had all been a distraction. Whilst Amanda was looking one way, McAllister's men swooped in and stole Shane away. Was their intention to torture him? To demand he tell them where Ewan was? But Shane was a cop. Surely they wouldn't risk tangling with him?

The elevator doors opened and Amanda was running down another corridor. She reached the glass-fronted gym and skidded to a halt. Amongst the array of expensive equipment lay Shane. He was on his back on a bench press. The muscles in his upper arm tensed as he raised a large dumbbell above his chest. He sat up when Amanda entered the gym.

'Hey,' he grabbed a towel draped over the edge of the bench press and wiped it across his face and the back of his neck. 'You're back.'

'I didn't know where you were.' Amanda found the weight of a punchbag behind her and leaned against it so that she wouldn't crumple into a ball on the floor. The wine in her system was making her emotional. Irrational. 'I went back to the room and when you weren't there—' her knees buckled as she released a ragged sob.

'Hey,' Shane scooped her up into his arms, his skin damp with sweat, and pressed her against the punchbag. He carefully stroked her hair out of her eyeline, tucking it behind her ear. 'I would never leave you.' The promise was soft against her cheek. 'I just had to get out of there. Had to work out some of my tension.'

'He wants me to go to his place. Tomorrow.'

'Shit, right. Okay.'

'I can't sleep with him,' Amanda trembled fearfully, realising how things might escalate. 'I can't go that far, I just—'

'Shh, you won't have to. We'll work something out.' Shane kissed her temple and raised his hand to caress her cheek with his thumb.

'Don't run from me.' Amanda wasn't sure if she was talking to Shane or her memories of Will. The wine was blurring all her thoughts together.

'I'll never run from you.'

'But you left me. Before.'

When her relationship with Shane had broken down a knife had wedged itself in Amanda's side. It was always there and she'd learned to live with the dull ache it provided. But sometimes the knife turned, and when it did she was overwhelmed with fresh pain, relieving the trauma of that goodbye all over again. Shane refused to accept her dalliances within the darknet and his feelings forced him towards the door. Amanda had let him leave but he'd been the one to cross that threshold, to set fire to all that they'd had.

'I was young and I was a fool,' Shane's body was pressed against hers. 'Tell me you want me and I'll never leave again. I swear. I'll be yours forever.'

'I…' The air in the gym was too hot and clammy. Amanda wanted to get out, wanted to breathe in fresh air and kick off her shoes and slide out of her red dress. 'I need you.'

Were want and need different things? Shane's reaction told her that they were. He dropped his arms, releasing the pressure between them. Amanda staggered forward, away from the punchbag.

'Let's get you to bed to sleep off all that wine in your system,' his shoulders were slumped in defeat.

'What wine?'

'Your lips are stained with the stuff. You've been drinking red wine. You never could handle it.'

'I'm fine,' Amanda insisted with a grandiose air, right before she almost toppled out of her shoes. Suddenly moving in a pair of five-inch heels felt more like walking on stilts.

'Get those things off.'

Amanda kicked off the shoes with a flourish, giggling, and started for the door. Shane scooped down and grabbed them before following her out of the gym. The carpeted floor of the hotel's corridor felt blissfully soft against her bare feet.

'Come on twinkletoes, bedtime,' Shane guided her towards the elevator and pressed the button for their floor. Amanda's mood shifted from playful to sleepy during the ascent and by the time they entered their room her eyelids felt leaden and her body was stiff. Shane had to help her over to the bed, where she collapsed against her pillows, eager to fall asleep.

'Okay, well, goodnight,' he pulled the sheets up over her.

Amanda could sense him walking away, retreating from her bedside. 'I want you,' she whispered, on the cusp of sleep. 'I want you so much it scares me.'

11

Gregg McAllister's main residence wasn't located in Glasgow. It was closer to Edinburgh, nestled away in the countryside just beyond the city. He had an apartment in Glasgow. But he hadn't invited Amanda there. She read the email he'd sent her again, sent to a ghost account Amanda had set up for herself. The address already familiar to her thanks to her investigative searches via Google maps.

'So he's invited you to his main house?' Shane had folded himself into the chair beside her. Starbucks was bustling around them so Amanda had to keep her voice low.

'His main house, yeah.' She slid her phone across the table, allowing him to read the message Gregg had sent her earlier.

'This place has got to be, what? An hour away?'

'More like two,' Amanda frowned at the map she'd pulled up on her laptop.

'Two? How are you even supposed to get there?'

'He's sending a car for me.'

'Jesus.' Shane shook his head. 'I mean, why couldn't he just invite you to his apartment here in the city?'

'I don't know.' Amanda guiltily chewed her lip. She felt like she did know. She'd flirted with McAllister and told him that they needed privacy. His mansion would offer them complete solitude. There'd be no city lights, no place for her to run to. And the mainframe. It had to be there. She nervously reached for her cup of coffee and had to force a gulp down her throat which was constricting as her thoughts began to run away from her.

'Want me to follow in my car?'

'No.'

'No?' Shane repeated dubiously. Her response had been fired off a little too quickly for his liking.

'I mean,' Amanda lowered her cup back down and squared her shoulders in an effort to calm down. 'It would be too suspicious. Too dangerous. I need him to believe that I'm just going there to, you know.' She gave a brisk shrug.

'To fuck him.'

'Christ, Shane. Do you have to be so crude about it?'

'I'm just telling it like it is, Amanda. How he'll be seeing it. All the flowers, the pomp, the gesturing, it's all just to get in your pants.'

'He could actually just be an old-school romantic for all you know.'

'Are we really having this conversation? Are you really defending him?'

'No. Course not. I'm fully aware of the reason I'm supposedly going to his house. I just don't need reminding about it.' She looked at Shane, into his green eyes which regarded her a little too keenly. He was scared. His fear radiated off him. He wasn't the calm, in control Shane that Amanda was used to seeing back home, back where he was a high-ranking officer, who was well regarded by locals. 'You know you don't have to look so scared all the time,' Amanda reached out and playfully nudged his arm. 'It's all going to be fine.'

'The problem is that I know exactly what you're dealing with. I just don't think you do.'

'I'm fine. I'm on top of it all. I have a plan.'

'A plan?'

With a satisfied grin Amanda spun her laptop around and let Shane look at the screen where she'd been exploring sleeping pills and how to turn them into strong sedatives by combining them with other medicines.

'Your plan is to take a nice long nap?' Shane cocked his head at her.

'Not me. Him. While he sleeps I hack into his mainframe and then get my ass out of there. By the time he wakes up I'll be long gone and the cops will already be on his doorstep, ready to take him in.'

'So you're essentially going to slip the guy a roofie?'

'Exactly.'

'And how do you intend to do that?'

'By distracting him while I lace his drink with it.'

'Distract him how?' a hard edge crept into Shane's voice.

'That brings me to the second part of my plan,' Amanda explained brightly. 'Come on, let's go.'

'Go where?'

'You'll see.'

*

'So I need a man's opinion.' Amanda nodded at the storefront that was filled with mannequins wearing sexy lingerie.

'I really don't know about this.' Shane had one hand tangled up in his hair as he eyed the shop warily. 'It's just…' he sighed and shoved both hands into his jeans pockets. 'Shopping. And this kind of…stuff.' He could barely maintain eye contact with the red balcony bra and French knicker set on display in front of him.

'It'll be fine,' Amanda tugged on his arm and drew him inside the store. 'Like I said, I need your opinion. I need an outfit that will be distracting.'

'You're distracting enough just as you are,' Shane grumbled as he reluctantly followed her. 'Just strip off completely, that'll distract him.'

'Strip off completely?' Amanda turned around and saw Shane's face reddening.

'No. Shit,' he squeezed his eyes shut in frustration. 'Don't do that. Keep some clothes on. I just meant—'

'Good to see that shopping still makes you nervous,' Amanda pulled him deeper into the store, towards the lingerie section. 'Just don't hyperventilate when we walk past all the vibrators,' she teased.

Amanda didn't own any sexy lingerie. When it came to her undergarments she tended to keep things pragmatic. She had a few pairs of black lace pants, some nice bras. But nothing that actually matched. She'd never felt the need to dress up in stockings and suspenders. With both Shane and Will things had quickly become too comfortable for that. Sex had been an extension of feelings; it was never all that... sexy. At least in terms of her wardrobe.

'Oh, jeez.' With her hands on her hips, Amanda admired the impressive array of lingerie on display. There were pants of varying colours, materials and size, from a skimpy thong to a fuller French knicker. There were bras that promised to give the kind of cleavage that a glamour model would envy and then there were bodices and brassieres which could pass as costumes for a burlesque dancer. Amanda had no idea what was deemed sexy. 'I'm a bit out of my depth here.' She pulled Shane, who as a distraction had been staring at his phone, to stand beside her and he grumbled as he slid it back into his pocket. 'What works?' she gestured at the wall of lingerie.

'God, Amanda,' he took a step back, as though one of the bras had reached out and scratched him. 'You said you just wanted my opinion on what *you* picked out.'

'Yes, but,' she gestured helplessly at the wall.

'Urgh,' Shane groaned. 'Fine.' He steeled himself and scanned all the lace and silk items. 'You want to keep it simple yet sexy. I'd go for a black and lace bodice, with full pants and suspenders.' He clicked his fingers, 'And stockings. You have to have stockings.'

'Wow.' Amanda began gathering together the items he'd suggested. 'That was surprisingly... specific.'

'Yeah, well, you asked.'

'I know, but,' Amanda was just about to select a pair of stockings. She figured a black pair would be best. 'I mean when we were together, I never...' she looked at the assortment of luxury underwear she was holding. 'I didn't dress up in this stuff.'

'Yeah, I know. You kept it simple and that was hot.'

'So when did you develop a keener appreciation for high-end lingerie?'

Shane sighed and bowed his head, suddenly really interested in his shoes.

'Oh, right.' Amanda's cheeks started to burn. 'Jayne. Right. Of course.'

'Some women enjoy dressing up in this stuff,' he replied defensively.

'Some *women*?' Amanda exclaimed as she strode towards the dressing rooms. 'God, Shane, how many were there?'

'You can't have expected me to be a monk after we broke up,' he said hotly as he followed after her. 'I mean, you went and got bloody married.'

Amanda stopped and turned back to look at him, her pile of red and black lace lingerie squashed against her chest. 'I'm sorry I said anything. Of course I didn't expect you to be a monk. I'm just,' she fingered the extravagant fabric of the bodice, 'I'm scared. This,' she hugged her bundle tighter, 'none of this is me.'

'Just say the word and we go back home right now and figure something else out.' Shane placed his hands on her shoulders, protectively shielding her not just from the store but from the rest of the world.

'I have to do this. For Ewan.' She swallowed against the lump in her throat. 'For Will.'

'I understand.'

'But can I even do this?' Amanda looked sadly at her gathered garments. 'I struggle to be sexy.'

'You really don't.'

'Please,' she scoffed as she pulled away from him and continued towards the changing rooms. 'I've never even worn suspenders before. I'm possibly the least sexy person in the world.'

'You're really not.'

Amanda felt Shane's eyes on her right until she closed the curtain and disappeared into the dressing rooms.

*

'So are you going to try them on for me?' Shane teased, kicking at the black and pink stripe bag from where he lay sprawled out on the hotel bed watching television.

'Nope,' Amanda replied primly where she sat at her laptop. There was another bag beside the one full of lingerie from the local chemist, filled with sleeping tablets and allergy medicine. She just had to work out a safe combination of the two that would create a strong sedative.

'But what if it doesn't look right?' Shane pressed.

'It looks fine.'

'There might be a button missing at the back that you didn't spot.'

'There are no buttons.'

'You really don't want me to see you in it? After you dragged me into that bloody shop.'

'I'm just embarrassed, okay?' Amanda looked away from her laptop, satisfied that she'd figured out how to create a sedative. The next part of her plan was using the right coding to access the hidden parts of McAllister's mainframe. She had two USB sticks out on the desk, small and discreet enough to fit in the garter she'd bought. She'd use them to house all the data she pulled from McAllister's computer. Once she found it. Once he was asleep. She needed an awful lot of things to come together for her plan to go without a hitch. Because things had to go without a hitch. She was too terrified to contemplate an alternative outcome of events.

'If you're embarrassed in front of me what about in front of him?'

'Huh?'

Amanda was distracted by an incoming message from Turtle82.

A simple encryption code will do the trick. You want bank a/c numbers, listing of transactions.

T.

Amanda could create an encryption code in her sleep. She closed the laptop and gave Shane her complete attention.

'Maybe you should think about getting comfortable in the lingerie,' he suggested delicately. 'Because when you wear it for him you want him to believe that you're... up for it.'

'You're right.' Amanda sighed and stood up, grabbing the striped bag as she headed for the bathroom.

Wearing the lingerie felt strange. The bodice was like a vice around her ribs and it pushed her boobs up so much that they almost met her chin. After she'd carefully pulled up the stockings and attached them to the suspenders she returned to Shane feeling painfully self-conscious. Her entire body itched with the desire to pull on a towelling robe and just hide away.

Shane looked away from the television, his eyes instantly glued to her the second she walked in.

'Does it look all right?' Biting her lip, she looked down at her legs, at the garter she'd pulled up her thigh. She hoped it'd be sufficient for housing her USBs.

Shane said nothing. He just stared.

'Oh, God, it looks awful, doesn't it? I'm not going to be able to pull this off. I just don't have it in me to be this kind of weird double agent and pretend to like someone.' Folding her arms across her chest, she started to double back towards the bathroom when Shane sprang from the bed and reached out for her. He carefully placed a hand against her waist as if he were afraid to touch her.

'You look stunning. Truly, Amanda. I swear that you'll distract him, no problem.'

'You think so?'

'I know so,' he tentatively took a step towards her. 'You look devastatingly sexy.' He raised his hands to cradle her face in his palms. 'But even without all the ribbons and lace what makes you beautiful, what makes you sexy, is *you*. You're the strongest person I know, Amanda. And the bravest.'

'Tell me I can do this.'

'You can do this.' Shane stepped forward so that their bodies were touching. Amanda was on fire. She remembered how it felt to have his lips pressed against hers, his hands exploring every inch of her. It had always been so natural, so comfortable. And just like riding a bike she'd never forgotten how to do it, how to fit their bodies together in perfect symmetry. The tip of Shane's nose touched hers. 'Don't go.'

He said the plea so breathily that Amanda almost missed it. 'What?'

'Don't... don't go,' he repeated, his words gaining strength.

'Shane, I have to go,' she stepped away from him.

'I can't,' Shane's hands became fists at his sides, 'I can't handle the thought of him *seeing* you like this. Hell, if he touches you I think I'm actually going to lose my mind.'

'He won't touch me,' Amanda insisted. 'He'll be unconscious before he even realises what's going on. I searched the darknet for the right recipe. The formula I've worked out is odourless and tasteless and will leave him sleeping like a baby for a good twelve hours.'

'But what if he does touch you? Because, believe me, once he sees you looking like that it's all he'll be able to think about.' Pushing his hands through his hair, Shane stalked over to the window, his body tense.

'I'll text you when I've managed to get away and meet you at the rendezvous point we picked out in the woods. Remember the one, just beyond the main road?' Amanda continued pragmatically, keen to keep their focus on the plan.

'Don't. Go.' Shane pressed his palms against the window and dropped his forehead against the glass as he gazed down at the city.

Amanda came and stood beside him, gently placing her hand on his shoulder. Beneath them people surged along the street, caught up in their own dramas, oblivious about what was going on several storeys above their heads.

'I do this one last thing and this is over.'

'If he touches you I'll kill him.'

'Shane—'

'I'm not messing around, Amanda. I'll strangle him with my bare hands if I have to.'

'You're not thinking straight.'

'How can I think straight?' He drooped against the window. 'My whole world is upside down right now. You. Me. How did we get thrown so far off course? You were meant to be my forever.'

As teenagers, forever had truly felt like an infinite word. But now, over a decade later, they both understood what forever really meant. That the length of a lifetime was unpredictable, you had to live for the moment rather than planning for a future that might not even exist. At sixteen when you promised someone forever you maybe promised the rest of the summer. But now, forever was a real promise, one you could make good on.

Amanda's laptop beeped from where it was placed on the desk. She could feel her soul trying to splice itself in half as she glanced over at it. She desperately wanted to stay with Shane, to give in to the ache in her heart. But she owed it to Will to protect his son, to ensure that Ewan could grow up to one day promise someone forever.

'It'll be him.' Amanda withdrew from Shane and went to the desk. Sure enough the email was from McAllister.

> My driver will pick you up at 6 from the train station like
> you asked. I can't wait to see you xxx

Three kisses. For a man like McAllister that felt like a lot. Amanda checked the time. It was already 5.15. Soon she'd have to leave.

'I need to be at the station for six,' she popped open her suitcase as she spoke and rummaged around its contents until she found a dark green shirt dress which she quickly began buttoning up over her black and red bodice.

'You're not getting changed?'

'I fail to see the point.' Next came her long beige mac and some ballet pumps. 'This way I'm almost all set to go once I get there.'

Into her handbag went her home-made sedative along with her phone. Then she placed the two USBs discreetly within her lace garter.

'So what time should I start heading out there?' Shane asked grimly, his eyes red as if struggling against the pressure of holding in tears.

'Give it a few hours.' Amanda untucked her hair from her coat and hurriedly pulled her fingers through it. 'Maybe eight or so. That should give me enough time to…' she pursed her lips together, not wanting to finish the sentence.

Enough time to seduce a monster. She was heading out to dance with the devil. She felt like Belle in *Beauty and the Beast* when she bravely forsakes her freedom to save her father from the ghastly master of the castle. But in that tale there had been a man within the monster.

Amanda smoothed her hands down her coat and tried to steady her anxiously racing heart with a few level breaths. She was going to McAllister's home. To the scene of the fire which had claimed the lives of his daughters. Erin and Kelly. He couldn't bear to say their names, but Amanda already knew them, had read about them in newspaper reports.

Was McAllister all man or all monster? She supposed she was about to find out. Her hand was on the door handle, pressing down.

'Amanda.'

She turned back to look at Shane who remained at the window, looking broken.

'No matter what happens tonight. No matter what you feel you need to do… I love you. I figured you should know that.'

12

Amanda sat in the back of the chauffer-driven car noting every minute that passed, feeling each mile that opened up between her and Shane. She couldn't let herself think about what he'd said to her before she left, not now. She needed her mind sharp. If she dwelled on Shane's admission too much she risked turning her back on the mission and she needed to go through with this, for Ewan. It took less than half an hour to leave the city. Tightly packed rows of houses and colossal stacks of flats gave way to open countryside. Rolling hills tumbled off into the distance, thick with heather. A setting sun turned the sky to rust.

As the car kept moving, the knot in her stomach grew larger, tighter. She sensed that she was getting close to McAllister's home. It was twilight when the car finally threaded through dense woodland before slowing and stopping at the foot of heavy iron gates. Shadows gathered around the car, momentarily kept at bay by the weakening light of dusk. The car idled for a moment and then the grand gates parted like opening arms, beckoning them inside.

McAllister's home was a mansion. When the car turned and halted, she was able to take in the immense structure in all its glory. The house surged up out of the land like some gothic edifice. Long leaded windows looked out on the surrounding woodlands and black double doors remained sealed at the entrance.

Climbing out of the car, Amanda craned her neck to take in more of the grandeur. Stone gargoyles peered out from the corners of various edges, giving the grey walls of the mansion a sinister edge. It looked like something out of Grimm's' fairy tales. The house stretched away from her, both in height and length. She was unable to take in all of it from where she stood beside the car, its engine still ticking over thanks to the long drive in.

The driver was at the far end of the vehicle, hauling Amanda's overnight bag out of the boot. Little did he know that instead of containing some cosmetic essentials and a change of clothes it was packed with a flashlight, sleeping bag, running shoes and energy bars – everything Amanda would need to survive a night in the woods if it came to that, if she somehow struggled to find Shane in the dark. She scanned the high stone wall which surrounded the home. Even from a distance she could see the digital blinking of security cameras. Once McAllister was passed out and the USB within her garter full of vital information she'd need to knock out the power for the entire complex. She could easily log into the local grid and ensure that casa de McAllister was without any electricity for an hour or so. That way she could slip out into the shadows, unnoticed. At least that was the plan.

'Ah, welcome.' The black doors opened and McAllister stepped out, looking more informal than usual in a loose fitting shirt and dark jeans. His hair was still moussed, his eyes filled with an excited glint. 'I was starting to wonder when you'd get here.'

'It's quite a drive. I'm surprised you live so far out of the city.'

'This place,' McAllister looked up at the vast windows, the gargoyles, 'it has a power over me. I just can't leave it. Too many memories I guess.'

He guided Amanda through the black doors and into his home. The building was just as impressive on the inside. A long hallway led towards a sweeping staircase which split itself in two as it ascended up towards the first landing. There was wood panelling everywhere. It covered every wall. Even the floorboards were mahogany, though they were largely covered by ornate rugs.

'It's like a castle,' Amanda uttered, struggling to take it all in. It reminded her of the stately homes she'd visited on school trips as a child. Homes owned by earls and lords.

'It's a little ostentatious,' McAllister agreed, leading her into what Amanda assumed was the main living room. A stoked fire roared in the large stone hearth, bordered by a cluster of sofas and armchairs made of thick red velvet. 'But then I designed it to be.'

That's when Amanda saw them. She peered round at the panelled walls and noticed the framed pictures of two girls adorning almost every spare inch. They were sat together on a swing, smiling. In another picture they were on a beach, arms wrapped around each other's waist, hugging with a tightness only sisters could have. They were blonde with their father's grey eyes. And they were always smiling. There wasn't a picture where they were sombre.

'Come,' McAllister was standing beside his giant fireplace, beckoning her over. But Amanda was bewitched by the images on the wall. The girls looked so full of life, so beautiful. If she strained to listen she thought she might hear their distant laughter as they ran down a hallway together. 'Amanda?'

'These are your daughters?'

And this is where they died.

Even though the fire burned brightly on the other side of the room, Amanda felt a dip in the air around her as a chill crept up her spine. Why would McAllister stay in the place where his daughters died? In their tomb? Did he just linger there to cling to the memories of happier times, praying that he'd one day hear the soft tinkle of their unburdened childish laughter echo off the panelled walls?

'Aye, that's them.' His voice was soft, almost drowned out by the crackle of the fire.

'They're… they're beautiful.'

'This was their home,' Gregg turned away from her to face the flames, leaning both hands upon the high mantle of the fireplace. 'It's why I can't leave.'

Amanda kept looking at the pair of smiling faces. She couldn't imagine their beauty twisted by fire.

'This was never a home for children.' Gregg's voice was rough with regret as he bowed his head against his chest. 'She saw that. I didn't. I endangered them and…'

Her legs were automatically carrying her over to him. Was Shane right? Was she powerless to resist a broken man? Amanda gently placed a hand against Gregg's back.

'I think it's nice that you want to stay here. To be close to their memory.'

'You do?' He turned to face her. The fire behind him hissed as a large log snapped.

'Yes. I do.'

Her own perfect home was still waiting on her return. Though Will hadn't died there he lingered in every room, upon every pristine surface. His footsteps would forever haunt the small landing. Amanda's hand fluttered up to her throat as she blinked away tears. She wasn't sure she had the strength to ever go back to the home she'd shared with her late husband.

'Why don't we go somewhere,' Gregg looked over at the shrine to his lost daughters, 'a little less crowded?'

Amanda followed him down more hallways. Up wooden staircases that creaked and past countless closed doors. Gregg gave her a brief tour as they moved through his grand residence: 'That leads to the wine cellar. That goes to my games room. That's the music room.' But he didn't open any doors. It was a whistle-stop tour. Amanda did her best to commit everything he said to memory. Since the second she'd entered his home, she'd been plotting her way back out, which hallways she'd need to fumble her way along in the blackout she was planning.

'And this,' Gregg paused before yet another closed wooden door. It was on the second floor. Looking down over the banister, Amanda could see the main hallway and the sparkle of a chandelier winking out from what looked like a dining room, its doors thrown open. 'This is my room.'

Amanda followed him inside. It was more of a luxury apartment than a bedroom. Two floor-to-ceiling leaded windows looked out onto the countryside which had been lost to impenetrable darkness. A few lights twinkled distantly on the horizon but it was obvious that the mansion was extremely isolated.

A grand raised sleigh bed provided the centrepiece for the room. It was flanked by two doors, both open, which led into a state-of-the-art bathroom and a walk-in wardrobe lined with designer suits.

Opposite the bed was a large chest of drawers which looked antique, above them a flat-screen television was suspended against the wall. And tucked into the far corner was an ornate desk atop of which sat a closed MacBook. Amanda's heart thudded so strongly against her ribcage that it almost caused her to topple forwards. That was it. The mainframe. It made sense that McAllister would keep it close by, in his private quarters.

Amanda looked up, trying not to appear overly interested in the laptop and saw the outline of a safe etched into the ceiling.

'I think I'm supposed to say that this is where the magic happens,' Gregg gave her a playful grin. 'But, call me old-fashioned but I believe that a lady should be wined and dined before being more thoroughly entertained.'

He left the bedroom and Amanda remained in the centre of the room, briefly dumbfounded. Why had he even shown her the bedroom if they were just going to leave? A preview of what was to come perhaps?

*

Gregg's chef put on a sumptuous meal for the couple. Amanda sat at the polished wooden dining table feeling woefully out of place as she ate braised lamb and enjoyed a perfectly baked soufflé. Every room felt like it was fit for a queen. Long velvet drapes had been drawn across the windows, allowing the chandelier to sparkle like a glittering sun. Even the cutlery was the finest silverware.

Eventually, when dinner concluded, Gregg encouraged Amanda to join him in the drawing room. In there the walls were lined with bookcases stacked full of leather-bound tomes. To spend several hours browsing the titles would be blissful but Amanda knew that she had to stay focused. Shane would soon be leaving the city to come and rendezvous with her. The clock was ticking.

'I like to enjoy a decent Scotch after dinner.' Gregg was reclining in a leather armchair, a crystal tumbler in his hand. He'd previously poured himself a drink from a nearby decanter.

Amanda sat down in the chair across from him. She knew she needed to up her game, to lure him back to the bedroom, to the laptop. 'It's so warm in here.' She gingerly unbuttoned the top of her shirt dress and then hoisted up the hem to reveal the top of her stockings. Gregg almost choked on his drink.

'Well, it's certainly just got a lot hotter.' He made a swift recovery, his eyes hungrily taking her in.

'Why don't I get you another drink?' As she made the suggestion, she pursed her lips and let her fingertips graze the top of her bosom. Thanks to the lingerie she'd squeezed into she looked like she had more than an ample amount of cleavage. She watched Gregg turn from a gentleman to a wolf. His gaze became intense as he licked his lips. Amanda got up and went to retrieve his glass. Her fingers closed around it as he seized her waist and pulled her onto his lap. His booze-laden breath was warm against her neck.

'You know, we don't even have to go back up to my bedroom. We could have some fun together right here.' He purred the words into her ear as his hands fondled and caressed her curves.

Amanda bit down on her tongue, using the pain to draw together her senses so that she could mentally distance herself from his touch. His warm hands were gripping her buttocks, sliding over her breasts. The intimacy of it burned Amanda. She couldn't handle the heat, the pressure. She thought she could play the femme fatale but she couldn't. Not in person, not like this. She needed to be behind a computer screen to be strong. Here she was exposed and vulnerable and so alone.

There had been so much darkness beyond McAllister's windows. So much emptiness.

He kissed her. Square on the lips, with force. And Amanda had no choice but to kiss him back. As his tongue pressed against hers, she imagined she was curled up with someone else. She allowed him to keep exploring her body with his hands, for the kiss to deepen. When they eventually pulled apart, Amanda was looking into Shane's kind green eyes. But when she blinked, McAllister was back there, smiling at her with satisfaction.

'Let me fix you that drink.' Amanda seized the glass he'd placed on a nearby table and hurried over to the crystal decanter. She had to remind herself how to walk. Her legs had turned to jelly and her heart was racing from a dangerous cocktail of fear and confusion. Why hadn't it been Will's face she'd imagined when she'd kissed McAllister?

Because it would have been too painful.

That had to be it. Imagining Shane somehow felt like less of a betrayal. Didn't it? Amanda turned her back on McAllister who was sprawled across his chair, openly staring at her. She shook out her hands, wishing they'd stop shaking. As she reached for the decanter with one hand she discreetly slid the other into the top of her garter and found the dissolvable pair of tablets she'd hidden there earlier. She quickly dropped them into the glass as she poured in the scotch. As the drugs hissed she coughed to cover the sound.

If her calculations were right, then once McAllister had taken a sip it would be less than ten minutes before he was unconscious. It was a risk to leave him in the drawing room, where one of his staff could easily find him. But Amanda didn't have time to be picky. She needed to get back into the bedroom, crack the password on his MacBook and then load all his dirty secrets onto her USB. She had to hope that her instincts were right – that the laptop in the bedroom acted as McAllister's mainframe.

'Here,' she handed the glass to McAllister. The tablets had completely dissolved. There was no hissing. The Scotch was flat, the colour of old varnish.

'Thank you, darling.' He went to raise the glass to his lips and then stopped, nodding at the bookcase behind her. 'Did I ever tell you that I have a first edition of Bram Stoker's *Dracula*? Seems fitting for a place like this don't you think? I reckon it's just there.'

Amanda turned towards the bookcase. There were so many ancient texts on display, titles etched in fading gold leaf. She breathed in their musty odour as she scanned their spines – a collection of deep reds, browns and blues. Nothing bright. Nothing vibrant. Nothing new. What must a collection of this calibre be worth? She was dizzy at the thought of it.

'I'm not sure it's here.' She glanced back at McAllister as he took a sip from his glass.

'Is it not? That's a shame. I was going to give it to you.'

'To me?'

'It's essentially the story of a lonely man who is searching for true love.' He held her in a penetrating gaze.

'A man who is also a monster,' Amanda countered, staring straight back at him. 'A man who ruthlessly kills innocent victims just to feed on their blood.'

'But love makes monster of us all, doesn't it?' He blinked. Once. Twice. Amanda saw his eyelids getting heavy, starting to droop. McAllister leaned his head against the back of his leather chair and his breathing slowed. Amanda tentatively went over to him.

'Gregg?' she breathily called out to him. McAllister didn't stir. 'Gregg?' she barked his name loudly. McAllister's eyes remained closed, his chest steadily rising and falling with each breath. Amanda clicked her fingers in front of his face. Nothing. She clapped her hands together inches from his nose. Still nothing.

It had worked. Giddy with triumph, she stepped back from him. Her dress was half unbuttoned and hanging off her shoulders, her hair wild around her head, but she didn't care. All that mattered was getting access to that laptop.

The journey back to the bedroom felt far too long. As Amanda crept up the staircase and along the landing she held her breath, expecting someone to find her any minute. She had a list of excuses stored in her mind, held on the tip of her tongue in case of such an event.

'Gregg told me to meet him in his bedroom.'

'I was just going to use the bathroom.'

'He fell asleep and I went for a wander. I got lost.'

But she didn't need to use any of them. Amanda arrived back at McAllister's bedroom undetected. She opened the door and ran inside, making a beeline for the MacBook. Sitting down at the desk, she pulled the USB from her garter and placed it in the side of the laptop. The hacking program she'd designed lit up the screen as she opened up the device. With a flourish of commands she told her program to figure out McAllister's password. It took less than a minute to crack it and then she was in.

Amanda worked quickly. She opened files, ran searches for hidden information and continually backed everything up to her USB, which blinked red as it remained wedged in a portal, working just as furiously as she was. Turtle82's guidance ran through her mind. She needed bank details. Proof of money changing hands. Something to implicate McAllister in his dark deeds without question. And it took Amanda just over ten minutes to find it. She stared at the detailed list of transactions upon the screen, at the litany of sins McAllister had committed.

There was money attributed to drugs. To the clubs which served as a front for dealing the said drugs. And there were names. So many women's names. And they weren't being paid. They were being paid *for*—

Amanda felt sick as she loaded the data onto her USB. McAllister didn't just deal in drugs, he also dealt in lives. He was part of a sex trafficking ring. Amanda felt more resolute than ever to put the monster behind bars.

13

The MacBook whirred as Amanda's USB blinked furiously, uploading all the vital data. She hoped she'd gathered enough information, that Turtle82 would have all they needed to send the authorities an anonymous tip-off.

Only how anonymous would it be? Amanda's hands froze above the keyboard, her fingers flexed, ready to type. McAllister *knew* her. Or at least he knew Amanda Preston. But she didn't really exist, she was just a product of what might have been.

Looking beyond the laptop screen, towards the windows of McAllister's bedroom, Amanda saw an endless stretch of darkness. The distant lights which had previously punctured it were gone. Was Shane sat in his car somewhere out there?

Pulling in a slow breath, Amanda mentally went back over how she'd leave the mansion. First she had to allow the darkness outside to penetrate the complex, to let every inch of it be swallowed by shadows. And that meant a blackout.

The MacBook pinged. The upload was complete. Amanda plucked the USB stick out of its dock and returned it to her garter. Her fingers danced across the keyboard. She was hacking into the local electrical grid system. In just a few minutes she'd have complete access and she'd be able to execute a blackout.

She could barely breathe. Around her the vast house moaned and creaked but Amanda barely noticed. Her fingers hammered against the keyboard, filling the bedroom with a symphony of tapping sounds.

'Nearly,' the word whistled through her lips. In her stomach she felt like she was auditioning for Cirque du Soleil, flying through the air on a trapeze and somersaulting. She felt giddy and infinite. It was almost done. When the house was plunged in to darkness she'd make her escape. With the USB in her possession she'd have everything she needed to avenge Will, to bring McAllister down. She felt drunk and delirious just thinking about it.

Over.

It was all almost over.

She was going to be able to go back to her old life. Back to Ewan. Back to her mother. Back to Shane.

Her stomach shifted with uncertainty. Her finger was poised above a single button. Once she pressed it, the blackout would be triggered along with a chain of events which were about to change her life forever. She sucked in a breath, closed her eyes and—

Amanda froze. Her entire body turned to stone as she felt the barrel of a gun press against the back of her head.

'Well, well, what have we here?'

It was McAllister and he sounded so calm. Too calm. Amanda didn't dare turn around and face him.

'Let's just close this.' Keeping the gun against her head, he leaned over her and with his free hand closed the laptop. Amanda felt like she'd been plugged into the nearest socket – every nerve within her felt electrified, sparking anxiously in preparation for fight or flight.

But how could she fight? Or run? The pressure on the back of her head was a deadly reminder of how easily McAllister could plunge her into an eternal darkness.

'Well, *Mrs Thorn*, it seems our delightful evening together has turned rather unpleasant.'

Thorn.

He said her surname like he could feel it sticking into his side, grimacing as he passed Will's chosen pseudonym through his lips.

The muscles in Amanda's body tightened.

'Ah, you're wondering how I knew,' McAllister sounded amused. He briefly released the gun from the back of her head and spun her chair around so that she was facing him. Amanda tried to read his expression but she kept looking into the barrel of the gun which was aimed squarely at her temple. 'Did you think me a fool?'

Somehow Amanda managed to shake her head.

'I've known who you were from the moment you walked into my club with your friend.' There was no weight added to the word *friend.*

Amanda tore her eyes away from the gun to look at McAllister. She shuddered at the maniacal grin upon his face. He dragged his free hand down his face, laughing lightly to himself. The gun trained on Amanda never so much as lowered even a fraction of an inch.

'I mean, I have to hand it to old Jakey Boy, he's got good taste.' McAllister took a step towards her and Amanda recoiled even though she had nowhere to go. It was so surreal to think that less than a half hour ago she'd shared a passionate embrace with the man now toting a gun at her. 'You intrigued me,' McAllister continued. 'When you showed up in Rumours, I figured I'd go along with your little game. See what you wanted.' He looked past her, at his laptop. 'And now I know.'

'You killed Will.' Amanda spat through clenched teeth. McAllister blurred in her vision through the tears that were silently washing down her cheeks.

145

'Jake,' McAllister tersely corrected her. 'I killed *Jake*. Only I didn't. Someone did it for me. As you've figured out by now, I'm not the kind of man who likes to get my hands dirty.' The mask had slipped and McAllister had revealed the monster he kept hidden beneath his expensive suits and crooked smile.

'And Evie?'

'Oh, Evangeline,' he drew the name out, enjoying watching Amanda squirm. 'I heard that Jake's *wife* OD'd. Such a shame. Makes me wonder why you've even bothered coming up here since you're not his real wife.'

'You're an animal.'

'I'm a businessman,' McAllister calmly countered. He released her from his gaze to glance back towards his bedroom door. Amanda shifted in her chair, wondering if she could run, and where she could go. 'When someone crosses me in the business world I have to send a message, ensuring that they or anyone like them, don't get to cross me again.'

'Will was a good man.' Amanda clung to her memories. The first time she'd seen Will he'd made her heart race. He'd seemed so mysterious back then. And he made her feel so safe. In his arms she'd been certain that nothing could ever hurt her.

'Jake. His name was Jake. He lay you down in a bed of lies, sweetheart. Not that I blame him. It's such a shame that you couldn't have delayed spiking my drink for another couple of hours. I'd have liked to have tasted what made Jake forget himself like he did.'

McAllister grinned at her. There was no warmth in the smile, no compassion. Just a wolfish hunger.

'I suspected you might spike my drink so I switched it when you weren't looking. I figured you wouldn't be able to resist a glimpse of a first edition. What was in it by the way? I had one of my men try it and he's dead to the world now. I mean, he isn't actually dead, is he? He will wake up?'

Amanda clenched her jaw and blinked away her tears. Why hadn't she been smarter? Why hadn't she anticipated that McAllister might have been on to her all along? She'd turned her back to him, admired his collection of books and given him ample opportunity to make the switch.

Because she was desperate.

The truth stabbed at Amanda as sharply as any knife ever could. Her desperation had made her reckless and now she was going to die. She'd failed Ewan. And Shane. She'd failed everyone.

'I'd be impressed if you'd killed him,' McAllister waved the gun at her. 'It would have shown a level of commitment I didn't think you had in you.'

He took another step closer, standing just a few inches away from the chair. Amanda pressed her spine against the back of it, trying to keep as much distance between her and McAllister as she possibly could.

'You know,' he twisted his head to look at his bed. 'We've got a few minutes before everyone comes to join us. I told them to hold off for a bit. I figured I could still get to enjoy what's on offer.' McAllister's free hand surged forward and pulled at the front of her dress. The buttons popped open with little resistance, revealing all the black and red lace and satin beneath. 'Oh my. Well it seems a shame to let such a fancy get-up go to waste.'

As he leaned in, his hand groping for her waist, Amanda reacted. She slapped him hard across the face. Hard enough to redden his cheek.

'Ha,' McAllister gave a hollow laugh as he straightened, massaging the right side of his face. 'You've still got a bit of fight in you. I respect that.'

Amanda didn't see the gun coming. McAllister moved with frightening speed, smacking the butt against the side of her face, causing Amanda to almost topple to the floor. As she steadied herself she felt the warmth of blood trickling down from the corner of her mouth. Gasping, she fought against the pain and made herself look up at him. Her cheek felt like it was on fire.

'I'm guessing that your little plan was to take something from my laptop, something incriminating, and have me locked up. Right?'

Amanda was silent.

'Only that's a decoy. Of course it is. I'd never keep my actual computer on display like that. I had another tech nerd like yourself draw up a load of false accounts for you, let you think you were onto something.'

He must have seen the surprise in Amanda's eyes.

'I know all about you, Mrs Thorn,' his eyes glistened with malice. 'I know about your hacker past. About all your darknet friends. You don't get to where I am without knowing how to watch your back. I have people constantly watching mine. And in turn I pay people to watch theirs. Who's watching your back, Mrs Thorn? Because it sure as shit ain't Jake anymore.'

Shane.

Amanda needed to get a message to him. Needed to tell him to get the hell away from the mansion, to get himself somewhere safe. To protect Ewan.

'Not that Jake did protect you. Because at the first sign of trouble he ran, right?'

'He was protecting—' When Amanda opened her mouth to speak she tasted the coppery bitterness of her own blood.

'His son.' McAllister interrupted. 'He thought he was protecting the boy. Only he wasn't. He came back for *her*. You must know that by now, right? I would never have hurt the kid. Jake knew that. You saw the pictures of my girls.'

Amanda hung her head.

'They were my angels and I lost them to this world that I live in. You can't imagine that kind of pain. You feel it with every beat of your heart. It's fucking awful. I wouldn't hurt a kid, no matter how big a prick they have for a father.'

'Revenge.' Amanda lifted a hand to swipe at her bloodied mouth. When she lowered it the back shone with a streak of bright crimson. 'You'd kill someone's child because someone killed yours.'

'No,' McAllister's voice hardened. 'I mean, I *use* my tragedy. I don't usually have pictures of my girls plastered all over the place, it'd be somewhat maudlin, don't you think? But I wanted you to see them. Thought it might help me get in your pants a bit quicker.'

Amanda turned away from him, hating herself for how willingly she'd allowed herself to be lured into his trap.

McAllister grabbed her chin, forcing her gaze back upon him and holding her head in place.

'I would *never* hurt a child. In this game there are rules. If someone hurts me, I get to hurt them back. It's that simple.'

'Evie,' Amanda fought to get her words out against the pressure being applied to her jaw. McAllister was squeezing her chin, tightening his grip. 'She was innocent.'

He gave a dark chuckle and released her. 'No,' he took a step back from her. 'She was about as innocent as you are, sweetheart. Seems old Jakey had a knack for getting women to do his dirty work for him. You should have just let it be.'

Four men burst into the room behind McAllister. All wearing black. All carrying guns. They gathered around him like a pack of hungry dogs awaiting their next command.

'You should have gone home when you had the chance, Amanda. You should have gone home and never looked back. And who knows,' he gave a flippant shrug, 'maybe I'll change my policy on killing children just for you. So that all your efforts in coming here weren't in vain.'

Amanda was screaming. 'Don't hurt him! Don't hurt Ewan! He's just a boy!'

McAllister gave a subtle nod and his men encircled her. They forced her to her feet and roughly placed her hands behind her back, binding her wrists together with a plastic tie. Then they started pushing her towards the door, not caring when she almost tripped over her own feet.

'Please,' she pleaded with them, looking between their blank faces. 'Don't let him do this. Just let me go. Please.'

'Shut her up,' McAllister barked from where he stood outside of Amanda's line of sight. A fist connected with her cheekbone and then everything went dark.

*

The cold snap of evening air against her face woke Amanda up. She was outside the front of the mansion, beside the car which had originally brought her in from the city, her hands bound behind her back. Her shirt dress fluttered around her like a flag at half-mast, revealing her expensive lingerie. To her left was a burly guard who held a rifle against his chest. His mouth was set in a hard line and he kept looking towards the house and the front doors where McAllister stood, his head bent in discussion with another guard.

'What will he do to me?' Amanda wondered weakly. It seemed strange that she wasn't already dead. Her face throbbed with the promise of a vast bruise. She could feel the blood gathering beneath the skin, her body desperately trying to repair the damage that had been done.

The guard didn't respond. He just kept looking ahead, towards his master.

A minute stretched by like an hour. The evening air snapped at her, infecting her with a chill which crept into her bones.

'I'll scream,' Amanda threatened boldly.

'No one will hear,' the guard replied stoically, not turning to look at her.

Shane might.

Amanda knew that he was out there in the darkness somewhere, waiting on her call. If she screamed, if she curdled the night with her desperate cries would he hear? Would he call the police? But when they arrived would it be too late? Amanda looked at the gun in the guard's embrace and felt her boldness ebb away.

'In case you get any ideas.' A fresh guard strode up to her. Had he heard her threat? He pressed her against the side of the car and then sealed her mouth closed with a thick piece of duct tape. Amanda shrieked against its sticky surfaces. All her cries now muffled. 'That ought to shut her up for a bit,' the guard announced flatly before moving away from her again.

Another minute passed. Amanda tried to concentrate on her breathing. She knew she couldn't give in to the rising tide of panic within her. Her head needed to remain level. Her mind alert. But she felt like she was in quicksand and each time she so much as moved she sank ever deeper, ever closer to her demise.

'Okay then, let's head out.' McAllister was striding over. He'd changed out of his shirt and jeans and now wore a dark suit. Against the shadows of the night it looked almost jet-black. Even his shirt was black. He seamlessly blended in to the darkness around him. 'Come, Amanda,' he reached for her cheek and Amanda jerked her head away. But his movements were not as restricted as hers. His hand found her face and he ran his thumb against her fresh wound. 'We're going to go for a little drive. Okay?'

Amanda shook her head furiously and screamed against the tape. She needed to stay at the mansion. Shane could find her at the mansion.

'I truly wish things hadn't ended up this way.' McAllister leaned in close and whispered in her ear, 'Just think, you could have been upstairs screaming my name in ecstasy right now. Instead you're about to be screaming for a very different reason.' He stepped back, his cologne lingering in the air. Amanda heard a car door open and someone climb inside. McAllister was gone; she desperately looked between his guards. Several had approached her, coming at her from all sides.

'Right, let's go.' The tallest guard grabbed her shoulder and started marching her around to the back of the car. Amanda looked at the polished rear end of the Rolls-Royce Phantom in which she'd previously enjoyed a pleasant ride out of the city.

A different guard leaned forward and popped the boot. It eased open, revealing its carpeted interior. Amanda tried to back away, sensing what was happening, but strong arms prevented any sort of escape, pushing her towards the boot.

'It's really not so bad,' the guard who'd grabbed her shoulder lifted her up with ease and bundled her into the boot like she were a sack of potatoes. 'Just watch out for the speed bumps.' This made all the guards chuckle together.

The base of the boot was rough against her cheek, the carpet coarse and unforgiving. She could already feel the fibres starting to make her itch. But that was the least of her concerns. Wherever they were headed, she knew that for her it was going to be a one-way journey. Amanda peered out at the guards, pleading with her eyes for them to have mercy on her, to let her go. Instead they slammed down the lid of the boot, sealing Amanda in musty darkness.

14

The darkness was a vessel. It took Amanda away from the mansion. As she lay on her side she could feel the rumble of the car's engine vibrating through her body. Her senses became distorted. Initially she tried to follow her journey, tried to interpret each bend, each turn. But it quickly became too difficult.

She felt her tears soaking into the rough carpet against her cheek, her ears filled with her own muffled, anguished cries.

McAllister was going to kill her.

Her mind refused to entertain other possible solutions. McAllister didn't believe in loose ends or forgiveness. When the lid of the boot opened up again Amanda would probably be minutes, even seconds, from certain death.

Screaming against the masking tape, she squirmed around the boot, desperately trying to free her hands. The plastic that bound her wrists together was tight. Unforgiving. But she had to try. If she didn't get out of the car before it reached its destination then she was dead. She tried to keep her thoughts pragmatic, to stem off the hysteria which gathered inside her like a growing storm. She had to get out of the car. If she got out she had a chance of surviving – a slim one, but it was still a chance.

The plastic chord dug into her wrists. The more she moved, the more it painfully pressed against her. Amanda's fingers became damp with her own blood as the plastic cut through her skin like it was butter. The pain burned but she refused to let her herself feel it. She kept writhing her hands together, trying to work them free of their restraints.

The car made a sharp turn and Amanda was flung against the other side of the boot. Her face smacked squarely against metal. She felt the jarring force of the impact down to her bones. Something warm trickled down from her nose. More blood. But Amanda couldn't dwell on it. There would be time to assess her wounds later when she was out of the car, back with Shane. When she was safe. If she ever got to experience safety again.

Rolling onto her back, she arched her spine to prevent her hands being compressed by her own weight. She noticed a chink of silver light in the distance, near the wheel arch. It wasn't much since there was only the moon and stars out to offer any light, but it was enough to guide her, to allow her to trace the outline of the boot, to figure out where its locking mechanism was. If she could just give the right spot a couple of really good kicks then—

There was a bump in the road. Amanda bounced loosely around the boot, crashing against all sides. She thought of the rag doll she'd loved as a little girl, of the doll's yellow string hair and black button eyes. After a visit to the beach her doll had become covered in sand, her pretty gingham dress darkened and soiled.

'She needs washing,' her mother had announced primly, plucking the doll out of Amanda's grasp.

'No,' a six-year-old Amanda had whined. 'I like her covered in sand. She's more like me now – an adventurer.'

Corrine had just tutted and put the doll in the washing machine. Horrified, Amanda sat and watched the sixty-minute spin cycle through the clear plastic door as her poor rag doll was thrown around the steel drum and lost in a sea of foamy water.

Another bump in the road. Amanda tumbled around the boot, doing her best to use her legs to steady herself as she braced for the next sharp turn. When it didn't come she returned to being on her back and tried to place her feet directly beneath the catch on the boot. The only positive she could find in her situation was that the boot of the Phantom was pretty roomy.

Amanda flexed her legs, testing the distance up to the roof of the boot. How long had they even been driving? Where were they going? She recalled all the names in the digital ledger she'd uncovered. McAllister had claimed it was all falsified, but what if that was just a bluff? What if she'd actually found exactly what she'd been looking for?

She delivered a blunt kick up at the catch. Her feet connected with the roof with a dense thud but nothing jangled, nothing sounded like it was being knocked loose.

Was McAllister going to turn her into a name on his list? Was he going to sell her into sexual slavery?

She kicked again. Harder this time. The boot responded by remaining locked tight. Mocking her with its durability.

'Mmphf.' Amanda wanted to turn the air blue in frustration but the masking tape pressed across her lips sealed in all of her expletives.

She kept kicking. Harder and harder, she smacked her feet against the roof of the boot, willing it to suddenly pop open. Then she could climb out and run. To where, it didn't matter. She just knew that she needed to run.

The sound of the car engine changed. It went from a steady rumble to a soft rattle. It was slowing down. Amanda shifted, panicked. They couldn't have reached their destination already. She needed more time. She needed to escape.

Her heart dropped into her stomach when her fears were confirmed. The engine died away all together. Even in her dark prison she knew that they'd ceased moving. A moment passed and then she heard a car door opening and heavy footsteps.

'Noooo.' She manoeuvred herself onto her back. If these were to be her last moments then she'd at least go down fighting. She bent her knees, preparing to kick madly the second the boot lifted up.

*

'The key to being a good swimmer is to kick furiously.' Mrs Maddox loomed large at the side of the community swimming pool as she looked down at the gaggle of fresh faces she was currently teaching.

Amanda bobbed up and down in the chlorine-laced water beside a little boy called Daniel. They both clung to the handrail, which prevented them from floating away from the edge of the pool like bounty from a shipwreck.

'You need to stretch your legs back in the water and just kick. Throw up as much water as you can.' Mrs Maddox had a perm so tight that Amanda wondered how it didn't make the old woman's brain ache. She placed one hand on her wide hips and drew her whistle up to her mouth. She blew into it. One sharp, shrill note.

Amanda started kicking. She stretched out her legs as far as she could and thrashed them about in the water. She tasted chlorine as the turquoise water of the pool got splashed against her face. Her mouth was open as she laughed. She wished she was in the ocean, tasting salt instead of chemicals. But her parents had insisted she learn to swim. Only then, they'd said, could she go down to the beach and roam about freely on her own.

'Keep kicking,' Mrs Maddox ordered, her voice a fog horn across the water. 'Kick as if your life depended on it.'

*

The boot opened with a soft click. Amanda started kicking. She blindly thrust her legs out, hammering them back and forth.

'Grab her, will ya?' she heard McAllister's voice before she felt the tug of strong arms grabbing her elbows and hauling her out. She landed a few kicks against the guard as she was pulled out of the boot, but he didn't even register their impact. 'Christ, girl,' McAllister was standing a few feet away from her, his eyes sweeping over her face. 'You've certainly managed to make a mess of yourself in there.'

How did she look? Was her face bloodied? Her eyes red and swollen?

'Now…' McAllister took a menacing step towards her.

Amanda frantically scanned the area around her. The guard's grip was tight on her arms, preventing her from running away. In the moonlight she saw that they were on a road. A long one which winded away into the shadows. There were no trees, just open highlands which allowed a fierce wind to power over to them.

'I'm rather fond of my Phantom,' McAllister cocked his head at her. 'It's arguably my favourite car in my fleet.'

There was something upon the wind.

Salt.

Amanda closed her eyes, breathing it in. For a blissful second she allowed herself to pretend she was back home, back upon the cliffs, near her mother's rose garden.

'I can't have you kicking about in there and damaging my favourite car.' McAllister's voice was low and sinister.

They were near the coast. Amanda knew it as she filled her lungs with the salt-laced air. So where exactly were they going? Did McAllister have a coastal home? A private air field nearby? A boat?

Amanda's knees weakened at the thought of a boat. The guard dug his fingers into her arm, keeping her standing up straight. She imagined herself crammed into the damp depths of a cargo boat, sailing away from Scotland as though she were nothing more than a damaged package. Who would be waiting for her on the other side of her journey? And how would Shane ever find her?

'The next time I hear you kicking my beloved car,' McAllister leaned in close, moonlight reflected in his eyes, 'I'm going to stop this car and have one of my men break both of your lovely long legs. Are we clear?'

Amanda nodded furiously.

'I'm glad you understand. Now, be a good girl and be nice and still for the rest of the journey.' McAllister eased back from her and walked away.

The rest of the journey.

So it still wasn't over. Amanda didn't know whether to be relieved or even more terrified. A journey on a boat was becoming more and more likely. Her mind raced with possibilities of where she could be going.

Europe?

Africa?

Where?

And why?

The guard clutching her arms scooped her up and tossed her back into the boot. Amanda rolled onto her side, keen to catch one last glimpse of the starlit night sky before the boot was slammed shut, returning her to her darkened vessel.

*

She didn't kick again. She believed McAllister when he said he'd break her legs. He probably kept a hammer under his car seat for such an event. And how could she hope to run with broken bones? The engine hummed as the car bounced along winding roads. In the darkness Amanda did her best to assess her current wounds. There was a throbbing in her left ear and her nose was damp with blood. Both cheeks were filled with a deep ache. Even her arms were starting to grow sore from being continually flung around the boot. And her wrists. They stung like the plastic tie had been swapped for barbed wire bracelets.

The car kept moving and Amanda stared into the darkness, imaging shapes within its depths. She tried to imagine Shane. He'd be sat out in his car now, waiting on the edge of the woodland. Did he intermittently peer at the treeline, expecting her to suddenly burst out of the shadows and come running towards him? How many times had he called her phone? Was he now realising that she wasn't coming back?

Amanda cried. Her tears mingling with the blood upon her face.

He'd said that he loved her. Before she'd left the hotel those had been his parting words to her.

And she hadn't said it back.

*

'I love you.'

The fire crackled and for a moment Amanda thought she'd misheard what Shane had said. She studied his profile in the amber light of the flames. He wasn't even looking at her, he was staring at a large piece of driftwood which had just caught light.

'What did you say?' she tugged on his arm, drawing his attention towards her face. His green eyes glistened but his lips twitched nervously. 'Shane?'

'I said,' he pulled in a deep breath, puffing out his chest, 'that I love you.'

Amanda blinked at him. Once. Twice.

The sound of John snoring disrupted the moment. He was on the other side of the campfire, curled up on his side, using his hooded jumper for a pillow.

'These last couple of weeks,' Shane leaned forward and began wringing his hands together. 'We've been hanging out together more and well—'

'But we've not even done it,' Amanda blurted. 'We've just kissed and hung out without John a bit,' she threw her slumbering friend a guilty sideways glance. 'I didn't realise it was… you know. Serious.'

'Really?' Shane's eyebrows shot up his forehead. He clenched his jaw but said nothing else.

'I mean, I have feelings for you, of course I do. But this, us,' she gestured between them, 'It's so *new*. We haven't even told our parents that we're dating or anything.'

'Jesus, Amanda. Love doesn't have a timeline or anything.'

'I know but—'

'I'm sorry if I don't fit into the weird schedule of romance you've got in your head but I saw you looking into the fire and I felt something in my heart and I just *knew*. So I just went with my feeling and said it. I didn't expect you to say it back or anything.' He stood up, dusted the sand off his baggy jeans and began walking down the beach, away from their fire.

'Shane!' Amanda hurried after him.

'What?' he spun around, his frustration etched into his sixteen-year-old features.

'I…' Amanda wasn't even sure she actually knew what love was. All that she did know was that it was meant to be forever. Her parents had loved each other, and even after her dad died her mum went on loving him, even though he was a ghost. Love was infinity. Love was everything.

'You don't feel the same. It's fine,' Shane remarked tersely.

'No, I do.' Amanda held his arms and looked up into his eyes. In her heart she knew that if she ruined this moment, if she let him just sulk away down the beach she'd regret it forever. Shane was like oxygen. She needed him to survive. A world without him just wasn't a world at all.

'Are you scared to say it?' he questioned tenderly.

'Yes,' Amanda admitted as she looked down at her feet in frustration. 'But only because it scares me. Because when you say it – it changes everything.'

'I know that.'

'And you said it anyway?'

'I said it anyway.'

'But it's like…' she chewed her lip, searching for the right words. 'I don't want to say it and then lose you.'

Amanda thought of the walls in her house covered in her father's image, how the place had become a shrine to him. And in her continued devotion to her husband, Amanda's mother got to go to bed alone every night. Corrine always said that she didn't mind, that her memories kept her warm, but Amanda wondered how true that could be, especially during the bleak winter months? Loneliness surely lingered on the fringes of her mother's existence, testing her previous declaration of love.

'You'll never lose me.' Shane sealed his promise with a kiss.

'Ever?' Amanda gazed deeply into his eyes as they parted, the tips of their noses still touching.

'Never ever.' He kissed her again. 'I'll be here for you, Amanda. Until the end of time. And even after that. I swear it.'

'I love you.' The words came easily. Amanda said them and saw Shane's features soften. He opened his mouth but someone bellowed from behind, speaking before he could.

'Oh my God you two need to get a *room*. I'm seriously getting sick of being a third wheel, guys!' John shouted from where he'd woken up beside the fire, his hair matted and sprinkled with sand.

Hand in hand, Amanda and Shane headed back to the warmth of the flames.

*

Amanda's head sagged against her chest. The car took a corner and she braced herself with her legs so that she didn't go tumbling all over the place. The memory of the night when she'd first told Shane that she loved him was keeping her warm, was keeping some of the denser shadows at bay. He'd been right back then, about how love didn't keep to any sort of schedule. It just… happened.

With Will it had just happened. Like a hurricane he'd swept into her life and it'd been impossible not to get pulled along by the sheer force of it all. He was strong and spoke his mind.

And he lied.

Amanda squeezed her eyes closed, refusing to cry anymore. Will might have lied to her throughout their marriage but he'd had his reasons. And ultimately he'd loved her. He'd used his final breaths to tell her as much.

Her chest heaved. With each grumble of the engine, Amanda knew she was creeping ever closer to her own end. Either McAllister was going to haul her onto some ship destined for God knows where or he was going to shoot her point-blank and watch her lifeless body drop into a shallow grave. Shane didn't factor into either of those scenarios. Amanda was going to be denied a chance to see him one last time, to tell him how she felt.

The car bounced over a bump and Amanda's head ricocheted up at the roof of the boot, hitting it so hard that she almost saw stars.

Just hold on.

She tried to find the will to remain focused. She didn't want to become a ghost, a memory to keep Shane warm on lonely nights. She wanted to see him again. To see Ewan and her mother. Her desire to live burned within her, keeping her strong. The car engine began to slow again. They were stopping.

15

Again Amanda heard the distant opening of a car door, heard gravel crunching underfoot as someone approached the boot. It popped open and a blast of cold air blew in. It swept across Amanda's bloodied face, carrying with it the scent of the sea.

'I want her on her feet and over there.' McAllister was giving his orders. A guard whose face had become familiar pulled Amanda from the boot. She shivered in her shirt dress and lingerie. A fierce wind billowed around them.

'I don't have all night. Let's get this wrapped up so I can get back home.' The orange tip of a freshly lit cigarette illuminated McAllister's features.

The guard put his hands on Amanda's shoulders and pushed her forwards. She had no idea where she was going. She deliberately stumbled her footsteps to give her a chance to look around. They were at the side of a narrow road and, from the sparse bracken and the power of the wind, Amanda sensed they were up high.

'Keep going,' the guard increased the force pressing against her shoulders. 'Some of us want to be back in bed before dawn.'

Amanda kept moving through the darkness. Then she saw it. The entire world fell away and she was looking at the ocean. Its rough surface distorted the moon's reflection. Waves powered towards the cliff she was standing upon and roared up at her in greeting. She stopped moving. Her legs locked.

'I said let's keep going,' the guard smacked her squarely in the centre of her back, knocking the air out of her lungs.

'I imagine she's scared.' McAllister came and stood beside Amanda. As he lowered his cigarette from his lips, he pushed a plume of smoke out from behind his teeth. 'Isn't that right, sweetheart?'

Even in the darkness she could see the sinister smirk that he directed at her. 'You've figured out how your story is going to end and I imagine you're not liking it all that much.'

Amanda heard the waves thrashing at the rocks below. She had to make her entire body rigid to stop her knees knocking together.

'But I thought there was something rather poetic about it,' McAllister extended his arms, gesturing grandly at the cliff edge which he boldly walked towards. The guard smacked Amanda's back again, signalling that she was to follow. But she couldn't? How could she? McAllister was looking to recreate the death she'd so narrowly escaped all those years ago. He was breathing life in to the nightmare that had haunted her for so long.

'I would say you inspired me,' he continued, never turning his back against the sheer drop behind him. He looked down, plucked a fresh cigarette from his pocket and then looked back at Amanda. 'But in truth, we often send discontents to their watery grave this way. The authorities always attribute it to suicide.'

A flame flickered madly in the wind as McAllister went to light his cigarette. He cupped his hands near his mouth, shielding it. Then, after taking a long drag, he looked at Amanda and laughed.

'And you couldn't be a more perfect candidate. Your husband left you and went missing. You never found him and in your grief you flung yourself off the top of this here cliff. It's drama. It's Shakespeare.'

Amanda protested but her sounds were just murmurs against the duct tape.

McAllister nodded at his guard and Amanda was thrown forwards. Her body dropped against the ground as she fell at McAllister's feet. The earth beneath her smelt damp, still holding the moisture from a previous rainstorm. She drank it in, focusing on how real it was. Her senses clung to the odour, reminding her that for the moment she was still alive.

'Damn, lad, keep her on her feet.'

The guard grabbed Amanda's hair and pulled. He kept pulling until she'd frantically managed to scramble back onto her feet, which wasn't easy when she didn't have the use of her hands. She was now so close to the edge that she could see the dramatic drop, the jagged rock face which plummeted down into the dark waters below.

'If only you'd had the sense not to repeat your fake husband's mistakes.' McAllister shook his head ruefully and then flicked his cigarette over the side of the cliff. Amanda held her breath as she watched it fall and keep falling. And then it was unceremoniously eaten up by the waves which continually beat against the rock face, like hands hammering on a door that would never open.

'So here's what we're going to do.' McAllister pulled something from his pocket and Amanda saw the moonlight shine off its smooth surface. She tried to stagger backwards but the guard was holding onto her shoulders, keeping her rooted to the spot. McAllister stepped towards her, brandishing the small blade in one hand. 'First,' he leaned around her, grabbing her wrists. The knife disappeared from view and she felt the pressure around her hands ease. He'd cut away the plastic tie. But before she could even think about claiming back the use of her hands, the guard's thick palms replaced the tie, keeping her arms pinned behind her back. 'I don't need your body washing up on some beach still bound and gagged. Can't have anyone suspecting foul play now, can we?' McAllister stepped in front of her and ripped the duct tape off her mouth in one swift motion. Amanda gasped, both from the pain and the sudden new ability to be able to breathe properly again. She sucked in deep gulps of sea air. 'Well, now we get to see if you can float.'

'Wait,' Amanda surged towards him, held back by the guard. Her words felt raw in her mouth. 'Please. Please don't do this.'

'You came here to *ruin* me.' McAllister sounded like he was more than just offended. He was outraged. 'What did you think would happen when you poked the bear, *Mrs Thorn*?'

'You killed Will. You killed my husband.' Amanda was screaming, using her words like bullets in the hope that one of them would connect with McAllister's chest and knock him down.

'*I* did no such thing.' He held his hands up defensively, smiling. Mocking her. 'If *Jake Burton* got shot up on some hillside then it's just because his shady past caught up with him. He and that fool friend of his tried to pull a fast one on me. I never give someone a second chance to cross me.'

'He was a good man.'

Amanda clung to her memories of Will. In the dead of night if a strange sound woke them up he'd be straight out of bed to investigate it, showing no regard for his own well-being. He was brave and kind. Amanda realised she was sobbing. Her shoulders shook with every mournful howl.

'Jake got what he deserved,' McAllister seethed. 'Just as you will. Did you really think you could come into my home and deceive me?'

'I know it's not all made up, the data on the file,' Amanda raged. 'You trade people like you trade drugs. You're a fucking animal that needs to be put down.'

McAllister grabbed her neck. He squeezed as his thumb grazed the centre of her throat. 'There's still fight in you yet.' He pressed his body against hers. 'I like that.'

If Amanda had possession of her hands she'd have punched him right in the face. Instead all she could do was squirm in protest, unable to shake off the guard's powerful grasp.

'And yes, the data on the file is all true. I make my money in ways other people might deem distasteful. But it's my life, my money. My conscience.'

His other hand slipped between Amanda's thighs and she froze. She felt his fingers creep along her garter. McAllister's body eased closer into hers and Amanda jerked forward. Their foreheads connected with a dull thud, causing him to stagger back. Her head pounded but she didn't care. She'd tear the flesh from his bones with her teeth if she had to – anything in order to stay alive.

McAllister cursed as he massaged his temple. 'Fucking bitch.' He paced away from her, regaining his composure. 'Did you think I wanted to have you? Don't fucking flatter yourself. I'm used to bedding women a lot younger than you. A lot more beautiful. I do not need to resort to raping some desperate slag out on a cliff edge.' He looked at her and the hate burning behind his eyes mellowed as a satisfied smile pulled on his lips, causing his scar to lift up his cheeks. 'What I wanted was this.' He produced the USB stick Amanda had stored away.

She fought against the guard's grasp, desperate to reclaim the only leverage she had on McAllister.

'You want this?' he dangled the slim piece of plastic in front of her like she was a playful puppy. 'Then go fetch.' McAllister slung the stick over the side of the cliff. Amanda kept her eyes on it as long as she could, until it was eaten up by the ocean. 'I hope it was waterproof,' McAllister remarked as his gathered guards sniggered. 'Now it's your turn.'

With a nod from his master the guard pushed Amanda forward so that she was standing directly on the edge of the cliff. As she wavered, trying to stagger back, she sent stones skittering down into the watery depths. She tasted something metallic. It wasn't blood. It was her own fear. Closing her eyes, she tried to imagine she was somewhere else. Anywhere else.

The last time she'd faced such a drop into angry waves her father had reached down and grabbed her at the last second. Like a real life Superman he'd appeared above her, the sunlight creating a halo around his head. He'd pulled his little daughter back from oblivion.

Amanda continued to fight against the guard, hoping and praying that Shane had somehow miraculously found her and that any moment she'd hear the squeal of his car braking before he ran over, knocked the guard to his feet and grabbed Amanda in the split second before she toppled over the edge.

'It pains me to do this, Amanda. Truly.' McAllister was standing close to the edge, shouting to be heard over the hungry roar of the waves.

'Then don't!' Amanda yelled. 'Be the man I met in the club. Be the man who your daughters would be proud of.'

McAllister thrust his hands deep into his pockets. 'Do you know that I heard them screaming?'

He wasn't looking at Amanda, he was looking out to sea.

'The fire, it moved like it was alive. And it was fast. Too fast. I couldn't get to them in time. But I got to hear them scream as their bedroom burnt down around them. Have you ever heard someone scream as they're burned to death?'

'No.'

'It's a sound that sets into your bones like a rot. A sound that haunts you in the dead of night. I'll never forget having to listen to my daughters die. Going through something like that it changes you, hardens you.'

'You're the reason they died.'

'True.' McAllister gave a slow nod. 'I angered a man who I shouldn't have underestimated. The next day, I went to his home and gutted him, stomach to sternum.'

'But it didn't bring your girls back, did it? You don't have to be a monster.'

'It was never about bringing them back,' McAllister chortled. 'It was about revenge. I mean, isn't that the reason we're both stood here? Why I'm currently freezing my bollocks off? Revenge, even more than love, is a potent motivator. We can pretend to be civilised, with all our politics and laws, but ultimately people still want an eye for an eye. And you sought me out as revenge for Jake.'

'Because you killed him!'

'No,' McAllister countered coolly. 'Because he lied. Because he left. And since he's dead you can't take your anger out on him. But me, I'm the perfect target. Or so you thought.'

'I'm not mad at Will,' Amanda shrieked her declaration into the wind. 'He did what he felt he had to do. And I loved him. Despite it all, I loved him until the end.'

'Well aren't you a worthy recipient for wife of the year?' McAllister deadpanned. 'Hold on to that thought on the way down.' He nodded at his guard and Amanda screamed. She wasn't ready. This couldn't be it. She flailed against the guard behind her, sending more loose rocks down the sheer face of the cliff. Her heart had settled in the pit of her stomach as she teetered on the precipice.

'Don't do this.' She was pleading for her life. She needed to be sick. She needed to scream.

The guard pushed her forward and then snapped her back into place. Amanda lost control of her bladder. She felt warmth pouring down her inner thighs and she started to shake. Was McAllister actually planning on killing her or just toying with her? She couldn't tell anymore.

'I hear that from this height, when you land in the water it's like crashing into cement,' McAllister bowed his head and looked down. The sheer drop into the waves was just a few inches away from the tips of his polished shoes.

'My cousin broke his back when he got drunk and jumped off a bridge,' the guard holding Amanda offered unhelpfully.

'Was that Andrew?'

'Aye.'

'So is he in a wheelchair now?'

'Aye. But he can still get about well enough. He's got his own flat and a girlfriend.'

'Good for him.'

The dark sky was weakening, turning from black to grey. The wind pressed against Amanda and her captors, as if trying to knock her off the edge.

'Boss, the weather's really picking up,' the guard commented.

A light drizzle started to silently fall around them. Amanda turned her head skyward, hoping it would wash away some of her blood and tears.

'Okay then, let's wrap this up.' McAllister gave another curt nod.

The guard pushed Amanda forwards. Her feet left the rocky edge and she was held in mid-air, suspended above the rocks below. She couldn't scream. She couldn't even breathe. Her heartbeat pounding in her ears like a war drum. And then she was snatched back, her feet once again grazing the rocky ground. The guard released her and Amanda crumpled like a puppet whose strings had been cut. She hugged her knees to her chest and sat there, shaking.

'Ach, come now, Amanda,' McAllister came and stood before her, stooping down to offer her his hand. Amanda looked up at it through strands of her hair which gathered in her eyes. 'You didn't really think I'd let one of my guys throw you over the edge of this here cliff, did you?'

Amanda still couldn't speak. She remained huddled in a ball like a beaten animal. Was that what this all had been – a mind game? Punishment for daring to try and ensnare McAllister in a digital net? Was he now going to spare her life after toying with it?

'Don't be proud now, girl. Let's have you back on your feet.'

Looking beyond McAllister, Amanda could see his men climbing back into the waiting Phantom. It was actually over.

'Take my hand and let's forget about all this, okay?'

His hand was still extended towards her like an olive branch. Reluctantly she took it. Her bloodied wrists burned with fresh pain as he hauled her up onto her feet. Amanda looked down at her legs uncertainly. Only moments ago she'd been held in mid-air. The ground beneath her feet almost didn't seem real, like it was all still an illusion and Amanda didn't know what to trust.

'Don't look so scared.'

McAllister had returned to being the man in the club. His grey eyes crinkled in the corners as he offered her an apologetic smile. 'You were the one playing me the whole time. You can't be all that surprised that we ended up here.'

Amanda tried to pull her hand away from his, to wipe at her eyes, but she couldn't. He locked his hand around her wounded wrist and then reached for her other arm before her mind could catch up with what he was doing.

'Like I said,' his words were soft but his touch was hard. His hands dug into Amanda's wrists, causing her to yelp. 'I wasn't about to let one of my guys throw you off this cliff.'

The roar of the waves grew louder and Amanda realised he was pushing her back towards the edge. She was once again a fly in his web, too weak from shock to fight back.

McAllister smiled wickedly at her. 'Not when I could have the satisfaction of killing you myself.'

'No—' Amanda's eyes widened as he released her wrists and pressed his palms into her chest. She fell back as the wind tangled itself in her hair. She was still looking at McAllister, at his twisted smile, as she continued to fall. There was nothing behind her. No ground to drop against. And a saviour didn't come. No hand appeared over the edge to grab her, to haul her back up. Even the wind wasn't powerful enough to sweep her back to safety. Amanda just kept falling.

16

Amanda flailed in the air, each of her limbs scrambling about, trying to find something to grab onto but finding only emptiness. She felt like she was falling through space and that when she landed she'd be sat amongst the stars.

It took just over two seconds for her body to hit the water. They were the longest seconds of her life. The water had turned to slate during her descent. She smacked against it, the impact jarring every bone in her body. She couldn't breathe. Her lungs had been flattened by the crash. Amanda sunk down into charcoal waters. Then the needles came. They pricked against every inch of her body, sharp and unrelenting, trying to tear the flesh from the bone. The cold was savage. Amanda was dropping deeper into the darkness. She vaguely recognised the weakening light of the moon hovering above, ripples distorting its face. It looked as though it were in another world.

Something pushed against her right side. It was strong and determined. It tossed her around like flotsam and only released her as she smacked against the rocks of the cliff. Pain shook through her body. Amanda's hands scratched at the slickened surface of the rock, using limpets to cling onto, to power herself up towards the rippling moon.

The force came again, pressing her more firmly against the rocks. Amanda's head snapped forward and bounced off the stone. She kept holding on even though a part of her longed to let go, to drift down into the blissful depths of the water. She knew there would be no pain there, just respite.

Amanda broke through the surface of the water, clinging to the rock. Her arms trembled. She sucked in a vital salty breath, as desperate as a newborn baby. Around her the world was shaded with charcoal. A reluctant sun had yet to replace the moon overhead. Amanda looked down at the water around her, the surface briefly glassy, like a doll's eye before the white crest of a wave broke through it and powered towards her. Amanda curled against the rock for protection. The wave came like a punch. Her arms kept shaking. She didn't have the strength to hold on for much longer. And the cold – it gnawed on her bones like she was already a carcass. If she stayed on the rock she was going to die. Her thoughts were slipping away, becoming increasingly incoherent.

'Keep kicking,' she heard the booming voice of her old swimming instructor, Mrs Maddox. 'Kick as if your life depended on it.'

Amanda waited for the next wave to recede and then released the rock. She kicked. She kicked with everything she had. Whilst her legs cooperated, her arms were less compliant. They felt stiff, as though they were now made of wood. Amanda thrashed them in the water as she kept kicking, slowly making progress away from the dangerous rocks.

Each time she raised her head enough to take in a breath she inhaled more seawater than air. She choked against it, continually kicking. Where was she even going? She didn't know this shoreline, there might be miles of cliffs or she could be mere metres away from a shingle beach. Amanda prayed it was the latter. Her mind zoned out as she just kept kicking. Piece by piece her whole body went numb, succumbing to the cold.

Amanda didn't notice the tide that helped take her ashore. She was single-minded in her determination to just keep kicking. When she eventually reached the shallows she crawled forward, her hands sinking into the wet sand. She hauled her body away from the shoreline, away from the icy waves, and collapsed face down in the shingle.

*

'So… this?' Will swept his gaze along the beach.

'Yes, this,' Amanda nodded as she squeezed his hand which was firmly interlocked with her own, 'this is my little slice of heaven.'

'It's a beach.'

'But it's *my* beach. This is where I grew up.'

'It's certainly… pretty.'

'Look, here,' Amanda eagerly pulled him towards a collection of rocks which threaded their way out to sea. 'This is where I used to go exploring in all the little rock pools. I'd find all sorts in my little net, like crabs and limpets.'

'It's nice.' Will took it all in with his usual stoic demeanour.

'And here,' Amanda pulled on his hand, taking him away from the rock pools and further down the beach. 'This is where my dad and I would race.' The sand stretched away from them, extending towards holidaymakers who were just dots on the horizon enjoying the sunshine.

'It really is beautiful, Amanda,' he released her hand to loop an arm around her shoulders. She instinctively leaned in to him. 'You're lucky to have grown up somewhere so idyllic.'

'So when do I get to see where you grew up?' she squinted up at him in the sunlight.

'Oh, no way,' Will furrowed his thick brow. 'You showed me your little slice of heaven. I'm not about to repay you by showing you a wedge of hell.'

'I bet it wasn't that bad. You're just being dramatic, trying to maintain your rugged image and mysterious demeanour.'

'No, it was.' Will kept looking at the people distantly bouncing around in the waves, their laughter carried over to them on the warm afternoon air. 'It really was awful, Amanda. It's a place I'd never wish to take someone like you.'

'Someone like me?' Amanda tensed, wondering if he was insinuating something unsavoury about her.

'Someone *unspoiled*,' Will clarified with a light smile. 'You see the world in such a wonderful way. I'd never want that to change.'

Amanda found herself looking up at the cliffside which loomed up above them. 'Bad things are everywhere you know, even in heaven,' she whispered absently.

'But when bad things are surrounded by goodness, you can overcome them. When it's all bad all the time, that's when it starts to change you, to corrode your soul.'

'Is your soul corroded?'

'No, because I got out. Sometimes the past just isn't worth revisiting,' he hugged her tight against him, drawing her attention away from the cliff. 'Trust me, Amanda. My past is just a collection of bad times. We're better off staying here, in your little slice of heaven.'

*

Amanda's eyes slowly opened. She saw the world on its side, a sea of stones sweeping away from her beneath a heavy pewter sky. 'Where?' She felt the stones around her hands, against her face. With a grunt she tried to stand up. Her body limped back towards the ground. 'Come... on,' she urged herself to try again. All of her joints felt like they were bunged up with glue. Amanda groaned and panted and eventually scrambled onto her feet.

She was on a deserted shingle beach. It was a small outcrop bordered on three sides by ominous dark cliffs. The sea roared behind her menacingly, reminding her of its presence. Amanda staggered forward and then dropped to her knees. She coughed and felt the icy ocean water churning around in her lungs. She tried to raise her left hand towards her chest but it remained lifelessly draped against her side. Her right hand was more obedient. Amanda smacked it against her chest. Once. Twice. The third time was the charm. She doubled forward as she retched seawater. Her purge splashed upon the shingle. Amanda slowly straightened. She noticed the red blotches upon her legs that would become bruises, the swelling around her right kneecap. Those were just the injuries she could assess. Everything else would have to wait. She was alive. For now.

Amanda laboured her way up the beach, her movements slow and cumbersome. At the end she found a narrow wooden staircase which led up the cliff, towards civilisation. She wilted against its shanty banister. Her legs felt like two blocks of ice. They were too stiff to make it all the way up the stairs. But what choice did she have?

Amanda started to climb. She yelped with every step, grimacing against the pain. By the third step something changed. The brittle morning air of a dull day was replaced by the hungry fires of a furnace. Amanda felt like she was being boiled from the inside out. Her right hand released the

179

banister to tug at her clothes. She was so hot in them. If she could just take them off and cool down a little she'd feel better. Her right hand fumbled at one of the few remaining buttons on her dress but before she could undo it her head sagged against her chest and then she dropped against the staircase and everything went black.

*

'Daddy, aren't you coming to bed?' Amanda hugged her little rag doll to her chest and looked up at her father who was leaning against the kitchen sink, his eyes focused on the little window before him. Amanda lifted her gaze to see what held her father's attention so raptly. She saw only darkness, without the guiding light of the moon, the sea and the sky bled together into one indecipherable mass.

'I'll come up soon, sweetheart.' He briefly abandoned his vigil to give his daughter a gentle smile.

'What are you looking at?' Amanda hopped onto one of the chairs at the kitchen table and continued to watch her father with interest.

'Did you hear on the news?' He nodded at the radio which was plugged in on the far side of the kitchen countertop, lit up and emitting a low murmur of voices. 'A fishing boat went down four miles out. Choppy waters out there tonight. Treacherous.'

'Will the fishermen be okay?' Amanda tightened her grip on her dolly.

'The lifeboats have headed out to them,' her dad gave a tense nod. 'Hopefully they'll get there in time.'

'And if they don't?'

Her dad slowly turned away from the sink, his shoulders sagging. 'Remember how Mummy and I are always telling you how dangerous the ocean can be?'

'Uh-huh.'

'And how important it is to be a strong swimmer?'

'Uh-huh.'

'But sometimes being a strong swimmer isn't enough. If the lifeboats don't reach the men in time it won't matter if they're the greatest swimmers in the world. The cold will get them.'

'The cold?' Amanda's eyes bulged in her head. The cold was everywhere. Especially in winter.

'At this time of year the water is icy cold. Spend too long in it and you're at risk of hypothermia.'

'Hyp-no-turn-in-her?'

'Hypothermia.' Her dad's stony expression softened with a brief smile. 'It's when your body has been exposed to the cold for too long and your core temperature starts to drop.'

'What happens?' Amanda scooted forward, to the edge of her seat.

'Well,' her dad looked back towards the window, 'I'm telling this to help you understand, not to scare you, okay?'

'Okay.'

'When you reach a certain level of cold, your body actually starts to think it's too hot. People with severe hypothermia can start shedding their clothes as their minds become irrational. Of course, that's the last thing they should be doing as it just quickens the process of freezing to death.'

'They *die*? From the *cold*?'

'From prolonged exposure to extreme cold, Amanda. It couldn't happen here at home where you have access to warm fires and nice thick clothes. But out there...' he was gazing at the dense darkness beyond the window. A drama was unfolding that was hidden from his eyes. 'The fishermen, they don't have much time,' he concluded sadly.

'So why aren't you coming to bed?'

'Because when they are rescued, and God willing they will be, a few of us will head over to the lifeboat house with hot drinks and warm food for the rescuers. The fishermen will be sent over to the hospital.'

'And they'll get better?'

'Yes, sweetheart, they'll get better.'

'Daddy why aren't you out there with the lifeboats helping?' Amanda wondered innocently. She watched his shoulders tense, his head bow slightly.

'I'm not a strong enough swimmer,' he admitted with a sigh of regret. 'My bad knees, they always held me back.'

'Oh.'

'That's why it's important for you to work hard in your swimming lessons, Amanda. To listen to what Mrs Maddox says. That way, one day, you can be out there helping those in need, just like I wish I was.'

'You wish you were out there?' Amanda looked beyond the window, horrified. She'd much rather be tucked up warm in bed than out on the icy sea.

'There's no nobler cause than helping others, sweetheart. Of course I wish I was out there trying to save the fishermen. I'd try and save everyone if I could.'

*

A seagull shrieked. Its pitched cry forced Amanda to open her eyes. She was crumpled against the step, one hand still on the wooden rail. Her body was still burning. She gasped, feeling every nerve in her body fiercely protest. A feral sense of self-preservation told her to keep moving. Amanda tightened her hand around the rail and forced her beaten legs to straighten. She screamed out as her knees felt too raw in their joints, like she was grinding bone against bone and wearing her own skeleton away.

The steps loomed ahead of her, snaking their way up the cliffside. Maybe there'd be a road at the top. Amanda could flag down a car and ask for help and—

She braced herself as she took the next step and then the next. She didn't dare look down at her haggard appearance. Would anyone even stop for her? Or would she look too horrific for even the kindest strangers to slow down?

She needed to happen upon someone like her father. Someone who was always putting the needs of others before their own.

He'd have stopped you falling.

Amanda repeated the truth she'd clung onto for so many years.

He'd have always saved you.

If her dad were there now he'd scoop her up into his arms and carry her the rest of the way. But he was gone. So was Will. And Shane would have no idea how to find her, where she'd gone.

The wind pummelled against the side of the cliff, challenging Amanda's endurance. It scratched at her cheeks, trying to bring her back to her knees.

I can do this. I can do this. She played the mantra on repeat in her mind as she took the steps one at a time.

Finally she reached the top. How long had it taken her? An hour? Maybe two. Because the ache in her bones told her that it had taken a lifetime. She'd never been so tired, so strung out.

Holding her limp left arm at her side with her right hand, Amanda looked about. She was on an open stretch of road that turned off onto bracken-laced highlands. Everywhere was still. There wasn't a car in sight. The only movement came from the wind which blew in off the sea and tumbled over the battered landscape.

'No,' Amanda wilted in defeat. She'd come this far. How could she be expected to go any further? Maybe she should just lay down in the middle of the road and wait for someone to find her?

Numbly she tottered along the road, feeling light-headed. She felt like she was walking in a dream as her heartbeat became weaker and weaker.

Then she saw it. It stood beside the road, its glass surfaces smeared by time and salty air. A phone box. An uneasy mix of euphoria and nausea swirled within Amanda as she staggered towards the phone box, hoping it worked. When she sealed herself within its small glass walls she didn't even care about the overwhelming stench of urine. She fumbled for the receiver and looked uncertainly at the keypad. Her instinct was to punch in her mother's number, to call home. The landline number for the little cottage had never changed, the numbers were etched into Amanda's soul. But Corrine couldn't help. She was miles away. Amanda began dialling a mobile number after requesting to reverse the charges. Her teeth were chattering so much that she wasn't sure she'd even be able to speak. She called Shane. But would he even pick up? He was supposed to be waiting for her somewhere on a roadside. She didn't even know where *she* was now.

Amanda clutched the receiver with her right hand and leaned against the phone booth. There was a poster above the phone, full of emergency numbers and, at the top of it, a name. A location. The letters tensed together, trying to prevent Amanda from reading them. She frowned at the poster as her call connected and she heard the first ring drag out.

'Ot...' Amanda tried to form the letters. Her tongue was loose in her mouth, it sat there thick and useless. 'Ot-ter...'

'Hello?' Shane picked up after the second ring. He sounded desperate. And afraid.

'Ot-ter-well...'

'Amanda, Amanda is that you?'

She couldn't respond. Not properly. It was taking all she had just to pronounce the name of the damn place.

'Amanda, Christ, I've been going out of my mind here! Are you okay? What happened? Where are you?'

So many questions. Amanda's head pounded with the delivery of each one.

'Ot-ter-well Bay,' she spat out her location finally and sagged within the booth.

'What?'

She groaned. She didn't have the strength to say it again.

'Otterwell Bay? Is that where you are?'

'Hmpf.' She was losing her ability to speak. Her head throbbed and her body burned as if coated in an invisible fire. 'Come,' she pleaded as her knees buckled. She fell to the floor of the phone booth, the abandoned receiver hanging just inches away from her.

'I'm coming!' Shane shouted out to her. 'Just stay where you are, Amanda. I'm coming.'

Amanda closed her eyes. She was so very tired. She thought about her father keeping a restless vigil at the kitchen window on a dark night and wondered if the lifeboats ever did reach those fishermen in time.

17

'Amanda, Christ, what happened?'

'Look at you, did he do this to you?'

'You're shaking. Amanda stay with me.'

Shane's voice was distorted. Amanda felt like she was still underwater. He sounded so far away.

In his arms she felt like she floated over to his waiting car. The landscape started to tilt, like she'd just stepped off the waltzers at the local fair.

'Just take deep breaths, okay. You're going to be fine, I promise.'

He was bundling something around her, something which glistened in the fragile morning light. Amanda looked down at the foil blanket which had been draped around her shoulders and tucked against her sides. If her mind was more tethered to her body she'd have teased Shane for being so obsessively prepared. Only he could have a foil blanket in his boot as part of his roadside kit. The boot of Amanda's car was sparsely filled. There were running shoes, some plastic boxes for when she did the food shop and a bag crammed full of energy bars and a soft blanket. The bag had been Will's idea.

'In case you break down,' he'd explained simply as he dropped the bag into her boot.

'Will.' Amanda whispered his name through cracked lips.

'No, it's me, Shane. Will's… Will's gone, remember?'

'Gone?'

The car pulled away from the side of the road as a sledgehammer connected with Amanda's head. Her eyes snapped open wide as she shifted frantically within her foil blanket.

'Just rest, we'll be at the hospital soon.'

'No,' her chest ached as she forced out the protest. 'No hospital.'

'Amanda, you're very badly hurt. You need medical attention. This isn't up for debate.'

Will was gone. Dead. McAllister had been the puppeteer who executed the order to kill him. And now he'd tried to kill Amanda.

'No. No hospital,' she wheezed out the words.

'You're bleeding and I'm pretty sure you're hypothermic. You need to see a doctor.'

'He can't know I'm alive.'

Shane slowed the car and watched her from the corner of his eye. 'Who can't? McAllister?'

Amanda did her best to nod. Why was her body being so unresponsive? All of her senses were dulled. She shivered beneath the foil. The fire against her skin had gone, leaving just an icy sensation that continued to cling to her.

'Why can't he know you're alive?'

'Because,' Amanda winced at the pain in her chest. How much of her had been broken when she was pushed off the edge of the cliff? 'Because he tried to kill me.'

*

The motion of the car rocked Amanda to sleep. She closed her eyes and sat shivering under the silver blanket, her skin breaking out in sweat. She slipped past the point of caring where she was going. If Shane insisted on taking her to the hospital then so be it. She imagined one of McAllister's lackeys slipping in after visiting hour was over and pouring something deadly into her drip. Amanda would be powerless, forced to sit and wait for the poison to be fed into her system. She was so tired. Too tired to care anymore.

'Amanda!'

Her eyes opened. The car had stopped. Shane's face was directly in front of hers, pale and concerned. He clapped his hands again, just centimetres from her nose.

'You fell asleep,' he was hurriedly scanning her face, taking in all of the damage on display. 'You can't fall asleep in case you have a concussion.'

'I'm fine,' Amanda grumbled, nuzzling against her seat as the words began to come a little easier to her. She wanted more sleep. Sweet, blissful sleep.

'You have two choices,' Shane told her sternly. 'Either you stay awake or I take you straight to the nearest hospital. Your call.'

'He pushed me himself,' she recalled dreamily. 'He toyed with me and then—' She winced as a searing sharp pressure bloomed behind her skull, the memory too painful to conclude.

'He pushed you? Pushed you where? If he did this to you, I swear to God, Amanda, I'll kill him myself. With my bare hands if I have to.'

'Don't,' Amanda pulled in a ragged breath, 'don't take me to hospital. Don't give him chance to finish the job.'

Shane lingered beside her, reluctant to move. He cupped her face with his hands. He was so warm to the touch, Amanda shuddered at how good it felt. It was like she'd forgotten how it felt to just be warm. She only remembered being either on fire or frozen.

'I won't let him hurt you again.' He said the words with such sincerity. 'If it's too dangerous to go to hospital then fine, we'll just return to the hotel.' He kept holding her face but dropped his gaze. 'I'll help you as best I can, but if you deteriorate in any way, if you show symptoms of internal bleeding, we'll have to take a chance with the hospital, do you understand?'

'If he knows I'm alive he'll kill me,' Amanda whispered the brutal truth. McAllister needed to believe that she'd died in the icy waters beneath the cliff. She'd have to use the darknet to plant a false story online about her body washing up on some beach. Just like Will had done, she was going to have to fake her own death.

'Okay, okay.' Shane released her and shifted back into the driver's seat. It was raining beyond the car. A curtain of drizzle gathered before them, obscuring the road ahead.

'Just take me back,' Amanda pleaded. 'To the hotel. I'll be fine.'

*

'We will stay awake all night if we have to,' Amanda's eyes were bright with excitement as she stood in her garden upon her freshly laid lawn and looked up towards the velvety blackness of the sky.

'All night?' Will grumbled as he carried the telescope out through the French doors. He was tucked up inside a white woollen turtleneck jumper Amanda had bought him the previous Christmas.

'Well, the reports said that the meteor shower could happen anytime between two and four.'

'Couldn't they be more specific?' Will placed the telescope beside Amanda on the lawn and eyed the night sky dubiously.

'Between two and four is pretty specific.'

'Some of us have to actually leave the house tomorrow to go to work.'

'You can go to bed if you want.' Amanda bent her knees and peered into her telescope. She carefully adjusted its angle so that she was looking upon the cratered face of the moon. 'I just figured you might want to witness such a special cosmic event.'

'I could just catch the footage on TV later.'

'Do you want to be a spectator in your life or a participant?'

Will gave her a lopsided smile. 'Sometimes I think you should have been a politician.'

'Oh yeah?'

'Yeah. You're pretty good at talking people into things.'

Amanda stepped away from the telescope to allow Will to peer through it. 'Wow,' his breath fogged around him. 'I never realised how beautiful the moon is.'

'Now you understand why I wanted to spend a thousand pounds on a telescope.'

'Sadly, yes.' Will straightened and reached for her, tucking her against his side like it was where she belonged. They slotted together so perfectly. Amanda sighed wistfully. 'Seeing the moon like that, it does kind of make the big spend seem worth it. Though I hold to the fact that a thousand pounds is a lot to spend on anything other than a car.'

'Do you think they'll look like balls of fire or shooting stars?' Amanda looked between Will and the sky. He smelt of home. She nuzzled against his jumper.

'Shooting stars, I guess.' Will tightened his arm around her. 'I mean, that's what shootings stars always were, right? Meteors.'

'Uh-huh.'

'So will you make a wish?'

Amanda giggled and leaned back to look up at her husband. 'Make a wish?'

'What's so funny? It's a shooting star, people make wishes on them.' The darkness concealed most of the blush which was creeping up Will's neck.

'People,' Amanda raised her eyebrows, 'but not Will Thorn. You're too pragmatic for that.'

'I make wishes from time to time.'

'My dad used to say that wishes were just dreams with wings.'

'So will you be making one, a wish?'

'Will you?'

'I asked first.'

'Fine,' Amanda leaned towards the telescope. 'I'll wish for more of what I have. More time with you, in our gorgeous home.'

'That's a nice wish.'

'And you?'

'I'll wish…' Will focused on a distant star. His eyebrows knotted together and for a moment he looked lost against the sheer infinity of the universe. Then he shook his head and the moment passed. 'I can't tell you what I wish or else it won't come true.'

'Oh, no fair, I told you mine.'

'Nope, not saying. You need to allow a man to have some secrets.'

'We have no secrets,' Amanda started to realign the telescope, not wanting to miss a moment of the meteor shower. 'I even know about that disgusting thing you do with your toenails.'

'Which is what?'

'You chew them. I've seen you. In some countries that is grounds for divorce, you know.'

'Damn, my darkest secret and you figured it out.'

'I'm a smart girl,' Amanda quipped.

'Hence the telescope.'

'Hence the telescope,' her lips curled into a smile as she stepped back from her expensive purchase, satisfied that the alignment was just right.

'Okay, well, it's one now,' Will lifted his wrist to check his watch. 'If this celestial event is occurring between *two and four* we're going to need a shedload of coffee to make it through the night so I'd best go and put some on.'

'Sounds good.'

'Because you're not falling asleep on me.' As he doubled back towards the welcoming glow of the house, he pointed towards Amanda, 'We're in this together, you and me, we're making some wishes tonight no matter how tired you get.'

*

The traffic thickened as they drew closer to Glasgow. Amanda bowed her head against her chest, unsure which hurt more – her injuries or the ache she felt in her heart whenever she thought of Will.

'How are you feeling?' Shane's hands were tight against the wheel.

'Tired.'

'Just tired?'

'And I ache. I ache badly.'

'Drink this.' Shane handed her a bottle of water.

'Can't I have something warm?' Amanda slowly unscrewed the lid off the bottle. Her fingers felt bloated and awkward. 'Maybe we could stop for coffee or something.'

'You need to warm up properly first. Once I'm satisfied you've regulated your core temperature you can have coffee.'

'Coffee would be good,' Amanda held the bottle to her lips and drank deeply from it.

'We could still go the hospital, you know.'

'No,' she shook her head in defiance. 'I'm relatively in one piece. I can't risk going to hospital, I can't risk him finding me.'

'You said he pushed you?'

'Can we just get back? I don't think I've ever been so exhausted.'

Time passed in a ribbon of roads and grey skies. Amanda's eyes fluttered open just as the car began to slow.

Shane turned into the multi-storey car park that their hotel used. He slid into an empty space and killed the engine. 'Are you sure it's even safe to be here?' He leaned forward and searched the darkened corners beyond the dashboard. 'I mean, don't you risk him coming to look for you?'

'He thinks I'm dead,' Amanda coughed, reaching for her door handle. 'We just have to keep it that way.'

'Wait.' Shane sprang out of his seat and powered around to the other side of the car. He opened Amanda's door as wide as it would go and looped an arm around her waist, helping her up onto her feet.

'Jesus,' she winced as she stood up. She felt like during the journey into Glasgow the metal of the blanket had sunk into her skin and fused with her skeleton. She was so stiff. Her joints painfully ground together as she staggered away from the car.

'Can you walk?'

'Barely.'

How far was it to the lobby? To the lifts? To Amanda's battered legs it felt like a million miles.

'We can't risk someone seeing you like this,' Shane desperately looked around. His body tensed as he settled on something. 'We need to take the stairs.'

'What?'

'I'm sorry, Amanda. But if someone sees you in the lift, or the lobby, they'll call an ambulance. I didn't spot any CCTV cameras on the stairs. It's our best option.'

A dry sob bounced over Amanda's sore lips. 'How…' She tried to balance most of her weight against Shane, 'how bad do I look?'

'Honestly?'

'Honestly.'

'Okay. Well,' Shane drew in a breath, 'your face is caked in dried blood. There's a gash on your forehead that keeps weeping, your arms and legs are covered in bruises, your clothes are all ripped up and you're white as a sheet. Other than that you look great.'

'Thanks.'

'And,' Shane began pacing towards the door marked with a sign for stairs, 'from the way you're carrying your left arm, I reckon you've dislocated your shoulder.'

'Ouch.'

'Ouch indeed.' Keeping Amanda held against his side, Shane struggled with the door and eventually pulled it open. An endless maze of metal stairs criss-crossed above them in a dizzying spiderweb.

'We can't do this,' Amanda gazed up at the stairs and tried to shrink back towards the door.

'We can and we will. We just have to take it one step at a time. Okay?'

'Okay.'

The stairs seemed endless. Amanda feared that she had no energy reserves left to call upon. She did her best to power through her pain. Shane helped her as much as he could but she had to use her own legs, had to place one bloodied foot in front of the other.

'Just keep going,' he intermittently whispered to her, 'you've got this.'

He pushed me. The words echoed through Amanda like a heartbeat. She kept climbing the stairs, kept going ever upwards.

He pushed me.

In McAllister's mind her broken body was probably still being tossed around by the tide. Was he back behind the walls of his mansion now, enjoying a dram of whisky beside a roaring fire? Had he toasted his success? Laughed with his goons about how they'd taunted Amanda until she'd wet herself with fear.

'How much... farther?' Amanda's lungs burned. She wanted to just collapse in a heap. She didn't care if anyone saw her. But no one came. No one else was crazy enough to use the never-ending network of metal stairs when there was a perfectly good system of lifts located in the lobby. Had they taken the lift, then Amanda would be in her hotel room by now, sprawled out on the soft bed. Her bones throbbed with longing.

'Nearly there.'

Shane kept giving the same response. *Nearly there.*

They seemed to perpetually be *nearly there.* Amanda felt like she were trapped in some nightmare where she was constantly trying to find an exit but one never presented itself. She was always just *nearly there.* She was reaching her threshold for tolerance, for pain.

Amanda dropped down onto all fours, her right hand pressing against the grid of the metal step whilst her left hung limply at her side.

Shane kept climbing the stairs. His footsteps rang out around her.

'Here,' he called back breathlessly. 'It's this door. This is our floor.'

Amanda tried to get up but there was no tension in her arm, no power to push her up. She'd turned to jelly. 'I can't,' she admitted tearfully. 'I just need to rest. Just for a minute.'

'You can rest all you want once we're back in the room. Come on.' Shane retraced his steps to her. She expected him to haul her back onto her feet, to keep up his mantra about how she could do it. Instead he lifted her off the ground, carefully placing her damaged body over his shoulder. Amanda tensed as her chest burned and her bones ground together to sing a symphony of agony. But the fireman's lift was better than walking. Shane panted and slowly ascended towards their floor. He thrust open the door and staggered out into the corridor. It seemed strange to suddenly be in such plush surroundings. The walls were painted a soft shade of grey, the floor covered in plush carpet and music was playing like a delicate whisper.

'Nearly… there,' Shane grunted as he pressed on. Amanda rested against his back, seeing their journey from a bizarre perspective. She looked along the corridor which was thankfully empty.

Shane kept moving, not daring to stop even to draw in a necessary breath.

It was what Will would have done.

Amanda stiffened in surprise at her own thought. But she knew she was right. Will would have scooped her up, hauled her over his shoulder and carried her up the stairs, just as Shane had done. Sure, with Will it would have been more effortless, he'd been a hulk of a man. But the thought process would have been the same – they both would have wanted to save her. Shane was doing everything he could to save her; he'd even ignored his instincts and not taken her to hospital at her behest.

Finally Shane was opening the door to their room. Amanda felt relief wash over her as they went inside and left the rest of the world out in the corridor. Shane carried her over to the bed where he carefully lay her down. Amanda looked up at him, she could feel her eyelids starting to swell. Would she be sporting one black eye the next day or two? She didn't dare go near a mirror, she imagined she looked horrific.

'Thank you,' she breathed as Shane began searching his luggage for the first aid kit he'd inevitably packed.

'Of course.'

'No, really,' she rolled onto her side, grimacing as she felt her injuries constricting and ripping, and reached out for Shane with a shaking right hand. She noticed that her fingers were caked in dirt and blood. 'You saved me.'

Shane looked at her and he didn't seem to see any of her injuries, just the girl he loved beneath them. He gave her a tender smile and then went back to his search.

'You saved me,' Amanda repeated as she dropped onto her back once more and stared up at the ceiling.

Maybe Shane's hand hadn't reached out over the cliff edge at the crucial point when she fell, but he was still her hero. He'd still saved her.

18

Amanda drifted in and out of sleep. In her waking moments she saw Shane hovering over her, mopping her brow with a wet flannel or renewing the dressings on her cuts. She ran a fever. At the height of her delirium she saw Will standing at the end of her hotel bed. His skin was grey, his eyes sunken and his clothes were caked in leaves and mud.

'Will.' She tried to sit up, tried to reach out for him, but there was an awful pressure upon her chest, keeping her pressed against the bed. 'Will.' She choked on his name. He said nothing, he just lingered at the foot of the bed, his gaze vacant.

The room started to smell of rot. Amanda was certain that it was coming from Will. He was haunting her, punishing her for leaving his body alone in the woods like a dead animal.

'I had to,' Amanda's lips trembled as she flitted between being too hot or too cold. 'I had to save your s-son. S-stop looking at me… like that. Will, s-say something.'

But he never spoke, he just stood, and to Amanda that was worse. She wanted to hear his voice, even if he was yelling at her, even if he was telling her that she'd let him down. At least he'd be saying something.

'I did this for you,' Amanda told him repeatedly. 'For you. And for your son. You can't hate me for that.'

On the third day Amanda's fever broke. She woke up to sunshine streaming in through the window and Will was gone.

'How are you feeling?' Shane was instantly by her side, he looked gaunt and deep shadows gathered beneath his eyes.

'Um,' Amanda looked down at herself. She wore the nightshirt she'd previously packed. Pulling back the covers, she saw her legs. Red welts were turning blue as they bruised. The swelling on her knee had started to go down. 'I feel more like myself, I guess.' She looked to where Will had been standing. Particles of dust danced in a beam of sunlight.

'You got sick,' Shane leaned over and placed his palm against her forehead. 'I got all the medicine that I could from the chemist and it seems to have worked.'

'Thank you.' The words didn't seem enough but they were all Amanda had.

'I dressed your injuries as best I could. Really you need a shower to thoroughly clean them all out, if you're up to it?'

'Yes.' Amanda closed her eyes at the blissful thought of a shower. She yearned to have the caress of warm water running down her battered back. 'A shower would be amazing.'

'Okay, but first,' Shane dropped his hand and looked at her left shoulder. 'Your shoulder is still dislocated; I didn't dare try to reset it while you were battling the fever. But, Amanda, it does need resetting.' His voice was calm but there was an edge to it, like he was delivering a warning.

'Then, reset it,' Amanda shrugged and turned, directing her left shoulder at him.

'It's going to hurt.'

'Okay.'

'A lot.'

'I said okay.'

Shane didn't seem satisfied by her response. He got up and began rummaging around the room.

'I'm sure it'll be fine,' Amanda assured him. 'I'm already in a lot of pain, what harm could a bit more do, so—'

'Bite down on this,' he thrust a hand towel at her.

'Are you serious?'

'Extremely. You have to trust me on this, Amanda. It's going to hurt like hell and I can't risk you screaming the place down.'

Amanda shoved the hand towel into her mouth, clenching her teeth around it. 'M-kay.'

'I'll do it on three.' Shane stood beside the bed with one leg raised up on it. He placed both hands around Amanda's left shoulder, holding on tight as though he were about to take part in a game of tug of war.

'Readme,' Amanda's words were muffled against the towel. A dagger forced its way through her skull, driving itself into her brain. Tears pooled in her eyes. She was back in the boot of McAllister's cars, back listening to the soundtrack of her own muffled anguish.

'One.'

Amanda tried to blink away her tears and the memory.

'Two.'

She could feel the rumble of the engine. Her heart beat echoed in her ears.

'Three.'

The pain sent the memory up in flames. The boot was gone. Amanda screamed against the towel, letting the fluffy fabric absorb all her agony. Her left shoulder burned as though Shane had just driven a hot poker through it. Flames fanned out down her arm, burning her, crippling her. She spat out the towel, panting.

'Okay, it's done. I'm sorry for the pain, but it's done. Are you okay?' Shane stroked her hair back from her damp brow.

'Fuck,' she still couldn't catch her breath. 'You weren't kidding when you said it'd hurt.'

Regret pinched at Shane's face. 'But at least now you can shower and use both hands,' he offered by way of consolation, reaching out and helping Amanda stand up.

'Did you happen to pick up any pain meds from the chemist?' She rubbed at her aching shoulder. Her bones were so sore, they felt brittle and worn down.

'Some.'

'Good, because I'm going to need them.'

'You'll feel better once you shower.'

*

Amanda stood beneath the hot water until her skin turned pink. She washed the seawater out of her hair, the sand from beneath her nails. She washed away the shame, the suffering which McAllister had caused her. Then she just stood with her face upturned to the shower head and let the warmth flow over her. It felt good to be warm. To be clean. The small hotel bathroom filled with steam and still Amanda didn't get out. She wanted to stay in the shower cubicle forever, hot and safe.

The door was ajar and some of the steam was trickling out. Shane raised his voice to be heard over the force of the water, 'Hey, you okay?'

Amanda moved to lean against the smooth tiled wall, letting the water forge a river down her back.

'Do you need me to help you get out or anything?'

He was treating her like an invalid. Which, Amanda looked down at her battered limbs, she supposed she currently was. She turned off the water. 'If you don't mind, then yeah, that'd be great.' Stepping out of the cubicle, she saw Shane nervously lingering on the edge of the steam. 'Can you hand me a towel?'

He nodded and quickly thrust a hand towel at her.

'Something… bigger?' Amanda prompted.

'Crap, yeah, sure.' He sounded nervous.

Amanda pulled the sheet towel from his grasp and began to dry herself. But it wasn't easy. When she tried to bend or turn, her bones throbbed, pleading with her to restrict her movements.

'Um, can you help dry me?' Amanda shyly extended the towel back towards him. 'I'm…' she looked down at her pink flesh, at her feet which had turned red. 'It's a struggle. I'm still in a lot of pain.'

'Yeah, of course, absolutely.' Shane began to tentatively pat at her skin. He didn't roughly run the towel over her like she were a wet dog, he just kept patting and dabbing away as though she were made of porcelain.

'Dry me, don't paw me,' Amanda teased. She noticed Shane's pained expression and she was about to remark that there were worse jobs in the world than having to towel-dry your ex but then she saw what troubled him. Her whole body was a patchwork quilt of cuts and bruises. The large mirror on the far wall was becoming unfogged with steam and revealing her tarnished reflection.

Her legs were scratched and bruised, along with her arms. When she turned, Amanda saw the dark shadows on her back, creeping their way up her spine. But it was her face that troubled her the most. When she locked eyes with her reflection she slunk back. The blood had been washed away but the blue bruises remained. Both of her cheeks were engulfed in them like some sadistic war paint. She had a matching pair of black eyes and a cut lip that was just starting to heal. A long gash ran across the length of her forehead, releasing a faint trickle of blood which traced a line down to Amanda's chin.

'He did this.' Amanda stared at herself in disbelief. It was like looking in a fairground mirror at the funhouse, only instead of being taller or really squat Amanda got to see the broken version of herself.

'We need to just focus on letting you heal.' Shane cloaked her in the towel.

'He pushed me.'

'You said that before, what did you mean?'

Amanda drifted back into the hotel room. She shuddered beneath the towel, away from the trapped heat of the shower.

'Here,' Shane went over to a large paper shopping bag that was tucked up in the far corner of the room. He pulled out a trio of soft flannel pyjamas and also a long-length nightgown adorned with Wonder Woman. 'I thought you might want something comfortable to wear, but I wasn't sure what you'd go for.'

Amanda looked at the items which Shane displayed on the bed. She reached out and stroked the pyjamas. They were deliciously soft to the touch.

'And these,' he hastily added two pairs of slippers to the arrangement and some striped slipper socks. 'Just pick what you want.'

Amanda pulled on the soft pyjamas and the slipper socks. She noticed that Shane turned away as she did so. Her wounds marginally eased within the gentle fabric. She sat down on the bed and rested a hand against her stomach, realising how hungry she was. 'I feel like I could literally eat a horse,' she joked.

Shane handed her the room service menu and remained standing, watching her like she was painting in a gallery he was struggling to discern the meaning of. 'You said he pushed you?' Shane crossed his arms against his chest and waited.

'Yes.' Amanda kept her head bent, focused on the menu. 'Ooh, a cheeseburger sounds good. Or macaroni and cheese. What are you going to get?'

'He pushed you – where? Down the stairs?'

'Actually, I might go for pizza.'

'Amanda, answer me.'

Slowly she closed the menu and raised her head to meet his penetrating gaze. In the bathroom mirror she'd noticed that the sea had stolen some of the brightness from her blue eyes.

'He didn't push me down the stairs.' A tear journeyed down her cheek.

'Then what did he do?' Shane whispered.

'He pushed me off a cliff.'

Shane clamped a hand to his mouth and turned away from her.

'I think my head's still bleeding I might need some new plasters or something—'

'That fucking *bastard*!' Shane roared. 'He pushed you off a *fucking* cliff! He could have killed you!'

'I'm pretty sure that was his intention.'

'Amanda, how can you be so calm about this? What the hell happened at that mansion? Why did he do this? That man, he…' Shane was at a loss for words. He paced back and forth, puffing out his cheeks.

'He made my greatest nightmare a reality,' she concluded flatly for him. 'And I let him do it. I went there, knowing how dangerous he was, but I thought I knew better. I thought I was smarter. I was wrong.'

'Amanda, you cannot blame yourself for this.'

'Oh, I don't.'

'What he did to you—' Shane spun around and punched the wall. His knuckles connected with plaster with a muffled smack, leaving a slight indentation.

'Right now I don't have the mental energy to think about what he did. I need to focus on healing.'

'I'll kill him. I'll kill the prick. I'll rip his fucking eyes out.'

Not when I could have the satisfaction of killing you myself. Those had been the last words McAllister had said to Amanda before he pushed her. And now she understood the sentiment implicitly.

'If anyone's killing him, it's me.' Anger swam in her veins, travelling to every inch of her body and pushing back any feelings of pain.

'Ridiculous,' Shane scoffed. 'All *you* need to do is rest and focus on getting your strength back. All right?'

'First I need to eat,' Amanda tapped the menu in her lap.

*

When Amanda woke up the television was on. The dull drone of distant voices had slowly pulled her away from sleep. With a struggle she sat up and rubbed at her eyes. She felt well rested. It was surprising how effective a long shower and a decent meal could be. She'd barely finished her macaroni and cheese when she felt her eyelids drooping south, her body relaxing into the softness of the mattress.

'What time is it?' she yawned. The television provided the only light in the room. It glowed on the far wall like an animated night light.

'Three.' Shane was sat up on the other side of the bed, the remote resting in his hand.

'Three?' Amanda shot a look at the window. Sure enough, the world outside seemed shrouded in darkness.

'I didn't mean to wake you, I'll turn this down,' Shane began lowering the volume with the remote control.

'No, it's okay.' Amanda rubbed at her eyes some more. They were so sore. 'Three? Why aren't you asleep?'

'I can't sleep.' Shane's attention never drifted away from the glowing screen. He watched it with a scary intensity, like a hawk studying a field mouse.

'Have you slept at all?'

'No.'

'What are you even watching?' Amanda looked over at the woman on the screen who wore a formal blue blazer and spoke with authority. The news. Shane was watching the twenty-four-hour news channel. 'You really need to try and sleep.'

'There has to be something.'

'Something?'

'On the news, about McAllister. There has to be something. How can he throw someone off a cliff and no one says anything about it.'

'Because only his men saw.'

'*Someone* must have seen *something*.'

'It was remote and it was the middle of the night.'

'Are you making excuses for him?'

'No,' Amanda sighed, 'I'm making excuses for the situation. For the lack of valid witnesses.'

'I'll keep watching, there must be something.'

'Actually,' Amanda awkwardly scrambled out of bed and grabbed her laptop. It felt heavier than she remembered. She opened it up, the blue glow of the screen illuminating her face. She was about to log in and then she hesitated. The online world had always felt like a safe place, somewhere she was able to hide in plain sight if she so wanted. But now, when she saw her log-in screen, her spine tingled with a sense of apprehension. How safe was her digital world? Did McAllister have eyes and ears there too, tracking her every move?

'Go back to sleep, you need to rest.'

'First I need to ensure that McAllister thinks me dead.' Amanda traced her fingers along her freshly bandaged temple before taking the plunge and logging in.

'What are you doing?' Shane looked away from the television.

'I'm just going to plant a false story about a body washing up on a beach or a fishing boat catching me in their nets.' She knew exactly where to go, how to leak such a lie to the world to make it look convincing.

'No.' Shane snapped her laptop closed. Amanda barely had chance to withdraw her fingers in time.

'Christ, Shane, what did you do that for?'

'I'm not having you fake your own death.'

'But if I don't—'

'He'll what? He pushed you off a cliff, Amanda. He doesn't expect you to get washed up somewhere. In his mind you're just gone.'

'You can't know that.'

'I do know that.' Shane's gaze became distant. 'I've worked a lot of homicide cases where bodies surface alongside a river, or on a beach. Once we finally trace the killer they are always stunned that the body was found, that they were able to be tied to the crime. When someone throws a body into the ocean or a river, they assume it's gone for good.'

Gone for good.

Is that what McAllister was striving for? To erase any trace of Amanda from the earth, to forever condemn her to exist only in memory?

'I don't want you to play dead for him. I want you to get better and then we'll go back home and turn our backs on this whole fucking mess.'

'It's just one little article. One little lie.'

'And if it snowballs?' Shane raised his eyebrows at her. 'If it gains momentum, if someone links your name to the body, if your mother ends up getting a call that you're dead, how do you go home then, Amanda? You couldn't say you miraculously rose up out of the grave, you'd have to disappear to maintain the lie. You'd have to abandon your life and everyone you know.'

'Like Will did.'

The words hung between them.

'He was trying to protect someone,' Shane said stoically after a moment. 'You'd be creating a lie just to protect your original plan.'

'What if he goes after Ewan? I need to check on him, make sure he's okay,' Amanda scrambled for the hotel room's phone but Shane rested his hand on her shoulders and eased her back against the pillows on the bed.

'I imagine that'd be more trouble than it's worth. To McAllister, pretty much everyone connected to Will is dead. He got what he wanted – his payback.'

Amanda looked at her laptop. 'Could you give it all up, your life, your identity if I commit to my lie?'

Shane massaged the back of his neck and watched the television. 'If you asked it of me, then yeah, I could.' He dropped his hand and turned to face her, his green eyes glistening with tears. 'But, Amanda, please don't ask that of me.'

19

Amanda watched the sun rise. She opened the curtains in her hotel room and sat on the bed, waiting for the shadows of night to recede. As a new day dawned a blue sky appeared above the city, cloudless and bright. The early morning light glistened against the windows of distant buildings, making the skyline look as though it were infused with diamonds.

She heard the door creak open as Shane returned from the gym. He'd been there since four in the morning, sweating away his frustrations. 'You should be resting.'

'I can't sleep.' Amanda felt caught between exhaustion and exhilaration. Her body longed for rest; each time she lay down her bones pressed themselves against the bed, wanting to become absorbed by its delicate softness. But while her body was tired, her mind was unbearably alert. Thoughts bounced off one another like bubbles in a glass of Coke. There was so much activity going on behind Amanda's temple that she felt a constant ache behind her bruised eyes. 'I keep thinking about it all.'

'Amanda.' She felt the bed sag beside her as Shane sat down. He began to gently massage her shoulders. 'I can only imagine how terrifying it was to go through what you did. But it's done now. You just need to rest and let your body heal.'

'There were names,' Amanda muttered bleakly. 'So many names, I see them when I close my eyes. They dance through my mind like I'm trapped in the *Matrix* or something.'

'So what happened to the USB?'

Amanda shot her laptop a dirty look where it sat upon the nearby desk. Technology had let her down. 'He threw the USB off the cliff,' she swallowed against a lump that was forming in her throat, 'before he threw me off too.'

'You need to try and forget,' Shane kept massaging her shoulders. 'You need to try and rest.'

'There must have been fifty, sixty names. Women, girls, who he had plucked from their lives and brought here to be sold as slaves. How can he just get away with that?' She spun around and stared into Shane's green eyes, searching their gentle depths for answers.

'You could report him. Tip off the local cops,' he offered weakly with a shrug.

'The case would be dead in minutes without any evidence, you know that.' Amanda struggled to her feet, refusing Shane's assistance. 'And he'll have wiped that entire laptop the second he got back to his house.'

'So what then? The only choice you have is to let this go.'

Amanda knew that the last thing she could do was to let it go. She was going to finish McAllister. She'd seen the true extent of his monstrous nature and she wasn't about to not at least try and end him, to stop his plague of torment upon countless others.

'The beach.'

'What?'

'The tide… it brought me to the beach.' Amanda hobbled back and forth, pressing her fingertips against her temple. If only the bubbles would settle, just a bit, to grant her direct access to her jumble of memories. 'Otherwell… Otterby…'

'Otterwell Bay?'

'That's it,' she snapped her fingers at him and stood still. 'Otterwell Bay. The tide dragged me there and then I found a phone box.'

'Okay…'

'Maybe the USB washed up there too?'

Amanda felt rejuvenated by the injection of hope she'd just given herself.

'Look—'

'We go there, we check the beach and who knows, maybe we find it. If it's not too waterlogged I should hopefully be able to recover its data, and then bam, we've still got him.' She closed her hand into a tight fist.

'I'm not taking you back to Otterwell Bay.'

'Why not?'

'Because you need to rest, that's why.' Shane got up and began stalking towards the bathroom. Amanda went after him, forcing her aching legs to move quickly.

'Shane, I've been resting for *days*. A bit of fresh air, it will do me good. Besides, I'm going crazy being cooped up here all the time.'

'It's too risky.'

'This might be my only shot at bringing McAllister down.' Amanda grabbed Shane's gaze and drew him towards her, pleading with her eyes as she looked up at him. 'All those names. There were just so many. They will all be someone's daughter, sister… wife. They deserve to be found, don't you think?'

Shane looked doubtful but Amanda recognised the way he leaned his head to the left, it meant he was reluctantly giving in to her demands. 'You have to sleep on the way and when we get there you can spend twenty minutes on the beach. That's it, do you understand?'

'Yes.'

'And wrap up warm.'

'Sure.'

'And be prepared for the fact that in all likelihood we won't find the USB, Amanda.'

'Uh-huh.'

'You're basically looking for a needle in a haystack.'

*

Amanda didn't sleep during the drive out of the city. Instead she gazed absently at the rows of buildings which thinned away to the rolling heather-clad landscape of the highlands. The early morning blue sky remained, bathing everywhere in glorious golden light. Leaning back in her seat, Amanda let the vibrations of the car soothe the deep ache in her bones.

'Okay, it's just up here,' Shane repeated the information that the satnav had just given him.

Amanda straightened and peered out the windscreen. They were almost two hours out of the city. They hadn't passed another car in miles. The road they were on was bleak and desolate, even in the sunshine. It wound its way along the shoreline, twisting and turning, meandering as though it had no destination in mind.

The phone box was on the side of the road. Amanda looked at it and shrivelled within her hooded jumper and loose-fitting joggers. She couldn't bear to wear anything tight against all her bruises.

'Are you really sure about this?' Shane slowed the car and then stopped. He looked at her, his fingertips grazing the key in the ignition. 'We could still go back.'

'I need to at least look for it.'

Amanda climbed out of the car and an icy breeze immediately tangled itself up in her hair. She furiously knocked the blonde strands out of her eyes. The low ponytail she'd hastily tugged her hair into earlier was proving to be not as proficient as she'd hoped. Some of her looser layers had broken free and now danced about her head as they were manipulated by the wind.

The small shingle beach looked miles away. Amanda paused at the top of the cliff, looking beyond the wooden staircase which twisted its way down between the rocks. Her palms became clammy, her heart beat quickening. If she closed her eyes she could still recall how it felt to fall and just keep falling.

'That's a long walk down,' Shane's hand was quickly on her shoulder. She felt stronger with him by her side.

'Yep, it is,' she agreed with a tight nod. She could barely recall climbing the stairs when she'd clamoured up from the beach. Adrenalin had made her feral that day, moving purely on instinct and she considered it was the only way she could have survived. If she'd stopped, even for a moment, and considered what she was up against she'd have fallen down and never got up again.

'Look, if you're not up to it—'

'I have to start pushing myself at some point, else I'll never get better.'

Amanda boldly approached the stairway which led down to the beach. Though her bones ached, nothing was broken. She'd thankfully sustained only surface injuries and she wasn't about to let some bruises weaken her, not anymore, not when she could be standing so tantalisingly close to the one piece of evidence which could destroy the monster that was McAllister.

The stairs creaked as they walked down them, the wood weary and fragile from decades being pounded by relentless winds.

Just as it had been the day Amanda washed up upon it, the beach was deserted. A few seagulls danced against the blue sky before diving into the water like kamikaze pilots.

'Where do we start looking?' Shane was pacing along the beach, head bent as he focused on the shingle beneath his feet.

Amanda tasted something metal. Closing her eyes, she drank in the sea air, focused on the shrill cry of the sea gulls. She needed to centre herself, needed to push back the memory of what had happened upon the beach. Like a piece of driftwood she'd been tossed ashore. Using what little strength remained in her arms she'd crawled along the sand and shingle.

'We need to focus on the shoreline,' Shane called over to her.

Amanda blinked. A brisk breeze slapped across her cheeks as if also committed to bringing her back into the moment.

'The shoreline, yes.' Amanda trudged over to the waves. They lapped idly against the mosaic of shingle, lacking any of the destructive strength they'd had further along the coast, where Amanda had fallen.

Been pushed, she corrected herself. Fallen sounded too much like an accident and there was nothing accidental about what had happened to her.

'What colour was it?' Shane asked as he stooped down to rummage amongst some wet stones.

'Black.' Amanda rolled her eyes in frustration. Why hadn't she picked a colour that would stand out, like neon pink or lime green? There had to be a hundred black stones glistening amongst the shingle. When she bought it black had felt discreet, classy even. Had she known she'd end up searching for it on a beach made of shingles she was certain that she'd have made a different choice.

'Black, okay.'

Amanda walked along the shoreline. She bent down, ignoring the pain that shot through her, and searched the shingle, digging deep but finding only sand.

An hour passed. Shane ran over his allotted time frame without even noticing. All that they'd found were two cans of Coke, a thick piece of driftwood and several slim black rocks, which from a distance could almost pass for a USB stick.

'It's not here,' Shane was doubling back towards her. Amanda looked out at the sea, currently so placid beneath a turquoise sky. She pleaded with it to release its secrets, to give back to her something so vital. 'We really need to go. We've stayed here too long as it is.'

'It has to be here.' Amanda ran from him, further along the beach. She kept her eyes glued upon the thousands of chipped stones at her feet. The USB had to be buried amongst them somewhere. If she'd washed up on this beach, then why hadn't her little storage device? She dropped to her knees and started to dig.

'Amanda, stop!'

'I'll dig up this whole bloody beach if I have to,' she dragged back the shingle with her hands.

'It's not here,' Shane was grabbing her shoulders, trying to force her back onto her feet.

'No, let me look,' Amanda wailed as she shook him off. She kept digging for the USB, not caring that her damp fingers were starting to resemble pink prunes. She had to take McAllister down. If she didn't he'd just keep on hurting innocent people. It wasn't just about Will anymore. There were the names on the list and—

'It's okay.' Shane knelt beside her and wrapped her up in his arms. She hadn't even realised that she was crying. A choked sob broke from her lips and Amanda burrowed herself into his embrace. 'I'm sorry it's not here, Amanda. Truly. You looked, that's all you can do.'

'He can't keep on hurting people,' she shook, her tears soaking into Shane's navy jumper. 'He tried to… to kill me.'

'I know,' Shane squeezed her harder. 'But he didn't kill you, and that's what matters to me. If I lost you…' |He kissed her forehead and they remained locked together on their knees until clouds started to roll in overhead.

*

By the time they were back at the hotel it was raining. Wet streaks swept across the glass of the window, the sky now a sombre shade of grey.

'It could have waited,' Shane tossed a small white box over to her and shook the rain drops out of his hair. Amanda smiled appreciatively at him.

'You know me and technology,' she eagerly began to open the sleek box. 'Besides, I need to call home and check in on my Mum and Ewan. Thanks for going out to get this for me while I napped.'

'No problem.' Shane peeled off his damp jumper and Amanda felt her attention drift away from her shiny new phone. She stole a glimpse of his smooth chest, his taut muscles as he rummaged in a drawer for a dry top. As he tugged it on she quickly looked back at her device.

'You got me the newest model,' she noted with approval.

'I figured you'd only moan if I didn't.'

Amanda emptied the box of all its contents. It felt good to have a phone again. She'd have to update everything with a new number and passwords, but she didn't care. It was better than attempting to remotely connect to her old phone which was still somewhere at McAllister's mansion, bundled up in the overnight bag stuffed with energy bars and flashlights. Had McAllister's guards gone through it? Were her belongings now in a shallow grave somewhere within the mansion's grounds?

My things are evidence. Evidence that he tried to kill me.

Amanda instantly dismissed the naïve thought. A man like McAllister was too smart to keep any evidence lurking around his home. There would be no trace that Amanda was even there; like the girls upon his terrible list, she'd just cease to exist.

'What if your mother asks about the new number?' Shane raised his eyebrows at Amanda as he smoothed out the creases in his clean jumper.

'She won't. And when I'm back I'll just update her phone myself before she can realise it's changed. My Mum will always just answer.'

'Fair enough.'

With her new phone activated, Amanda typed in the number for the little cottage. One ring became two. Three. On the fourth her mother picked up. She sounded out of breath.

'Mum, are you okay?' Amanda gripped the phone with both hands, wishing there was some way she could teleport through it and be back home in the next breath.

'Oh, that boy,' Corrine chuckled. 'He's had me running round this house like a blue-arsed fly. Hide-and-seek,' more chuckling. 'With a time penalty system! Can you believe it!

After ten minutes, each passing minute equals minus one point. Amanda, I'm on minus *sixteen*! He's a little Houdini that one. Do you know where I found him last time?'

'No, where?' Amanda relaxed her hold on the phone and leaned back against the pillows on her bed. It was blissful to lose herself in the innocent fun of what was going on at her mother's cottage. It was a world Amanda was keen to return to. Was keen to preserve.

'The laundry basket,' Corrine chortled with delight. 'Wedged in amongst all my towels! Can you believe it? I won't even tell you how long it took me to crack that one.'

'It sounds like you two are having fun.'

'Yes, we are,' Corrine enthused. 'And… are you?' her mother's voice changed from joyful to detective in a heartbeat. 'How are you and Shane finding Vegas? Have you been to many shows? Have you gambled?'

'Two shows,' Amanda turned and reached for her laptop. She tapped on the mouse pad and read from the screen. 'Cirque du Soleil was just amazing. We loved that one. And we even went to see Britney Spears, to be, you know, nostalgic.'

Across the room Shane crinkled his nose up in disgust. Amanda pressed a hand to her chest to suppress her laughter. It bubbled around in her sore lungs, replacing mirth with pain. Wincing, Amanda dropped back against her pillows.

'What else do you have planned?' Corrine wondered eagerly. 'Maybe a visit to a little white chapel perhaps'

'Mother!' That seemed a distasteful suggestion even by Corrine's standards.

'I meant to sightsee,' her mum quickly clarified. 'They're a tourist attraction, you know, along with being a wedding venue. And no one would judge you, Amanda,' Corrine's tone became haughty, 'You've been through such a lot lately. And to lose Will and have to take in a son who you'd never known about, no one would judge you for seeking solace with another man. Someone familiar, someone who you know.'

'Christ, Mum,' Amanda could feel her cheeks burning.

Shane glanced over with interest and mouthed, 'Are you okay?'

Nodding, Amanda forced a smile, knowing it was time to end the call. 'We're just about to head out for an all you can eat brunch.'

'Brunch?' Corrine echoed shrilly.

'Brunch, you know, it's later than breakfast but earlier than lunch. So kind of the two combined – brunch. It's still early here.' Amanda hoped she was still successfully managing to keep up the time difference charade.

'Sounds like an American thing.'

'It is.'

'Okay, well,' Corrine sounded reluctant to leave, but then she bellowed something away from the phone, 'I said the time penalties didn't apply when I got a phone call! Ewan, we'll have to start again!'

'Sounds like you've got your hands full. Hug Ewan for me. I'll call again soon, Mum. Bye. Love you.' Amanda disconnected before Corrine had chance to say anything else.

'Are things okay back home?' Shane wondered cautiously.

'Yeah, they're okay. You know my mum, inappropriate as usual.'

'What did she say?'

'Nothing,' Amanda waved a dismissive hand through the air. 'Shall we eat? Talking about brunch has made me hungry.'

'Sure,' Shane tossed her the room service menu. He watched Amanda as she studied it. 'You know, we could just go back, get involved in all the fun going on back home ourselves.'

Amanda kept reading the menu and pursed her lips as she shook her head. 'We can't go back yet.'

'The USB stick is gone. It's over, Amanda. And you're a lot stronger than you were. We should think about—'

'I'm not going anywhere until McAllister has paid for all that he's done.'

'But, Amanda—'

'I haven't worked out how I'm going to do it yet, but I will. I owe it to Will. I owe it to the names on that list.'

'Amanda—'

'And I owe it to myself,' she concluded sharply. 'Can you tell me, truthfully, that after what he did, you'd just be happy to go back home and pretend it never happened?'

Shane's face hardened. 'No,' he said after a long pause. 'I wouldn't.'

'Then it's settled,' Amanda handed him the menu with a fake smile, 'we stay here until we bring the bastard down. And tonight I'll have the cheeseburger with salad, not fries. Thanks.'

20

'Daddy,' Amanda pulled her blanket up to her chin, her voice a frightened whisper, 'there's a monster outside, I can hear it.'

'A monster?' her dad slowly lowered himself down and sat on the edge of her bed. The little night light in the corner of the room did its best to try and banish away the shadows which clotted together like molasses.

'Can't you hear it?'

Something rattled along the side of the wall. Like bones shaking in a bag or long fingers feeling their way along the house. Amanda shrieked and pulled her blanket higher.

'There,' she cowered towards her father. 'It's outside and it keeps growling and scratching at the walls, like it wants to come inside.'

'Oh, Amanda,' her dad's hands were warm as he smoothed down her hair and gave her a gentle smile. 'That's not a monster, sweetheart. That's just the wind.'

'How do you know?' She didn't dare release her tight grip on her blanket. Had her father been outside? Had he challenged the darkness and its depths?

'Because there are no monsters.'

Amanda shook her head, refusing to believe him. What next – would he tell her there was no ocean or sky? The monster was outside, she could hear it desperately trying to get in. It roared around the walls of her small room, confirming its presence.

'Daddy, you've made it angry,' she dove beneath her blanket, burrowing deep.

'Amanda,' her dad peeled back the blanket, re-exposing her. 'There are no monsters. What you can hear, it's just the wind whistling around the house. It will die down soon.'

'There are no monsters?' Amanda sleepily settled against her pillows. If her father said it then it had to be true.

'No, there aren't.' He tucked her blanket in around her and kissed her forehead.

'But if there were?' Amanda wondered as her dad retreated from her bed. He was almost at the door beneath which the welcoming yellow light of the landing crept into the room. His fingers grazed the handle as he turned back to her.

'There are no monsters, Amanda. I promise. Try and get some sleep.'

'But if there was a monster outside,' she pressed, determined to get an answer. 'And it was really trying to get in the house. How would you stop it?'

Her father dusted his hands through his hair and drew his eyebrows together. He glanced down at the golden light of the landing which pooled around his feet and then yawned.

'Well?' Amanda peered at him, her eyes bright with curiosity.

'If there was a monster outside,' he conceded with a sigh, 'which there isn't. But let's pretend there was, for a moment, and it was trying to get in the house.'

'Yes,' Amanda was nodding along with him, 'what would you do?'

He thought for just a second. 'I'd have to kill it,' he responded simply. 'Because I'd do anything to keep you and your mother safe, you know that.' He doubled back across the room and gave Amanda another kiss on the forehead. 'Now try and get some sleep and remember that monsters aren't real, okay?'

'Okay.'

This time when he made for the door Amanda didn't call him back.

*

Amanda reluctantly opened her eyes. She'd wanted to stay in her dream, close to the memory of her father. Close to a place where monsters weren't real and she'd known complete safety.

'Hey,' Shane was already up. He was at the end of the bed buttoning up a shirt, his hair damp and flat against his head. 'Did you sleep okay?'

'I know what I need to do.' Amanda sat up. When she slept she was able to forget about her battered body, about her navy bruises. But when she awoke all the fires within her body started up again. Groaning, she slumped against her pillows.

'What do you need to do?' Shane was still preoccupied with his shirt.

'I need to kill him.'

'What?' he abandoned the final button and stared at her, mouth agape.

'McAllister, I need to kill him.'

'Christ, Amanda. First you just wanted to put the bastard in jail and now you want to *kill* him? We're leaving, *today*. I'm not going to sit around here and watch you lose your mind.'

'I'm not losing my mind,' Amanda declared stridently. She scrambled out of bed, wanting to present herself as strong, self-possessed, not a weakling still resigned to convalescence. 'In fact I think I'm finally seeing things clearly.'

'Pack your stuff; we're leaving, *right now*.' Shane clicked his fingers at her as if he were ordering a disobedient dog.

'He's a monster, Shane.'

'I don't care if the guy's fucking Dracula himself, you're not putting yourself in danger again. This is too much, Amanda.'

'If he lives, more people suffer.'

'Their blood isn't on your hands.' Shane was unzipping her bag and throwing open drawers. 'Besides, the second you take him out, some other lowlife asshole will rise up to take his place.'

'If he lives, I don't get to go home.' Amanda walked over to him, placing a hand on his arm to urge him to cease his manic packing. 'And I want to go home, Shane. I want to resume my regular life, I don't want to have to drift into hiding like Will did.'

'You don't know that he'll still be looking for you.'

'You don't know that he won't.'

'Amanda—'

'Years,' she stated bluntly. 'McAllister hunted Will for years, even though he'd faked his own death, left his wife and son. It still wasn't enough. To a man like McAllister nothing will ever be enough, he deals only in absolutes.'

'This is madness.' Shane ceased packing.

'It's my only shot at getting my life back. At keeping Ewan safe. On saving the names on that list.'

'You're talking about committing *murder*.' The veins in Shane's neck throbbed. He'd built his entire career on locking up people who did exactly that. Murderers, killers. He helped bring them all to justice.

'I'm talking about killing a *monster*,' Amanda raised her chin and held his gaze, 'and you remember reading fairy tales as a kid? The only way we are going to get our happy ever after is if we kill him.'

*

'I don't like this.' Shane was several verses into his complaint. He'd been reciting it since they left the hotel.

'What's to like?' Amanda muttered as she sat in the corner of the café, bent over her laptop. Her black eyes were concealed behind aviator sunglasses. The long sleeves of her hooded jumper and joggers hid the rest of her wounds. Her blonde hair was gathered at the nape of her neck in a loose bun.

She'd dared to peer inside the windows of the white van parked outside the hotel but there was no one sat behind the wheel. Her heart was a jackhammer in her chest as she hurried past it and continued down the street.

'Are you sure it can't be traced?'

'Certain.' Amanda was focused on her computer, but Shane kept sending furtive glances around the café.

'But what if someone sees?'

'No one will see.'

'How do you know?'

'I know.'

Amanda's fingertips pounded her keyboard. She knew what she was looking for and exactly where to find it. Once again she was trawling the murky depths of the darknet. She'd found an online store that specialised in guns and promised untraceable transactions.

'What about the payment?' Shane lifted his coffee to his lips, there was a slight tremor which ran through his hands. 'They'll be able to trace that.'

'No, they won't.'

'They will.'

'No, Shane, they won't,' she raised her head to frown at him. 'I'm paying in bitcoin.'

'In bits of coin?'

'No, *bitcoin*,' Amanda stiffly corrected him, taking care to keep her voice low. 'It's a digital currency used online. Completely untraceable.'

'A digital currency?'

'I invested in a couple of hundred a few years ago when bitcoins were first launched. They've more than doubled in value since then.'

'Really?'

'One day there will be just one global currency and it will probably be bitcoin, or another incarnation of something very similar.' Amanda enjoyed prophesising about the future when it came to technology.

'So you're paying with this… bitcoin?'

'Uh-huh.'

'And delivery? Will someone hand it to you down a back alley in a brown paper bag?'

'Hardly,' Amanda rolled her eyes. 'For a cop you're not all that switched on, you know,' she added teasingly.

'I'm in homicide, not weapon and drugs trafficking.'

'Good job,' Amanda cracked a smile, 'because you'd be wasting a lot of resources with all your back-alley monitoring.'

'Fine, so how does it work?' He placed his drink down and roughly shook his head. 'Actually, no, I don't want to know.'

'Okay.'

'But it will be delivered?'

'That sounds like you want to know.'

Shane clenched his jaw. 'Fine. Tell me.'

'It's all about PO boxes these days.' Amanda's gaze danced across the screen. Her transaction was almost complete.

'A PO box. Right.'

'So I'll just finish my order and—'

'Let me see,' Shane dragged his chair around to the other side of the table. He swallowed as he looked at the purchase Amanda was about to make.

A 9mm pistol. Silver. It was apparently 'light and easy to use.' Ammunition supplied.

'You, um…' he awkwardly stabbed his finger at the screen.

'What?'

'You need a silencer.'

He was so close that Amanda could feel his leg pressed up against her own. She watched him out of the corner of her eye, 'A silencer?'

'Yeah,' Shane coughed nervously and pulled the laptop closer to them. 'However you plan to use this, it'll be better if it doesn't make a sound, trust me.'

'You're suddenly awfully knowledgeable.'

'In my job you get to understand the way a killer's mind works,' he said grimly. 'When it happens, you want it to be fast, quiet and clean. When it comes to murder, that's the holy trinity that everyone is aspiring to.'

'Shane?' Amanda saw a shadow pass over his face, hardening his features.

'I'm essentially helping you commit murder.' He dragged a hand down his face. For a moment he looked completely lost. 'Everything I stood for. Everything I worked for. I'm flying directly in the face of it for… for you.'

'I know,' Amanda said softly, chewing her lip and watching him. He looked so young bathed in the glow of the laptop. But the deep lines around his eyes, the creases in his forehead, were evidence enough that he was no longer the boy who she played with on the beach.

'I'm risking it all for you,' he was starting to sound annoyed. 'Does that make me a fool?'

'No.'

Shane just stared at the laptop. 'I fear that it does.'

*

A day. That's how long Amanda needed to wait for her darknet purchase to be delivered. It was going to be left in a PO box near Glasgow train station.

'You shouldn't come,' she'd decided this as soon as her acknowledgement email had come through. Shane was watching the news, his back to her as she sat on the bed wedged up against a mound of pillows, her laptop resting on her upper thighs.

'Of course I'm coming.' Shane didn't turn around.

'No, you shouldn't. In case something does go sour. I don't want you getting implicated in this.'

'I think I'm already pretty implicated, don't you?'

'Shane—'

He swivelled around, momentarily ignoring the stern-faced man on the television delivering the evening news. 'You jump I jump, remember?'

'No,' Amanda closed her laptop with an angry flourish as laughter tumbled out of her, as brilliant in clarity as the jangling of silver bells. 'You...' she pressed a hand to her chest. Laughing hurt. Almost as much as sneezing did. It forced her swollen, aching muscles to work much more than they'd currently like to. 'Shane, you can't quote *Titanic* at me about this.'

'Why not? You used to love that film. Do you remember when you made me hold you up on that rock on the beach pretending we were on the bow of the ship?'

'Ha, yeah, I remember.'

'John called us sad and sulked off.'

'I think he was starting to feel a bit like a third wheel at that point.' Amanda lowered her hand, her laughter subsiding.

'Jokes aside, the sentiment is there, Amanda. We're in this together, there's no going back now. Tomorrow, we'll both go and collect your... delivery. Okay?'

'He dies.'

'What?'

'At the end of *Titanic*, Jack dies. Even when they both jump, they don't both make it.'

'Amanda,' Shane reached for her leg and placed his hand on it. 'It's just a movie. And together, we're going to be fine, I promise. We're not on a sinking ship.'

Sinking deeper into her pillows, Amanda eyed him warily. 'Aren't we?'

*

The next morning brought rain and lots of it. It bounced off the pavement and ran in rivers along the gutter. Amanda walked arm in arm with Shane, their heads bowed against the watery onslaught from above.

'We could call an Uber,' Shane had suggested when he opened the curtains and saw the leaden sky outside.

'No. There can be no record of our going to the station today. We have to walk. Heads down to avoid any CCTV cameras.'

The bottom of Amanda's joggers were already soaked through. Her shoes squelched with every step. But they were nearly there.

She'd clocked the van when she left the hotel. It stood faceless and passive, and yet its presence felt like the sword of Damocles over her head.

'It's weird how it's always there, don't you think?' She tucked in close to Shane and edged his attention in the direction of the van.

'It's just a white van, Amanda. They are all over the city.'

'But it's *always* there.'

'Maybe they work in the hotel.'

'Then why not use the car park like everyone else?'

Shane shrugged and kept walking, head bowed against the rain. Amanda glanced back at the van and wondered if she was slipping into some strange state of paranoia. Maybe it was just a van. And maybe she was going crazy with worry, maddened by always having to check over her shoulder, always having to fear what lurked in the shadows.

People hurried all around them, huddled beneath umbrellas. Rainwater had been walked into the station, streaking the floor with damp, muddied stains. Amanda pulled down her hood and shook herself off.

'I'm at least buying an umbrella,' Shane started stalking towards a nearby shop. 'It's pouring it down out there and I'm not getting soaked a second time.'

Amanda waited, suddenly feeling awfully superfluous to the flow of activity going on around her. People craned their necks at the arrivals screens, shook off their overloaded umbrellas and fired off swift messages on their phones. No one was looking at her. No one was staring at her as if they knew the real reason she was there – that she had no train to catch. No one noticed her at all.

'Okay,' Shane returned, brandishing a long black umbrella. 'So where now?'

Amanda was reluctant to keep going. She felt weighted with anxiety. Her stomach churned like the time she'd scrambled up into the attic of the cottage to cop a feel of her freshly wrapped Christmas presents. At the time, she'd known that she shouldn't have been there, her heart kept an anxious beat as she scurried around, pawing at all the brightly coloured items.

'Come on,' Shane took her hand and helped her feet remember how to move. She numbly let him lead her deeper into the station. 'This is where we need to be, right?'

Six rows of PO boxes, neatly stacked together like lockers at a public swimming pool. Amanda thrust her hands deep into her pockets. She was about to steal fire from the Gods – about to do something which could have dire consequences for everyone she knew. Everyone she loved.

'Just go,' she hissed at Shane through clenched teeth. 'I've got this.'

'I'm not going anywhere.' He stubbornly remained at her side.

'Fine.'

They were taking too long. If anyone was watching them, keeping an eye out for strange behaviour, then they were surely ticking every box. Amanda pushed her shoulders back and tried to appear nonchalant as she approached the second row of boxes.

'She said it was 218,' she spoke loudly, confidently. Like she was just picking up a package which had been shipped over from a distant cousin.

'218, that's here.' Shane found the right box faster than Amanda would have liked. He hovered beside it, hopping from foot to foot, restless.

'Oh, right, thanks honey,' Amanda gave him a saccharine smile, doing her best to keep up some sort of charade of normalcy. She approached the keypad and punched in the number that had been emailed to her. She almost didn't want it to work. As she pressed in the final 4 she held her breath. There was a bright chirp of confirmation and then the small metal door swung open. Amanda had to force herself to look inside. She half expected thousands of bullets to suddenly pour out, to pool at her feet as every security guard in the vicinity came running over, drawn to her illegal activity.

But nothing bounced against the floor. Inside there was a simple square package in a cardboard box. It looked completely unassuming, like a regular Amazon order.

'Is that it?' Shane was peering in along with her.

'I guess so.' Amanda was about to reach in and grab it, but Shane beat her to it. He retrieved the box and didn't dwell on its details. He just clamped it at his side and gave Amanda a curt nod.

'Okay, then, let's get going. Lucky I bought this umbrella.'

He was being so calm. Amanda wanted to take the package, shoulder her fair share of the burden, but she knew he wouldn't have it, and she couldn't risk rousing suspicion by fighting with him over it. Remaining cool and composed, Amanda closed the PO box and, arm in arm with Shane, she began to drift back towards the exit of the train station. Her heart was beating so loud that it was deafening.

Up in the attic of her mother's cottage no one had caught her as she sat amongst the dust and cobwebs feeling the hidden stash of Christmas presents. Amanda must have sat up there for almost an hour, merrily trying to decipher what her gifts were simply based on size and shape. Clothes were always a disappointment – light and flat. But a box, that always caught Amanda's attention. Especially a heavy one. When she finally climbed down from the attic there was more than just dust that clung to her though. Guilt dug into her pores. Whilst her parents were out shopping she'd betrayed their trust. Amanda considering leaving the panel to the attic ajar, leaving a clue about her dalliances. She wanted to get caught, to be berated for going up there. It would surely help remove some of the guilt. She closed the hatch, leaving it looking exactly the way it had before she went up into the attic. Her parents never figured out what she'd done and on Christmas morning she'd been suitably surprised by her array of presents to keep her secret safe. But the guilt never left. Amanda just learned how to wear it.

21

The package looked so innocuous sat in the middle of the bed. Amanda stood chewing her nails as she regarded it. She scanned every edge, every corner, not daring to take her eyes off it for a second as though it were a bomb that could go off at any moment.

'Are you going to open it?' Shane was standing beside her, equally reluctant to be in too close proximity to the box.

'Do you think I should?'

'At some point, yes.' Then he sighed. 'Although in an ideal world you'd just throw the bloody thing away and we'd be done with all this mess.'

Amanda shuffled away from him. She headed for the plastic bag full of items she'd hastily grabbed at the chemist on their way back. Rummaging in its depths, she pulled out the multipack of disposable gloves and carefully snapped on a pair. Amanda returned to the foot of the bed and steeled herself with a deep breath.

'Right.' She leaned forward and, slowly, carefully, reached for the package. It was heavy. It felt like it contained a pair of really expensive shoes or several DVD boxsets. She plucked the tape that sealed the box loose and then lifted its lid. The gun was nestled in a medley of styrofoam balls. There was no purchase receipt, no label for a return. Just the weapon. Amanda closed her fingers around the gun's hilt and withdrew it from the box. It was heavy. She quickly had to share its weight between both her hands.

'Where's the silencer?' Shane remained focused on the box. He pulled on a pair of bright blue disposable gloves before rooting through the aerated balls. 'Here,' he pulled out a short black cylinder. 'This attaches to the barrel.'

The gun was resting in Amanda's palms. She offered it to Shane, relieved when he took it from her, easing her burden. He twisted the silencer into place, then he checked the gun's magazine and whether the safety was in place.

'You really know what you're doing,' Amanda noted as she watched him. She'd cradled the gun like it was a grenade whilst Shane was now holding it at arm's length, looking down its barrel.

'I've held a gun before.' He turned the weapon over, checking both its side.

'I haven't.'

Shane stopped, his arms stiff and extended. 'You haven't?'

'No,' Amanda could feel her cheeks getting hot. 'When would I have?'

Shane smoothly placed his hand around the barrel of the gun and offered the hilt towards Amanda. She stepped back, suddenly unwilling to take it.

The curtains in the room were drawn and all of the lamps were on, filling everywhere with garish yellow light. Amanda suddenly felt the brightness burning against her eyes. She shielded herself with her arm, feeling like a mole that had been forced out into the baking sun.

'If you're serious about this then the first step is learning how to hold the damned thing,' Shane offered it towards her again. He held it with such confidence. There was no tremor in his hands, no sweat upon his brow.

Amanda felt her chest start to tighten. When Will had aimed his gun at her, his body had been just as stoic, like all his limbs had been cast in stone. He didn't even flinch when he turned the barrel of the gun towards his wife.

Amanda lowered herself against the end of the bed, a hand against her chest. She couldn't breathe. When had Will learned to manage a gun? Was it during all the years he lived in Glasgow? Was it just another thread to add to the growing ball of yarn that was all his lies?

She remembered how it felt when McAllister wedged the tip of his gun against the back of her head. It was like someone had dropped ice down her spine making everything go numb. Twice someone had held a gun at her. And now... now she was supposed to become the thing which she was trying to vanquish. A murderer. A monster.

'You're having a panic attack.'

Amanda heard the rustle of paper as Shane placed a brown bag into her hands.

'Breathe into this. Slow and steady. In and out. Okay?'

Amanda breathed.

In.

Out.

Had Will sourced his gun on the darknet or through an old prison contact? Did it even matter?

In.

Out.

The pain in her chest eased. Amanda lowered the bag from her mouth and looked at Shane. Her face felt hot and blotchy. She noticed that his hands were empty. Where was the gun? Before she could spin around in a panic, he rested his hands on her shoulders and looked deep into her eyes.

'It's back in the box. With the safety on. It's fine. Amanda, I need you to calm down, okay? Just keep breathing nice and slow.'

'I can't do this,' she looked down forlornly at the crumpled bag in her hands. 'I can't kill someone.'

*

'Why are we here?'

The hotel's gym stank of old sweat. It was late in the evening and all of the equipment was empty and unused. Amanda ran her clammy palms down the front of her T-shirt. The short sleeves exposed the dark bruises that ran up her arms like a Jackson Pollock style tattoo. Her hair was pulled back from her face in a high ponytail.

Shane had insisted that she spend the afternoon resting. Somehow she'd managed to fall asleep in the same room as the gun, to forget about it altogether. And it was still up there, locked away in the hotel room's small safe. While they were down in the gym. Amanda folded her arms against her chest and looked over at Shane, waiting on a response.

'You need to get your strength back.' He scanned the various pieces of equipment and then led Amanda over to a punchbag. He wore a skintight T-shirt and loose-fitting joggers. He looked sculpted, sleek, his hair still tousled from when he'd lay in bed beside Amanda while she slept, gently reassuring her whenever she got trapped in a nightmare and twitched and whimpered.

'Right now, you're afraid,' Shane told her. 'Will broke your trust, McAllister tried to kill you. You've got so much to be afraid of. But you've never been the kind of woman to give into fear.' He punched the bag once, directly in its centre. The hook which it hung from shuddered. 'Find your strength again and the fear will ease.' He stepped back from the punchbag and nodded. 'You try it.'

Amanda lamely bundled her fingers into a fist, ignoring the persistent ache in her joints and smacked the punchbag. It stayed rigidly in place.

'Again.'

She smacked it. It stayed in place.

'Again.'

'Look, Shane…' With a sigh she stepped back from the punchbag. Why did she need to bother learning how to throw a punch if she had a gun? Surely that was the entire point of such a weapon – to eliminate the need for physical prowess? 'This is all pointless.'

'He threw you off a cliff.'

She froze.

'He knew that if the fall didn't kill you the trauma of it would scramble what remained of your sanity, fuck you up beyond repair. Did it make you think of your dad?'

Tears gathered behind her eyes – her knee-jerk reaction whenever she thought of her beloved father.

'He wouldn't have let you fall, but you did. And Amanda – you survived. You never needed a knight in shining armour to come riding up, not when you were capable of saving yourself all along. You're your own hero. You don't need to hold onto your dad like you do.'

'He saved me,' Amanda said through gritted teeth.

'You saved *yourself.*'

She could feel her chest getting tight again.

'If your dad was still around, if Will was still around, they'd come railroading in to save you. But I'm not them, Amanda. You told me that you wanted to do this, that you wanted to save yourself so I'm going to let you. Prove to me you can do it.'

'Shane—'

'He threw you off a cliff!' Shane was shouting now. 'Will lied to you. About who he was, about what he'd done. He had a *wife*, Amanda. And a *son*. What does that make you?'

She hit the punchbag. She hit it with everything she had. She put all her pain, all her frustration, behind her arm and then let her fist smack against the smooth exterior. Then she did it again. And again. She kept punching the bag, making tiny jabs in its centre. Its hanging hook started to quiver and she didn't stop she just kept pounding its exterior, trying to beat her way through to its core. Her knuckles burned and sweat poured down her forehead and onto her neck.

'Okay, okay,' Shane grabbed the bag, holding it in place as Amanda lunged at it a few more times. 'I think we're done.'

Gasping, she stepped back and dropped her hands to her knees.

'Did that feel good?' Shane was standing over her, offering her a towel.

Amanda straightened and swept the back of her hand across her brow. She didn't take the towel. 'You're right,' she was struggling to catch her breath. 'You're not like Will. Or my dad. They'd have never pushed me like that.' She moved away from him and started heading towards the door, eager to return to her room and just drop against the soft bed.

'You needed pushing,' she heard Shane shout after her as she stormed off.

*

Amanda needed space. The hotel room was starting to feel too small, the gun's presence within it too big. Even locked away in the safe, Amanda was acutely aware of it. It was the giant elephant in the room which she had to get away from. Pulling on a hoody and her sunglasses, Amanda grabbed her laptop, tucked it under her arm and dashed out before Shane could catch up with her and talk her out of leaving.

It was quiet in the nearby café. The oaky aroma of coffee enveloped Amanda in a warm embrace as she stepped inside. After ordering a latte she headed over to a booth on the back wall and opened up her computer. She'd always been soothed by technology. As her fingers glided over the keyboard and typed in her access details, the tension in her chest eased away completely.

Whenever Amanda logged onto the Internet it felt like diving into the ocean. The wealth of information at her fingertips was fast, verging on limitless. And if she swam around enough and explored who knew what treasures she might discover?

The laptop beeped with a notification. Amanda instinctively opened up the relevant box and immediately stiffened in her seat. Numerous messages had been sent to her darknet account, all from Turtle82. Amanda nudged away her coffee, losing her desire for it. Her tongue felt too large in her mouth like it had turned into a sponge which had absorbed all the moisture in her body.

She couldn't risk opening Turtle's messages. It would be an indication that she was alive and something told Amanda that she couldn't trust Turtle, not anymore. She ran a few programmes which would enable her to open up the messages undetected.

How did it go? Waiting on data transfer from you.
　　T.

It's been days. What's happened to you??
　　T.

I'm starting to fear the worst. Did you catch the
Carp or was it the other way around? Either way
I'm going to have to go dark on here, it's too big a
risk. Carps have a tendency of biting back.

Thanks for your help, Lambchop. Did you see the
list? The names? My sister is on there.
　　Hope you're safe.
　　T.

Amanda deleted the messages. Then her history. Turtle
almost seemed concerned in their correspondence, but she had
to read between the lines. Maybe Turtle's sister truly was
named on that awful list, maybe this entire mission had been
concocted so that they could get some vengeance of their own.
But there was still the possibility that it had all been a set-up,
that Turtle knew McAllister and was feeding information back
to him. Amanda wanted to believe that their desire to bring
down McAllister had been fuelled by a pain as raw as her own.
But belief was dangerous, now more than ever.

Frustration made Amanda feel restless. If only she'd found
the USB stick. Then she'd have a way to put McAllister away.

She thought of the gun, locked away in the safe. Sleek and
silver. She did have a way to end McAllister. A very permanent
way.

'There you are,' Shane burst over to the booth, setting down across from her. His words were like shrapnel, embedding themselves in Amanda and agitating old wounds. 'I've been worried sick, looking everywhere. You really scared me.'

'I just needed some space.' She felt like a sullen teenager who'd been caught trying to sneak out of the house.

'S-space? Seriously?' Shane stuttered over the words.

'I do need to save myself.' Amanda chewed her lip and continued to stare at her laptop. What pained her the most was that Shane was right. Both Will and her father had always been so quick to jump to her defence when really they needed to teach her to fight for herself. And she intended to fight. If McAllister lived then Amanda had to remain a ghost. She was ready to do what Will should have done years ago – to bring the monster down once and for all.

'It's dangerous to just be walking around the city on your own.' On his frantic walk from the hotel to the café, Shane had seemingly gone past annoyed and reached angry. His cheeks were red, his forehead damp with a sheen of sweat. 'What the hell are you playing at, Amanda?'

'You need to teach me how to use it.' She closed her laptop and stared at him.

'What?'

'You know what.'

'Amanda—'

'I have to save myself and I can't do that if I'm having a panic attack every time I'm around it.'

Shane dragged his hands through his hair and didn't meet her gaze.

'I can do this,' Amanda drank in a deep, calm breath. 'When I was thrown off the cliff I managed to get to the shore. I saved myself. I can do it again. I'm strong enough.'

'I've never doubted your strength.' Shane dropped his hands but still didn't look at her. 'It's mine that I question.'

'What do you mean?'

'It's already gone this far,' Shane squirmed uncomfortably in his seat. 'I let you come here. I let you go alone into the dragon's lair and look...' he gestured towards her and then rubbed at his eyes. 'I should never have let you go,' his voice dropped to a whisper.

'Shane, I had to go. It was my only chance to get access to his computer, you know that.'

'I didn't mean then. I should,' he leaned back, stretching his long legs out beneath the table, 'I should never have let you go. Not ever. If I'd just listened to my heart instead of my head.' His eyes were misted when he finally looked at her, causing their brilliant green to shimmer with sadness.

'Shane—'

He got up so abruptly that Amanda tensed in surprise. He powered over towards the counter and ordered himself a large coffee which he drank in silence as they walked down darkened streets back towards their hotel.

*

Amanda was freshly showered as Shane helped her get into bed. Her hair was braided down her back and slightly damp. But she needed sleep. Snuggled up in her comfortable new pyjamas, her joints were already turning to wood, keen to heavily drop against the mattress and be swaddled by the duvet.

At night her wounds sung their painful symphony much louder than they did in the day. The shoulder which had been dislocated would throb and the skin around it would burn.

'I'm like an old woman,' Amanda joked as she dropped into bed, her head blissfully sinking into the mound of pillows.

'A very sexy old woman.' Shane offered a crooked smile. Once she was all tucked up he drifted back to his side of the bed and turned the TV on, keeping the volume low.

'You've used a gun before, right?' Amanda sleepily rolled onto her side to face him.

'Yeah.'

'In training?'

'Yeah, in training,' Shane nodded and kept watching the television.

'Have you ever,' Amanda nuzzled against the soft pillows, 'you know, shot someone?'

'No.' His jaw clenched. 'But I know people who have.'

'Did they say what it was like?'

He nodded. The movement so slight that for a moment Amanda thought she might have imagined it.

'And?' she pressed as she tried to pull herself back from the cusp of sleep. But she was drifting, her body already giving way to the blissful warmth all around her. Her eyelids had become metal shutters, keen to close for the day and not open up again until morning.

'What do you want to know?' he sharply turned to her, his eyes ablaze. 'It *changes* people, Amanda. At least the good ones. I've dealt with death enough to know a killer when I see one. It's as if, when you take someone else's life, a part of yourself just checks out.'

'And you think that'll happen to me?'

'I think killing someone, being the one who pulls the trigger, is a lot harder than either of us can imagine.'

'If it changes me, will you still care about me?' Amanda's mouth opened wide as she yawned. Her eyes closed. 'I want to change,' she muttered dreamily. 'I want to go back to being the girl on the beach by the bonfire. I want to go back to believing in forever.' As she drifted off to sleep, she didn't see Shane looking over at her, his eyes filled with pain and longing.

'I never stopped believing in forever,' he whispered before turning off the television and lying down on his back beside her, letting the darkness of the room seep in around them.

22

'So where are we going again?' Amanda turned to look at Shane. His attention was focused on the road ahead as he drove them out of the city.

'I told you,' he came to a stop at some traffic lights, 'it's a surprise.'

The rain had moved on. Deep puddles lingered in dips in the road but the sun would soon devour them. The sky was blue and cloudless. It was going to be a beautiful day.

'What sort of surprise?' Amanda fidgeted against her seat belt. It was already digging in too tightly to her sore ribs.

'The sort that requires patience.'

The lights turned amber and then green.

'I hate surprises.'

Amanda had felt unsettled since Shane had mentioned that they were going out. He'd been cryptic about plans, just telling her that they were going somewhere and that she should be prepared for a relatively long drive.

'That's true, you have always hated surprises,' Shane agreed.

'Then why spring one on me now?' Amanda was watching him, studying every twitch in his clenched jaw, trying to read his expression like a map which would lead her to her answer.

'Because—'

Amanda's phone started to ring. They both glanced over at the front pocket of her hooded jumper where she'd stuffed it before leaving the hotel.

'Are you going to get that?' Shane had to force his gaze back onto the road.

'Uh.' Amanda fumbled in her large pocket. Her stomach tightened in on itself. Bile was creeping up her throat as she pulled out her phone. A thousand panicked questions jumped up in her mind.

What if it was McAllister?

What if he'd found her?

What would he do now he knew that she was alive?

She'd transferred all calls to her old phone to this new one, but what if that'd been a mistake made in haste?

The questions died down when Amanda saw the familiar number on the display screen.

'Hey, Mum,' she said as she drew the phone up to her, exhaling shakily.

'Amanda.' Corrine breathed out her daughter's name. She sounded deflated.

'Mum, are you okay?' It was morning which meant late night in Last Vegas. Her Mum shouldn't be calling at such an hour. Unless there was something wrong.

'I'm…' there was a long pause. 'I'm tired. He keeps calling for her in the night.'

'Who?'

'Ewan. For his *mother.* He's like a little candle. All day he burns so bright but I fear there won't be much left of him soon. He's unsettled, Amanda. As any little boy in his situation would be.'

Amanda closed her eyes, pushing away the surrounding scenery as the car drifted out of the city.

'Some days he has no appetite and others he eats like a little wolf. He's depressed, confused. Maybe I should take him to see Dr. Townsend?'

'Mum—'

'And he hears voices,' Corrine lowered her voice as though sharing a secret. 'At night. When he's not calling out for his mother he says he hears voices in the garden, below his window.'

Amanda's eyes flew open and she surged forward, clutching the phone tightly and straining against her seat belt. 'He's hearing *voices*?'

'I mean, obviously he's dreaming,' Corrine was sighing, Amanda could imagine her clutching a small sherry in her free hand, trying to calm her jangled nerves.

'Yes,' Amanda agreed tightly though she wasn't convinced.

'So should I take him to see the GP?'

'No. Wait.'

Wait until I've killed the man who might be responsible for those voices. Wait until I'm home and that Ewan is completely safe.

'Is there any chance you could get an earlier flight back? I know there's only four more nights left of your holiday, but he's… he's lost and I don't think I know how to help him find his way.'

'Mum—'

'He keeps asking after you and Shane.' Corrine released a deep sigh. 'And his father.'

'I get that he's a bit scared and unsettled—'

'He's a smart boy. All the toys in the world can't distract him from what's really going on. He thinks that you aren't coming back. He thinks that everyone has abandoned him.'

'That's not true.' Amanda's voice caught in her throat. Abandoning Ewan was the last thing she was doing. She was out here *for* him. To protect him indefinitely. The accusation of abandoning the boy felt like her mother had slammed her into a brick wall.

'But he needs to *see* that.'

'Tell him that there's only four more nights and then I'll be back.' Amanda clutched at her stomach. It constricted painfully as she told what could very well be a lie. If things went south with McAllister then she wouldn't be coming back at all.

'You really can't get an earlier flight?' Corrine pleaded. 'He seems so fond of you, Amanda. Seeing you would really lift his spirits, I know it would.'

'I'm…' the truth was a grenade which would destroy everything.

I'm not done here. I still need to murder the man who had my husband hunted down and killed.

'I'll see what I can do, but don't go promising him anything, Mum. Changing flights can be expensive and I'm not sure I can afford it. It's only four more nights.'

'What do I do?' Corrine whispered. 'When he wakes in the night screaming out for his mother? How do I answer his cries?'

'Tell him…' Amanda pulled at a loose thread on her joggers. 'Tell him that his mother is gone but can still hear him. And that Shane and I will soon be back.'

'He'll make me promise.'

'Then promise.'

'Because you are coming back, Amanda. Aren't you?' the doubt in her mother's voice stabbed at Amanda like a knife. She could feel tears clotting beneath her eyes.

'Of course,' she assured Corrine hoarsely. 'God, Mum, of course I'm coming back. I'm not just going to abandon that poor little boy.'

'It's just that you've been through such a lot and you didn't ask to be a mother but the role has been thrust upon you. And Will, you must be dealing with that. I wouldn't blame you for wanting to just run away from it all.'

'Is that what you'd want to do? Run?' Amanda felt oddly defensive of her actions. She wasn't running. She wasn't fleeing from her responsibilities she was fighting. Fighting to give both her and Ewan a safe, secure future.

'I never ran,' Corrine said coolly. 'No matter how bad things got, Amanda, I never ran.'

'But did you want to?' Amanda challenged.

'No. Running only gives you distance, not closure.'

'Mum, I'm not...' The car started to twist down country lines which cut a line through the rolling hills of heather. 'I'm not running. I hope you know that.'

'I know that because you're coming back. Right?'

'Right.'

'Promise me.'

'Mum?'

'I'm going to have to promise *him*, so perhaps you could do me the courtesy of promising *me*.'

'I'm coming home, Mum. I promise.' Amanda hoped with every fibre of her being that this wouldn't turn out to be a lie.

'Good, because I'm going to hold you to that,' Corrine's voice was losing its edges.

'You do that.'

'Four more nights?'

'Four more nights and I'll be home.'

'I hope you're having fun out there, Amanda.'

'Yeah,' Amanda deadpanned, 'tonnes.'

They drove for just over an hour. They seemed to have followed the rain as when Shane pulled off the road onto a gravel car park the ocean of blue sky overhead had been replaced by pewter clouds.

'So,' Amanda climbed out of the car and looked around, 'my surprise is a drive out to some remote field? Awesome.'

'Not just any field.' Shane moved around to the back of the car and opened the boot. The sound of the lock releasing unnerved Amanda. She felt like she'd suddenly slipped and was falling. Her hands reached out and caught the car door just in time to help her stay on her feet. Shane didn't notice. He was too busy taking something out of the boot. 'This is a shooting range. I found it online. Looks like it's barely used these days.'

He moved away from the car with the box in his hands. Amanda's knees buckled and she flailed against the car.

'You brought…' she could barely form her words, 'the *gun*? You brought the bloody gun out here?' The whole time they'd been driving it had been stashed away in the boot, silent and deadly.

'Amanda—'

'*This* is my surprise?'

'You need to focus,' he thrust the box into her hands. 'You're the one who was so determined to do this but you can barely be around the thing without falling apart. How are you going to compose yourself to actually use it?'

Amanda's hands trembled against the box.

'You can't give in to your fear. I'm not trying to be cruel, I'm trying to help you get some clarity. Come on.' Shane strode off, the gravel crunching underfoot as he moved beyond the small car park to a cluster of trees. Amanda felt obliged to follow, the weight of the box unpleasantly heavy in her hands.

There was a clearing at the heart of the trees in which four straw torsos were arranged on wooden poles.

'The website said that the TA uses this site but only on weekends,' Shane explained factually, like he were a tour guide in a museum.

Amanda looked at the four effigies. They lacked heads or arms. Their bodies were just tightly packed straw held together by string.

'I'm going to teach you how to load, aim, and fire. You got it?' Shane relieved her of the box and pulled some disposable gloves from his back pocket before opening it up. 'This is your safety, your magazine,' he handed a pair of gloves to Amanda before permitting her to take a closer look. 'And of course the trigger.'

The surface of the gun was polished. Someone had taken great care in its manufacture.

'Hold it,' Shane offered her the gun.

Amanda felt her body trying to pull back, like a magnet being repelled, but she fought against the reaction. Clenching her teeth together, Shane raised her hands and closed them around the hilt of the gun. He released the barrel.

'Now, aim it.'

Amanda used both hands to keep it level and steady. She turned towards the quartet of straw bodies positioned some ten feet away.

'Just hold it for a bit, get used to the weight.'

Her upper arms throbbed but Amanda remained stoic in her stance.

'Okay, that's it. You're doing great.' Shane came in close, checked the line of her arms, and lowered her shoulders. 'Now, when you're comfortable,' he stood at her side, 'shoot the far left one in the chest.'

Amanda's finger found the trigger as she carefully manoeuvred herself to face the far left torso. Her palms were damp and she felt unbearably cold, like her teeth could start chattering at any second.

'You need to squeeze the trigger but really commit to it once you do. The safety is off. Give it a shot.'

Her mouth was so dry. Amanda kept the gun steady, pulled against the trigger. When she pulled, a force was unleashed from within the gun which made her stagger backwards. It happened so fast that for a second she didn't trust her senses. The only sound was the snapping of straw as the bullet connected with the torso's upper right shoulder.

'Christ,' she looked down at the gun which remained in her hands.

'It definitely packs a punch,' Shane commented. 'Now, go again. This time really focus on hitting the target directly in the chest.'

Amanda fired off four more shots. None of them landed in the centre of the straw torso. They were always a couple of inches shy of the mark.

'I keep missing.'

'A good aim takes years to perfect,' Shane massaged her shoulders which were now aching. Each time Amanda squeezed on the trigger she felt the power of the shot cross over into her and echo into her bones. 'You'll get there.'

'I don't have time to get there.' Amanda handed Shane the gun and snapped off her gloves in frustration. She walked over to the four torsos, drawing up close so that she could survey the damage she'd caused. 'Four more nights,' she shouted over her shoulder. 'That's all we have left. Then we have to go back,' her fingers explored the fibres of straw which had come loose. Softer, as if sharing a secret with the dummy torso, she muttered, 'Ewan is expecting me. He needs me.'

'Well, we can't come back here tomorrow as it's Saturday.'

Amanda wasn't listening. She circled the torso, stalking it. She suddenly felt predatory, like a cat that had just noticed the sparrow sitting quietly on the garden fence. She made her fingers into the shape of a crude gun and poked at the straw. It would be hard to miss a shot from such a distance. In fact it would be impossible.

'So do you want to practise some more now?' Shane was trying to get her attention.

Amanda prodded the torso again. Jabbed it sharply in the centre of its straw chest, right where its barley heart would be. If she couldn't shoot accurately from a distance then what she needed to do was eliminate the distance completely. But how was she ever going to get close enough to McAllister to shoot him at point-blank range?

*

'I should have killed him when I had the chance.' Amanda had felt tormented the entire drive back into the city.

'And what, got yourself killed in the process?'

'I should have stabbed him or just clawed his bloody eyes out with my bare hands.' She surprised herself with her vitriol but she was mad. Verging on furious. Each time it felt like she had McAllister within her grasp he managed to slither just out of reach.

'If this is about the shooting, then I can do it.'

'No,' she turned down Shane's offer for the fourth time. 'I have to do it.'

'Amanda—'

'This is about me being my own hero, remember?'

'Yes, but I'm not about to let you get yourself killed.'

'I won't, I'll be fine.' Amanda sounded so convincing that she almost managed to fool herself.

'We can practise some more. We can—'

Amanda groaned as she cradled her left arm against her chest.

'Do you ache?'

'Uh-huh. A lot.'

'We probably overdid it a bit today. Pushed you too hard. I'll run you a bath as soon as we're back at the hotel.'

'A bath?' Amanda's sagged in her seat as she imagined the blissful sensation of warm bubbles caressing every inch of her sore body.

Once they returned to the hotel Shane was as good as his word. He ran Amanda a hot bath and set about ordering room service, leaving her to enjoy its fragrant warmth. It felt good to settle down amongst the bubbles. The heat massaged all her aches, helping them fade away. Amanda closed her eyes, loving how her whole body tingled with delight.

*

'I ran you a bath.'

Amanda had just burst in through the front door. She still had sweat pouring down her forehead and clinging to her cold skin. There was still ice on the cars outside. The tip of her nose had turned into a cherry.

'You what?' she gasped, trying to get her breath back.

'While you were out jogging, I ran you a bath.' Will was sat in the living room in the middle of the sofa, carefully working his way through the newspaper he was holding.

'Oh, wow.' Amanda swept the back of her hand across her slick brow. 'You didn't have to do that.'

'I figured you might want a bath when you got back.'

'You figured right.' Amanda eagerly kicked off her trainers. She raced for the stairs and then doubled back, peering into the living room. 'You know, I could get used to this being married lark. I mean, are there other perks besides freshly run baths?'

'Oh,' Will turned to flash her a suggestive grin, 'there are lots of perks. Just you wait and see.'

'Maybe…' Amanda flirtatiously lifted up the hem of her T-shirt, giving Will a flash of her pale stomach, 'you could join me, if you like?'

Will abandoned his paper as though the pages had suddenly set on fire.

*

Amanda slowly opened her eyes. The water around her had grown cold and the bubbles were all flat. Her joints creaked like rusted pipes as she carefully manoeuvred herself out of the bath. The lingering steam provided little warmth so she hurriedly bundled herself into the nearest towel. She gazed at the flat surface of the water.

'Hey,' behind her the door opened. 'You were taking a while so I thought I'd check in on you,' Shane explained apologetically, already retreating when he noticed that Amanda had successfully got out of the bath on her own.

'He's everywhere.'

'What?' Shane pushed the door open a bit further, looking confused.

'Will.' Amanda wilted as she dropped down onto the toilet lid. 'There are memories of him *everywhere*. Even,' she gestured at the water with a limp hand, 'having a bath reminds me of him. He's everywhere. How am I supposed to deal with that?'

Shane opened the door fully and came and knelt beside her. He brushed his fingers down her damp cheek. 'I wish I knew the answer, Amanda. I guess that, in time, it will get easier.'

'Will it be worse when we go back, when I'm in my home? The home we shared? I don't know if I can handle seeing him everywhere all the time. I feel... guilty. Like if I hadn't chased after him he might still be alive. Along with Evangeline.' She dabbed at her eyes with the corner of the towel.

'I'll be right there with you. Whatever you go through, I'll be by your side to get you through it.'

'What if—' she choked on a sob. 'What if my mum is right? What if I am running?'

'Amanda, you're not running.'

'Maybe that's why I'm so determined to face McAllister, because deep down I don't want to go back.'

'Don't say that.'

'Am I running?' Amanda asked tearfully.

'You're not running.' Shane cradled her cheeks with his warm hands. 'You told me that you didn't want to run, that you didn't want to live like a ghost. You're here because you're fighting for your future, Amanda.' Then he added, hopefully, 'For *our* future.'

'I can't shoot him from a distance' Amanda dropped her chin, unable to meet Shane's gaze.

'Then don't. You'll shoot the fucker in his sleep if you have to.'

'I need to find a way to be alone with him. Some place where he can't call for help or get away.'

'Look, just let me do it, Amanda. Let me kill him.'

'No,' the word shot from Amanda like a bullet. 'This is on me, Shane. I have to do this. I have to be the one to end him. You understand, don't you?'

'No. But we'll figure this out.' Shane withdrew his hands and stepped back. He leaned down to help Amanda stand up. 'Whatever we need to do to finish this, we'll do it, okay?'

'Okay.'

'You're not running away from your problems being up here, Amanda. You're facing them.'

23

'You wander down a darkened tunnel. You're completely alone.'

The large metal garage door creaked loudly in the wind.

'And the stench of rotting flesh fills the air.'

'Thanks for that, John,' Amanda rolled her eyes and fiddled with the dice in her hand.

'As Dungeon Master it's my job to embellish,' John puffed out his chest from where he sat at the head of the small foldout table, wedged into a plastic patio chair just as Amanda and Shane were.

'Rotting flesh, really?' Shane challenged as the wind hammered more fiercely at the garage door.

'It's a *dungeon*,' John raised his eyebrows so that they nearly met the paper crown he was wearing. 'It's highly likely that people are left to rot and die in a dungeon. Hench the smell.'

'Okay, okay.' Amanda started to shake the dice she was holding. Her black Linkin Park T-shirt swamped her slender frame and her hair was still a muted shade of lime green from when she'd dyed it for Halloween the previous week. 'I'm in a darkened tunnel. Which stinks. And I'm alone.'

'Only you're not alone,' John announced grandly, a sly smile pulling on his lips.

'But you just said that I was.'

Undeterred, John continued. 'Out of the shadows creeps Declamore, the oldest and the most powerful vampire in all of the seven realms.'

'Hey, no fair,' Shane smacked a hand down against the table, causing it to wobble precariously. 'You made us both abandon our physical weapons when we entered the second level. We're armed only with magic now!'

'I offered you a *choice*,' John stated sagely. 'You could have abandoned your weapons *or* your magic in order to pass through the portal to the next chamber.'

'Yes but—'

'Besides,' John held his palm up towards his friend but did not engage him directly, 'Tarquin the Destroyer is currently subdued by a sleeping curse, is he not?'

'Yes,' Shane grumbled, folding his arms across his chest and sinking low in his chair.

'Which means that you, Morgana the Wise,' John stared expectantly at Amanda, 'must choose how you wish to face this foe.'

'She gave up her silver blade,' Shane stretched out his arms in protest, getting frustrated. 'And you know her magic isn't strong enough to take on a low-level vampire, let alone Declamore. Why did you even bring him in, John?'

'Because I am Dungeon Master,' John threw Shane a venomous look. 'It is up to *I* to make the rules. Yours is not to challenge them.'

'Ours is just to do or die,' Amanda muttered, still jiggling the dice against her palm.

'So what will it be?' John gestured towards her like she were some lucky contestant on a television quiz show. 'How will you take on the dreaded Declamore?'

'We're completely alone?'

'You're completely alone since Tarquin drank from the forbidden chalice and thus fell under a sleeping curse.'

'I told you not to do that.' Amanda arched an eyebrow at Shane who was once again slumped in his seat on the other side of the small table.

'I was thirsty.'

'You're also meant to be asleep,' John snapped, 'so hush.'

'Um,' Amanda chewed her lip as she kept twisting the dice around the palm of her hand. 'I mean, I could run, but he's too fast. I can't fight him with my magic and I have no weapon. There's nothing I can do.'

'Think harder,' John urged, 'there's always *something* you can do. Everyone has a weakness, it's just a case of finding it.'

*

'He needs to be alone,' Amanda drummed her fingertips against her laptop as Shane paced around at the end of the bed.

'Completely alone,' he snapped his fingers towards her. 'If one of his goons is close by then that's it because they will undoubtedly be armed. A guy like McAllister, he'll always have someone shadowing him. Maybe intercepting him at the club somehow will be our best bet.'

'He goes jogging.' Amanda sat up straighter.

'He what?'

'Jogging. Every morning, at dawn. He told me that he likes to run through the woods which border his estate. That he likes to be alone with his thoughts.'

'Okay...' Shane didn't sound particularly convinced.

'Of course,' Amanda began shaking her head, 'maybe that was just another lie he told to try and gain my trust. But...' she picked at the ends of her nails, 'it seemed real. When he told me.'

'It was probably just a lie, Amanda. Something else he fabricated to try and make himself seem more human.'

'But it's all we've got.'

Shane sighed.

'If I apprehend him when he's jogging then at least he's alone, away from his house and his hired muscle. It's a shot, Shane.'

'It's a risk,' Shane's voice was hard with resistance. 'I bet the prick doesn't even own a pair of trainers.'

'Isn't it at least worth investigating? I mean, we're running out of time.'

'Jogging?' Shane's shoulders sagged.

'Jogging.'

'Okay… we'll look into it.'

*

Amanda rotated her shoulders, doing her best to push past the dull ache which throbbed in her left side.

'I should be doing some investigating,' she objected as she set her feet apart in a strong stance and bunched her hands into fists.

'You will,' Shane nodded at her, 'but I need to make sure you're strong enough to do this. Especially since you keep insisting that it has to be you, not me. Hit it again.'

Amanda drove her arm forward and punched the bag which was hung a few inches away from her.

'Good,' Shane noted with approval. 'Again.'

Her muscles were starting to ache. As were all her joints and they'd only been in the hotel gym for fifteen minutes.

'Okay,' Shane gently guided her away from the punchbag and went over to a treadmill. 'Maybe we should focus on your stamina for a bit.' He started typing numbers into the treadmill's digital display.

'My stamina is fine.'

'When you apprehend him, if things go wrong, you need to be able to run away.' Shane looked at the treadmill. 'Show me you can run.'

Amanda reluctantly climbed up and the small conveyer belt at her feet began moving, forcing her to start jogging. It didn't take long for a sweat to break out all over her body and for her chest to start burning.

'Don't push yourself,' Shane was standing close by, watching her. 'Just see how far you can go.'

But Amanda wanted to push herself. Shane was right – she needed to recover her ability to run. She started to jog faster on the treadmill, her feet tirelessly pounding to keep up with the increased speed. Sweat dripped into her eyes, but she kept going. Every bruise on her body felt like a needle stabbing down towards her bones but she kept running. She needed to be fast. And strong.

Her knees buckled. The treadmill threw her off like she was an unwanted piece of trash and her back sharply connected with the tiled floor of the gym. 'Argh,' she gasped as the air was knocked out of her lungs.

'I said not to push yourself,' Shane was quickly helping her back onto her feet.

'What choice do I have?' she snapped as she stepped back onto the treadmill.

'No, we're done for today. You need to rest,' Shane was moving his hand towards the machine's digital display but Amanda swatted him away.

'I can do this,' she insisted breathlessly.

'Amanda, you're already exhausted.'

'I need to keep running. Let me keep running.'

*

For the next six hours, Amanda ran, stopping only for toilet breaks and to devour energy bars and bottles of blue liquid which promised to replenish essential electrolytes. Shane looked on with a thunderous expression, but Amanda refused to stop. Her body had once been strong, she needed to remind it of the power it held in its bruised muscles.

As she ran she closed her eyes and imagined she was back in the woods near her home with leaves crunching underfoot as she hurried through the trees. A lacy patchwork of sunlight covered the floor and the leaves whispered as if sharing secrets. Amanda breathed in the sweetness of wild flowers, the damp undertones of a previous storm. This was her safe place. This was where she ran to cleanse her mind of all the cobwebs that got tangled up in her thoughts. When she ran she was free, even though her problems kept biting at her heels. If she just kept running they couldn't keep up, they could only chase her. That's how she knew that McAllister was telling her the truth about his morning jogging routine – it was the one chance he had to outrun his past, to try and briefly forget about his beloved daughters.

'Okay, we're done.' Shane switched off the treadmill and Amanda crumpled against him, her legs numb. 'I'm not sure what you were trying to prove today but—'

'I can run,' she rasped. Even though they were numb, she knew her legs had remembered how to sprint. 'If he chases me, I can run.'

'Great,' Shane frowned at her, 'but right now it looks like you can't even walk.'

Amanda tried to stand up but failed. She fell against Shane, looking like a newborn deer struggling to get its balance.

'Fine, here we go,' Shane scooped her up in his arms, holding her against his chest.

'You don't need to *carry* me,' Amanda said, indignant.

'How else will you get back to our room? Were you going to crawl? Or maybe sausage roll along all the corridors?'

This made Amanda laugh. She had the bizarre image of her rolling lengthways along the corridors, slow and steady, round and round, just like she used to roll down the sand dunes at the beach with John and Shane. Only they liked to show off; as Amanda rolled, they did cartwheels and roly-polys. At least Shane did, John's attempts never quite came off right.

'You're pretty heavy, you know that?' Shane commented as he stepped sideways into the lift, taking care to bundle Amanda's long legs inside before the doors neatly closed together.

'Are you calling me fat?' Amanda teased.

'I'm not calling you fat,' Shane panted and repositioned her in his arms, 'just *heavy*. There's a difference.'

'Is there?'

Luckily the hotel was quiet as they headed back to their room. It was late on a Saturday afternoon and most of the guests were already attending weddings and functions in the large convention rooms on the lower floors.

'Finally,' Shane pushed open the door to their room and stepped inside. He kicked the door shut behind him and then froze, Amanda still in his arms.

'You going to let me down anytime soon?' she asked, squirming.

'Huh?' Shane blinked like she'd just broken some spell he'd been under. 'Um, yeah.' He lowered her to the ground and Amanda headed for the bed, her legs still feeling unreliable in managing her weight.

'Urgh,' she made a starfish across the bed, stretching out as much as she possibly could. Her muscles burned in a pleasant way, like she was stretching out a spring which had been boxed up for too long.

'Did, um...' Shane slowly moved deeper into the room, scratching at his head. 'When you and Will got, um, married, did he carry you, you know, over the threshold?'

'No.' Amanda was staring up at the ceiling, at the faint cracks in the paint, enjoying the tingling sensation which was journeying through her body. It felt good to finally be resting. But it also felt good to have been running again. She hadn't realised how much she'd missed jogging through the woods.

'No?'

She felt the bed sag as Shane sat down.

'To carry me across the threshold would have been too... traditional. In some ways Will was a mega-traditional guy, but not others. And our wedding was small, modest. Why?' She raised her head to look over at him.

'I just wondered,' Shane was staring at the blank screen of the television.

'At the time,' Amanda scrambled so that she was sitting up, 'I figured he was just this low-key guy who didn't want a fuss. Now I realise it was because it was all old news to him. He'd probably done the whole big wedding thing. I'm sure he carried Evangeline across the threshold of their little flat.'

'Amanda, I—'

She reached for Shane's arm, silencing his apology. 'I'm joking. Will would never have wanted a big wedding no matter the context.'

'Would you?'

'Would I what?'

'Want a big wedding?'

'What do you think?' Amanda scoffed and lay back down. The cracks in the ceiling were so faint, like relics from another time.

'You always wanted to get married on the beach at dawn.' Shane lay down next to her, his fingertips grazing against hers.

'You remember?' Amanda turned her head to face him.

'Of course,' he gave her a smile that was tinged with sadness. 'You said that getting married at dawn felt more poignant than at sunset, since it was about the beginning of something, not the end.'

'Uh-huh.'

'Jayne wanted a big wedding.' He rolled onto his back and looked up at the ceiling.

'She did?' Amanda kept watching him.

'She wanted a huge dress, a big venue, a horse and carriage.'

'A horse and carriage? Wow. She had it all figured out then.'

'Only I didn't.'

'Want the horse and carriage?' Amanda asked teasingly. 'I can't say I blame you. They aren't the speediest mode of transportation. I see you as more of a classic car man.'

'I didn't want to marry her,' Shane admitted softly. 'Not at any single point in our relationship did I want to marry her.'

'But you would marry someone? One day? Right?' Amanda was tired. The soft duvet was relaxing her tight muscles, caressing them and luring her to cross over the precipice into sleep.

'I would, yes,' Shane confirmed. He sounded far away, like Amanda was perhaps dreaming his response. 'One day I want to get married on a beach. At dawn.'

*

'Dammit, John, I'm just going to die, aren't I?' Amanda was getting frustrated. She continued to shake her dice, knowing that when they hit the table her fate would be decided.

'Firstly, stop calling me John,' he glowered at her, 'from eight until midnight on a Wednesday I'm Dungeon Master, we've been over this. Secondly, you don't necessarily have to die, Morgana the Wise. Think about it.'

Amanda thought. She was in a darkened corridor, unarmed. The magic she possessed could create a ball of fire and some lightning, but they were useless against a vampire as powerful as Declamore.

'He's getting closer,' John said menacingly. 'He'll soon be upon you. What do you do?'

'Christ, John, you've not even given her a chance,' Shane protested.

'You can smell his putrid breath, you hear the hiss as he extends his fangs, about to pounce—'

'I'll roll a six!' Amanda was so excited she jumped up in her chair.

'And, if you roll a six?' John was pointing at her, wearing a crooked smile of approval.

'He can turn me!'

'Yes,' John clapped his hands in triumph.

'What? No!' Shane intervened. 'She can't let him *turn* her.'

'Why not?' John asked blankly.

'Yeah,' Amanda agreed. 'Why not?'

'Because then,' Shane pulled at the frayed edges of his sleeves, 'she will be a vampire.' He couldn't meet his friends' gazes. He looked down at the table, at the dungeon they were currently playing through.

'So?' John and Amanda demanded in unison.

'If she's a vampire, Morgana and Tarquin can't continue onto Talbaton together. Once the sleeping curse lifts they were supposed to venture there together, to engage in the battle for the Golden Isles. But it's a land permanently bathed in *sun*. So Morgana won't be able to go.'

'True,' John stroked his chin. 'But to roll a six and get turned by Declamore is her only chance of survival.'

'If she doesn't roll a six?' Shane demanded.

'Then he'll devour her in the darkness and there will be no one to help lift your sleeping curse.'

'Dammit,' Shane pounded his fist against the table.

'I have to throw a six,' Amanda was whispering to the dice she was still clutching, rolling them between her palms.

'And become a vampire?' Shane stared at her, looking hurt. 'What about Talbaton?'

'Shane,' Amanda heard John grumble in disapproval so she quickly corrected herself, 'I mean, *Tarquin,* if my only chance of surviving is to become a vampire then that's what I'll have to do. That way I can still lift your sleeping curse.'

'But what about our future?'

'That's the thing,' John swept a hand above the table, gesturing to their game, 'our fate is indeterminable. We cannot predict what lurks around each corner, what dwells in the depths of the shadows. All we can do is roll the dice and hope for the best.'

'Let him kill you, we can start over,' Shane was looking at her, pleading with her. 'The best bit about the game is exploring places together. If you become a vampire we won't be able to do that.'

'Roll a six and you'll be immortal,' John countered, 'and powerful enough to take on deeper, more dangerous dungeons.'

'This is ridiculous,' Shane threw up his hands in frustration. 'Just roll the damn dice already. It's almost midnight and my mum will be pissed if I'm late home again.'

Amanda shook the dice one final time and then released them from her grasp with a flourish, letting them roll across the table. Whatever she did next was going to seal her fate one way or another.

24

The steam from the bathroom followed Amanda as she headed back towards the hotel bed. Her wounds throbbed against the towel which she kept tightly wrapped around herself, her damp hair dripping down her back.

'Feel refreshed?' Shane glanced away from the television to lock eyes with her. Beyond him the city sparkled beneath a blue sky.

Amanda rolled her neck, feeling the pinch in her left shoulder and dropped down onto the bed. 'Everything aches,' she grumbled.

'Then you shouldn't push yourself so much.'

'Can you...' Amanda tucked her hair back and raised her left shoulder towards him. The skin was dark, a maelstrom of black and blue. 'It's still bothering me. Could you take a look at it?'

'Sure.' Shane tentatively touched her bruised shoulder with his fingertips, gently applying pressure.

'Argh,' Amanda grimaced through clenched teeth.

'This hurt?' he applied more pressure.

'Uh-huh.'

'Can you roll it around for me? Just move it a little?'

Amanda moved her shoulder, feeling the sinewy resistance of her battered skin.

'The joint seems fine,' Shane concluded, 'but it is badly bruised. There might even be a fracture somewhere.'

'Going to hospital still isn't an option, not yet.'

'I know.'

'So?'

'More pain meds. Less overexertion.'

Amanda rolled her eyes and pressed her hand against her side. Her ribs continued to ache. They felt like tree branches which had been worn down to their delicate inner core, with no sturdy bark to protect them. Each breath, each sneeze, each bubble of laughter came with a flash of brilliant, bright pain.

'How are you holding up?' Shane was watching her, his brow furrowed.

'I'm still in one piece.' She winced. 'Just about.'

'Want me to check you over?' His fingertips were still resting on her shoulder.

In the bathroom Amanda had pivoted and turned in front of the misted mirror as much as she could but her assessment of any lingering damage was limited.

'Okay,' she gently withdrew from Shane and rolled onto her front. 'Could you check my back? I can't see it in the mirror.'

'Sure.'

The weight on the bed shifted as Shane sat beside her.

'How does it look?'

'Um.'

'What?'

'The towel. I can't see through it.'

'Ah.' Amanda sheepishly wriggled out of the towel and let it drop to the ground. She held her breath, suddenly feeling exposed. 'Um... Shane?' she whispered after the seconds drew out between them.

'Yeah, uh,' he coughed several times. 'There's...' He traced his finger down her spine and Amanda closed her eyes. His touch sent delicious shivers racing through her body which silenced the sirens of pain that were continually screaming out.

'Some bruising here,' he drew out a map of her afflictions with his fingertips, 'and some redness here. But everything looks to be healing. All of the swelling has gone down, the cuts are closing up nicely.'

'So I look okay?'

His hand lingered at the base of her spine. 'Uh-huh. Absolutely,' he replied quickly with a bit too much enthusiasm.

'Great,' Amanda slowly started to roll onto her back. 'Because I was wondering if you'd check my front too? Just in case there's something wrong that I've failed to pick up.' Her heart was frantically pounding against her sore ribs but she didn't care. This was the most alive she'd felt since the morning Will had left her. Even her battered body couldn't cage what was swirling around within her.

Shane didn't meet her gaze. His head was bent, focusing on his hands which were now resting in his lap.

'How are the bruises?' her voice was breathless, verging on seductive.

'Amanda...' Shane clenched his hands into fists, as if he was fighting against something she couldn't see.

'My ribs still ache and there's a constant pain in my side.'

With a strained groan he let his fingertips glide down the canyon between her breasts. 'There's bruising,' he whispered, stroking her side. The sensation was both awful and amazing. Amanda tensed against the sheets, grabbing handfuls of the crisp white fabric. 'By the looks of it you probably bruised some of your ribs.' Shane drew closer as if he was coming in for a better look. He smelt of sweat and fresh coffee. Letting her eyes flutter closed, Amanda drank him in. 'And then,' he gently touched her outer thigh, 'there are some lacerations, but they are healing well. I'd say the main problem is your shoulder. But it will get better, it just needs time.'

Amanda opened her eyes. Shane's face was inches from her own, his breath warm against her cheeks.

'How are you feeling?' he asked as his eyes searched the depths of her own.

'Better,' she curled her body towards his. 'You always make me feel so much better.'

'Amanda…' he closed his eyes, his voice raw with longing.

'Hold me,' Amanda laced her hand around the back of his neck, 'bring me back to life.'

His lips were on hers instantly. He kissed her softly, tentatively. But as she melted into his embrace the kiss deepened. Amanda allowed herself to let go. She felt like she was floating as the burden of Will fell away from her. The bed became a cloud and Amanda gasped in delight. She was free.

Shane remembered just how to hold her, to touch her. Every movement was infused with fiery passion yet there was a tenderness in their connection. A tenderness which only time could breed.

'Amanda,' he murmured her name into her damp hair. 'Amanda, I've missed you so much.'

She closed her eyes and sucked in a breath, her toes curling. 'Yes,' she gasped, 'I've missed you too.'

*

There was still sunlight outside when Amanda got off the bed, unfurling her long legs. The golden hues of late afternoon glistened off distant windows. Amanda looked out on the city.

She was dressed in one of Shane's T-shirts, her hair an uneven tumble down her back from where it had dried while she slept.

After they'd reconnected Shane had slipped out. Amanda had been sleeping, curled up and content beneath the duvet when she vaguely heard the door click open and then close. She'd drifted away on another cloud, but now she was fully awake and the room felt empty and cold. She shivered beneath the T-shirt and hugged her arms against her chest.

The city was alive beneath her. Cars slowly meandered up the street, outpaced by the people who briskly walked beside them, unencumbered by traffic lights and congestion. Amanda pressed a hand against the glass and kept watching. The white van was still stoically beside the curb, its constant presence mocking her. She'd run its number plate through several searches online and come up with nothing.

It was easy to observe up in her ivory tower, to imagine where people were going, to add whimsical details to their lives. Amanda liked to think that every event which had led these people into the city had been a joyous one. But maybe someone was running up the street frantically searching for a lost loved one. Maybe someone else was still reeling from the sting of betrayal, just as she had done.

Amanda spun around, abandoning the bustling vista of the city. The bed was empty, the stark white sheets crumpled. Where had Shane gone? She smoothed her hand along his side of the bed. There was no lingering warmth. It must have been over an hour since he'd left.

'He's coming back,' Amanda whispered to herself. 'He promised he'd never leave. He's coming back.'

Amanda's body betrayed her. She wanted to sit up, to wait on Shane's return, but instead she sagged down against the disturbed sheets, allowing their softness to envelop her. Her hours in the gym had taken a mighty toll. Now her body was demanding rest and lots of it. Her eyelids closed and she rolled onto her back, drifting away from the stillness of the empty room.

*

'Coffee.'

'Coffee?' Amanda rubbed at her eyes and turned her head in the direction of the deep voice which had just spoken.

'Coffee.' Will was at her bedside, holding a cardboard cup out towards her. Amanda noted the label, it was from the café beneath her flat. She gave him a crooked smile and sat up.

'Have you been out?' she croaked, wishing she sounded more polished first thing in the morning.

'Briefly.' Will waited for her to settle herself against her pillows and then handed her the coffee.

'To get this?' Amanda lifted her drink.

'Yep. I did look through your cupboards but you didn't seem to have much in.'

'Yeah,' Amanda raked her free hand through her hair. 'I keep meaning to go out and get some essentials.'

Her latest freelance job had turned into a rabbit hole. She'd dropped down it at the end of the previous week and she'd just kept falling. Her client was demanding; every time she completed something there was a new problem, a new solution she had to find in a timely manner. The fog had only cleared when she was around Will. And when she was with him the last thing she wanted to do was drag him to Asda for the food shop.

Amanda laughed self-consciously. This was Will's first time in her flat and the cupboards were bare. The only things left in the fridge were two cans of Coke and a half-eaten takeaway pizza. Amanda was living like a student. It wasn't the impression she'd been hoping to give to the guy she'd just started dating.

'You forgot to get coffee?' Will tilted his head at her as he sat down on the edge of the bed.

'I know, I know,' Amanda threw her hand up in submission, 'I *love* coffee. I'm a Gilmore when it comes to my coffee consumption and yet here we are. And now you know how scatterbrained I can be when I get stuck into a job.'

'A Gilmore?' Will frowned, his thick black eyebrows pulling together.

'It's a thing from a show I love,' Amanda waved at him, batting the question away. 'But you're not supposed to see this side of me. Not yet.' She groaned as she nursed her coffee. 'You're supposed to see the together Amanda. The Amanda who always irons her clothes and gets to places on time. Shambolic Amanda shows up later, much later.'

'I like the shambolic Amanda,' he tenderly stroked his fingertips against her cheek. Amanda chewed her lip, recalling how amazing it had felt to have his strong hands exploring her entire body the previous night. 'This is the real you, and that's who I want to get to know.'

'I'm sorry I didn't have coffee in,' she whispered, smiling at him.

'It's no problem,' he mirrored her warm smile. 'I like that I got to go out and get you some. I like taking care of you, Amanda.'

She looked at him. At the mountain of a man who was perched on her bed bathed in pale early morning sunlight. He was all strength and power, a raven-haired Greek God. But in her bed he'd shown a softer, gentler side. Will Thorn was two extremes, held together in a muscular package. No wonder his eyes always seemed to glisten with some inner mischief. He was the jester and the hangman, the pauper and the prince. Will was everything Amanda had been searching for – a gentle giant.

'I promise that next time I'll have some coffee in,' Amanda insisted.

'Next time?' Will's smile widened and Amanda thought her heart might burst from sheer excitement.

'Yeah,' she managed to remain coy, her fingers pulling at the stickered logo on her cup, 'I'm hoping there will be a next time. Aren't you?'

'Most definitely,' Will's voice was rich with sincerity. 'I'm hoping for many, many more next times.'

*

The door clicked open. Amanda stirred in her sleep and swept the hair out of her eyes. Someone was moving around at the end of the bed. And she could smell coffee. The oaky aroma was like a bolt of lightning as it struck her senses. Amanda fought against the sheets bundled around her as she sat up.

'Hey,' Shane had his back to her as he placed the cardboard cup holder down beside the television.

'Hey.' Amanda swept her gaze across the room, towards the window. The blue sky had darkened, turning to indigo as she slept. 'Where…' she coughed, resenting the accompanying ache in her chest. 'Where have you been?'

'The gym.' Shane was approaching her, cup of coffee in hand. 'And then I went to grab some coffee. I thought you might want some.' Before he handed her the drink he pressed a soft kiss against her lips. It helped burn away the remaining remnants of sleep, but as they parted Amanda still felt a sting in her soul. She took the coffee and hoped that her anguish wasn't written across her face. 'Did you sleep okay?' Shane's voice remained buoyant and happy.

'Yeah,' Amanda looked down at her cup. 'I slept fine.'

'It's okay, you know.' Shane was raising his own drink up to his lips.

'What is?' Amanda blinked uncertainly at him.

'To, you know,' he shrugged nervously, 'not jump straight back into being *us*. I know that one time isn't going to bring us back to that point. Hell, I don't even know if I want us to get back to the point. If anything I want us to be better, stronger.'

Amanda just stared at him, unsure what to say. How could she promise him a future when she didn't even know if she was going to survive the week?

'But I'm getting ahead of myself,' Shane shook his head, casting his train of thought to the wind. 'The point is that I know things aren't simple. I know you're still mourning the loss of your husband. But I'm willing to be patient, Amanda. I hope you know that.'

The coffee cup was warm in her hands. Her palms were wrapped around it, eagerly absorbing its heat. 'Then don't leave.' She kept her head bent to the cup, unable to meet Shane's gaze.

'I'm not going anywhere.' He put down his drink and hurried to her side. He sat next to her and tucked a golden strand of hair behind her ear, grazing her cheek with his fingertips. 'I'm here for you, always.'

'When I'm sleeping.' Amanda bristled and leaned away from him. 'Don't leave when I'm sleeping,' she whispered, on the verge of tears. 'I woke up and you were gone and—'

'Christ, I'm sorry, I didn't think,' Shane was wrapping his arms around her, pressing her head against his chest. 'I would never, ever, just up and leave you.'

Her heart leapt up into her throat. She was back in her perfect home, living her perfect life. Only it was shattered. The far side of her bed was empty and Will was gone and he was never coming back. All of her wounds sung a mournful melody in unison, causing her to slump against her pillows, powerless against her grief. 'That's what he said.' She bowed her head.

'Amanda, I *promise* I won't leave you. I love you.'

'He made a vow,' she sniffed as she pulled away from Shane's embrace, furiously wiping at her eyes. 'He married me and he made a vow to never leave. But he did. He broke the biggest promise that he made to me. And I understand why. I've grieved for him, for Will, for everything we lost, and now he's gone. I know that in a way he was never really there with me, not completely.'

'Tell me what to do.' Shane gripped her hands in his and looked into her eyes. He was a boy again, drowning within the rising tide of his emotions. 'Tell me how to make you feel secure. Tell me how to make you believe that I'll never leave.'

'I… can't…' Amanda shook her head. She couldn't answer him because there was no answer to give. Promises were just words that could be broken. Just as prayers were wishes with wings. The words held no weight on their own. They required actions to take root and become something substantial, something you could cling on to. 'Just don't leave.' On her lips it sounded like such a simple request.

Shane kissed her. Again and again he kissed her, each one a miniature promise of a greater commitment.

'I won't leave you,' he told her fervently. 'Ever. Do you understand? I swear to you, Amanda, I'll always be here.'

25

Amanda's laptop whirred as it frantically churned through data. She flexed her fingers above the keyboard, her gaze focused on the screen with laser precision.

'Hey… are you awake?' She didn't turn towards Shane as he shifted beneath the covers. She remained hunched over her computer, the glow from its screen illuminating her face in the darkness. 'Amanda?' Shane was sitting up and creeping across the bed towards her. 'Is everything all right, can't you sleep?'

The names.

She squeezed her eyes shut, blocking out her laptop for a moment.

Will.

All of McAllister's dark deeds danced around in her mind on a maddening carousel ride that never ended. Even in her quietest moments the thoughts found her.

Evangeline.

So much death. So much chaos. Losing his beloved daughters had hardened McAllister against the pain he inflicted on others. The trauma had hollowed him out so that now he was just a walking shell incapable of feeling empathy.

'It's late, you should rest.' Shane nuzzled against her neck, his lips grazing her skin. It was almost enough to distract Amanda from her current task. 'Come on, go back to sleep.' He drew back from her, tensing when he glanced at the laptop's screen. 'Shit, Amanda, *this* is what you're doing at three in the morning?'

Amanda said nothing. She zoomed in on the map she was studying, wishing the satellite camera could somehow penetrate the latticework of trees which obscured her view.

'That's his house, isn't it?' Shane pushed himself off the bed and turned on the light. He'd seen the gothic stone structure in the centre of the map, like the heart of a flower, with the dense woodlands which grew out of it like long, languishing petals. The picture had been taken in the autumn, when all the leaves had glowed yellow and gold. 'Amanda, you need *rest*. It's the middle of the night, can't this wait?'

'There has to be a route through these woods,' Amanda traced a finger along the screen, letting it delicately glide across the image. 'I can't make it out from the satellite image, but it has to be there. I just need to find it.'

'Maybe it's really not there,' Shane stretched and yawned, assuming the role of Devil's Advocate with ease. 'Maybe the jogging thing was just another lie, all part of the bigger yarn he was spinning.'

'It's not a lie.' Amanda could still see the pictures on the wall of the smiling little girls. Their cherub faces were so sweet, not tainted by time or cynicism. Youthful optimism had oozed from every pore, just like it did with Ewan. McAllister had insisted the pictures had been placed there for her benefit but Amanda wasn't convinced. He might protest otherwise, but she saw him for what he was; a bitter, haunted man.

'This whole jogging thing is too tenuous, I don't like it.'

'All I need is to find his route.' Amanda pulled her laptop closer, scrutinising the image in as much detail as she could. If these were the woodlands behind her home, where would she go? She'd want a route that was a circuit, a never-ending loop. It didn't need to be challenging, full of steep hills and sharp turns, the whole point of her morning jog was distance.

The trees which bordered McAllister's home were tightly packed, forming a maze of twisted branches. But Amanda knew there had to be a clearly defined route somewhere.

'Can we go there, tomorrow?' She was still studying the picture.

'What? *There?*' Shane pointed at her laptop accusingly, as if the device had somehow wronged him.

'Uh-huh.'

'We're not ready, Amanda. You're still too weak to face him.'

'I'm not going to face him.' She opened up a new tab in her current window.

'Then why do you want to go there? To sightsee?' Shane was being sarcastic. He used to always hide behind sarcasm when he got really mad.

Amanda pursed her lips and tapped out commands on her keyboard. 'Sort of.'

'Sort of?'

'I need to find the route,' she stated factually. 'First, I need to go and pick up some digital cameras. Then we need to go the woods.'

'Cameras?' Shane was shaking his head. 'For-for what? You're not making any sense.'

Amanda finally closed her laptop. It whirred for a moment and then the little fruit symbol on its cover dulled and it was still. 'I need to figure out his route,' she rested her palms against her precious device, 'to do that I need to see what's going on inside the woods. I need you to help me hide some cameras that I can remotely access. Ideally I'd have them with motion sensors to avoid draining the batteries unnecessarily.'

'You want to go and booby trap the woods?'

'No,' Amanda straightened. 'I want to go and spy in them.'

*

It was easy enough to get the digital cameras Amanda wanted since they were in a city. Shane went in on her behalf as she was still wary about being spotted around Glasgow. Even though McAllister wasn't looking for her, fate could still decide to cruelly intervene and have their paths cross before Amanda was ready to face him.

'The guy figured I was into studying wildlife,' Shane dropped the cameras into Amanda's lap before climbing into the driver's seat. He kept going on about deer. And grouse.'

'We're hoping to study a more formidable creature,' Amanda muttered as she started removing the packaging from each camera and syncing them up to her laptop.

A faint mist followed them out of the city and lingered in the rear-view mirror for several miles.

'Are those things waterproof?' Shane wondered, his hands resting on the steering wheel.

'To a point,' Amanda reached for a discarded box. She scanned the text on it and nodded. 'As long as they're not submerged.'

The rain became pellets which bounced off the car's windscreen. 'Up here it rains so much they might as well be submerged.'

Amanda smiled flatly at Shane. The term submerged was troubling her. She only had to think of it to feel the icy pressure of water all around her, trying to squeeze out the last breath from her lungs. What if she really wasn't ready for all of this? What if the trauma of what had happened with McAllister was too fresh? Too real?

The car cut a path through the rain which had become a curtain upon the road. The windscreen wipers battled furiously against it. 'Some summer,' Shane noted dryly.

All of the cameras were now online. Amanda tested each of them multiple times to be sure. With the press of a button she could remotely access their feed, see what they saw.

'Every morning at sunrise I go jogging through the woodlands that border my home. I run until my lungs burn and my legs go numb and I find that it helps.'

Amanda replayed the moment with McAllister in her mind. *Every morning*, he'd said. Not just some mornings. Not just when he could be bothered. It was a daily routine, habitual. *At sunrise.* So just as dawn was creeping over the horizon threading sunlight through the canopy of leaves.

Until my lungs burn and my legs go numb.

Distance. It was always about distance. He was trying to outrun his demons.

'What if someone sees us?' Shane tightened his hands against the wheel. 'When we're traipsing through the woods, one of McAllister's guys could easily spot us. He might even have cameras of his own dotted throughout the place.'

'It's a chance I'm willing to take.'

'I don't think you've thought this through.'

'No, I've thought it through,' Amanda slammed her laptop closed, not caring as it whirred feebly in protest. 'I've thought about it over and over. In moments that should just be mine; when it's dark and I'm sleeping I think about it. It invades my every thought, even my unconscious ones. I have to do this, Shane. The woods offer me my one chance at getting McAllister alone.'

'We could still just go back.' The rain was easing, the windscreen wipers no longer having to thrash around with such vigour.

'We can't,' Amanda stated tightly. 'You know we can't.'

'Do you ever regret it?' Shane turned down a side road at the satnav's behest.

'Regret doing all this?'

'Regret meeting him. Marrying him. Cracking open the Pandora's box that contained all his secrets?' The car bounced along a dirt road.

'Do I regret *Will*?' The question alone felt like a betrayal. Amanda drew back against her seat, her arms hanging heavily by her sides like she were a broken butterfly.

'Well, do you?'

They were close to the woods. A dense treeline bordered them on either side of the road.

Amanda thought about Will. About how he could flash her a smile that was both sexy and shy in equal measure. How he would curl up with her on the sofa with one arm always protectively draped over her shoulders, pulling her close. It would be so easy to tarnish all her memories, to let the truth of who Will really was bleed into them, distort the happiness that they held. But Amanda had boxed away every moment of her marriage, preserved them in her mind.

'No,' she choked out the truth she'd been holding on to too tightly. 'Not even for a second.'

'What about me? Do you have any regrets about me?' Shane stopped the car, they'd reached their destination but his hands remained on the wheel, his knuckles white.

'Don't turn this into something which is you against him,' Amanda threatened. 'I can't go back and change things, Shane. Neither of us can. We can only move forwards. And unless we accept that we'll just be stuck in the past forever.' She climbed out of the car and slammed the door. Then she remembered herself.

Amanda fearfully bent her knees and crouched beside the car, searching the gentle stirring in the woods for something more sinister like a footstep. Or a gunshot. But all she heard was the soft melancholy chorus of distant birds and the rustle of wet leaves.

'Okay, well, this is it,' Shane climbed out of the car and joined her, keeping his voice low as he peered into the woodlands close by. 'This is where I parked up and waited. Our rendezvous point. The house is a half-mile straight through there.' He pointed at the tightly packed tree trunks. They gathered together like nature's army, blocking the way up to McAllister's fortress.

'Okay then, let's go.' Amanda waited for her feet to obey her but they remained in the mud beside the car, sinking.

'Is this safe?' Shane placed a hand on her back and angled his body to shield her from the treeline. 'What if we've just walked into some kind of trap?'

'I've pulled myself out of a trap before.' Amanda drew in a deep breath, tasting the damp earth, and straightened. Her heart started to keep a nervous beat. 'We just need to keep quiet, that's all.' She pulled up the hood on her khaki coat, doing her best to blend into the foliage around her.

Both she and Shane wore green. Green coats, green combat trousers. Short of smearing mud across her cheeks Amanda hoped she'd done enough to be able to slip through the woods unseen. She reached the treeline and pressed on. The rain lingered in a heavy mist but Amanda was grateful for its presence. It meant that the ground was soft, that her steps fell on damp leaves and wet mud, muffling the sound.

The woods were beautiful, even in the strained light of a wet afternoon. Tall trees stretched up towards the grey sky, their twisted branches threading together like withered arms. Green leaves fluttered and fanned out overhead so that each tree wore a glorious mane. The leaves flooded the woodlands with colour, pushing back the bleakness of the slate sky.

Amanda crept forward, keeping her body low. Her pockets were stuffed full of the little digital cameras, each waiting to be hidden away within the woods. The silence was unnerving. The deeper Amanda ventured, the more it felt like she was entering a vacuum of sound. There was no distant hum of traffic, no rumble from a plane passing by overhead. She felt like she was standing in a different world, in her own personal piece of Middle Earth.

'Hey.' Even though Shane whispered, the sound startled Amanda like it were a yell. She bristled and searched the nearby trees for him. He was crouched beside a grand oak, gesturing at something in front of him. Amanda hurried over. 'This looks like a track, doesn't it?'

It certainly did. Amanda ran her eyes along the rugged mud track which swept through the trees in a perfect curve before turning and disappearing from view.

'Yes, this must be it,' she fumbled in her pocket for her first camera. She wedged it in the hollow of a nearby tree which overlooked the track. Its black eye blended seamlessly into the shadows within the darkened trunk. 'I need to plant some more.' She scurried along the track. Though she didn't walk on it directly, she lingered at its edges. She knew better than to leave obvious footprints for McAllister to find – a little trail of breadcrumbs for him to follow.

'What happens after?' Shane was watching her balance a camera on a fallen tree and then cover it in a carpet of leaves.

'After?'

'After you've… you know… ended McAllister?'

'We go home.'

'I'm thinking closer to the event.' He nudged the fallen tree with the tip of his boot. 'What happens to the cameras? They're covered in your fingerprints, linked to your computer. If you leave them here you might as well plant a sign saying, "It was me. I was here."'

Amanda instantly ceased touching the camera, holding up her hands as if the object had just bitten her. 'Crap.'

'So what was your plan?' Shane pressed.

'Dammit.' Amanda felt the weight of the other six cameras in her pocket. She'd only planted two so far.

'Forgive me for thinking like a cop but we need to be pragmatic about this.'

'Yes,' Amanda was nodding, feeling numb. 'Yes we do.'

Her hands had been all over the tree. All over the cameras. And her footprints, they traced an uneven route all the way back to Shane's car.

'Shit.' Her knees dipped into the mud and she cradled her head with her hands. 'I wasn't thinking. I was just so focused on finding him and—'

'Two cameras, that's it?' Shane began to rub his hand in circles across her back.

'So far.'

'Two. That will have to do.'

Yes, but—'

'I can find two. When we come back, two is a reasonable number for me to retrieve. No more.'

'But our fingerprints? And footprints?' Amanda lowered her hands and looked at them as if she no longer recognised them as her own. As if they'd betrayed her.

'The rain will take care of that,' Shane tilted his chin towards the sky. The darkening clouds hinted that the mist would soon intensify. 'This time we've been lucky.' He helped Amanda onto her feet and dusted off her knees. 'Next time we need to be smarter, more prepared. You need to wear gloves. Your hair has to be under a hat. Wear shoes several sizes larger than what you usually wear.'

'Right,' Amanda was nodding as she tried to create a mental checklist for herself.

'I slipped up today.' Shane hung his head as his cheeks reddened.

'What, no, this was me.' Amanda reached for him and traced his jawline with her fingertips. 'I was too eager to trace the damn jogging route. I wasn't thinking straight, I'm sleep-deprived and—'

'You're clouding my judgement.' Shane gently lowered her hands away from his face. 'This... this thing between us. Whatever it is, it's messing with my head. I'm getting jealous and being impulsively reckless and if I keep this up I'm going to get us both killed.'

'This *thing* between us,' Amanda laced her hands around his waist, drawing him to her, 'is what's keeping me glued together. Without you I'd have fallen apart long ago.'

'Amanda—'

'Without you I'd just become a ghost. I'd allow myself to disappear. You give me something to fight for. A future to hope for.'

'What about Ewan? Isn't he future enough?'

'*You're* what makes the future bright.' Amanda grazed the cold tip of her nose against Shane's. His green eyes glistened as they held her in place. 'I want Ewan to be safe. I want him to have a home, to be able to grow up into a man. 'But you,'

293

Amanda leaned in close so that their hearts were beating just inches apart, 'you're the light outside on the porch that always leads me back home. I *need* you, Shane.

'If he'd never left?' Shane's hands were on the small of her back, holding her against him. 'If he'd always been the man he'd said he was?'

'I refuse to live in the past.' Amanda wished there was a map she could follow back to simpler times, back to when they had sand beneath their feet rather than mud. But she couldn't go back. There was only the present and what lay beyond it. 'I can give you my future, isn't that enough?'

'Yes,' Shane kissed her, his hands feeling their way up her back and getting tangled up in her hair. 'Yes,' he declared breathlessly when they parted, 'that's enough.'

As they retraced their steps back to the car, Amanda wondered just how much of a future she had to offer Shane. Were there decades stretching out before them or mere days? Maybe even just a few hours? Everything would be decided the next time Amanda ventured back into the woods.

26

Amanda drummed her fingertips against her temple. Her head was bowed as Shane frantically paced around the hotel room.

'You just can't do this,' he lamented for the fourth time, throwing his hands up towards the ceiling.

During the drive back into the city he'd changed. There had been an hour of stony silence and when that broke Shane was no longer Amanda's ally. She had no idea what sort of thoughts had hounded him as they drove away from the woods but he was suddenly resolute that they abandon their plans.

'It's too risky. Even... even if you pull it off. *If* you pull it off, Amanda. And it's a big if. You're going to get caught.'

'I'm not.' Amanda kept tapping her fingers, trying to drown out the worst of her own thoughts which echoed Shane's feelings.

'There will be something that will link you back to the murder. No crime is perfect. People always get caught.'

'Not always.'

'Amanda!' His face twisted with frustration as he said her name. 'I'm telling you that you can't do this. I won't let you. If you kill the bastard or not, you go into those woods and I'm losing you either way. He'll kill you or you'll get caught and locked up. I'm ending this madness. Now.'

'How will I get caught?' Amanda kept her voice level as she lowered her hands and raised her head.

'What?'

'Tell me, and be specific, how will I get caught?'

'The gun,' Shane gestured wildly at her, disgruntled.

Amanda pursed her lips, pretending to mull it over. 'You mean the gun I bought in an untraceable transaction?'

'Nothing is untraceable.'

'This is. Trust me. You know your world and I know mine. The darknet is completely safe in these circumstances. There are entire police divisions who are tasked with trying to crack into it and expose its secrets and they are failing woefully. It's a digital fortress. I bought the gun in an untraceable transaction with bitcoin that cannot be connected to me. I've always worn gloves when handling the gun. When I'm done with it I'll throw it into the sea. If it should somehow surface on a coastline somewhere it will just be an unregistered gun, devoid of prints. A red herring not worth pursuing.'

'Your DNA. In the woods.'

'Circumstantial evidence at best.' Amanda kept her voice firm, behaving like she was already on trial. 'Like you say, the rain will have washed most of it away. What remained could be explained away – maybe we went hiking together. But no one is going to be looking for my DNA. I'm not stored on some criminal database somewhere.'

'How do you know they won't look for your DNA?'

'Because we're in Vegas, remember?' Amanda smiled sweetly at him. She reached for her laptop and turned it towards him. 'I've been Photoshopping a load of pictures of us at all the sites there just in case we need to rely on it as an alibi. And it's a solid alibi, Shane. I hacked the airline, the hotel, booking us in, making us seem to physically exist over there.'

'People have *seen* you. Here.'

'No one can really trust their memory when it comes to getting a glimpse of a stranger. I'm just a tall blonde who was seen with McAllister. I could have been any number of girls.'

'His men know who you are.'

'And do you think that their records are so squeaky clean that they'll go running to the police when they find their boss dead in the woods? Good men don't end up working for a guy like McAllister.'

Something about her last statement caused Amanda's confident mask to slip. She coughed against the grief which had suddenly been set free and was trying to claw its way up her throat.

Will had worked for McAllister. He'd been a good man who made bad choices. He let the world around him become an anchor which held him down.

'I know you think you've got it all figured out.' Shane dropped onto the bed beside her and pushed the laptop back towards the mound of pillows at the headboard. His voice was softer now, his cheeks paler than usual as the blood drained out of them. 'But Amanda, there is going to be something you've missed. There always is in these sorts of cases. We need to stop this before it goes too far, before you do something you can't come back from.'

'Do you know how I feel when I think of McAllister?'

'I know you're hurt and—'

'Fire.' Amanda interrupted. 'Everything turns to fire. All my insides liquefy with my fury and I'm just this bubbling mass of hellfire. Feeling that way – it's corroding me slowly like I'm some wreck resting on the bottom of the ocean. I need to end McAllister. To save myself. To save all those other girls on his damned list. With the puppet master gone we can all be free.'

'That freedom will have a price, Amanda.' There were shadows in the depths of Shane's green eyes which spoke of all the cases he'd worked, all the murders he'd helped solve.

'It always does.' Amanda drifted away from him to retrieve her laptop. 'But it's a price I'm willing to pay.'

*

It was four in the morning and outside it was just starting to get light. The black cloak of night was beginning to weaken to a threadbare grey. Amanda hadn't slept. She'd tossed and turned beneath the covers, letting her mind race like a hamster on a wheel. When she was certain that Shane was lost to his dreams she got up and went to her laptop. She triple-checked all the Las Vegas information. It was there on the screen in black and white, a room booked in a luxurious hotel where she and Shane had stayed for two weeks. Tomorrow they would be checking out. And not just in Vegas.

The Glasgow hotel was booked under a false name. She'd tampered with the CCTV to remove any fleeting trace of her and Shane. Just like in Vegas the room was theirs for one more night. Then Amanda had to return home. Either in a body bag or on her own two feet, she'd be going back.

Amanda checked the details of her bogus flight home from Vegas. She set up the code which would tell the flight crew that she and Shane were checked in. She'd scramble all the seating records just as she had on the outbound flight to ensure that her absence went unnoticed. It was an airtight plan. One she'd learned from Turtle82.

She dragged her finger along the mouse pad and opened up her messages. There was no more word from Turtle. Did they still assume her dead and that was why they'd gone silent? Amanda frowned at the screen. There was a time when she loved the anonymity being online gave her. She could be anybody and nobody, a ghost drifting through the virtual world. But things were shifting in her life. She needed to be more present. More real.

Shane moaned in his sleep and rolled onto his side. For a half second, out of the corner of her eye, Amanda thought she saw a mass of dark hair flecked with silver resting on the pillow. She turned too sharply, caused her left shoulder to throb painfully. It was most definitely Shane bundled up beneath the sheet.

Amanda closed her eyes, allowing her mind to the place where it was so often forbidden to go. She thought of the wooded hillside on which Will had died. How he'd dropped to the ground, a toppled giant. She'd held him as the light left his eyes. Where was he now? McAllister had to have found him along with his dead men. Then what did he do with the body? There had been no reports of bodies washing up on a beach. Wherever McAllister had taken Will, Amanda knew that he wouldn't be easily found.

'Jeez, Amanda.' Shane was sitting up, running his hands down his face. 'You really need to get some sleep.'

'I did sleep, a bit.'

The lie seemed to satisfy Shane as he leaned in towards her. 'Good.' He gently kissed her shoulder. 'What are you doing?'

'Waiting.'

'Waiting for what?'

Amanda tapped a button on her laptop and dual images popped up side by side, filling the screen. It was so dark it was difficult to discern anything in them. But gradually details presented themselves, like the tall silhouette of a nearby tree.

'You're watching the camera feed?'

'Uh-huh. They went off a few times in the night with badgers and foxes, but I've logged in for a live feed since it's nearly dawn.'

Just as it was beyond the hotel window, the sky in the camera feed began to lighten, slowly exposing the woodlands in various soft shades of grey.

'If he doesn't come?'

'He'll come.' Amanda had to believe that at any second McAllister would come running past one of her cameras. She'd staked too much on this one plan for it to fail.

'Just don't pin all your hopes on it, okay?'

Too late.

'Okay.'

*

Half four came and Shane went to shower. Amanda listened to the distant hiss of the hot water and kept watching her live camera feed, kept scrutinising all the shadows.

Five a.m. The sun was a burning orb on the horizon. The leaves had their colour returned to them as golden light poured through the trees. Amanda sat rigidly on the bed, feeling despair welling up within her with each passing minute.

Five fifteen.

Shane was out of the shower, towel drying his hair at the end of the bed and asking Amanda something, but she didn't hear him. On the left of the screen there was movement. She held a breath, staring at her laptop as Gregg McAllister jogged into view. He wore dark grey joggers and a white T-shirt. His hair was slicked back and glistened like it was damp. He powered past the first camera, a quick blur of fabric and designer trainers. Then he was gone.

Amanda's eyes were on stalks as she stared at the other half of her screen. A moment dragged out, unbearable in length. This camera offered a better vantage point, looking directly down the jogging trail from its perch in the hollowed-out tree.

He appeared at the end of the trail as silent as a ghoul and began pacing towards the camera, his arms powering back and forth at his sides. His Glasgow smile was embedded deep into his cheeks. Amanda shuddered when she looked at his face. She could still see the wicked glint in his eyes as he pushed her over the cliff to her doom. Her hands started to shake against the laptop. They clattered noisily against the keyboard.

'Hey, are you okay?' Shane was beside her, the damp smell of the shower still clinging to him. He peered over her shoulder at the screen just in time to see McAllister jog out of the shot. 'Christ. You were right.'

Amanda kept shaking.

'Hey,' Shane gripped her shoulders, trying to turn her towards him.

'I wasn't about to let one my guys throw you off this cliff. Not when I could have the satisfaction of killing you myself.'

McAllister's parting words to her were a dark echo in her mind. He'd given her a wicked smile. Had he stood and watched her fall? Or had he waited until she'd been completely consumed by the icy water before climbing back into the comfort of his Phantom?

'No,' Amanda snapped her hands up from the laptop and held them in fists. They stopped shaking as a faint tremor danced through her body. 'I won't fear him.' She remained fixated on the screen which was now just a peaceful image of sunlit woodlands. 'I won't let him have that control over me.'

'Amanda?' Shane stroked her cheek and brushed away tears she hadn't realised had fallen. 'Say the word and we turn back now, okay? You don't have to face him again. We can just go back home, live out our lives together.'

'No,' she refused to be subdued by Shane's rose-tinted lies. If she didn't end McAllister, then there would never be any certainty when it came to their home, their future. 'I'm finishing this. Even if it's the last thing I do, I'm finishing it. Tomorrow when he goes jogging he won't be alone in those woods.'

*

Sleep came that night. It dragged Amanda under, coating her body in a feverish sweat as she tossed and turned.

'You're my husband,' Amanda tried to ignore how his breathing was becoming shallower. She focused on the light in Will's dark eyes, but even that was growing dimmer. 'I would follow you to the ends of the earth. You know that.'

'I love you,' Will rasped as he squeezed his eyes shut, battling against his internal pain.

'I love you too.' Amanda's tears had become a river that almost blinded her as she looked down at her fallen husband. 'Don't leave me,' she whispered, lowering her head towards his. 'I wish you'd never left me.'

'Never again,' the hand around her wrist tightened, just slightly. Already Will lacked so much of his former strength. 'I'll always be with you.'

'Don't go, Will, please, we can beat this. I can save you.' Amanda bowed her head against his and heard his final breath pass through his lips. 'No,' she shook as he remained with him cradled in her arms. 'No. Not like this.'

The moment of Will's death had been etched in stone on Amanda's soul. She rolled beneath the covers, whimpering as she relieved the trauma of losing him.

Will had been a river that would never run dry. Powerful, constant, a life source to all those around. And now he was just a memory trapped in the dark recesses of Amanda's mind.

'I'll always be with you.' Those had been his final words.

Amanda's eyelids fluttered open. The hotel room was densely dark around her and it took a few moments for her eyes to adjust. Shane was snoring softly close by, the sound bringing her some comfort. Stretching out her arm, Amanda found her laptop and opened it up. She read the clock in the bottom right corner. It was two a.m. In less than an hour the alarm would go off and she and Shane would embark on the final leg of her journey. Of Will's journey.

Ever since the morning when he'd left their bed as she slept, he'd been on a mission. A mission to save his son from McAllister's wrath. And now that mission had passed to Amanda. One final thing that she and her late husband had shared between them.

Amanda rolled onto her back and thought of the little boy, how he was probably sound asleep in the bed which had once belonged to her back at her mother's house. Did he drift off to sleep listening to the sound of the waves lapping against the rocks outside like she used to?

The seaside cottage was a safe place. It always had been. Even after Amanda's father died, the walls held onto the strength they had absorbed from him over the years. As a little girl Amanda used to love how the rose garden reminded her of the thorns which gathered around Sleeping Beauty's castle to keep outsiders away. Though they were a product of Maleficent's malice, they still made the castle secure and Amanda liked that, even as a child. She understood the need to feel protected from the outside world. She grew up believing there were monsters in cupboards and beneath the bed, even though her father assured her there wasn't.

Will's final wish was for his son to be safe.

If Amanda killed McAllister, then she would be truly honouring that. She'd be destroying the one monster which could penetrate the rose garden, could enter the house uninvited and destroy the tranquillity Amanda's father had bequeathed to his family.

Amanda quietly lifted herself out of bed and drifted over to the window. Her aches had dulled from a persistent buzzing to a dull drone. She looked out at the city. With its starry array of street lights and illuminated windows it had never looked so beautiful. Amanda was up in her tower, living out some twisted version of an urban fairy tale. She would vanquish the beast. She would avenge the man she had loved. And maybe, just maybe, she'd get her own shot at a happy ever after.

A watery memory rose to the surface, the faces in it forgotten by time so that only their voices lingered. Amanda was sat in GCSE English, struggling to focus. It became a common problem for her after she'd shared her first kiss with Shane. Her studies slipped from prominence and became a chore she had to trudge through to get back to the boy with the bright green eyes.

Her English teacher was stood, hand on hip, beside the blackboard, her grey shirt dusted with chalk. 'What this book is teaching us...' she tapped the dog-eared novel she was holding in her hand. Amanda's eyes strayed towards her own, unopened copy, which lay flatly on her desk. 'What it is telling us about the human psyche, the desire to evoke justice, to have an eye for an eye,' the teacher's voice droned on like a persistent wasp that Amanda wanted to swat away. But something stuck. Something managed to drill an anchor into her memory and ensure it stayed in place.

'When one sets out on a quest for revenge,' the teacher dramatically slapped her book down against her desk and stared at her class, her eyes two magnified watery spheres behind her thick glasses, 'you must first dig two graves.'

'Why two, Miss?' Roger Olsen's podgy hand was instantly up in the air, waving around for the old woman's attention.

'Read the book,' the teacher's lips quirked up into a knowing smile, 'and figure it out.'

27

In the hours that followed two in the morning the world always seemed still, like it was holding its breath in anticipation for the new day. Amanda wandered behind Shane down the stairs which led into the hotel's car park. They didn't want to risk being seen using the lifts and rousing suspicion. Their footsteps bounced off the stairs and the walls, pinging back to them in an endless echo.

Amanda had already checked out online. Shane had loaded up his car with their bags. When she'd closed the door to the hotel room, it was the last time she'd see the large bed covered in crisp white sheets or the city lights sparkling like scattered sequins through the window. There was no time to dwell on goodbyes. Amanda pulled the door shut, listening for the click of the lock and then hurried after Shane.

They saw no one as they powered down the stairs. They rattled down them like ghosts shaking their chains in the night. In the car park a blanket of silence covered all the vehicles. Amanda rested by the door to the stairwell, leaning forwards and waiting for her lungs to stop burning. Despite all the hours she'd spent in the gym she still hadn't regained all her usual strength. Her bruised bones continued to feel delicate.

'Amanda, come on,' Shane was whispering as he looked over his shoulder at her. It felt strange to be running around in the dead of night. While most other people slept, they were sneaking through shadows, locking up doors. It was both thrilling and dangerous. It reminded Amanda of being eight years old and tiptoeing down into the kitchen during the night and easing the biscuit jar off its shelf, trying to be as silent as possible. It was that delicious moment when you reached inside, stroked your fingers against a sweet treat and froze, waiting for the lights to suddenly come on as you were caught, or for the darkness to endure, so that you could continue in your illicit deed.

'Amanda.' Shane had stopped running. He was stood by the bumper of his car, studying her.

'I'm coming,' she jogged towards him, pulling her lips into a smile so that she wouldn't grimace. There had been so many stairs. Her legs felt unsteady and the fire in her chest refused to go out. But she couldn't let Shane know. If he saw that she was still as weak as she was he'd call everything off. And she needed him. She was about to cast herself into a sea of dangerous uncertainty and he was the life preserver she'd have to race to if things became too much for her to handle.

'Are you sure about this?' the crinkles of worry in the corners of Shane's eyes were becoming permanent.

'I'm sure.' Amanda strode past him, opened up the car door and climbed inside. The sound of the door closing snapped loudly through the car park. Like a gun shot. Amanda sunk low in her seat, breathing heavily.

She was once again in her green combats and coat, her hair slicked back in a smooth bun at the nape of her neck. The gun was inches away from her, in the glove compartment, swaddled in a towel Shane had brought. The gloves she'd need to hold it were tucked into her pocket. Her fingers twitched. She yearned to check her laptop, just one more time. Logging into her digital world always gave her such a feeling of calm. She felt genuine pangs of withdrawal when she was away from it for too long. But the laptop was in the boot of the car along with everything else. Thinking about the darkness of the boot made Amanda's stomach do a backflip.

'Then we're doing this.' Shane slid into the driver's seat and put his key in the ignition but did nothing else.

'Are we going or are we just going to sit here and stare into space all night?' Amanda tried to sound funny but there was no making light of the situation. She just sounded scared.

'Tell me to go home.' His hands were now on the wheel.

'Shane, we've been over this so many times and—'

'Tell me to go home.' He tightened his grip. 'Just tell me, Amanda. Tell me that we can put all of this behind us and just leave.'

'You know we can't do that.'

'But I'm going to lose you,' Shane's voice caught in his throat and he bowed his head.

'No, you're not.' Amanda reached for him. 'We've been over every eventuality. It will all be fine. And in a few hours it will all be over.'

What if you drop the gun?

What if you miss?

What if he's armed?

What if he's not alone?

Dark thoughts snapped at Amanda like snarling dogs, trying to tear at her flesh and hurt her. She closed her eyes, pushing them back, refusing to give them power. She knew what she was doing. She knew where McAllister would be, his route along the jogging trail. She could do this. She had to do this.

*

'So it's over?' Corrine pressed for clarity, leaning forward in her armchair, both hands still genteelly cradling her cup of tea.

'Yeah,' Amanda tugged on the sleeves of her jumper from where she sat on the sofa, her long legs curled up beneath her. Her own drink – coffee, black – sat untouched on a nearby side table.

'But you love Shane,' Corrine insisted. 'And he loves you. You two have been through so much together – college, university.'

Amanda cringed. She didn't need to hear the list or have a quick history lesson about her relationship. It was done. Over. Shane had made that very clear when he packed up his stuff and left.

'What happened?' Corrine squeaked. 'What did you do?'

'What did *I* do?' Amanda glowered at her mother. 'What makes you think it was something *I* did? Maybe he cheated!'

'Oh no, Shane's such a nice boy. He wouldn't do something like that.'

'Jesus, Mum.'

'So what happened?'

'He cheated,' Amanda declared bluntly, raising her eyebrows in a taunting gesture.

'Seriously,' Corrine passed over the declaration with a roll of her eyes. 'What happened? I know Shane would never cheat on you.'

'How could you possibly *know* that?' Amanda spat bitterly.

'Because he loves you. Every time he looks at you I can see it bursting out of him. He loves you much, Amanda. He'd stand by you through anything. He already has.'

'Yeah, well, he doesn't love all of me.' Amanda suddenly needed her coffee. She reached for her cup and drank deeply from it, not caring that it slightly burned as it slid down her throat.

'Of course he does.'

'No. He doesn't. Shane's changed since he joined the force. He's more… judgemental.'

'He's taken on a very serious job, Amanda. I imagine he's under a lot of pressure and—'

'He's perfect, I'm not. I get it.'

'That's not what I'm saying, Amanda, I—'

'I've always been *how* I am. *Who* I am. But suddenly that's not good enough anymore. Suddenly it's no longer okay for me to bend the rules.'

'Are you bending rules?' Corrine looked horrified. She placed down her cup and stared at her daughter, stricken.

'Nothing important.'

'Amanda—'

'The world is not black and white, Mum. Its shades of grey. And Shane used to get that. Only now he doesn't.'

'Have you been doing something…' Corrine lowered her voice and stared nervously towards the window and then back at Amanda, '*illegal?*' She paled as she asked the question.

'Define illegal.'

'Oh, dear God,' Corrine produced a handkerchief from her pocket with a flourish and began dabbing gently at her brow. 'What did you do, Amanda? What was so terrible that Shane felt compelled to leave you?'

'Nothing.'

The darknet and her adventures within it. But her mother would never understand that. Amanda broke a few laws but only for the greater good. She was like a digital Robin Hood, her and Turtle82 and a few other hacker friends. They helped take down corrupt organisations, expose married people who signed up to exclusive dating agencies with the intention of secretly cheating on their spouses. Once upon a time Shane admired her tenacity, her bravery. Now he just saw the litany of crimes she was committing. He'd become a cop first, a boyfriend second.

'You must have done *something*.'

'I was me,' Amanda shrugged. 'That's all I've ever been. And I'm not perfect, Mum. No one is. And Shane never used to care about that, now he does.'

'Oh, Amanda, you can't throw away what you two have over some petty argument.'

'I'm not.'

'But he loves you. He truly, utterly adores you.'

'Clearly not enough.'

'How can you be so hard about this?' Corrine was now wiping tears out of the corners of her eyes.

'Mum, Shane and I are over and I'm moving on with my life. I just came round here to let you know, not be lectured about it.'

'Do you think a good man is like a bus?' Corrine seethed. 'That you can just jump off one and then hop on the next one and ride it for as long as you like?'

'I don't want a good man,' Amanda was standing up. She was ready to leave. 'I want a great one.'

*

The darkness pressed in on them from all sides, challenging the strength of the car's headlights. They cut a clear path ahead but beyond their reach the world was lost to the night. The city shimmered distantly in the rear-view mirror like an abandoned jewel at the bottom of the ocean. Soon it would disappear completely.

Shane didn't speak as he drove. He just silently moved the car deeper into the countryside.

Amanda picked at the ends of her nails, looking down at her hands, wondering what they would prove themselves to be capable of.

'Do you remember when you left?' the question slid from her lips before it was even fully formed in her mind.

'Huh?' Shane's forehead crinkled as he was suitably confused.

'When we were together. In our apartment. You remember that?'

'Of course.' His green eyes remained focused intently on the illuminated strip of road ahead.

'You left because you were tired of me using the darknet.'

'What's your point?'

'My point...' Amanda shifted in her seat. No matter how she sat she could feel the stifling presence of the gun nestled close by. 'Is why are you here now? I'm about to commit a *murder*, Shane. That makes you an accessory, which is a whole lot worse than turning a blind eye to my online activities.'

Shane clenched his jaw but didn't reply.

'If we're caught you'll lose more than just your job. You'll go to jail. We both will.'

'Is there a question there somewhere?' He sounded angry.

The car careened around a corner, the headlights burning against a small rabbit who just had time to scramble out of the road to safety.

'I guess what I'm asking is why stick around now? When you wouldn't before.'

'Because I learned from my mistakes,' he told her briskly.

'Meaning what?'

'Meaning,' he swung the car around a tight corner, approaching it with a bit too much speed. It shuddered uneasily as it straightened out. 'If I had to choose between losing you and losing my job, my freedom. I now know which is worse.'

'But you're risking everything.'

'You're worth it.' He powered down a length of straight road. They were drawing ever closer to the woodlands within McAllister's estate. 'Now can we just drop it please?'

Amanda pulled at a loose thread on her coat. She wondered if she tugged hard enough if the whole thing would just unravel.

*

The first night had been the worst. Amanda had stood in the centre of her small apartment, letting the emptiness seep into her. She could still smell him in the bathroom. On his side of the bed. Even on the sofa. His cologne had burrowed deep into the fabric throughout the place, embedding itself upon the home like a permanent tattoo.

Amanda felt restless. She tidied the kitchen cupboards, rearranged all her knick-knacks in the living room area and made and then re-made her bed. Midnight crept by and she didn't even notice. She felt Shane's absence everywhere. Only he wasn't really gone, not like her father had been. Amanda went to the window and drew back her thin curtains, gazing at the pale glow of a nearby streetlight. Shane was out there, in the world. Maybe he'd gone back to his parents or perhaps he was crashing on John's couch. But he was no longer in Amanda's world. She regretfully glanced back at the emptiness.

She just needed to readjust. That's what she told herself. Shane had been such a huge part of her life for so long that losing him now was obviously going to be a shock to her system. But she'd get over it. She'd recovered from far greater loses before.

As she ambled towards her bedroom, finally resigned to the fact that she needed sleep, she wondered what her father would say if he were there to witness the collapse of her first big relationship. Would he be annoyed as her mother had been? Relieved? Would he tell her that this was her chance to spread her wings and see the world? To grow?

He'd left Amanda's life before he'd really had chance to impart any wisdom to her about love and matters of the heart. He'd only ever known her as his little girl.

'Love is a strange beast,' he'd declared one Christmas after several glasses of sweet sherry. 'It can be playful like a kitten or ferocious like a wolf. But no matter how love treats you, you can't ever shut it out completely, not forever. It will always scratch at the door, begging to be let back in.'

*

A crimson fissure cracked along the horizon. The darkness was distilling. Amanda rubbed at her eyes and grabbed a bottle of water that was resting at her feet. She needed to sharpen her senses.

'We're nearly there.'

Shane confirmed what she already sensed. An iron ball rolled around her stomach, crushing everything in its wake.

'I won't ask again if you're ready, because I know you are. You've shown me that you are. And I believe in you.'

Amanda nodded in gratitude. Shane's belief in her helped keep the wind in her sails. She told herself over and over that she could do this. That everything was going to work out fine.

'Where will we live?'

She blinked, startled. Her mind had drifted and she'd missed the start of Shane's question.

'Sorry, what?'

'When we go back, where will we live?' He was watching the distant sky as the fissure widened. A new day was imminently dawning. And for someone in the woods that morning it was to be their last.

'When we go back home?' Amanda had barely entertained thoughts of home. She was too fixated on the present.

'Yeah, when we go back. I mean, I know you've got your house that you shared with Will, but I didn't want to assume anything about that and—'

'I can't live there,' Amanda blurted. The apartment had become so hollow after Shane left and his absence wasn't permanent. There was no way she'd be able to tolerate the pure walls and sparkling surfaces of the home she'd shared with Will, not when she knew he'd never be coming home to tell her off for not using a coaster. It would be too painful to continue to exist in the world they'd built together.

'Then we'll find somewhere,' Shane said gently. 'Together. If you like?'

'Have you been thinking about it much? Going home?'

'Of course.'

The woodlands were up ahead. Dark and still shrouded by shadow.

Shane cocked his head towards her as he slowed the car. 'Haven't you?'

'Not… really,' Amanda admitted honestly. 'My head's kind of been stuck in the moment.'

And the past.

She felt like she was being haunted by all her previous choices. All her lingering heartaches.

'Well, I've been thinking about it.' Shane stopped the car. 'To be honest with you it's the only way I've been able to cope.'

'Really?'

'I couldn't do this. I couldn't drive you out here, let you buy yourself a bloody, gun,' he shrivelled as he said the word, 'I couldn't do any of it unless I knew we were working towards a tomorrow together. I can't believe that this is the end, Amanda. Even though there's a gnawing fear within me that thinks that it could be.'

Amanda nodded and stared at the glove compartment. She felt that fear too. It was in a constant orbit around her and occasionally it crashed against her like a meteorite, destroying the part of her that it touched.

'Everything is going to be fine.' She lifted up the hood of her coat. 'I'm going to go and kill Gregg McAllister and then we are going to go home. Together. Everything will be fine.' She hoped with all her heart that she was right.

28

The morning air was damp. It was filled with the lingering remnants of a cold night. Despite the canyon of dusky pink that was expanding on the horizon, the woods remained clotted with shadows.

Amanda stood beside the car, tentatively scouring the darkened treeline. She'd already pulled on her plastic gloves which made her look like a misplaced surgeon and the gun was tucked into the waistband of her jogging bottoms. Each time she breathed in she felt her skin prickling around its solid shape.

'We need to go now.' Shane crept away from his car, keeping his body low to the ground. He slipped into the shadows and Amanda watched the darkness absorb him. She didn't know if she was ready. She drew in more damp air, filling her lungs to capacity. She clenched and unclenched her hands, listening to the static ripple of the plastic gloves.

Will.

His presence was everywhere. It crackled within the trees along with the whispering of their leaves. He was the reason Amanda was stood at dawn on a remote dirt track about to enter woodlands that were laced with danger.

Had Greg McAllister left his sumptuous home yet? Or was he knelt down in the grand hallway, still lacing up his trainers? Amanda glanced at the digital clock on the car's dashboard. Minutes were slipping by as she pointlessly deliberated what she needed to do next. She already knew the steps to this dance. She'd rehearsed them in her mind a thousand times.

Her fingers flexed as though squeezing an invisible trigger. She could do this.

It was darker in the woods than she'd anticipated. Any milky pre-dawn light was banished entirely by the solid wall of trees that packed in tightly around her. Amanda crouched low to the ground, just as Shane had done. She took small, fast steps between trees, pressing herself up against their rough bark as she snatched an anxious breath.

'Amanda,' Shane whispered her name and then reached for her arm. They dropped closer to the mud, huddling together. 'I think the first camera is just up here.'

She looked beyond him and amongst the various shades of grey she saw the unmistakeable outline of the hollowed-out tree in which she'd placed a camera. The previous morning it had filmed McAllister jogging by.

'I'll go grab it while you move onto the next one, okay?'

'No. We'll get it after.'

'I'm not risking there being any record of what goes down here,' Shane scurried away from her. Amanda blinked and slowly stood a little straighter. He was right. The camera was fitted with a motion detector and she couldn't risk it going off. Unless...

The gun prodded her in the back. Reminding her that all was not lost. Not yet. But if everything did go wrong. If she fumbled the shot, if McAllister had time to produce a weapon of his own – wouldn't she want to record him killing her? Wouldn't that be a noose she could posthumously wrap around his neck?

She hurried in the direction Shane had gone, following the sound of snapped twigs and rustling. His hand was in the bowels of the tree when she found him, plucking free the little digital camera.

'What if *he* kills *me*?' Amanda grabbed his arm, staying his hand.

'What?' He sounded distracted. Annoyed. Amanda threw a fearful glance along the jogging trail. How much sand had slipped through the hourglass since she'd left the car?

'Leave the camera,' Amanda told him briskly. 'If things go wrong it'll film him killing me. It'll be evidence.'

'We won't need evidence.' Shane shook her off and roughly removed the camera and stepped back from the tree, away from the jogging trail.

'Shane!' She was on his heels. The camera needed to go back. It needed to be a back-up in case she failed.

'We won't need evidence,' Shane repeated, his voice low but filled with rage. He drew her close enough to see the glint of something sharp when he partially opened his coat. A knife. He'd taped it to the inner lining. 'Because McAllister isn't leaving these woods alive.'

'Shane…' Amanda couldn't stop looking at the knife. It was long and sharp. The kind of blade you'd use to cut through the toughest meat. Shooting a man was one thing. With that kind of execution you were permitted a level of distance. But using a knife? That required hand-to-hand combat. That required proximity. And a level of ruthlessness that Amanda knew she didn't possess. 'Will you…' she pointed at his coat, '*can* you use that?'

'Of course I can,' he growled at her.

'This is *my* thing.' She stepped back from him, almost tumbling over a fallen log. In her mind she saw everything going wrong, her carefully laid plans unravelling at the seams. She'd miss her shot, McAllister would pounce on her, shoot her first. He wasn't the kind of man who believed in leaving room for ambiguity. Not a second time. He'd shoot her right between the eyes, turning out the lights before Amanda even had a chance to realise what had happened. Shane would swiftly come seeking her, and when he saw her laying fallen on the ground he'd chase down McAllister. Would he plunge the knife into his back or spin him around first? Would he want to watch the older man bleed? And then what? Shane would stumble out of the woods, alone, drenched in blood that wasn't his own. Amanda couldn't let that happen. He needed to leave the woods as the same man he came in as.

'If things go wrong just get the hell out of here. Go take care of my mum. And Ewan.'

'Do you really think I could just run?'

'Shane—'

'Surely you, more than anyone else, understand the need for revenge?'

A bird distant heralded the new morning. Its cry was caustic and raw. The sound shredded down Amanda's spine and she pressed against the nearest tree.

'Just don't do anything stupid,' she pleaded before gathering herself and hurrying towards the location of the second camera.

As she picked her way through the trees, straining her eyes in the dim light to check for rocks and tangled roots upon the ground, Amanda could hear the echo of Will's final moments all around her. With Ewan at her side she'd fled into similar woods not too long ago. They'd left the warmth of the cabin and hidden like hunted animals amongst the trees. Will, always brave, always formidable, had sacrificed his life to save his second wife and son. The boom of the gunshots still trembled deep within Amanda's bones.

She continued to scurry between the trees. The rustle of leaves behind her told her that Shane was following. She found the tree trunk where she'd placed the final camera. Her gloved hand knocked off its cloak of leaves and closed around it. And then she hesitated.

If you die here at least let it film him killing you.

Her mind was still intent on going against Shane's wishes. If only she'd found her USB when she'd returned to the beach, if only someone had filmed McAllister launching her off the edge of a cliff. Technology had always been her friend, her lifeline. How could she ignore it now to rely solely on the barbaric weaponry of a single gun and a knife?

'Give me the camera.' Shane's breath was hot against her cheek. He'd caught up with her as she deliberated her next move. 'There isn't time to argue, Amanda. Give it to me.'

Numbly she obliged. She twisted the camera free of its nature-infused perch and handed it to Shane.

'I'm going to be *just here*,' he was creeping back into the shadows, pulling away from her. He was like the tide. Amanda yearned to just go with him, to let him take her wherever he went. She suddenly didn't want to be alone. 'You need to *hide*,' he ushered his final warning and then he disappeared behind a tree.

Amanda looked around. The jogging trail curved away from her in the strengthening morning light. Above the latticework of leaves overhead, the sky had turned to a softer shade of charcoal. Birds were singing to one another, urging the other woodland animals to rise from their slumber. Amanda placed herself beside a grand oak tree, pressing her stomach against its barked centre. She leaned to the left and peered at the jogging trail which lay empty. Then slowly, carefully, she slid the gun out from the waistband of her joggers and held it in her gloved hand. With a soft click she removed the safety, just as Shane had shown her to. The silencer was twisted upon the barrel of the gun. The weapon was ready to take a life.

Amanda held her gun at her side. She could feel its weight dragging against her wrist. She remained pressed against the oak tree and she waited. The trees ceased rustling, no longer sharing secrets through their network of leaves. Even the birds were no longer singing. It felt like all around her, the woods were also waiting. Did they know what was about to happen? Was the soft earth and ancient trees preparing to welcome another soul into their midst?

Dawn had arrived. Though its light was weak it meant that the jogging trail was completely lit up until it dipped out of Amanda's eyeline. Sunlight sparkled on dew-speckled leaves and tufts of green grass. Amanda felt a single tear slide down her cheek as she wondered if this was to be the last day she'd live to see.

29

'Dad was a good man, wasn't he?' Amanda resisted the urge to scratch at the sleeves of the black woollen dress her mother had picked out for her that morning.

'He was the best kind of man.' Corrine lifted a crinkled white handkerchief to her cheeks and dabbed at her tears and smeared mascara.

The cottage was finally empty. All of the mourners and well-wishers had moved on having issued heartfelt condolences and eaten their weight in finger sandwiches. Amanda swept her gaze around the living room, still not quite believing that her father wasn't about to burst through the door any minute. She couldn't imagine him in the long wooden box they'd committed to the ground just hours earlier.

'Your dad, he always put his family first.' Corrine's handkerchief was now streaked with black but she continued to dab at her cheeks and panda eyes. 'There was nothing he wouldn't have done for you and me. He'd have given us his last penny if we'd asked him of it.'

'What do we do now, without him?' Amanda hugged a small crochet pillow to her chest. The date of her father's accident had been carefully stitched into it. A 'gift' from Mrs Simmons who lived further down the street. Amanda couldn't wait to take the pillow down to the beach and watch it burn on the next bonfire she made with Shane and John.

Shane had stayed longer than most people had. He let Amanda cry against his shoulder and barely spoke, as if he knew that words had no weight on days such as these.

'We are tasked with the unfortunate demand of carrying on.' Her mother ceased dabbing her cheeks and stood up with purpose, eyeing all the empty china plates littered around the room.

'What do you mean?'

'Your dad is gone. It's us, the living, who now get to suffer.'

Amanda whimpered into the pillow, letting her tears sink deep into its fabric.

'Your dad would want us to be strong.' Corrine started to stack the plates up. She had to be careful as it was the finest china she'd used for her guests, the set which she'd once received as a wedding gift.

'But I just want him back,' Amanda wailed. 'This is so unfair.'

All she wanted was a hug from the man who meant the world to her. Instead she'd had to put on an itchy black dress and say goodbye to him forever.

'Life is unfair.' Corrine was taking her stack of plates into the kitchen, finding comfort in her current pragmatism of attending to chores.

'He was a good man,' Amanda chased after her, still clutching the unfortunate pillow. 'The best man. You said so yourself. So why did he have to die? How is that right?'

Corrine dumped the plates into the sink and spun around to look at Amanda. Her eyes misted with fresh tears which she didn't bother to dab away. 'There is no right or wrong when it comes to death. Good men, bad men, even the best men, they will all be forced to meet their maker at some point. None of us can escape that fate.'

*

The next ten minutes felt like an eternity. Amanda's muscles were tight. She was pressed against the tree in a permanent state of alertness. Every chirp of birdsong or rustle of leaves sounded like a jackhammer going off. Her sanity began to gnaw in on itself.

What if McAllister wasn't coming?

What if he knew that she was waiting for him?

What if some of his best guys were currently heading her way?

She was driving herself mad with the 'what ifs'. But the doubt-filled questions kept coming, falling like an avalanche around her.

What if I'm too late?

Footsteps. Light, yet unmistakeable. Amanda held in a breath and barely moved a muscle as she inched her head out from beyond the cover of the oak and glimpsed along the jogging trail.

McAllister was coming. He was running directly towards her, arms powering at his sides. He wore grey joggers and a white T-shirt. His hair was slicked back, perhaps still damp from his morning shower. This was it.

If Amanda stayed where she was he'd just run past, move deeper into the woods without ever knowing that she'd been there lurking, watching his every move. Doing nothing proved to be a tantalising proposition. Amanda entertained how it would feel to just watch him run away, to not endanger his life or her own.

But then she remembered the weight of Will's lifeless body in her arms. The warmth of his blood as it flowed out of him and stained her hands. He'd been her oak tree and though he'd done his best he could never completely shield her from the darkness of his past. Amanda tightened her grip on her gun and moved away from the tree's protection. It took her several strides to plant herself in the middle of the jogging trail.

McAllister ceased running. He slowed to a halt three feet away from her, panting. There was a sheen of sweat across his forehead which wrinkled with confusion.

'Jesus, am I seeing a ghost?'

He smiled at her. Genuinely smiled, almost laughed, like he was being reunited with an old friend. Amanda wasn't about to be fooled by his false warmth. She showed her ace as she raised her gun and aimed it squarely at his chest. McAllister staggered back in surprise and slowly lifted his arms up above his head.

'My, my, it seems you and Jakey boy had more in common than I thought.'

'You killed him.' Emotions were coursing through Amanda like a potent black tide, desperately trying to drag her under. But she needed to keep her head above water, needed to stay focused.

'I did no such thing. We've been over this.' McAllister's grey eyes danced over her. He sniggered when he saw the faded shadows of her bruises upon her face. 'You look like somebody gave you a well-earned beating.'

'I have you to thank for that.' Amanda spread her feet, squared her shoulders, just like Shane had showed her how to do when they had practised.

'You're spunky, I'll give you that. I figured you'd be fish food by now.'

'You figured wrong.'

'Still nursing that death wish though, aren't ya?' The left side of McAllister's mouth lifted into a crooked smile. 'I mean, why seek me out like this? Unless you want to finish what we started?'

Amanda bristled as she felt him undressing her with his eyes, devouring her with his hungry gaze. Though his hands remained above his head McAllister seemed completely unfazed by the gun currently aimed at his chest. Raising his hands was just paying her gesture lip service. This was clearly not his first time being held at gunpoint, which didn't surprise Amanda one bit.

'You killed Will and then you tried to kill me.'

'Tried, failed,' McAllister gave a flippant shrug. 'And here you are, set to live another day. Provided you put that toy down and turn around. I'm willing to forget that you were ever stupid enough to show up here. I'll carry on imagining you as a bloated corpse floating around in the big blue.'

'You're not a man who shows anyone mercy.' Amanda's arms were beginning to struggle with the weight of the gun but she didn't flinch.

'Sweetheart, you need to stop aiming that thing at me unless you intend to use it.'

'I intend to use it.' Amanda's words were like nails – hard and sharp. She kept telling herself to focus, that she was at the finish line, all she needed to do was break through the ribbon and cement herself as the winner.

'Bullshit.' McAllister narrowed his eyes at her, his lips curling into a snarl. 'I bet you don't even know how to use the fucking thing. Stop wasting my time, Mrs Thorn. Or are you going by Miss Thorn now? Who the hell even cares? Step aside.'

McAllister lowered his arms and took a bold step forwards but Amanda held her ground. She kept the hands wrapped around the gun level, her aim steady.

He cocked his head at her, looking like he was caught somewhere between amused and annoyed. 'I tell you now, lassie, that you don't have the guts to kill someone.'

'You know nothing about me.'

'I know that you're not from Jake's world. I bet that's what he liked about you – that you were so *pure*.' Venom coated the final world.

'You mean like your daughters were?'

That struck a nerve. McAllister's neck snapped back as though she'd just given him whiplash. 'Careful what you say, sweetheart.' He still managed to sound menacing and dangerous even though she was the one holding a gun.

'What about all the girls you smuggle into the country for a life of sexual slavery? I imagine they were pure before you ruined them. You ruin everything you touch. You're toxic. You're poison.'

'I'm done listening to this bullshit. Either shoot me or get the fuck out of my way.'

Amanda tightened her grip on the gun and pressed her fingers against the trigger. All she had to do was squeeze and McAllister would be gone. Dead. But was he right – did she have it in her to kill someone? To be a murderer?

Before going into the woods she thought she'd covered every eventuality. She wore her gloves, used the darknet to cover her tracks, to give her an airtight alibi. She didn't stop to consider that she might be the very thing standing in her own way, that her conscience might prevent her from crossing a line.

'Jake got what was coming to him and so did you,' McAllister was getting angry. His cheeks turned crimson as he spat out his hate-filled words. 'When you tread on a scorpion, you better hope you crush its stinger else it'll turn around and hit you right back, only it hits a lot harder.'

'Will Thorn was my husband.' Amanda thought of the man she'd married, the man she'd lay in bed with and dreamt beside. Even though he'd wrapped himself up in so many lies Will Thorn did still exist. He'd been the man who stroked Amanda's forehead when she had a nightmare, who cleaned her car and restocked the oil without asking, who insisted on them eating dinner together every night to ensure they had quality time together. He had loved her. That part had never been a lie.

'Will Thorn was Jake Burton. Stop being such a stupid bitch and holding onto his lies. I'm over this little reunion of ours. You're not going to kill me.'

'I've watched a man die in the woods before.' Amanda was crying but her arms remained stiff. She refused to let her aim dip, even for a second. 'I can do it again.'

McAllister lunged at her and she squeezed the trigger.

*

'Did I nearly die today, Daddy?' Amanda sat wide-eyed on the garden bench. She didn't know how to process the feeling of staring into the void and having the void stare back. The old bench creaked as her dad sat down beside her. He didn't look at her, instead he let his gaze drift towards the horizon so that they were both staring at the sun as it dipped towards the water.

'It was a close call,' he admitted, lacing an arm across her shoulders and tugging her closer to him. 'You certainly scared me and definitely shaved a few years off my life.' He gave a low chuckle.

'What if I'd fallen?' Amanda remained completely serious. For her there was no mirth to be found in what had happened earlier that day. Her stomach was still on a frantic spin cycle because of it.

'But you didn't fall.'

'If I had?'

'Amanda—'

'What if you hadn't been there to catch me?' Amanda looked away from the setting sun, at the low-lying clouds which had been stained red like heavenly rubies. She watched her father scratch at his cheek and realised that her question had provoked him to do some serious thinking. This filled her with a weird sense of pride. She was always trying to impress her father, to prove to him how smart she was.

'Today, I was there.' He lowered his hand from his cheek and rested it flatly against his knee. The corduroy trousers he wore had been thinned by many years of wear. Once upon a time they'd been the colour of strong coffee but now they were more of a delicate beige. 'But you know, I won't always be there.' A sad sigh escaped from his lips as he turned from the sunset and bowed his head towards her. 'I'll always be here,' he tapped at her chest with his finger, 'and here.' The tip of his finger touched her forehead. 'But not always *here.*' His hand was resting on his lap once more.

'So what happens when you're not here to save me?' Amanda's shoulders began to shake. She was about to cry. It would be a mournful, haunting sound like all the other crying fits she'd had that afternoon. She wanted to shake off the shadow which had attached itself to her back and clawed its long fingers into her slim shoulders. She didn't want to have to wear it for the rest of her life.

'Someday you're going to have to figure out how to save yourself.'

'What about Mummy?'

'Mummy and I won't always be around.'

'Then who will save me when I fall?'

'You will, Amanda.' He smiled at her, his eyes warm with pride. 'You're so bright, and so adventurous. But *take care*. You really scared me today, the cliffs are no place for little girls to be playing.'

'I wasn't *playing*,' Amanda objected, pouting. 'I was *searching*. For nests.'

'Well then the cliffs are no place to go searching, either. You have to be careful, sweetheart. The world can be a dangerous place.'

'Because of bad people?'

Her father chewed the inside of his cheek as he considered his response. 'I mean, sometimes, yes.'

'And places can be bad too, like the cliffs?'

'Amanda, what you need to remember…' he turned her to face him so that his eyes bore into her own as though he was trying to create a clear highway for the information he was about to impart. 'No one is inherently bad. Just as no one is inherently good.'

'What does that mean?'

'Bad people can do good things. Good people can do bad things.'

'But they're still bad though, right?'

He looked away from her. At the light leaking through the rose bushes. The sun had almost been completely swallowed up by the sea.

'I know it's a lot to grasp when you're young, but try not to be too judgemental, Amanda. Good, bad, they are such definitive ways to see the world. It's like a beautiful painting – from a distance it's this wonderful image, but up close it's a tapestry of little brushstrokes. Always try and see things for what they really are, not the illusion. Especially when it comes to people.'

'So there are no bad people?'

'There are bad *choices*. And often in life your choices are what make you.'

'But you're a good person, aren't you, Daddy?'

'Because I choose to be. And I definitely try to be.'

'Then I'll choose to be good too.' Amanda nuzzled up against her father. He smelt of old books and coffee. The last light of the day glowed upon her dad's face. The swirling in her stomach stopped. Amanda was with her hero, her saviour. She was safe. 'When I grow up I want to be just like you – brave and good.'

*

There was no sound. The bullet charted a silent trajectory from the gun to McAllister's chest. Amanda wasn't even certain she'd fired it until he staggered back from her, his hands instinctively clawing at where his ribs met.

Clamping a gloved hand to her mouth, Amanda watched McAllister's white T-shirt bloom red. He dropped to his knees and stared up at her, wheezing out laboured breaths through his wounded chest.

'You... bitch.' His perfect teeth were tarnished by the dark treacle of his own blood. He hunched forward to spit some of it out.

He was still alive, still staring at her. If she ran now he'd be able to fumble in his pocket for his phone, rasp out a cry to help to the goons stored back at his mansion. A helicopter might be flown in to help hurry him to a hospital so that doctors could spend the rest of the day saving his pitiful life.

Amanda kept her gun held stiffly in her hands and aimed upon him. 'This is for Will.' She fired off a second shot. McAllister instantly dropped to the ground. He was on his side, his eyes wide as blood trickled out of the fresh hole in the centre of his forehead. For a moment all Amanda could do was stare at him. His blood was seeping out into the mud of the jogging trail, the colour leaving his face.

'We need to get the hell out of here.' Shane was dragging her away, pulling her back to her senses. She felt like she was drifting in a bubble, like a bomb had just exploded right beside her, muting the rest of the world. As she staggered away from Gregg McAllister's fallen body, her senses came hurtling back at her with the force of a freight train. The birds were still singing, though their melody was deafening. The rustles of the leaves felt like sinister whispers sharing secrets, all of which were about her. The woods were no longer tranquil and beautiful. They were terrifying.

30

The wind dragged cold fingers across Amanda's cheeks. Despite the blue skies, icy air tumbled inland off the waves which continually battered against the rocky face of the cliff. Amanda tasted the salt of the sea, embraced the sharp slap of the wind.

'Let's just get this done and get out of here.' Shane's focus darted back and forth along the empty road behind them as though he were a spectator at a tennis match. Despite his anxieties no other cars crept along the coastal route as Amanda stood at the cliff's edge, gun in hand. 'If we leave now we might get back home before its dark.'

Home.

Amanda's tears were warm as they tumbled towards her chin. She'd been fighting to save what home meant to her for so long that she'd been left feeling hollow. All of her old wounds throbbed, eagerly reminding her of their presence. Clenching her jaw, she flung the gun free from her grip. It dropped towards the waiting waves like a sinking stone. Her eyes followed it as it fell, a lump forming in her throat.

Not too long ago she had been the one to tumble down into the icy water. She stroked her gloved hand against her left shoulder, remembering all too clearly the pain she'd felt on that traumatic day.

The ground beside her crunched. Out of the corner of her eye she saw Shane standing by her, his vigil of the road abandoned so that he could look out to sea. There were no boats chasing the horizon. They'd specifically chosen a desolate strip of coastline to dispose of their incriminating evidence. The sea was a rippled grey slab which in places reflected the brilliant blue of the sky above it.

'The gloves too.' Shane was stoic as he spoke, just as he had been since they'd left the woods. The vice-like pressure of their situation hadn't broken him. It actually seemed to have made him stronger, more focused.

Amanda looked at her hands. The plastic gloves were spotted with McAllister's blood – red pinpricks against the blue. She swallowed against the lump in her throat and turned towards Shane, revealing her tarnished palms to him.

'Fuck.' He drew his mouth into a tight line when he saw the blood. His green eyes narrowed as they swept over her coat. Amanda lowered her head and saw more red splashes, darkening the design and starting to blacken. In her haste to leave the woods and McAllister she hadn't noticed the bloodstains upon her person. 'You'll need to burn anything with blood on.'

Amanda shrugged off her coat as though it were already on fire. The gloves came next. She tore them off her hands and let them flutter to the ground like tiny brittle flags of blue and red.

'We'll find some woods and burn them there. It will draw too much attention to do it now.'

After bundling her soiled items into a plastic bag, Amanda got back into Shane's car. As they drove away from the cliffside, winding their way along the coastal road, Amanda found her mind taking her back to the woods. She kept wondering if anyone had found McAllister yet. His body would be cold now, starting to stiffen.

'I should have asked him,' she gave a regretful sigh and tried to focus on the blurred landscape beyond her window.

'Asked who what?'

'McAllister. About Will.'

'What about Will?'

'What he…' she twisted her hands together. 'What he did with… his body.'

'Amanda—'

'I know it's a terrible thought to entertain. But…' she swept away the birth of a tear, 'he's just gone. Completely. I don't have part of him to bury, to mourn. I'm just left with this great hole in my life that he used to fill.'

'You don't need to visit someone's bones in order to remember them.'

'I know that. It's just,' she sighed and shook her head, letting her icy blonde hair fall over her shoulders, 'I wanted *something*. And one day I fear that Ewan will yearn for something too. I guess its closure. With Will so utterly gone, do I get any?'

'What would you even put on a gravestone?'

'I don't know. Loving husband, father, the usual.'

'I meant his name.'

Amanda froze. She felt like Shane had just skewered her against the car seat with the piercing arrow he'd thrown. She had to remind herself how to breathe.

'I wasn't trying to be a dick,' he told her softly, glancing over and seeing her muscles stiffen and her cheeks pale. 'I was just… wondering.'

'Will Thorn.' Her response came like a knee-jerk reaction. 'I'd put Will Thorn.'

'But that wasn't his, you know, *real* name.' Shane was treading carefully, trying not to crack any of the eggshells beneath his feet.

'He was Will Thorn to me.' Amanda didn't bother to wipe away her new batch of tears. 'He will always be Will Thorn to me.'

*

It was dark when Shane pulled off the road just east of Bristol at a scrap of woodlands that were bordered on all sides by rolling fields of farmland. Amanda waited in the car while he took the plastic bag of her ruined clothes and doused them in petrol.

Home was so close now. She could almost smell the roses in the garden, feel the refreshing breeze of the southern coast getting tangled up in her hair. No cars had chased them down the motorways. When they stopped at service stations no one stared at Amanda as though they'd just seen her face on the news above the caption *most wanted*. If Gregg McAllister had been found, and she was certain that he would have been by now, no one had connected her to the crime. To his guards she was nothing more than a ghost. To the rest of the world she was on board a long haul flight coming home from Las Vegas. The only things that could place her at McAllister's side when he died were the items which were about to go up in flames.

Amanda climbed out of the car and reached Shane just as he dropped a single match into the dampened pile. Flames quickly burst to life, a brilliant flash of amber and orange against the bleak night.

'We should pretend it's one of our beach bonfires,' Shane joked as he placed his arm around Amanda's waist. She leaned against his side and watched the flames. They tore through her coat and caused the fingers of the plastic gloves to curl and blacken.

'Do you think it's really over now?' The heat from the fire fell against the couple in radiating waves. Amanda peered up at Shane, saw the flames reflected in his green gaze.

He cleared his throat and hugged her tighter. 'Yeah, of course.'

'I don't want someone calling me in four or five years telling me that they know what I've done. That they are coming for me.'

'That won't happen.'

'How do you know?'

'Because I won't let it.'

The fire didn't crackle. It just roared softly as he continued to pillage the piles of clothes offered up to its fury.

'Do you think that Will thought it was really over for him? That he'd outrun his past?'

Shane considered this for a moment. 'I think he did, yeah. Else he wouldn't have planted so many roots. But he did – he got married, he bought a home. He was planning for a future, Amanda.'

'Do you think he ever intended to return to Evangeline and Ewan?'

'I can't answer that.'

'I used to like that he was this collection of secrets all jumbled together. It made him seem so mysterious,' a bittersweet smile spread across Amanda's face.

'And now?'

'I like that I know you. I know you almost as well as I know myself. There's no surprises between us.'

'You don't think that will get boring?' Worry crept into Shane's voice as he turned to face her, cradling her face with his hands.

'No,' she pressed her lips against his. 'I don't.'

They kissed as the evidence burned. They lingered in the woods until it was just ash which Shane then scattered to the wind.

'So, are you ready?' he was walking back towards the car. The sky was full of a thousand stars and the smell of smoke still lingered in the air.

Amanda felt strangely at peace. As though since Will had left she'd been shackled to his secrets and now those restraints had been removed. 'Ready?'

'To go home?' Shane nodded at his car.

The mileage on the car. Speed cameras. Amanda looked at the vehicle and saw a thousand new ways she could be caught. She felt like she was standing in snow, desperately trying to cover her tracks but in doing so she just created new ones. But she refused to live on a knife edge. If Will had managed to exist beneath the vast shadow of his past and all his previous wrongdoings then so could she.

'Yeah,' Amanda smiled and it felt genuine. 'I'm ready to go home.'

Six Months Later

Amanda stood at the French doors her eyes fixed on the distant ashen sea while her hands were clasped around a floral porcelain mug filled with fresh coffee.

'Will it snow soon?' Ewan popped up at her side, dressed as a Power Ranger. He pressed his little palms against the doors and widened his eyes as he peered out at the landscape.

Beyond the garden of the small bungalow the world fell away and plummeted towards the sea. The sky was ripe with swollen silver clouds and there was a bite in the air which hinted at the imminent arrival of snow.

'If it snows I promise we'll go and build snowmen on the beach,' Shane offered with a smile from where he sat on the sofa behind them, reading a book and toasting his toes in front of the log fire.

'Snowmen! Yay!' Ewan bounced on the spot and then sprinted back into the centre of the living room and his pile of toys which were haphazardly arranged on the rug beside the hearth. Amanda continued to linger by the doors. There were still boxes along the far wall demanding her attention. But the unpacking could wait. It was Sunday and Sundays were family days. In a few hours they'd walk the short distance to her mother's cottage and when Corrine opened the front door the smell of roasted beef would instantly greet them. 'So when do you think it will snow?' Ewan tilted his head at the man reading on the sofa.

'Any day now, champ. Just be patient.'

'If it snows do I have to go to school?' This question was divided between Amanda and Shane.

'I guess that depends on how much it snows,' Shane replied, turning the page in his book.

'Well then I hope it snows loads and loads so that I get to stay home.'

Home.

The word tugged on Amanda's heart, drawing her away from the doors and towards the warmth of the fire. Tender flames tangled together in the black Victorian fireplace. They wound themselves around the freshest log like a pack of snakes trying to constrict it.

Shane leaned forward to squeeze Amanda's hand. He'd heard it too. The declaration of home. Right from Ewan's lips. The little boy was finally settled into his new routine, his new way of life. The adoption papers were filed away in Amanda's study. He was truly theirs. Truly home.

Sometimes he awoke from a dream asking for his mother. Occasionally he even asked for Will, although that was happening less frequently. His father seemed to be slipping out of his memories. Amanda fondly ruffled Ewan's hair and stooped down to grab the nearest toy.

'Who's this again?' she shook the toy, causing its wheels to rattle.

'That's *Lightning McQueen*,' Ewan explained, puffing out his chest. He gingerly took the toy from her and rolled it across the carpet, making engine sounds. 'He's one of the fastest cars around. Wanna see?' Ewan leapt up, his *Thomas the Tank Engine* slippers softly pattering across the floor as he hurried in the direction of the kitchen and its tiled surfaces. 'Come on,' he called to no one in particular.

'I'm coming.' Shane marked the place in his book and followed after the little boy.

Amanda looked around her home. Everything still smelt new – from the sofas to the plush rug beneath her feet. Even the furniture was new. Shane had spent an entire weekend piecing it all together and cursing the invention of flat-packs. But his hard work had paid off. The little bungalow was now a home; warm and inviting. Ewan's bedroom looked out towards the sea and Amanda had painted the walls a vibrant shade of blue and adorned it with Marvel decals. Ewan loved it. He had bounced up and down on his bed when he was first allowed inside, bursting with gratitude.

Amanda and Shane's room also overlooked the sea. The bed they shared was adjacent to the window, allowing her stunning views of moonlight dancing on distant waves as she drifted off to sleep.

'Look how fast he is,' Ewan's bright voice floated in from the kitchen.

Amanda smiled and sipped at her coffee. She stepped closer to the fireplace, letting her hand rest upon the mantle. There was still so much unpacking to do. Every room was filled with boxes. But there was one box Amanda had opened up immediately when they moved in. Carefully placed towards the top of it were two framed pictures. They now stood at either end of her mantelpiece like a pair of bookends holding the fire between them.

In the picture closest to the kitchen, Amanda stood beside Will, smiling madly like she'd just won the lottery. He was smart in his suit and she was pretty in her modest dress. Whenever Amanda looked at the picture her heart skipped a beat. Will was so alive in the image, so handsome.

'This is your dad,' Amanda had explained to Ewan as she positioned the picture.

'It's a wedding picture.'

'It is.'

'Of you and my dad.'

'That's right.'

'So you were married to my dad?'

'I was.'

'Then what about my mummy?'

Amanda knew that one day she'd have to sit Ewan down and explain what had happened to his parents. But she wanted to spare him the grief of such a conversation for as long as she could.

'He was married to your mummy too. For a time.'

'Oh.' Ewan had studied the picture at length as if hoping that his father would somehow reveal some of his secrets to him through his captured smile.

'You don't think it will confuse him, having that picture up?' Shane had queried that night as they lay in bed together.

'No, I don't,' Amanda curled against his chest, loving the feel of his beating heart. 'I think it's good for Ewan to see it. Will was his father. He should know about Will's past because it's ultimately part of Ewan's story.'

And the topic had been dropped.

Amanda wandered towards the second picture on her mantelpiece. She was again wearing a wedding dress only this one was lace and it swept behind her in a pretty fishtail. There was a suited man beside her but it wasn't Will. Shane's green eyes sparkled, jumping out of the photograph, bright with joy. He wore a pale grey suit and had his hands on Amanda's hips as he looked deep into her eyes. Behind them the sun was rising over a gentle ocean, turning the sky the colour of pink rose petals.

We hope you enjoyed this book!

Carys Jones' next novel is coming in autumn 2017

More addictive fiction from Aria:

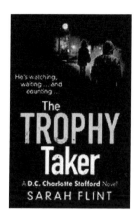  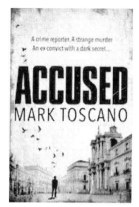

Find out more
http://headofzeus.com/books/isbn/9781786690708

Find out more
http://headofzeus.com/books/isbn/9781784978969

Find out more
http://headofzeus.com/books/isbn/9781784978907

Acknowledgements

A huge thanks needs to go out to the amazing Aria team; Caroline, Sarah, Yasemin and Nia. They continue to be extremely supportive of me and my work and I'm so grateful for all their guidance.

To my very patient husband, Sam, thanks for listening to all my frantic rambles whenever I ran plot ideas past you.

Lauren Graham – you kept me doubly entertained whilst writing *Last Witness*. I embarked on an epic *Gilmore Girls* marathon when I started the book, I also read your new novel *Talking as Fast as I Can* and you always managed to put a smile on my face. You truly are an inspiration.

Thanks as always to Rollo, my insanely adorable cavalier for keeping my feet warm while I wrote at my laptop and for always sensing when I needed a cuddle.

Finally to everyone who read *Wrong Number* and connected with Amanda and her story. I love hearing from readers, I love hearing about if you were a Team Shane or a Team Will. I value your support and enthusiasm for the series so, so much. Every Tweet and email you send me about my books is genuinely cherished. Thank you.

xoxo

About Carys Jones

CARYS JONES loves nothing more than to write and create stories which ignite the reader's imagination. Based in Shropshire, England, Carys lives with her husband, two guinea pigs and her adored canine companion Rollo.

Find me on Twitter
https://twitter.com/tiny_dancer85

Find me on Facebook
https://www.facebook.com/CarysJonesWriter/?fref=ts

Visit my website
http://www.carys-jones.com/

Also by Carys Jones

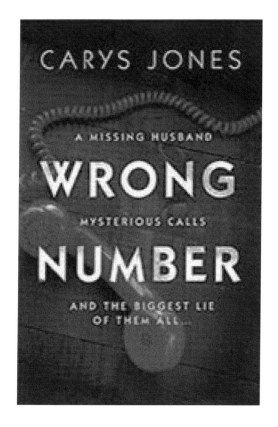

Find out more
http://headofzeus.com/books/isbn/9781786692481

Visit Aria now
http://www.ariafiction.com

Become an Aria Addict

Aria is the new digital-first fiction imprint from Head of Zeus.

It's Aria's ambition to discover and publish tomorrow's superstars, targeting fiction addicts and readers keen to discover new and exciting authors.

Aria will publish a variety of genres under the commercial fiction umbrella such as women's fiction, crime, thrillers, historical fiction, saga and erotica.

So, whether you're a budding writer looking for a publisher or an avid reader looking for something to escape with – Aria will have something for you.

Get in touch: aria@headofzeus.com

Become an Aria Addict
http://www.ariafiction.com

Find us on Twitter
https://twitter.com/Aria_Fiction

Find us on Facebook
http://www.facebook.com/ariafiction

Find us on BookGrail
http://www.bookgrail.com/store/aria/

Addictive Fiction

First published in the UK in 2017 by Aria, an imprint of Head of Zeus Ltd

9 7 5 3 1 2 4 6 8

A CIP catalogue record for this book is available from the British Library.

ISBN (E) 9781786692498

Aria
c/o Head of Zeus
First Floor East
5–8 Hardwick Street
London EC1R 4RG

www.ariafiction.com

Printed in Great Britain
by Amazon